Jesus, Mary & Lucifer

VERSUS

Paul of Tarsus

& the Evil of his Church

Book 3. Apocalypse

By

John E. Hunt

"The intuitive mind is a sacred gift and the rational mind is a faithful servant. We have created a society that honors the servant and has forgotten the gift." Albert Einstein.

All characters appearing in this work are fictitious. Any resemblance to real persons, living or dead, is purely coincidental.

TABLE OF CONTENTS

CHAPTER 1. PRELUDE TO SÃO PAULO

SWITZERLAND. PAUL & CESARE

It was a beautiful day. A slight breeze gently rippled the waters of Lake Lucerne, the bright sun sparkling off the ripples. The deep green trees shaded the private and protected courtyard overlooking the lake. Paul sat, relaxed, in an elegantly carved chair, enjoying the moment. He slowly sipped a glass of fine red wine, waiting, but not impatiently. Watching the water but not really seeing it, he was enjoying a break in the day's chaos and savoring his plans for the future.

"You wished to see me, Father?" Cesare asked, as he walked up to Paul. There was a little anxiety in Cesare's voice because these conferences were usually not good news. What has he found out now? Cesare thought glumly. Which of my little projects stepped on someone's toes?

"Sit down, my boy, please," Paul replied, waving at the chair next to him. "Enjoy this beautiful day with me."

Cesare sat down, surprised, carefully watching Paul, who authentically seemed in a good mood.

"You've done nothing wrong," Paul added, "or, more likely, at least nothing that I know about," and Paul smiled cheerfully. "Here, have some wine." Paul moved his hand slightly and immediately a servant rushed over carrying a bottle and a crystal glass.

This is good, Cesare thought, eying the trembling servant filling the glass. When the glass was full, Cesare casually took it, ignoring the servant's obedient bow.

Paul twitched his hand and the servant backed away.

"Do you remember Lucretia's project? Do you recall the details?" Paul asked.

"Yes, Father." He furrowed his brow. "Most of it, I think."

"Well, it won't go as well as she planned," Paul announced. "First, things never do. Second, I have a deeper plan in mind, carefully hidden from her. On the rare chance that her plan works perfectly, it is just the springboard for the next steps. It will change the world if it works, my boy. Everyone wants to change the world."

"What can I do to help?" Maybe he will trust me to help?, he wondered. It's been years.

"I need a legend," Paul answered, leaning close to Cesare. "A cover story. I have the best and the brightest working on this problem, at least what they know of it. Let's have a backup. Not that you are not the best and brightest, my son, because you are. I need more than the best and the brightest—I need something really rare, which is competent help that knows the full plan, and that's you."

"And what do you want me to do, Father?" thrilled to be trusted and at the same time terrified of failure. I barely survived the last disaster, he remembered. And my brother didn't, but it really was his fault the plan crashed. Or, at least father thought so.

"I want you to set up a branch office in São Paulo, Brazil. Make it something technical sounding that doesn't make a lot of sense. What it does really isn't that clear," Paul explained. "This will be fun, actually," and he smiled. "Hire a confused idiot for the manager. Here is a list of the types of employees we need," handing Cesare a folder. "We want damaged, barely functioning people. People who could follow simple instructions badly, and complex instructions not at all. The company has been set up through a chain of countries so confusing that I can't follow where they start."

"With all respect, father, that would be why?" Cesare worried. "As Lucretia perhaps more eloquently demanded, I've got to have some idea of what's going on to do what you need."

"True. Listen carefully, and tell no one at all. It's harder to hire idiots than intelligent people when you have a specific project in mind, because you have to structure it so they fall, despite themselves, into success. But idiots can be wonderful, because they have no idea what's going on and so couldn't tell anyone if they wanted to; and if something unfortunate happens to them, no one is really all that surprised. I've used this trick over the centuries, and have had great success with it."

They talked for an hour, hashing out ideas, and finally came up with a focused set of next steps.

"I'm honored, father," Cesare blurted out. "Really! I generally, well, get pushed aside."

"I can trust no one else with this, my son. And it's a chance to prove yourself. This is a big step towards the new world, that new world which be our old world again, forever."

PAUL IN CONFERENCE

Paul sat in his room, looking out at the lake but not seeing it. His prior selves were standing in a circle around him. They had been pouring over the plans and possibilities, critically tearing the ideas apart and putting them back together again. They all thought, frantically trying to see any weaknesses.

"I like the deception," Constantine argued. "Having separate groups working at cross purposes is an excellent plan. If a single group knows the whole plan, they get sidetracked into ethics and morality and such other nonsense. Handing each of them an ethically defensible project that they will never see past is far more effective. The intersection of the projects gives us what we want, and they will never see it coming."

"Having different groups do different things, well, it's a lot harder to trace it back, because neither group can explain the whole story. It looks like accidental interactions," Cortés agreed. "When I had to work with the Spanish court, I always had at least three stories going with four groups because there was no one I could trust there."

"It's a bold stoke, a brilliant concept," Xerxes declared. "And I hate all this waiting."

The Adversary had been observing, sitting quietly in the corner of the room. "Damned if you do, and bored if you don't," the Adversary observed.

They all stared at him, disgusted.

"Just being helpful," the Adversary pointed out, shrugging. "I'm doing my job."

SÃO PAULO. CESARE FINDS A LEGEND

Cesare sat in a poorly furnished office in a seedy section of São Paulo. Paul's staff had researched the city, finally providing Cesare with a list of possibilities. After a few days wandering around the city, Cesare had decided on this office. Cesare then hired an elderly real estate agent with a known drinking problem to handle the transaction. Cesare had given the man cash, which the agent had used to pre-pay the lease. The agent then was found dead drunk, literally, outside a cheap bar in a shantytown, nicely removing the only witness. The agent was poor, his heart was weak, and he had no relatives, so when he died, no one asked questions. Cesare had the key to the office and a lease in the name of a nonexistent company when the dust settled. There's a risk in being here myself, he told himself, but there's a limit to using cutouts. Father and I discussed this over and over and I have to make sure that the people we hire are the right kind of idiots. Simple stupidity isn't enough.

He spent the next two days interviewing prospective employees. He met people who were competent but stupid; people who were incompetent but bright; and a very few people who both competent and bright. He was getting discouraged and then—Gold!

"I was working for this little company," the blonde woman giggled. "I was the office manager, I think. Well, I sat in the office more than anyone else did and I told some of the people what they should be doing. And no one told me not to be in the office and tell people what to do, so I must have been the office manager."

She was roughly forty-five. Promising, Cesare thought. There was an incurable mediocrity in everything about her, making the drab office seem even tawdrier by her presence. I'm assuming that she planned her outfit, Cesare mused, because women normally plan their outfits, despite the complete lack of evidence of planning here. This outfit is a classic, with each piece of the outfit flashy and cheap. She was proudly wearing stripes with checks, and while it was hard to be certain of all the specifics of the fashion riot sitting in front of him, he thought there was at least one contrasting pattern mixed in. The flashy but worn jewelry clashed with everything. Her hairstyle was an out-of-fashion cut that accented her sagging jowls more than anything else in her face structure and her roots were showing. Interesting, Cesare realized, because the contrasting roots are different lengths. I don't even know how that's possible. For a woman, it was astonishingly badly done. No, he thought to himself, it's more than badly done—I'd say that for any human over the age of three it would be almost impossible. He glanced again at the resume and saw nothing in her training or experience indicating an accounting background, so she must just be naturally gifted. A mass of tiny, useless acts of vanity, each individual item selected for its own characteristics, without any regard for the effect of the collection. All trees and no forest, no grasp of the totality at all. Perfect for my purposes.

"I thought my last position was very interesting," she bubbled, "but the office closed because they never made any sales. I wondered, really, because after a few months, I got bored sitting in the office and so I went out to give prospects sales presentations. I noticed after I had given several presentations that the company didn't have any order forms that I could use if I did make a sale. As I never made any sales, it wasn't a problem, but I thought it was a bit strange. It turned out they were some kind of marketing scam, I think the police told me. I went to the office one day and it was full of police! There were men going through the records and several policemen standing around the door. When I walked in the office, shouting that I was the office manager and wanted to know what was going on, the police arrested me! They took me to an interrogation room and asked me many questions. Evidently my answers satisfied them, because the police just shook their heads after a while and sent me home. It was so odd."

Hardly, Cesare thought. The police would be glad to just get her out of the room. But this a plus, because the police already know she's an idiot.

She wrinkled up her face, thinking.

I could use that picture to sell wrinkle cream with, Cesare thought. NO woman would ever want to look like that!

"Well, I've been unemployed for a while since then" she rambled on. I've interviewed with many businesses, but no one seems to need an office manager. You'd think with all the disorganization in the world, there would be a place for an in-charge, on-top-of-it professional, but I guess I've been knocking on the wrong doors."

Cesare coughed to cover a laugh. He really didn't have the slightest respect for others or their feelings and rejoiced in the crushing remark, but he didn't want to upset her. Not that she would be able to tell when she had been insulted! Pure 24 caret Gold, yup, he thought. Know thyself? I'm surprised she doesn't offer to shake hands with herself in the mirror in the morning. Not the brightest crayon in the box, now are we?

He went into his spiel about what the district office would do. He lost her after two minutes. Good, he thought. Most of the others hung on for at least ten minutes and half of them finally told me that none of it made sense. He kept going for ten more minutes, testing her. She was making notes, a serious look on her face. "And that's what I need done," he finished. "Is that something you could handle?"

"Certainly!" she giggled, nodding eagerly. "Staff this office, hire people with these credentials and train them. I can do that." She drew some random lines on her notes, arrows running in a circle. "I'm certain I can do what you need done."

"Good," he announced, with an odd smile. "You are hired. I've been talking to people for two days, and you are the only person who is competent enough for this challenging position." Given that no one in the world could make heads or tails out of the story he'd just spun, he suspected that she might really be the only person actually incompetent enough to run the office.

She beamed.

"Here is an advance check." He pulled out a checkbook and wrote out a large check.

Her eyes widened as she looked at the check. Then she actually jumped up and down in excitement. "Wonderful!" she gasped. "My family will be so proud when I tell them about this."

And I don't doubt it, Cesare realized. They all have her genes. Scary, actually. Dad is right about the world.

"I'll start looking for staff tomorrow. I can send resumes and information to this ah, e-mail address?" she asked. She stared at the e-mail address, puzzled.

She does know how to send email, doesn't she? Cesare worried, panicked for a second. He quickly added, "I'll have the computers installed tomorrow and they will show you an easy way of sending information to me. I don't want to waste your time on small matters like typing in e-mail addresses."

"Thank you," she beamed, obviously relieved. "Well, I'll be here bright and early tomorrow to get started."

"I'm glad we met," Cesare assured her. "I'll be looking forward to hearing about your progress."

NEW YORK. COLDMEN SACKING OFFICES

A large conference room high above the street, glass walls from floor to ceiling looking out over the wonder of the world that is New York. The room was full of anxious people, most nervously standing, ignoring the outside world as a useless distraction. On the long inside wall, there was a row of large monitors, portals into Coldmen Sacking conference rooms around the world. There were few smiling faces in any of the rooms anywhere in the world.

The senior partner who replaced Lucretia stood up and banged a gavel on the table. The chatter vanished, replaced by silence.

"Please sit," he gruffly ordered and there was a rattle of chairs, the muttering of social pleasantries and a few muffled hisses as people fought for territory Irritated, the senior partner glowered at the staff and the room became quiet. In a few minutes, everyone was seated.

"We are here to implement this exciting and visionary plan that Lucretia developed for this very important client of ours. As she is regretfully gone, I've been appointed Partner in Charge of this project. This client has advanced several billion dollars to implement this plan, with substantially more funds available if necessary. Now, we should be cautious about needing to ask for more funds, as Lucretia's experience in South America showed. We believe adequate resources have been committed to the plan for its success." There was a wave of nervous muttering around the room that stopped when he banged the gavel too loudly.

"You all have copies of the parts of the plan that you are responsible for. The partners have copies of the full plan. This plan has been discussed at the highest levels, and vetted by legal around the world, so it's approved, nay, blessed. But," and he stammered, "this has to be done right. Done right and there are bonuses. We won't go into the results for failure, but it's more than just no bonus, I can promise you." The partner stopped for a moment, staring at the table, gathering his thoughts. Alligators, and his stomach churned. Not where I want to be.

He looked back up at the group, a worried-looking mass of bodies. Confidence, he told himself. This can work, and it's really, really serious money if it does. He tried to smile to project assurance. It actually came out as more of a grimace. "Look, this is the plan that she worked up. If you don't think you can do it, you are saying that she was smarter than us. Is anyone saying that?" He was suddenly shouting, his anxieties taking over, and he was known to get belligerent when under stress, which was the polite description. 'Flaming asshole,' was what the staff thought, but they whispered it between themselves after work. "Because if you are saying she was smarter than you, then you can just leave now, and I'll find some people who can perform. Anyone?"

One young man in the back stood up. "I'm not having any part of this," he snarled. "This sucks. You can go to hell." The young man calmly walked out, slamming the door behind him.

"Get security," the partner hissed to an aide, "and follow him. Now."

The aide scurried off, dashing out of the room and chasing the man down the hallway.

"Anyone else?" the partner shouted, secretly astonished at the man's courage. The partner had thrown out that challenge many times before, and never had a taker. And he damn well may be right, the partner cursed to himself, desperately wishing he could run down that hallway. But we are committed now. I've got to keep legal on top of this every minute, because we need clean fingerprints here. Clean? Sanitized, actually. We're overthrowing a country here, I think.

No one answered or met his eyes as he glared around the room.

"Very good," he declared. "Okay, we start taking positions later today, gradually building our bets as events develop. We've done this before, people, it's our bread and butter. The traders will get orders from me when and how increase holdings and adjust our hedges. I can promise you we are throwing all our resources into this. There will be no rogue elephants, no creativity allowed! Everyone got it?"

People nodded. It was quiet. Tomblike, the partner realized. "Then this meeting is over," the partner ordered, banging his gavel too hard and scratching the table's finish. He studied the damage as the staff very quietly got up and filed out.

SAN PALO. THE OFFICE MANAGERS SPEECH

Staff all hired, it was time for the introductory meeting of the employees.

"I have carefully reviewed each person's resume, and we have a select group hired here," Ms. Amber Zima babbled happily, standing at the front of a fairly large room full of people. There were perhaps sixty people in the room, ranging across age, sizes, national origins, and levels of attire. The only common characteristic was an absence of anything in common.

She stopped, looked carefully at her notes, an incomprehensible arrangement of random words and thoughts, and then began reading her prepared speech. "Here is what we will be doing for the company," Ms. Zima announced. Cesare would have been proud of his handiwork, because the speech she gave was absolutely incoherent. Not mad or insane, but perhaps worse, a jumble of grammatically correct sentence structures conveying absolutely no message at all. A raving lunatic would at least have had a theme. The staff stared at her, and then at each other, wondering if the fault was in them or her. After perhaps five minutes, each person decided that she was just crazy, but they were being paid to be there, so they sat back. Forty-five minutes later, she stopped speaking. "So, everyone on board?" she giggled, beaming at the staff. The dazed faces quickly smiled and nodded their heads.

"Great," she finished. "I'll see you all tomorrow morning. I'll give you your assignments then. This is an exciting opportunity for all of us!"

The staff stood up and wandered out.

"I'm not sure about them," she mumbled to her office wall. "I explain and explain, and they don't seem to get the idea. Still, the boss wanted these specific people, and he pays well."

COLORADO. AN ECONOMIC SEMINAR

Jesus was sitting in a comfortable chair, munching a donut. This was the second presentation of the morning. The speaker, a respected professor and a well-known author, was not being well received because his message was, essentially, that things were not working. Jesus looked around, mentally counting up the number of people who had tuned out. They sat politely but the expressions on their faces clearly denied the speaker's words. We deserve the world we get, Jesus thought.

"The global economy can be compared to the physical world in many ways. As you know, the continents drift around the globe on top of tectonic plates. Very slowly, but they move. Fault lines in the earth's crust are created where the tectonic plates collide. When they collide, they create fault lines, and enormous stresses build up around these fault lines. When the stresses are finally too great, the pressure is relieved by earthquakes, volcanoes, and general chaos. It's no different for the global economy, but perhaps harder to understand, because the tectonic plates that collide are group stories embraced at very deep levels by different cultures. Those conflicting stories cause fault lines because, with an integrated world economy, actions that are best for the individual actor, whether that actor is a person, a group, a government, or other social structure, are not always best for the overall system. The simple example is the Ten Commandments, which are very good rules for keeping a village functioning. While the rules work for a village, they don't scale well. For any given individual, the rules may be very destructive, which you can see by analyzing the plot lines of most novels. Certainly, in scaling up the Ten Commandments to the international relations level, 'do not kill' has not been a good plan if you intend to keep your country independent."

"Let's run with the concept of fault lines, and look at how fault lines affect the financial sector. These fault lines are..." The speaker talked for several minutes.

Jesus listened carefully; making copious notes on the differences between countries with government plans for industrial growth and countries with a more "let it happen" viewpoint. "Where you have a country with an economic plan from the top, then the banking and industrial systems, which are funded according to the plan, are quite different from a country where there isn't a 'vision'. Now, visions are always popular, because the government can excite the people with big goals and cut deals with their friends at the same time—the best of all worlds for a politician. The problems are structural and hidden. For example, where economic plans are imposed top down, public financial information is very limited, because the government controls the flow of money, and perhaps doesn't want, or at least see the need for, public oversight. Typically, large banks and powerful industries are bound by private deals. That doesn't work at all well when they have to go outside their little world to seek money from a global economic system. The numbers provided to outside financiers are generally carefully complied and audited fantasies."

So that means that investments in developing countries really are a crapshoot, Jesus thought. Just what Cali's been arguing. That the data is nicely arranged on the page and in an attractive font, but it means nothing. Because behind the numbers are laws and structures that don't work the way we tacitly assume they will.

"Worse, where a country's leadership decides to rapidly build a country as an exporting power, all the focus is on building industry, shipping outside the country, and minimizing consumption in the country to maximize savings for investment. If the country succeeds, it finds itself wealthy, but with no consuming infrastructure. That is, they told people to save, not spend, and now that's all they will do. So the country is trapped in a race to export to other countries, impoverishing those countries by sucking money out, or its economy collapses because its citizens won't buy the stuff the country manufactures. Eventually the other countries have to stop buying stuff because they are broke, and the country's economic plan breaks.

"Now, where a country doesn't have a clear vision, people run amok, from the point of view of central planning, focusing on addressing real needs. It's a lot slower than a master plan, but much stronger in the long run. Of course, every country has a master plan for something, and all politicians have friends who need deals, so it's really a question of the level of government intervention."

The speaker talked for another ten minutes, before ending with, "Where you have a disconnect between the banking system on one hand, and the real work most people do each day on the other hand, you are going to have a crash. Ironically, this seems to happen in the most developed financial systems, where it isn't supposed to happen. The problem, which was unexpected, is that the developed financial systems have carefully tied risk and real life in little bundles that have little to do with each other. The non-developed financial systems, because of the private deals between friends, have quite different types of crashes.

"The practical problem is that bankers and investment advisors are smart predators. They first seek the unsophisticated, i.e., a fool and his money are soon parted. Because big piles of money are not generally held by fools, at least for long, then you have to find people managing money, such as pension funds, who know not that they don't know, or perhaps don't care. When the investment is signed off by legal and risk management, then the investment advisor can go home, his job safe and secure. But the most attractive target is the government itself, because it's all other people's money to a government.

"A lawyer in Kansas brought his son into the practice. One morning, a rancher walked in, furious. 'I raised those cattle—they grazed on the landowner's land, but I paid him for the grazing. Now he says they are his cattle!' The attorney told the rancher that the cattle would be his, and the man left, happy. An hour later, the landowner walked in, furious. 'He grazed those cattle on my land—they are my cattle!' The attorney told the landowner that the cattle would be his, and the man left, happy. The son looked at his father, puzzled. 'You told the rancher the cattle were his, and you told the landowner the cattle were his. That can't be.' The attorney looked at his son, and smiled. 'The cattle, my son, will be ours.' And that's the position of the investment bankers as they confidently look out over the steel and glass canyons where they ply their trade, watching the taxies deliver their prey to their door.

You sell to the government, and then it can print new money to cover the losses. All the bank has to do is to control the levers, Jesus thought to himself. And the investment banks certainly do control those levers.

NEW YORK. COLDMEN SACKING PARTNERS MEETING

The Partner in Charge was sitting in his office with several other senior partners. None seemed at all happy.

"We have orders to make this happen fast," the Partner in Charge grimaced. "And they are people who hold your feet to the fire."

"Literally, I've heard," another partners growled. "Remember that salesperson who sold them some guaranteed Russian bonds that quickly defaulted? He was found in pieces—well, most of him was found. We gave the buyers a full refund."

"Wwwhat did happen to Lucretia?" a third partner stammered. "Wwwas it these people, or others?"

The Partner in Charge stopped and stared out the window. "I don't know," he confessed. "This group told me they had nothing to do with it. They mentioned that there was bad blood between Lucretia and some, unspecified, others. I don't doubt that she had multiple enemies. She had a mind of her own."

"She was hell on wheels," another partner muttered. "I'm not sure she had anything but enemies."

"True enough," the Partner in Charge agreed. "But I do doubt the answers I've gotten. All the responses have been hasty and incomplete. But I'm not interested in pushing those people because they push back-hard! And really, what happened to Lucretia isn't our problem."

"It could be our problem if she is out there working against us, or slipstreaming with us, throwing off the numbers," the risk management partner pointed out, very worried.

"I do not believe that she is," the Partner in Charge mumbled. "I don't think that she's, well, alive any more. Assume she's out of the picture."

The other partners stared at the Partner in Charge for a moment.

"She deserved better," a partner commented sadly. "She was no joy to work with, but she didn't deserve this."

The Partner in Charge stared out the window, and then looked at the partners. "Focus on what we have to do, or we may know more about what happened to her than we ever wanted to."

The partners grimaced and then stood up and left.

DETROIT. WHAT IS REALITY?

Hal, Cali, Lucifer, Mary, Aliston, Lucretia, some of Vladimir's veterans, a few of Lucifer's staff, and the transferees from New York were meeting in the new conference room. Nearly thirty feet to the roof, brightened by a row of old factory windows high in the wall, the conference room was a work in process. Large rusted pipes ran far above, spanning the room and some of the windows were still darkened with grit, but the rest of the room was freshly painted and bright.

"It's thinking about change today," Hal announced. "We appreciate everyone being here, and especially these poor souls who transferred from the bright lights of the big city to the wild frontier here."

"The cost of living is cheaper," one of the transferees replied wryly.

"That was pretty much my initial assessment," Hal agreed, nodding. "But it grows on you."

"Like moss?" Cali inquired.

"And that's why we're here today." Hal observed cheerfully. "A rolling stone gathers no moss..."

There were general groans around the table.

"And we want to be that quick, adaptable company," Hal finished.

People shook their heads. "Where are the cheerleaders?" one of the transferees asked, looking around.

"Umm, we were not able to negotiate an acceptable contract with their union," Hal replied. "Well, here's the problem that we are dealing with: 'There is nothing more difficult to take in hand, more perilous to conduct, more uncertain in its success, than to take the lead in the introduction of a new order of things.'[1] And that joyful task is today's problem." Hal looked thoughtfully at the inert group before him.

"How about some donuts? They are great in this town," Hal suggested and was relieved to see some life in the crowd. Good. The other option was electric buzzers in the seats, and that really hasn't tested well. He motioned to an assistant, who jumped up, ran out of the room, and then ran in back in carefully carrying several boxes of donuts. Don't drop them, Hal worried. I can't guarantee your safety if you do, noting the feral expressions of the people impatiently waiting for their treats.

As the assistant fussed with the boxes, and the smell of donuts filled the room, people's eyes lit up. Everyone quickly walked over to the treats table and there was a short period of polite discussion, followed by intense, focused bargaining and some sneaky grabs. Eventually, everyone had the donut they wanted.

"Okay, we are on a sugar high, and the coffee is strong today, so we'll be bouncing off the walls soon. A good start for a meeting," Hal observed when everyone was seated. "You've all returned to the land of the living?"

There were nods and a few muffled grunts as people munched.

"We've seen the kinds of surprises that the world can offer in the past few weeks," Hal started. While assassination attempts, kidnapping, blackmail and character destruction is perhaps a little more than the usual, it isn't that far off in the world we are headed into. The various structures that order our lives are tottering, and we have to work out a plan for how to survive. When the elephant's dance, the mice have to watch out and right now, the dance floor is shaking. What about supply chain interruptions? What about supply chains vanishing, because of natural or other problems? What about demand vanishing if the economy weakens? What are the break-even, the let-it-burn, the abandon-ship, and the run-for-your-life decision points? Looking on the bright side, where can we make some money? Doing what we did yesterday is a worse idea than it was last week, and it will be even worse next week." Hal stopped and took a sip of his coffee. He shook for a second. "That's strong!"

"Is there good news coming?" Cali inquired, tapping her fingers. "My sugar high is starting to sag."

"No good news that I know of, which may be why my career as a motivational speaker went down in flames," Hal replied, shrugging. "Okay, here's the concept. The companies have to be more independent—closer to their feedback—so that they can adapt. We need to think about what kind of information we're looking for to see a disaster about to happen from a distance, or conversely, point out maybe something that people are not seeing. That's not asking much, just clairvoyance and perfect vision."

"In case you're wondering," Aliston pointed out to the transferees, who were looking distressed, "going back to New York isn't an available option. This will be corporate headquarters, so it's an exciting opportunity, like I told you."

"Perhaps more exciting than you mentioned," one of the transferees replied carefully. "But better here, planning, than in New York, getting memos after the 'famous plan' is in place."

"Ah, the legendary 'famous' plan?" Hal responded. "Make a plan, tear it up. All the day you'll have good luck."

Cali shook her head.

"We've been thinking about the whole idea of change, tied to, well, how we view the world, for a long time," one of the veterans reflected. "Business is a small subset of the events in the world. Life is change, at many levels."

"We need a flexible, adaptive group of people who are used to dealing with constant changes in business/life, and successfully adapting," Hal commented. "Is that asking for much?"

"We are building a fighting force of extraordinary magnitude," Cali announced. "You have our gratitude."

One of the transferees spit out his coffee, he was laughing so hard. There were mixed groans and laughter from the rest of the group.

"If it were only as simple as sword fighting," one of the veterans wished.

"Obviously, we're in Detroit," Hal continued, ignoring the laughter, "where GM over-organized itself into almost non-existence, a wonderful example of what not to do. It's being adaptive to change, not resisting change, that will keep us going."

"In all fairness," one transferee interrupted, "any huge organization like that runs aground eventually. Things scale up, but they don't scale down well. Elephants dominate the savannah until the food runs short and then little creatures feed on their remains."

"Very fair point," Hal agreed. "And a good lead, because we need to scale up when we can, but scale down when needed. Scientists have found pigmy elephant fossils on an island, so elephants can scale down. It's the time required to act that is the difference between survival and oblivion. So, what is change? Anyone?"

"Change is something different from now," a transferee volunteered.

"When someone says 'You've changed,' it simply means you've stopped living your life their way," another transferee mumbled.

"Marriage counselor, Aisle 2," a transferee noted. "Bring a mop."

The transferee who had made the remark laughed. "I think Aisle 2 got bulldozed. I'm happy to be in Detroit, leaving the mess back in New York."

"Pain makes people change," Jesus mused, more to himself than the group.

"We expect something, and change is a different result. Change is perception," a third transferee argued. "This guy gives a hot dog vendor a twenty to pay for a three-dollar hot dog. He gets his hot dog and he's waiting for his money back, but nothing happens. After a minute, he angrily asks the vendor, 'Where's my change?' The vendor replied, 'Change comes from within.'"

Boo! Hiss! Came from all directions.

"An affection for poor jokes," Hal observed. "You have a future in this company, sir. Get that man an extra donut!"

"How do we know change?" Hal asked. "How do we know what's actually happening? We read, talk to people, get someone's take on something they think happened. Anecdotes are not data—probably the world's most neglected truism. And the categories we use, sloppy moral categories like 'powerful and powerless', or 'selfish and altruistic', are manipulated and misleading. Every newspaper uses facts, woven carefully into both a story people will pay money for and that the newspaper can't be sued for."

"That's what the Internet is for—saying false things without getting sued," one of the transferees mused.

"Perceiving a situation should be a simple operation," Hal continued. "You just look and see what's around you. The problem is that surface simplicity appears because your mind has weeded out almost all of the events actually going on around you. Only a few things are pushed up to consciousness. What's pushed into consciousness is a complex calculation based on many factors, almost all of which we are unaware of. Imagine a circle labeled 'physical reality/real world.' Then another circle labeled 'social reality,'' and finally, a third circle, labeled 'your perceptions.' The circles overlap a bit, but a lot less than you'd guess. Now, that's important because, for example, where you have a strongly held social reality that doesn't actually overlap with the 'real world,' that's black swan territory. A train wreck in process."

"I'm asking you to face reality," Cali begged, staring at Hal.

"Whose reality?" Hal demanded, puzzled. "Yours or mine?"

"My reality and yours, that's whose," Cali pleaded.

"What are you saying?" Hal asked, frustrated.

"I'm asking you to face reality," Cali sighed.

"And so on and so on," Hal commented. "What is reality? The rallying cry for the hippies."

"We see only what we know," Lucifer announced.

"Facts show you only what you want to see," Jesus added.

"See a penny, pick it up. All the day you'll have good luck," Mary bubbled.

The transferees glanced cheerfully at each other.

"I knew corporate were out of their minds," one advised.

"Better to be in the asylum writing the plan than outside taking orders," another responded.

"They're wise to us," Jesus acknowledged.

"Moving right along," Hal smiled, "what's the underlying model of the world we use? Because that's what we use to recognize change. There are two possible encompassing models, really. First, a model that insists everything could be known, if we had better information, the classical mechanistic view of the universe. God the watchmaker, lots of little gears clicking away. Or second, a quantum model that argues the future is unknowable, not just unknown. If you have an unknowable future, you act and think a lot differently than if you are constantly looking for the gears of the clock structure poking through. Watching is astrology and omens, reading the tea leaves for hints of the already fixed to come. Unknowable is collecting information and seeing what it adds to, improvising with events."

"Now, when we are babies, we experiment with the real world," Cali remarked. "Babies are always doing stupid things to discover the world around them, because they don't realize the difference between fatal and not. Those who survive develop some techniques, call them 'schema,'—what's a meeting without fancy words?—that we use to interact with the world. These techniques evolve, and when we face something new, we choose an existing schema and use it, seeing what happens. If it works, we use it more often. Piaget called this assimilation—babies applying existing schema to new things. For adults, assimilation is a perfectly natural response to new technology, and as a result we often get it completely wrong. One of the biggest problems with a new software program, for example, is that you bought it because the old program wasn't adequate, but you want the new software to work like the old program, so you don't have to think. It's using the new program as a new program, it's changing your behavior that gets the results you want, but it's really, really hard. Who has time to rethink everything you run into every day?"

"Like career choices?" one of the transferees questioned cautiously.

"Actually, an excellent example," Hal agreed. "When you're in college, you make choices based on things you read and hear. Then you go to work and discover that there is a marginal, at best, relationship between what you thought the work would be and what it actually is. Why? The definition of what you expected was tied to some type of a measurement someone used. Underlying 'rethinking' is the very real problem of measurement. First, we measure some 'thing,' some attribute of the 'thing' that can be expressed as a number. Now, this measurement number may or may not relate to anything useful about the 'thing,' but at least we have a number, something 'real' to hold on to. That number may or may not be useful in predicting some behavior of the 'thing' measured, but we are so proud of the number that we then extrapolate that measurement to another 'thing,' and then make decisions on the data generated. At that point, our 'hard' data, sadly, is a figment of our imagination, but it's real numbers on a sheet of paper to show the committee."

"That's revealed truth!" a transferee exclaimed, standing up and waving her arms.

"You chose well with this group," Hal advised Aliston. "Crazy people—they fit in well here. Anyhow, measurement leads to the problem of the stick in the ground. We have a number, and we made a decision. Once a decision is made, that structures the next decisions and they all reference the initial decision. Most of the time, that makes sense, but sometimes, the initial decision is so far off because of changed circumstances that the stick in the ground makes future decisions impossible."

"Now, John Maynard Keynes had an answer for that problem," Cali pointed out. "'When the facts change, I change my mind. What do you do, sir?' But it's hard to do. You lose face with people, and worse, you feel inconsistent yourself. If I was wrong once, then I could be wrong again, that type of thought."

"Fortunately," Hal noted, "I'm wrong so often I don't have to worry about keeping track."

Cali bit her tongue as Hal glanced at her. "No, that's too easy," she replied, shaking her head.

"Let's look at the goal," Hal continued, smiling. "A device is easy to use when the possible actions are visible, and it's obvious what works where. That's a design rule for physical things, like doors, but the same idea applies to planning for the future. Even with that clear rule, how often are the doors in an office building impossible to figure out how they open until you push on them? You need a visual clue as to whether to push or pull, and which side to grab onto. Plans are the same, except more complex. If we have a plan, and we have an idea how the plan affects things, then we can pick a plan that matches a given situation. That worked pretty well hoeing the fields, because after the one-hundredth time, you had the parameters down pretty well. We don't get those kinds of clear plans anymore with all the changes in the world. Our minds are not hardwired to immediately grasp and act on many things we face today. Oh, we're pretty good at throwing rocks at small animals and reading facial expressions, but genetics, evolution, neuroscience, embryology, economics, and mathematics? "

"Back to Hal's intersecting circles—looking at the circle labeled 'yourself,' and the intersection with the circle labeled 'social structures.' You are different than they want you to be," Jesus observed. "Take my word for it, I know. William James asserted that we are the survivors of the successful killers, and while we may put on a happy and peaceful face, inside us, ready at any moment to burst into flame, are the smoldering and sinister traits of our ancestors. People under pressure revert to the norm. Unsophisticated native peoples are deadly serious about warfare. They exterminate their enemies when they can, while enthusiastically torturing captives, collecting body parts for trophies, and feasting on enemy flesh. I mention this because people, enmeshed in a structure that provides food, shelter, and protections for their children are dramatically different people from those either outside a structure or people whose structures have collapsed. You can't assume polite behavior after a crash."

"Are we having fun yet?" a transferee asked, "or does it get better? Is there a part coming about our happy retirement vacation home on the water?"

"Well, the meeting is almost over, for what that's worth," Hal answered. "Okay, what is my favorite topic?"

"Anemones," Cali responded, cheerfully. "Those strange little creatures that live on coral reefs."

"I love the clownfish," a transferee added. "Nemo was so cute!"

"Okay, if we are done having fun at my expense," Hal continued, "it's anomalies. Otherwise known as system deviances?"

"We love deviance," Aliston asserted and there were general nods around the room.

"I'm going to have to wrap this up quickly, I see," Hal sighed. "The troops are getting rebellious. Okay, in a nutshell, an anomaly is some part of the story that isn't working. Everything is a story. All stories have a chronology, a beginning and an end, and a background that it is played against. Just like any play, but an anomaly is something 'not right'. The problem is that we don't see the 'not right.' A great example was the gorilla in the basketball game. These professors filmed a basketball game and guy in a gorilla suit wandered in and out occasionally. The people watching the game didn't see the gorilla because they were told to watch a specific aspect of the game, and that's all they saw. They saw the game they were expecting and never even saw the gorilla! So why are we like this? A study studied scientists studying data denying desired deviances."

"Bet you can't say that five times quickly," Cali interrupted.

Ignoring her, Hal continued, "We resist anomalous information, assuming that unexpected results are a stupid mistake, because we are hard wired that way. Each of us, all the time, carefully edits reality, selecting evidence that confirms what we already believe. Which makes a lot of sense, because who can rethink everything all the time? It's a problem, though, because we are just as blinkered as a horse pulling a wagon, but we deny the blinkers. The anterior cingulate cortex, referred to as the 'Oh Shit! circuit,' affects our perception of errors and contradictions. Tied to that is the dorsolateral prefrontal cortex, which suppresses thoughts that don't square with our preconceptions. So think about this and try watching for the parts of the story that don't work. That's where the money and the opportunities are, if that helps. Fine, recess, everyone, we're out of here."

SÃO PAULO. THE BIOLOGIST'S STORY.

There were three groups of employees at the office in São Paulo.

One group seemed to actually do something more or less productive. They cleaned offices. Not really all that well, but they actually went somewhere and did something. Ms. Zima went and inspected their work and always found it satisfactory. Within a month at most, the crew was fired from that job and Ms. Zima would find them another office to clean until fired again. No one asked why they were fired. Ms. Zima just assumed their work was too high quality and looked for more work.

Another group was assigned to make a map of the city, marking off certain kinds of businesses. They really didn't understand what they were doing, but they wandered around town, made notes and marks on the maps they were given, and turned the paperwork in at the end of each week.

The third group was only three people and their work, as far as they had determined, was sitting in a different bar each afternoon and preparing a report about the service and the food. While they couldn't believe their luck at finding the job, they were, bluntly, barely functional at even that.

"I don't like this place," the tall one snapped. Ryan Flynnigan was his name. A man in his early fifties, he was angry. He was angry in the morning, angry at noon, and angry when he left work. The other two wondered if he was angry at home, but didn't really want to find out. Ryan railed for twenty minutes about perceived faults in the food, the beer, and the table he was sitting at before he finally annoyed another person in the restaurant enough that they went out in the alley to fight.

"That's five minutes longer than yesterday," the biologist commented. "Maybe he's mellowing in his old age."

"Doubt it," the other man replied. "What's amazing is that for a man as angry as he is and with as many fights as he gets into, he still can't pick people he can beat."

The other participant in the fight came back in, laughing, and loudly told his friends what an idiot the other man was. "Your friend, he is a fool," the man shouted to them, his fists ready.

"True enough," the biologist agreed.

The fighter turned away, disappointed.

"So, you were telling me about your life," the rough-looking man asked. "Wasn't sounding like all that good a time."

"No," the biologist replied, shaking his head. "It's been horrible, actually. My tribe was so proud of me, I was first one given the chance to go to college. So I went, studied hard. I earned a degree in biology, and then an advanced degree. I lost touch with the tribe. I was a long way away, working hard. Hell, I turned my back on them—fell into the world of the city, the civilized. Met a wonderful girl, and we were engaged." The biologist stopped talking, and gulped his beer down. Then he stared at the table for a few minutes.

The rough man sipped his beer and waited.

"We took a trip to a remote part of the country," the biologist finally continued, staring at his empty beer. "I was doing some research—there were some important samples out there. We were there for a few days with a group, camping, way out in the jungle. Suddenly, there was an attack on the group at night. She vanished along with several others.

"The next morning, the police were there. Something about how they were closed at night, so they were there by ten in the morning, only, say, twelve hours after the attack. They nosed around, wrote up a report, and were about to leave," the biologist muttered, making himself talk.

"I shouted at them, 'What about the tracks?' Shouldn't they follow the tracks? There were heavy foot tracks leading into the jungle—even a policeman could have followed them," the biologist sighed. "The police were angry, but they agreed. Three of them and I walked for ten minutes, following the tracks. When we were far away enough from the group so that no one could hear, they beat the hell out of me, told me to get out of the area immediately, and to never, never tell the police what to do again. They got a little carried away because I didn't wake up until about dark. Well, I couldn't go back, because they had told me to leave before dark or they would kill me. So I slept through the night in a tree. Being raised in the wild, a member of a, well, partly civilized tribe, has some advantages. They'd have figured the animals would have got me in the night, and forgot about me.

"The next day, I carefully followed the tracks," the biologist continued. "They had faded, but to me they were as clear as a paved road.

They led to a highway, where I could see that at least a couple of trucks had stopped, by their tracks in the mud. I had nothing else to do, nowhere to go, so I walked down the highway. I knew which way they went because the mud wore off their tires, showing me where they had gone. After a day's walk, I came to where they had pulled off down a muddy road, back into the interior.

"I waited until night," he mumbled. He stopped to sip the beer the waiter had just brought and then stared intently at the table. "Then I carefully, quietly went down the muddy road. It was good I had grown up in the wild, because I spotted the guard long before he spotted me. A stone took care of him, and I went on." He stopped again, and, grimacing, took a long drink from his beer, draining it. He banged the glass down on the table. "Then I heard trucks, and jumped for the brush. Two trucks roared by me, headed back to the road. Since I couldn't catch up to the trucks, I followed the path down to where the trucks came from.

"They were organ farmers," the biologist hissed. "All that was left in the camp was bodies with important organs missing. My fiancée was one of them. I stayed there for a day, in shock, and finally pulled myself away, back to the world. Searching the camp, I'd found labels and papers, enough to figure out the next step in the puzzle. So I spent four months following up. Net result: a visit from several large men in uniforms. It was made very clear that if I ever made any more trouble, I would be harvested. Very slowly. The only reason they were not killing me was because they thought that killing me might give someone the idea that what I had been shouting about, warning people about, had some truth to it. So they threw me into a psychiatric hospital. Surprisingly, I survived, and eventually they threw me out, bored with beating me.

"I tried to go back to the tribe, but they were gone. Driven out by the big landowners, thrown off the land by thugs. The big companies, the huge corporations who have offices near this bar, they can do anything. So, six months ago, I came here. I prowl about on little cat's feet, watching and waiting, but there isn't anything I can do to get back at them. Still, I wait. Natives learn that the jungle rewards waiting. And then this job popped up. It keeps me alive."

"That's not a good story," the rough man concluded. "Not good at all."

The biologist sat silently.

"Well, this job," the rough man argued, changing the subject. "It makes no sense. Nothing that we do makes any sense, and that manager? It's a good thing that woman's shoes don't have shoelaces, because she'd never get into work."

"So you?" the biologist asked, looking at the rough man. "What was your life?"

"I've kicked around," the rough man admitted. "Roughhouse work, physical labor where I can find it. This job? It's nice to do nothing and get paid for it. It gives me a chance to rest."

"I'm out of here," and the biologist suddenly stood up. "Talking about things, well, it makes me antsy. See you tomorrow." He stood up and left.

Roughhouse work, the rough man thought. Yeah, that's a good description for armed robbery, drug dealing, and extortion. And I know all about organ farming. What's really odd is that I swear they knew about that when they hired me. I've never had a job interview like that. He waved at the waiter and ordered another beer. There's a game on the TV, it's comfortable in here, and I have money. It's a good day.

New York. The Junior Partner

The traders started taking currency positions, hedging a multiplicity of currencies.

A floor down, the junior partner responsible for the day-to-day trading mechanics studied a thick printout, clearly baffled. What the hell was she doing? And I have to handle all this detail? How the hell am I supposed to get the transactions to run through all these little companies all over the world. It's impossible to keep track of what entity does what and when. He threw the printout to the floor in disgust. And I'll be out of here on my ass if it isn't done as ordered, he complained. Shit.

Wait!, he realized, suddenly excited. I know people in São Paulo—financial people. People I went to school with, people I can trust. Well, as much as you can trust anyone in this line of work. I don't see why all of this elaborate charade is needed anyhow. The partner told me that legal had vetted this and it is clean. So if it's legal, do it like it's legal. All this fooling around just makes it look like we had something to hide. Lucretia was just weird and all this elaborate planning shows her weirdness. He smiled, really happy for the first time in days. There are big commissions here. I'll bet I can get some side commissions and split them. That would offset the bonus that I was shorted last year. Shorted because of Lucretia, actually. I'll prove I can do this better than she could have, and I'll make some real money in the process.

He carefully went over his list of contacts, and decided who to approach. A fairly short conversation later and it was agreed. He was to get a side commission, the bank officer got a side commission, and everything ran through that bank. All of Lucretia's careful planning, running all the transactions through countries that would prevent anything from ever being disclosed, tossed by the wayside. All of the orders and transactions would be sitting happily in a bank in São Paulo, which became the central clearing house.

The risk compliance officer, who hadn't seen a copy of Lucretia's original plan because that was 'partners only & need to know', signed off because it made sense to run everything through that group of banks. They were financially strong, well thought of, and solid. The trading desk was overjoyed to run everything through one place so they could worry about the hedge, not the details. And the Partner in Charge, having handed the plan off to the staff with emphatic, shouted orders to absolutely, without the slightest deviance or creativity, follow the exact damn plan, never knew. At least, not until it was too late.

DRIPPING

Around the world, little reports started to pop up above the noise of daily life. Little snippets of information generated and sent out by official-sounding companies and agencies. Those companies and agencies were all actually empty shells, but who has the time to check everything? An escalating flow of serious-sounding documents, questioning, belittling, doubting, and attacking all the exports and products of Paraguay. At least in the executive outline, which was all the press reads. In the small print, there were weasel words and careful, delimiting statements. Responding to the attacks, more documents appeared, belittling, defending and denying the attacks. The responses were cleverly worded to actually strengthen a readers doubts and questions. What can be more tantalizing for an expert reader than a carefully reasoned defense, subtlety flawed, that in the end makes it clear things are even worse than the attacks imply? The excited reader concludes there has to be fire under all that smoke and shifts into gear.

Soon, there were papers citing papers, the small print in the original documents swept aside. The cascade of paper flowed around and around the world. Blogs picked it up, anxious to be on top of things, the big cheese leading their followers to a promised land. Computers hummed as money people started paying anxious attention. Because, as Lucretia foresaw, people run first and ask questions later if they think the markets are going to go down. Every product/manufacture, resource from or linked to the country: soy, drugs, and produce—everything they manufacture or grow or re-export was under attack, from all over the world. And then the real government agencies had to respond as the Internet chat built on itself.

The crisis began building on itself, as weak companies in Paraguay quickly saw their financing drying up. Then stronger companies were put under the bright lights, because in this world information flows at the speed of light, and no one wants to be the last to the exit. You don't have to be faster than the bear; you just have to be faster than the investment banker running beside you.

Lucretia's plan had buffers built into it. Buffers keep the financial wheels from spinning too quickly and coming off the machine. Paul's plan wanted the wheels off and so his staff tore the buffers out. Lucretia's vision of a huge wave, an amplification of events, built and built, moving towards the shore to break.

Days went by and the traders, excited, smelled blood. They were placing bigger and bigger orders, seeing incredible sums of money being made. They read the articles on the problems with exports and products, and little voices inside them asked what was really going on. All too convenient, they told to themselves in the night, but they were swept up in the excitement of the chase.

SWITZERLAND. AN UNWELCOME DISCOVERY

Then, one day, a junior accountant on Paul's staff was thumbing through the reams of daily reports. Everyone was happy, actually ecstatic, about the plan's progress and the profits so far and so reviewing the details had become a little cursory. 'Why look too closely when things are going well?' is the normal human daily magic. Don't look a gift horse in the mouth, all that stuff. But this junior staff accountant, casually checking the transactions, froze. He studied the transactions on the page. Then the next page, and the next. He suddenly realized, his gut twisting around itself, that all the transactions had been run through a consortium of banks in São Paulo. He began shaking as he worked through the thick printout, but each page had the same story. Not the plan, he thought frantically, holding his head. Not the plan I signed off on. Terrified, he unlocked a compartment in his desk, and pulled his copy of the plan out. He read the plan and read it again. And again, before letting it slip out of hands onto his desktop.

He sat, shaking, at his desk for ten minutes before he had the courage to go to the head accountant's office. He walked in and closed the door. He uttered five sentences and there was a roar from the head accountant, who rushed out of the room, down to the staff person's office, to check the reports himself.

Four hours later, the entire staff had finished checking and cross checking and cross-cross checking, and there was no doubt. Little red tick marks covered the printouts like spilled blood. The head accountant steeled himself and walked into Paul's audience room.

"Yes?" Paul asked, noticing him standing there. And then Paul looked more closely, seeing clearly the beads of sweat on the man's face and his soaked shirt. "Out, everyone," Paul snarled. "Now." People ran from the room.

When the room was empty, Paul demanded, "What?"

Three sentences from the head accountant, and there was a roar from the audience chamber. Paul called his key staff back in, and they started calling people. Including the wet work/cleanup group.

NEW YORK. COLDMEN SACKING

The Cardinal and Mother Superior were sitting in the conference room of the Coldmen Sacking office, looking quite displeased. Sitting across from them was the Partner in Charge, who was actually shaking, and several other senior partners who were trying to breath as quietly as they could to avoid notice. The only sound was the Cardinal's tense tapping on the table, a Morse code signaling fury.

The junior partner in charge of the transaction detail was led into the room by a smiling secretary. Her smile became a look of terror as she turned away from the junior partner, who noticed nothing. The secretary rushed out of the room, not looking back, and the door was closed behind the junior partner by one of the Cardinal's guard, who quietly stood in front of the door. The junior partner sat in the chair politely held for him by one of the Cardinal's staff. The junior partner didn't know the Cardinal or Mother Superior; he was just worried about whether anyone knew about the side commission deal. This type of thing happens all the time, he told himself, and it would be okay even if they found out. And if they don't like it? I made enough in the last week to leave this place forever.

"You didn't comply with the plan," the Senior Partner stated, trying to control his voice.

"Ah, no," the junior partner replied, nervously. "I looked at the legal review and as this investment was completely legal, with no questions, I analyzed all possible options. Because we could get a faster response and better prices running the transactions through the bank group in São Paulo, I did it that way." He sat back, defiant. "It was better for the plan and better for the firm, so I didn't see any reason to raise the issue. Hey, it was close enough to the plan!"

"You also made, oh, approximately $35M in the last week alone in side commissions," the Cardinal remarked, idly tracing a rune on the top of the desk. "Paid into your accounts in Hong Kong, after the transactions were washed through a dozen banks and jurisdictions. Interesting that you took the effort to cover those transactions. Your behavior would almost show a guilty mind." The Cardinal looked at the junior partner and smiled.

The junior partner flinched.

"Close only counts in hand grenades and horseshoes" the Cardinal commented, and Mother Superior laughed.

The junior partner gulped. "I think you misinterpreted..." he started to stammer.

"There are mistakes, and there are errors," the Cardinal growled. "An error is the incorrect execution of the right plan. A mistake is choosing the wrong plan. You chose to make your life simple by running everything through one bank and to enrich yourself on the side at the same time. Do you really believe your decision to be lazy and greedy will be rewarded?"

The junior partner sat terrified, his mouth open, shaking in his chair. The senior partners stared at the table, their faces frozen, knowing what was coming.

The Cardinal glanced at Mother Superior and nodded. She smiled at her guards. In a second, the junior partner was trussed up and shoved in a large laundry cart. "Get him out of here," Mother Superior ordered. "Keep him alive. I will interrogate him later." Her guards bowed and the laundry cart was wheeled out into the hallway. It was silent in the room as they all listened to the sounds of the cart fading down the hallway.

"Fortunate for you that he is a complete fool," the Cardinal announced, looking at the Senior Partner. "Had he the sense to say you were involved also, I could just kill all of you and get some pleasure out of this day. As it is, you live: for now. I need a complete, and I mean complete, report on what information is where, and the exposure that we face. I need to know whether the information that we are concerned with can be transferred to safety, or if the information is stuck forever at that bank and its records. You might as well continue running the transactions through São Paulo, as the junior partner was doing, until we figure out how much of a mess this is. There is no point focusing attention on us by changing our patterns at this time. But, do not fail me again."

The senior partner nodded, not even able to speak.

"These gentleman," the Cardinal continued, pointing to several boring-looking people sitting in the corner, "will stay and review your progress. They are quite bright, so don't try and fool them or hide anything from them. Should they feel that someone, anyone, at any level, is trying to hide or disguise things or in any way fool them, well, they have a direct line to Mother Superior, who will proceed with the questioning of the suspect individual. Mother Superior enjoys her work, but the people being questioned do not. Is that clear?"

All in the room nodded.

"Thank you, gentlemen," the Cardinal snarled, "for this meeting. I think we clearly understand what has to happen next." The Cardinal and Mother Superior stood and walked out, their guards following them down the hall.

"We need to get started," one of the dull men told the Partner in Charge. "Now. Mother Superior loves her work—I've seen her in operation. I never want to be the focus of her work, and I can promise you, gentlemen, you do not either."

NEW YORK, THE CARDINAL'S PENTHOUSE

Two days later, one of the dull men stood in the Cardinal's dining room, his report finished.

The Cardinal studied him, dismayed, and then glared out the window. "It's that bad?"

"It's actually worse, Your Eminence," the man stammered. "This is a list of the information that is at that bank group. They have all of these transactions, all of these orders carefully organized. Even a moderately bright investigator could back into the press releases and the timing of the orders and tie far too many things together. And there is no banking secrecy law that we can effectively use for cover."

"What would, hypothetically, fix the problem?" the Cardinal inquired. "Just hypothetically."

"The bank needs to vanish, physically, which is the only way of making sure the physical records and the information on the computers are gone. The backup data center—vanish. The bankers involved, and anyone they may have spoken to, bragged to, all 'poof'. That would head off any investigations," the man replied. "Hypothetically."

"Very good work," the Cardinal declared. "Thank you for your quick and comprehensive analysis. And, if you were to apportion blame to people who did not deserve our trust, well, Mother Superior would appreciate your thoughts." The man bowed and left.

The Cardinal rang a bell, and his butler ran into the room.

"My jet to Switzerland," the Cardinal sighed. "Now."

SWITZERLAND. THE CARDINAL'S REPORT

"And that is my report, my lord." The Cardinal sipped his wine and gazed out over the lake, bracing for an explosion.

"The lake is beautiful this time of year," Paul commented, toying with his wine glass.

"You seem to take the news well, my lord," the Cardinal observed, surprised but relieved.

"I had a backup plan. This kind of thing usually seems to happen and actually fits into another plan very well." Paul stood up and walked over to the edge of the balcony, resting on the carved stone, silent for a minute. "Here's what I'm thinking. Do you remember London in, oh, roughly 1850?"

"Yes," the Cardinal grimaced. "Filthy city—smelled like shit all the time. I had to go and feed money to Marx for years to keep him alive. It took days to get the smell out of my nostrils."

"It fixed itself, eventually. But all these megacities of the developing world are on the same unsustainable growth path London faced all those years ago. It's estimated that by 2015, the five largest cities on the planet will be Tokyo, Mumbai, Dhaka, São Paulo, and Delhi. Hard to believe, but all of them will have populations in excess of twenty million. Most of the people will live in shantytowns, squatters living in their own filth. Victorian London reborn, masses of crawling, dirty people sucking precious resources away from the rest of the world. There are a billion squatters on earth now, and at the rate things are going, perhaps a quarter of humanity will be squatters by 2030."

"Which nicely ties to your wish to crash all of this sooner rather than later," the Cardinal observed.

"True," Paul confided. "This isn't going to work, and we might as well try and save ourselves. What did that guy say, Taleb? He called the modern world a state of Extremistan. That meant that it's dominated by rare, very rare, events, but very powerful events."

"There really isn't any way of judging the effects of our actions," the Cardinal advised, studying Paul carefully. "So we may unleash the disaster we fear instead of creating the new world we seek. There are so many possibilities that it's beyond any risk analysis."

"Wicked problems," Paul answered. "That's what they call them today. Tied together, you yank on one part, the others pull tighter."

"And so you proposed to cut that Gordian knot? Decisive action, to the heart of the issue?"

"It takes a good man to prevent a catastrophe, milady, and a great man to make use of one," Paul quoted. "From *The Three Musketeers*—you should recognize that. It was, after all, attributed to one of your past selves."

"They were good movies," the Cardinal agreed. "In reality, I had the three musketeers murdered in the Bastille, but that's not as pretty a story."

SÃO PAULO. NEW WORK

There was a meeting at the company offices. The office manager sat down with the third group: the angry man, the biologist, and the rough man.

"The company has a job for you," the office manager bubbled. "I don't exactly understand it, but here are the instructions. You are supposed to do something with this stuff that is coming in next week. You will be working at this location from now on—it's at..." She squinted at the letter. "I can't read it, here." She handed the biologist the letter and then handed each of them a map. "Here is a key for each of you. Remember! Report to me at least once a week."

The men looked at each other, shrugged their shoulders, and walked out.

"Real work," the angry man muttered. "I'm sure it will be something demeaning. I'm so sure that I'm going to have a beer first." He walked off.

"How does he stay that angry?" the rough man marveled, watching the angry man stomp away. "You'd think he'd have a heart attack or something."

"And he's never even explained why he's angry," the biologist replied, staring at the man's back as he vanished into the crowd. "I don't think he even realizes that he is angry. Weird."

They walked over to the address the manager had given them. It wasn't far, and they had nothing else to do.

"Okay, this is interesting," the biologist observed, puzzled, as they stepped into the facility. He started examining the equipment very carefully. "This is a state-of-the-art biological facility with full biohazard systems." He looked around, astonished. "This equipment is almost new. Used, certainly," touching some of the equipment, "but in excellent shape."

"Used means it is harder to trace," the rough man pointed out. "It must have been difficult to find this exact equipment. Interesting."

"Well, let's see what we've got," the biologist remarked. He leaned over the desk and started leafing through the papers there. Then he sat down and started reading intently.

The rough man looked over his shoulder and shook his head. "Can't understand a bit of it."

"I can," the biologist replied. "I just can't believe it."

"Look, I'm going to the bar," standing up. "There is nothing for me to do here."

"I'll stay here," the biologist replied and he went back to reading. He didn't even notice the rough man leaving.

Two days later, the rough man walked into the facility. The biologist was sitting at the desk, making notes.

"So what is it?" the rough man asked. "Drugs?"

"Kind of," the biologist replied, biting his lip. "We're getting a shipment of something tomorrow and I've got the equipment ready for it. Some kind of biohazard? I have a guess, but I don't know exactly what. It certainly won't be what the shipping manifest says it will be"

"Is it dangerous?" the rough man blurted out.

"Not to me," the biologist warned. "Not to you if you touch nothing. Otherwise, it's deadly. Really fast, and nasty."

"Got it," hastily stepping back from the piece of equipment he had been tapping on. "Well, do you need me?"

"No," the biologist answered. "Not a bit."

The rough man left for another bar.

The next day, the biologist received the package, delivered in a plain box. No biohazard stamps, he thought. Nothing. Not even marked fragile. He carefully pulled the cylinders out and put them into the culturing equipment. For the next day, he was busy balancing the temperature and nutrients, but the instructions were pretty clear. The culture was growing nicely as he left for the night.

The next day, he took a sample, very carefully, and began to analyze it. And then analyzed it again, and again. Yeah, that's what it is, he thought. Biohazard? This is far beyond that. What could anyone want with this?

SWITZERLAND, THE CHATEAU

"So, that's the situation, Father," Cesare reported to Paul as they walked through the park-like setting of the chateau. "São Paulo is going well. That damaged group of idiots will make us proud. Anonymously, of course."

"Very good, my son," Paul declared. "Well, it should work. Remember, 'The very first essential for success is a perpetually constant and regular employment of violence.'"[2]

"Those who want to live, let them fight, and those who do not want to fight in this world of eternal struggle do not deserve to live,"[3] Cesare quoted.

"Reading from the same playbook," Paul agreed, nodding. "Now, what are we missing? It's always the details. One night Osiris slept with Neftis, thinking she was Isis. That was inattention to detail."

"And wine," Cesare added. "Usually there was some of that involved also."

"True, but from inattention to detail bad results can follow, and do," Paul replied, smiling. Then he frowned. "What are we missing here?"

SÃO PAULO. THERE ARE NO INNOCENTS

The biologist, the angry man, and the rough man were sitting at a bar the next day. The biologist had made sure that there was no one else sitting within earshot of them, first by bribing the bartender to turn the television up, secondly by bribing the manager to leave the surrounding tables covered with dirty dishes, and finally by bribing the waitress to seat people anywhere but at the tables surrounding them, even if customers demanded those tables, dirty dishes or not. The manager had offered to close the bar, but the biologist didn't like that idea. Too obvious, he thought. Hiding in plain sight, that's always the best. There may still be thugs from the corporations watching me.

"So, you have some news," the angry man demanded. "Are they firing us?"

"Hardly," the biologist replied. "But that shipment I just received? It's interesting. Dangerous, actually."

"Figures," the angry man growled, disgusted. "They want us to get hurt."

"Not hurt. Die is more like it. This is weapons-grade biological warfare. I've seen it in my research. Nasty stuff; it causes uncontrollable rage, leading to death after a couple of days, if you aren't killed while trying to kill something. Not something everyone keeps around the house. I'd guess Asian, probably Indian, by the seals on the cylinders."

The other men looked at him, astonished.

"Would it kill many?" the rough man asked.

"Hard to say," the biologist admitted. "You never know until you try with these toys. There are different levels of strength possible, and different ways of transmitting it. Full strength? Airborne? A LOT of people. Pretty much the whole city, I'm guessing. Lesser strength, not as many. But it's hard to think of any good reason other than killing a lot of people for it to be here."

"What exactly is it?" the angry man worried, rubbing his head.

"Spores. But something really sophisticated. Think of it, well as a kind of a parasite."

"Parasites like ticks?" the rough man scoffed. "Those are not that dangerous."

"Not that dangerous only because we are the spawn of creatures who were infected with what the ticks carry and survived. You have no idea, actually, how dangerous this stuff is. Parasites can be more dangerous than you can imagine," the biologist emphasized. "Plants have parasites, people have parasites, and bacteria have parasites. It's the nature of the world that every possible resource is used by anything that can use it. There are a lot of these spores that do odd things—things we don't really understand. Things we don't want to understand, is closer to the truth.

"For example, there is a parasite called Toxoplasma gondii. It's all over because it's carried by rats and cats. As much as sixty percent of the population is infected with it in some parts of the world. There is evidence that some of the infected people have their behavior permanently changed. The effects range from the levels of neurosis in a population; or poor reaction times, which can cause more traffic accidents; or short attention spans and little interest in seeking out novelty. There may be a relationship between infection and schizophrenia. Toxoplasma has been tied to these effects and it probably does a lot more."

"That can't be," the angry man argued. "People can't be controlled by little bugs like that."

"Actually, it's likely that there is lots and lots of manipulation of human hosts by bacteria and viruses," the biologist countered. "Medical research doesn't look for parasites as explanations for disease and behaviors.

Parasitologists look for these things, but there are not many of them, and it's hard to track and catch these effects."

"People study the little bugs for a living?" the rough man asked. "Yuck, what a life."

"There are airborne spores in Canada killing people. I took a lot of classes in this—thought it would be useful for my life here, until my life dissolved." He sighed and was quiet for a minute. "That one is called Cryptococcus gattii, a fungus thought to only live in tropical and subtropical climates. Surprise! It thrived in the Pacific Northwest, and has become more dangerous there. It attacks by releasing millions of invisible spores that infiltrate a victim's lungs and central nervous system, causing fatal pneumonia or meningitis."

"That's awful," the angry man gulped, momentarily stumped as to who or what to be angry at. "Just walking, you breathe in this stuff and wham?"

"Generally only if your immune system is weak. See, these spores carry all kinds of interesting biological things within them. Like retrovirus, a member of the same family of viruses as the AIDS virus. These viruses carry their genetic information in RNA rather than DNA, and they insert themselves into their hosts' genetic material and stay for life."

"Yeah, but that's science fiction that they can kill," the rough man disagreed. "Colds come and go, and they don't kill everyone."

"Colds are not genetically modified to kill," the biologist declared. "What's in those containers is. Viruses are tough, and there are ten billion viruses in an average quart of surface seawater. So mixing some of those little surprises in the DNA and RNA of the spores isn't that hard to do. Now, this bug we have at the office could never survive in the wild, because it kills its host so quickly. However, as a weapon, these spores are really marvelous. In a sick sense, of course," catching the glances from the other men.

"There was this movie," the rough man remembered, smiling, "... Shivers? I think that was it. There was a parasite that made everyone want to have sex all the time. That would liven the city up!"

"I don't think you grasp this! Did you see Alien? This spore/virus is a perfect organism. Its structural perfection is matched only by its purity of focus. It's unclouded by conscience, remorse, or delusions of morality, as it turns its host into exactly what the parasite wants."

"That's not possible," the angry man snapped, angry now at his confusion, shaking his head.

"Our DNA is only a shade different from that of chimpanzees, or a turtle or a lamprey. Body parts work essentially the same, the brains are made of neurons and neurotransmitters. If we had sense, which humans don't seem to, we would respect the Tree of Life and get along better with the rest of our family of life. Look, a parasite can control those DNA and RNA signals and then it can control us. Humans are not the overlords of the world, humans are food for parasites—a host for the parasites life plan, to be discarded when not needed anymore."

"I saw that Alien movie," the angry man interrupted, wincing. "The creature that burst out of the man's chest was horrifying! Nature bursts through our little worlds and it's terrifying. I still see it in my dreams sometimes."

"This can't be," the rough man muttered, uncertain.

"We don't understand our own DNA," the biologist admitted. "The parasites, the spores, they can take over part of our own DNA. Huge chunks of our human genetic material do nothing for you. This junk DNA doesn't make hair, skin, hemoglobin, or even help other genes. The junk DNA is a type of parasite that consists of little more than instructions for getting itself replicated faster than the rest of the genome. Some of the DNA chunks wander around, a selfish DNA, maybe you could call them genetic parasites. We are guessing that like conventional parasites, genetic parasites can harm their host. As they insert themselves at random places in the genome, they can cause disease. Because genetic parasites can replicate at a faster rate than their fellow genes, they have swamped the genome of many hosts, including humans. This stuff at the building can activate some of those genetic parasites, and away we go."

"How could it do that?" the angry man asked.

"Lots of ways. For example, if you damage the frontal lobes of the brain, you can unleash aggressive attacks. That happens because the damaged lobes stop being a brake on the limbic system, especially a circuit linking the amygdala to the hypothalamus. Make certain connections between the frontal lobe in each hemisphere and the limbic system and you have a mechanism to generate very, very aggressive behavior. Brings out the Berserker in all of us. As our lives prove, lots of people are happy to hurt other people. This just removes any doubts people might have had about their actions. And that's just one possibility. These new designer drugs get right into the brain. The spores, the parasites, they can do the same."

They were silent for fifteen minutes.

"Could a person have a gas mask and survive?" the rough man inquired carefully. "Just hypothetically."

"Yeah," the biologist replied. "The right kind, and careful decontamination, yeah, you'd survive in the chaos. It would be like a zombie movie, though, trying to survive."

"A survivor in a rich but empty town like this one could have a profitable opportunity," the rough man pointed out. "There's information, money, stuff out there."

"There's a lot of people I'd like to use that on," the angry man hissed. "All those thieves and whores that put me down over and over. I'd laugh to see them choke on their own vomit."

"Okay. That's an opinion. And, truthfully, there are some people I'd like to see inhale some of that. A lot of people, actually."

"Well, we're going to need gas masks," the rough man concluded. "Just in case it gets loose."

The others gave him knowing looks.

"Fine, if we're supposed to do something and survive, we're going to need masks," the rough man argued.

The biologist nodded. "Here" He wrote down a name and model number. "Something like this. Cash only! Maybe have someone else get them for you, someone who doesn't know you."

The rough man nodded. "I know how to do this." He left.

"He's a thief," the angry man whispered after the rough man left. "I know people who know people. He's a killer, actually. I couldn't figure out why he was hired. You notice I've not fought him! I'm crazy, but not that stupid."

"So, what's next?" the biologist wondered, surprised at what the angry man had told him. "Do we wait for orders?"

"We do," the angry man agreed. "Assuming we get a beer from that incompetent waiter sometime in our lifetime." He went off to yell at the waiter.

It's right there, at my fingertips, the biologist knew. Revenge against all of them: the slimy politicians, the corrupt police, and the huge corporations that answer to no one. Against all those who destroyed my tribe and my woman! But what about the others in the city, what about the innocents? Is anyone innocent? He sipped the beer that the angry man brought him. What was that novel? *Atlas Shrugged*? The disaster at the railroad tunnel? That was the breaking point. People knew it was going to happen, but they didn't stop it because if it hadn't been that disaster, it would be another. It's the structures—they are forcing the disaster. An individual can't change the future.

Later, in a run-down used goods store in a shantytown in São Paulo. In a back room, where the black market stuff was kept. "So, you're sure about this?" the portly man demanded, studying the rough man.

"Absolutely," the rough man replied. "This guy, he's an academic. A crazy guy, but he knows his stuff. This stuff can wipe out a bunch of people. When they are gone, the pickings are going to be wonderful. We have masks—no one else does."

"I'll track these masks down," the portly man promised. "Carefully, quietly. I think some special clothing, too. The more protection, the better. You don't know what they are planning to with this stuff? A timetable? It isn't here for a good time, that's for sure."

"No, I don't know," the rough man replied. "I wish I did. I've sent my kids out of town, way out of town. You should do the same, but really quietly. A mess like this, should it come down, well, people might dig deep. We don't want any strings back to us."

"I'll send my ex-wife tickets to a show in town," the portly man remarked and they laughed.

DETROIT. BRAZIL?

Everyone was sitting in the community dining room. The television was on in the background and the evening newscaster looked unusually serious.

"What's been happening in Brazil?" Lucifer asked, motioning at the screen with his taco.

Everyone watched the newsman on site in São Paulo talking animatedly about the recent financial events.

"Have you been following the papers?" Lucifer inquired.

"It's some kind of financial crash?" Cali replied, munching on her taco, "as much as I can follow it."

Hal was watching Lucretia closely. She had been talking and joking, but suddenly was staring intently at her plate, saying nothing, her mouth clenched. "You wouldn't know anything about this, would you, ah, sis?" Hal asked Lucretia carefully. "Coldmen Sacking had their fingers in this, as far as I can tell."

Everyone at the table looked at Lucretia, who was very carefully cutting her vegetables into precise squares, completely silent, avoiding eye contact.

"Well, um, I," Lucretia mumbled, quickly taking a bite of food and chewing slowly, still not looking up.

"It's okay," Hal observed, sitting back and watching her, nodding his head slowly. "We have plenty of time. I've noticed that when people answer a question like you just did, well, there's usually a story behind that answer."

Lucretia slammed her knife and fork down on the table. She looked up at Hal, her lips thin and tense. "Okay, well, I kind of prepared a plan for my evil master that he seems to have screwed up royally when it was implemented," she growled, and looked back down at her plate, furiously hacking the green beans.

"That's the problem with lesser minds," Mary suggested helpfully. "They just don't get the nuances."

"Evil master?" Jesus laughed. "I like that. You must have read the same comic books that Hal read in college."

Lucifer was looking carefully at Lucretia, who refused to look away from her plate. She was cutting the vegetables into smaller and smaller chunks, her knife cutting into the finish of the plate.

"Who would believe my daughter was in league with the forces of evil?" Lucifer remarked.

Lucretia glanced up at Lucifer and laughed despite herself. Then she sighed and pushed the plate with its savagely shredded vegetables aside. She stared at the television with a very worried look.

"And the evil plan was, in a nutshell?" Hal asked. "Just out of professional curiosity."

"Oh, destruction of the Paraguayan currency, crashing their economy, making huge profits on the currency speculation, and then buying up assets on the cheap. The usual investment banking routine, writ a little larger," Lucretia responded, defensively. "Well, it's what we do down there. Or did."

"A competent plan, too," Cali offered. "It seems to have worked."

"Not just worked," Lucretia confessed, giving up her attempt to keep secrets and looking around the table. "It's feeding on itself. There were dampers in my plan, but oh, no. That wouldn't have been manly! Go for the gold, and they are. A feint, a little damage, the prey recovers, and the world let's that go by. The Russian Third Armored Division grinding through a countries economy draws attention. Angry attention, from people with guns and armies. And this isn't done yet. Only about half of the plan is visible now—the other half is still building. I know. My plan." She pointed at herself. "It all started at once, but it was timed so the effects build on each other."

She suddenly stared intently at the television, startled. "Wait! What did he just say?" she shouted. "That can't be! Turn it up!"

Hal grabbed the remote and turned the volume up so they could hear. All stared at the television, a newsman standing next to a jovial middle-aged man in a well-cut blue suit. "And here we have the vice president of the bank which led the financial consortium rumored to be behind the recent events," the newsman announced. "The financial press is hailing you as a genius, isn't that correct?"

Lucretia stood up and threw her taco at the screen, which splattered all over the television. "Idiot! Fool! Moronic crawling dung beetle! Your mother was a hamster and your father smelt of elderberries! Shit!" She smashed her hand on the table and winced. She sat down, rubbing her hand, still staring at the TV.

"Ah, interpretation?" Cali asked. "Did I miss something here? I'm inferring, through your actions, that things are going to get worse?"

"I'd say that's a reasonable guess," Mary replied, carefully not looking at Lucretia.

"I like the tacos on the TV," Hal commented. "Look, the newswoman has a mustache. It's a good look for her."

Everyone avoided looking at or even near Lucretia, who was boiling with rage.

"Well, I carefully structured the transactions to flow through a host of small companies headquartered around the world, in odd little places with strong secrecy laws," Lucretia snapped. "I know that sounds clever and well, perhaps 'wrong' in the traditional street sense of the term, but it turned out that the law firm had a standard form for the situation with checkboxes for options. I was amazed. It took them maybe two days to get the whole thing in place." She took a drink to calm herself. Putting the glass down on the table, she stared at the table, taking a couple of slow breaths, and then looked back up. "And I did that because people lose interest if their questions are not quickly answered. You make it hard enough to track what happened, and eventually the world lets it go by. But no—Mr. Asshole here has to grab the limelight. Now the authorities will know exactly where to go to ask pointed questions. They will find all the information in one place, on nice computer disks. Bank officers and investment bankers fold like card tables under pressure."

"So, the scheme comes out," Goth Girl concluded. "Where is the problem? Justice prevails, life goes on. Could be worse."

"Is worse," Lucretia explained. "Paul isn't big on the 'justice prevails' routine. Neither are the very, very important people he had working with him on this. None of that can come out. Ever."

"Ah, I'm hoping I'm not connecting the dots here," Jesus interrupted, worried. "On one hand, the authorities will know where to look and the guilty will fold, thus ensuring everything will come out. But it can't come out. I'm thinking there is a bad end coming to this story?"

"The information has to disappear," Lucretia declared. "That means, oh, just thinking off the top of my head, the bank people, some of the investment bankers, the physical records, the computer records, and the backups. Also any nosy investigators, wives, children, mistresses, and drinking buddies—everyone who could know anything. Paul will insist, I'm sure of it."

"That would be his style," Lucifer agreed, nodding. "Actually, that was always his favorite part of the play."

"So, let's work backwards," Hal speculated. "One possibility would be a focused attack by a select team of special operatives. A big team. That takes out, oh, maybe five hundred people and a couple of large office buildings without damaging anyone else. Unlikely, to say the least. So that leaves the other obvious possibility, which would be wholesale destruction, which coincidentally takes out the problem people and information."

"When you say wholesale destruction," Lucretia continued, grimacing, "you need to expand the concept in your mind. A LOT has to vanish. It's a big city, those people are all over the city, and they all have to go away. I'd guess that Jericho is the playbook they are reading in Switzerland right now."

"That's really not good," Jesus broke in. "I have business interests and friends in São Paulo."

"You see," Lucretia confided, "it was complex, and there were a lot of people involved. There are people who carried out the transactions, and people who wrote the, well, perhaps unclear reports and opinions. People in regulatory agencies around the world. They all lied and cheated for money and were promised privacy. They won't take no for an answer. Then there are the historical conflicts between the countries down there. Lots of bad old stories and suppressed rage that people carry around with them. What has happened so far is only the beginning. The rest of the iceberg is still looming in the fog. They don't even see it coming-yet. The bad feelings are going to turn to psychotic anger by the time it's done. Isn't machismo the ruling behavior?"

"It is," Jesus replied. "They take their honor seriously."

"Well, their honor is about to be handed to them on a plate along with their heads, and selected parts of their reproductive anatomy," Lucretia observed. "My plan made money and walked, leaving pieces behind to satisfy everyone. I told Paul that pigs are slaughtered, and that's where this is headed. Umm, sorry about that," she apologized to the servant wiping off the television.

The woman gave Lucretia a forced smile and kept cleaning.

"Can it be stopped?" Cali asked, worried.

"No can do," Lucretia replied. "First, I don't think it is possible to stop it at this point. Things in motion stay in motion, all that physics stuff. Second, the person trying to stop it has shouted to the world that they know a lot about things no one should know anything about. They are setting themselves up for a long, long stint in a Brazilian jail, as they would be the first to be blamed. Assuming, they lived long enough to go to jail. You know, I used *The Art of War* for this. The 'an attack should be boulders down a mountain onto eggs,' and once the boulders start coming down, gravity takes over."

"You wouldn't like to help with the firm investments, would you?" Hal asked Lucretia. "I mean, quality work should be rewarded. Look, sis, you either came up with a plan or died. I know Paul's mind."

Lucifer was tapping his fingers, thinking. "Paul's not stupid," he pointed out. "Arrogant, vicious, and cruel, but not stupid. This may not be as accidental as you think."

Lucretia looked at Lucifer thoughtfully. "I did wonder," she answered. "There were parts of the plan specifications that didn't seem to tie neatly into what he said he wanted. I asked and Paul went into this monologue about how the Emperor makes strategy and the General carries out the tactics—a polite way of telling me to do what I was told and shut up. Yeah, there was something else in his mind."

"I'm thinking I should go down there," Jesus muttered. "Boots on the ground, and all that. I have contacts. I can ask around."

There was silence.

"You may not want to do that," Lucretia begged, biting her lip as she stared at Jesus. "Please. Worse is one of those relative terms that people define in their minds, only to be later surprised about just how bad it can get. 'Worst' is where this is headed. I'm sorry."

PARAGUAY REACTS.

"Look what they have done!" the President of Paraguay screamed. "They have destroyed our currency, our businesses, our reputation! It's all just smoke and mirrors, all lies and tricks, but we can't stop it!" He smashed his hand on the table and swore. He moved back from the conference table, holding his damaged hand, twice as angry.

"This is an enemy action," a cabinet member shouted, furious. "And we know what country hates us that much."

"The last time we went to war against them," another member of the cabinet observed quietly, "there were few survivors. And their army is much bigger now."

The cabinet sat there, glum.

"On top of everything, it's ruined most of us," a cabinet member groused. "There was no reason to think this would happen. All our stock holdings have crashed; the banks have called loans because of the currency problems. Most of the companies in the country are insolvent and the lawyers are starting to seize the carcasses."

"I want legislation stopping all collections," the President ordered. "For at least ninety days, maybe a year. The world community thinks they can screw us? Well, we can screw them back."

"What about the banks in São Paulo that led this?" another cabinet member demanded. "What are we going to do? I was so angry watching the news last night that I broke my television! Those idiots crowing about their investment ability and the vast amounts of money they made. It adds insult to injury, and we can't stand for it! The public is furious—at least the part of the public that has a clue about what happened. Most of them are just trying to get enough food for themselves and their families."

"We'll take steps," the President promised. "They want to play outside the lines? Turnabout is fair play and we can play outside the lines too. They think we are weak? Our fathers fought and died, but they didn't run. And we won't run either."

Plan B

"The federal investigators made their first visit to the bank," the Cardinal reported to Paul, using an absolutely secure line. "We have someone on the inside, watching. So, plan B?"

"Plan B it is," Paul acknowledged. "Your person—are they useful to you?"

"Yes," the Cardinal answered. "They are long-term staff, actually."

"Perhaps they should leave town then," Paul suggested. "And quickly."

Brazil, a cabinet meeting

"What about this Paraguay thing?" the cabinet member asked. "They have been torn apart, and it looks like it came out of São Paulo."

"It didn't, actually," the finance minister explained. "It came, well, from all over, as much as I understand what happened. It isn't clear, and people are not talking, but there was big money at work here. It was run through those banks, but it wasn't the banks' idea or plan."

"Can we get the word out that this wasn't the banks work? That is was someone else's plan?" a cabinet member asked.

"Not likely," the finance minister replied, frowning. "The bankers are so proud of themselves that they would never admit it wasn't their idea. As to what the real story is, that's another set of problems. I've had investigators beating on this and it's one stonewall after another. We had a couple of people start to talk and those people and their families turned up in the river. At least, we think it was them-the fish didn't leave much. The investigation ground to a halt."

"Don't the banks have a clue about what they have unleashed here?" another minister snarled. "They are grabbing all the headlines, pretending they did all this, to play up their power in the world. Meanwhile, I hear angry rumblings from Paraguay, very angry. We can't persuade the banks this isn't smart?"

"I've tried to talk sense into them," the finance minister protested, staring at the table. "With no success at all. They are the toast of the world financial news and they did make some substantial money out of it. Then, they know there are limits about what they can say. They don't want to end up in a river. So they can't say it was 'X's' idea, and they are not likely to admit they were puppets. No, we'll just watch and try and keep people calmed down."

"They practically destroyed Paraguay," a cabinet minister observed. "Those people are very, very angry people. Hot tempered in the best of times, and now?"

"We have moved troops into place, very quietly," the defense minister replied.

SÃO PAULO. THE BIOLOGIST & CESARE

It's the anniversary of my fiancée's death, the biologist thought bitterly. If you could call it that. He stood outside the biological facility, and stared at the huge logo on the proud, brightly glowing skyscraper a half-mile away. The company that harvested her, he thought, furious. Oh, through subsidiaries and cutouts, but I tracked it back that far. I even found their price list for organs. I was destroyed that day.

He walked into the building. There was a man sitting at the desk who the biologist had never seen before. A healthy middle-aged man, whose eyes looked older, much older. The man was smiling, but it was a cold, calculated smile.

"Who are you?" the biologist stammered, suddenly afraid.

"A friend," Cesare answered him. "I'm the person who hired you, well, told the office manager to hire you, and you've done wonderfully. You've grown the materials better than expected, actually."

"Thank you," the biologist replied, pleased despite himself.

"This is something to add to it," Cesare ordered, holding up a small cylinder.

"What does it do?" the biologist asked, knowing without being told.

"Your woman, slaughtered. They didn't even use an anesthetic, as I understand their procedures. They see it a waste of time and money to minimize the suffering of poor person under their knife" Cesare snarled. "And your tribe destroyed, your ancestors graves desecrated. Justice? Where is your Justice?" Cesare demanded as he stared intently into the biologist's eyes.

"Nowhere," the biologist shouted, furious, his mind swirling.

"Justice," Cesare offered, holding the cylinder high. Cesare smiled to himself at the biologist's naked hunger for the cylinder. Cesare held the cylinder out to the biologist, who grabbed the cylinder. The biologist held it tightly, staring at it.

"Add this to the culture. And then wait for my orders." Cesare stood up, clapped the man on the shoulder, and walked out, closing the door behind him.

The biologist smiled at the cylinder and then at the closed door. "Justice it is," the biologist announced to the containers. And he began to work. Who needs action when you have words? Well, they will see I have more than words.

Cesare was driven through the night to another city. He took an airplane from there, hopping to another city, switching passports at each new takeoff. Finally, he left Rio de Janeiro on his private jet. So?, he thought, leaning back in the seat as the plane reaching cruising altitude. He adds the cylinder, it grows, and the pressure builds in the containment facility. Takes, what did they estimate? Forty-eight hours? Then, Showtime!

CALIFORNIA. THE MINISTER

"You're sure about this?" the Minister inquired, looking doubtfully at the messenger. "This is quite a dramatic event that you are telling me is about to happen."

"One can never be sure about the future," Paul's emissary commented politely. "Especially something as dramatic as this. A clear, unambiguous reference might make it seem as though a person had forbidden knowledge before the terrible event. Still, perhaps vague references could put a gloss on your reputation if done correctly." The emissary bowed and walked out.

"Gloss? More publicity than could be imagined," the Minister admitted to the window, and shrugged. I'll play it up big, because Paul has something in mind, that's for sure. The next day, on his nationally televised show, his sermon proclaimed the disaster coming, punishment for the sins of man.

The news picked up on it and played with it, mocking him.

DETROIT. THE NEWS IS WRONG AGAIN

"That's not so good," Hal mused, watching the news story on the Minister's prediction. The news people are all bright, smiling faces and quick quips, laughing at the Minister's doom and gloom.

"Why say you so?" Jesus asked Hal.

"Because he's tied in with Paul," Hal replied, frowning. "And São Paulo is ground zero for the financial information that Lucretia is sure Paul has to destroy. Oh, he didn't say that city, but knowing what we know, I don't know where else it could be."

"I must go there," Jesus sighed. "There may be nothing that I can do, but I have to try."

"Dad!," Goth Girl protested. "Lucretia told you it's going to be really awful. You can't walk into the middle of that!"

"Do I have a choice?" Jesus demanded. "Those are my people. Don't worry," he promised Goth Girl, bending close to hold her. "I'll take guards, and I have resources there." He patted her on the back and then stepped back. "I'd better go. This won't wait, I'm afraid."

"But, Dad!" Goth Girl cried, holding onto him.

"Miss Dove!" Jesus demanded of Goth Girl. "You know I have to do this. You look at me and tell me I don't have a duty to go there."

Goth Girl looked away, crying.

"No one walks into a crisis that they think can't be solved," Hal broke in. "They make choices on the way, based on their hopes and expectations. Those are usually wrong choices. You're making an emotional choice to solve a real-world crisis. Failure is the usual result."

"Done that before," Jesus admitted. "But there are people down there I have to try to help." He patted Hal on the back, kissed Goth Girl on the cheek, and walked out.

Goth Girl glowered at Hal, who looked away at the floor.

SWITZERLAND, THE CHATEAU

"Now the city shall be doomed by the LORD to destruction, it and all who are in it," Paul pronounced to lake, standing on the balcony.

"In the scriptures," Constantine agreed, nodding. "Foretold, it was."

"It's a controlled burn of the forest—isn't that the ecological thing to do?" Xerxes laughed. "Isn't that what they are calling for?"

"If you cross the river, a great empire will be destroyed. Believing the response favorable, Croesus attacked," the Adversary retorted. "Look, I'm just doing my job," as they angrily stared at him.

SÃO PAULO. MORNING

The city came alive, a bright, hot morning like so many others.

People went off to work, to school. The unemployed, the shanty people, sat and stared at the big buildings in the distance.

Ms. Amber Zima walked happily into the door of the office and sat at her desk, carefully wiping the dust off of it.

And the pressure built in the containment facility.

The hours drift by, and it's late in the day. The biologist, the rough man and the angry man are at the facility.

"What will it do?" the biologist wondered to the other men as they sat in the control room. "How many will die?"

"Did they ask your fiancée?" the rough man growled. "Did they ask your tribe?"

The biologist put his head on the desk and cried.

"There are no innocents out there!" the angry man shouted. "They are all intertwined in it completely. The sweet-faced little girl sells food to the

51

corporate executive who kills through others. All tied together, completely. They all deserve it!" He shook his fists at the city.

"My fiancée, my tribe, all dead," the biologist cried, staring at the containment equipment. "And the wicked flourish. I'm dead inside, so what happens doesn't matter to me. But the people who killed her, killed my tribe, they will be dead, too."

"The innocents," the rough man spit. "They work for the killers, help the police. There are no innocents in today's world. Wait, what's that?"

There was a blinking red light on the control console. They stared at it, puzzled.

Exception handing is one of the weaknesses with a system, it turns out. If an alarm appears a few times a week, people know what to do. If it happens once in a while, or never before, then no one has any idea what to do. The problem with words in a manual is that until you have walked through an event at least once, words, which are general, don't mentally match actions, which are specific.

"Here," the biologist mumbled, pulling out the manual. He thumbed through, looking back and forth between the light and the manual. "Okay, when that blinks like that, then I need to adjust this pressure release, the instructions say."

"That seems clear," the angry man observed.

The biologist flipped a switch. "And...hmm...you do this." He turned a knob.

The containment vessel exhausted into the air, a cloud rapidly expanding above the building.

The angry man laughed at the sky, shaking his fists. The biologist screamed. And the thief moved for the door as he grappled with his gas mask—just a little too late. The generator exploded and the biological facility quickly burned to the ground.

CHAPTER 2. THE FIRST BELL: SÃO PAULO

Jesus was waiting, sitting in an elegant hotel room. His chair was cutting-edge modern; rather sparsely padded—designed for looks, not function, he thought. Like so much else is! If they can't get a chair right, what hope is there for anything else? He stared out the floor-to-ceiling windows, forcing himself to watch, waiting for the play to unfold. This room was part of a penthouse suite at the top of a five-star hotel. In other rooms in the suite, his guards conferred quietly, worried about the night to come.

Outside, the city throbbed with life, traffic and lights stretching out of sight. It was a clear night, the moon bright far above, watching over jungle and city with the same indifference. The bright lights thrust upwards proudly, to be absorbed by the dark sky. The night was hot, but his room was cool—pleasant, not cold. Perfectly adjusted, he thought, the privileges of wealth, and he smiled. What did I say? Actually, what was I supposed to have proclaimed? It is easier for a camel to go through the eye of a needle than for a rich man to enter the kingdom of God? That's not quite how I phrased it. But the churches do collect more with that wording. What if you used a big needle? There is a scale beyond human scale.

Grendel taught me things, but nothing as harsh as this, he lamented, staring out over the city. Hal told me Grendeline would be stronger, and I'm thinking I'm going to need her. Well, if I can face and accept her, there is that. I'm not like them—I can pretend, he hummed to himself.

He abruptly stood and paced for a few minutes, then stopped and looked out the window. "Of all men's miseries the bitterest is this: to know so much and to have control over nothing."[1] Remind me not to tell Lucifer I'm using his pretty slogans. Vanities, he thought, isn't that what Ecclesiastics laughed at? He looked out at the proud display before him, the lights flashing far into the distance, traffic flowing and the large buildings jutting into the sky. And this building? He looked critically at his room. It's the human version of a great tree, thrusting up, providing shelter for the creatures. But it doesn't give life back, it doesn't release oxygen into the air, there is no rotting of the leaves as it returns nutrients to the forest, no symbiotic relationship with the greater ecology. It's just pride and power, a denial of the real world. Still, it is cool, comfortable and the bed is soft, he thought as he stroked the silk and cotton fabric covering the sofa.

I long for the old days sometimes, he thought. Frenzied women dancing in the dark night, lit by roaring fires, from whose lips the god speaks, foretelling the future. I'd give a lot to hear another future than the one I know is coming. Why was it that women were always the mouth of the gods—always knew the future? Men were never worth a damn at that job. Weird.

There was a soft knock on the door.

"Come in, please" Jesus called out.

The door opened and a man stood in the doorway. "My lord, we have been notified by the lobby guard that a delegation of local officials has entered the elevators," his head guard reported.

"As expected," Jesus replied, looking at him and smiling. "Please keep the men get out of sight when they arrive. I doubt they are a danger, because they have no courage, but watch carefully. This meeting is useless, but it must be done. Have the men ready for the certain chaos to come."

"As you wish, my lord," the guard acknowledged. He closed the door behind him as he left.

Jesus absently watched the clock to the left of the sofa, it's red numerals glowing. Counting down, he realized, and grimaced. Why are my days numbered, and not, say, lettered? That was Woody Allen, I think. It won't be long now. There is nothing I can do! And if I could raise my hand, would I? "Don't expect me to cry; Don't expect me to lie; Don't expect me to die for thee," he hummed. What do you think, Kurt? Have they brought this upon themselves? Am I some cartoon superhero in tight pajamas to pull them out of whatever mess they danced carelessly into, so they can merrily go to the next one? I'm tired of that job description.

JOB

He suddenly found himself in a hot, dry room, looking out over the desert. A man there was, in the Land of Uz, he thought to himself wryly. This again?

What had Mary Magdalene snarled? Do you still cling to your innocence? Curse God and die, she spat as he stood at the entrance to the tomb. And I said to her, "You speak as one of the base women would speak. Shall we accept good from God, too, and evil we shall not accept? Life is all, it is what it is. To God, all things are good, only men deem some good and some evil."

"What does a man know of life?" she retorted. "Only a woman has life flow though her. Men must just mark time, doing important things in men's eyes." And she had walked away to the market. He missed her. She had been destroyed by Paul centuries ago, and he'd not taken his revenge. Why? Because there had been bigger plans, important reasons to not act. And those plans brought him to today, he thought bitterly, to this first-row seat, for a special performance of 'no exit,' writ large on the tablet of life.

And now the three friends came in to the room, and they sat next to him, as real as all those centuries ago. "Annul the day that I was born, and the night that said, 'A man is conceived,'" Jesus spoke as the men stood around him. He was overwhelmed again by anguish, feeling that all he had reached for was slipping away, felt the pain as he had not in centuries. "Let that night be barren, let it have no song of joy." There is no song of joy for what is about to happen.

"'For now I would lie and be still, would sleep and know repose, with kings and councilors of earth, who build ruins for themselves.' Who was it? Ozymandias? Yes, he told himself. So many of them over the long years. Proud, tall castles under bright dawns with brave, confident Kings and Queens standing on the battlements and then in the dark night, the jagged ruins of their castles. The happy celebrations under sunny skies, sheep bleating in flocks in the green fields lying before the white walls of the fortresses on the heights. The Kings of little lands fought, the Sun burning like fire on their bright and hungry swords. Victory and defeat; proud battlements fell as flames leapt high into the sky. And here we are again, another burning coming. All I have done, has it been for naught?

Eliphaz spoke to him. "You reproved others, you lifted others in trouble, but now trouble comes to you and you cannot stand it? Your virtues gave you security and hope before. Those virtues will bring you past this dark place. The innocent are not punished! The trouble that has come to you is for a reason, a just punishment for what you have done. Man is to wretchedness born, like sparks flying upward. Look at my own piety. I am better than most people—I can guide you if you listen. Follow my advice, and then you will be taken from your problems. Do you not know that your agony is reproof from God, who will heal you when you mend your sinful ways? Then you will be safe. This is what everyone knows, and you should know this yourself."

"It's always the group," Jesus replied, looking thoughtfully at the well meaning but frightened man. "If you deny the vision of the group, then you will truly see wrath fall upon you. You turn away from the real world, lovingly grasping and polishing your stories, holding the stories before you like a magic talisman to ward off evil. Well, at least to ward off the real world."

Jesus stood, pacing for a minute and then turned to the men. "You see what has happened to me," Jesus declared, "and you fear it may happen to you. So you defend God, you seek his favor by blaming me and praising him. You raise your hand against me as though that will be weight with him! You see him only as a petty prince of a small town, jealous of his power and privilege. You have no knowledge of what he is."

My days are swifter than the weaver's shuttle; they snap off without any hope. Bitter words, he thought, harder because they are true. Recall that my life is a breath. And why do you not pardon my crime and let my sin pass away? For soon I shall lie in the dust. You will seek me, and I shall be gone.

Bildad spoke. "Would God pervert justice? You are being punished because of your faults, which you refuse to see. Your faith is weak, a mere cobweb; you fool yourself in denying our advice. Your suffering is just and has fallen upon you because of what you have done—that is what all know. I will not stand with your foolishness and weakness. God will not spurn the blameless, nor hold the hand of evildoers. You go against his will by complaining, and that is why you suffer so."

The traditional moral calculus is a complete mathematical proof to those that embrace it, Jesus thought. Make the assumptions unquestionable and then the proof cannot be denied. Paul got that one right.

"Should a person bring grievance against Him?" Jesus demanded of them, again, as he has so many times over the years. It didn't go as I expected the first time I did it, he thought. "What is a day in court against the creator of the court, the law, the judge and the jury, the prosecutor and the witnesses also? Created by Him, should I call out and he answer me, I would not trust Him to heed my voice." It's the human, he thought sadly. I want to design the world as I want it, not the world as it is, as it must be. But do I sin by standing and asserting what I think? I am made by him, and must I not be what I am made to be? Thinking like that, round and round, makes my head hurt. "If I was guilty, alas for me, and though innocent, I could not raise my head, sated with shame and surfeited with disgrace." So, I can't win either way, he thought.

Zophar spoke. "I cannot listen to this sophistry, this smooth talk without denying it, without standing up against you. I do not know what crimes you have committed, but your denials only make the crimes more clear to me because all of this could not have happened without crime. Look to yourself—you deny and hide, and then you have the nerve to demand justification from God!"

Freud two thousand, five hundred years earlier, Jesus thought. All repression, projection, and denial. Zophar sees wrongdoing and piously makes little notes in a book that prove his superiority to all others.

"If you ready your heart, turn back from your evil ways, then God will forgive you," Zophar offered piously. "Then you will be whole again, and rise back into health. That is the wisdom of the tribe. All know and only you deny."

Jesus glowered at them, furious. "With you wisdom will die!" he shouted. "The smug man's thought scorns disaster, readied for those who stumble." Paul's teachings, Jesus thought bitterly to himself. The banking god of Paul, that dispassionate heavenly accountant, weighing the debits and credits carefully, fitting into a neat system of reward for the virtuous and punishment for the transgressor. That's not how it works, is it? There is no retributive justice in the universe.

Jesus stopped and stared out at the darkness past the city, trying to find where the jungle started. How did we deny Life? Jesus questioned. How did it go so far off the tracks?

"Naked I came out...naked shall I return there," Jesus announced to the men. "May the Lord's name be blessed. You do not know what you think you know. Why, my eye has seen all, my ear has heard and understood. I am no less than you, even though you despise the sight of me. You are all quack healers. Would that you fell silent and this would be your wisdom! Hear, pray, my dispute, and to my lips' pleas listen closely. Would you speak crookedness of God? Of Him would you speak false things? Would you be partial on His behalf? Would you plead the case of God? Would it be good that He probed you? As one mocks a man would you mock Him? He shall surely dispute with you if in secret you are partial. Will not His majesty strike you with terror, and His fear fall upon you? Your pronouncements are maxims of ash, your words—piles, piles of clay."

He stopped and thought for a moment. "Centuries later, I clearly preached, 'If you fast, you will bring sin upon yourselves, and if you pray, you will be condemned, and if you give to charity, you will harm your spirits.' Why? Because you seek to buy your way into God's favor, like Job's friends did." That was lined carefully out of the official book. They are not going to sell many indulgences with that as part of scripture.

And then the men condemn him more fervently, taking his statements as first, insults to them, but secondly and far worse-putting them in the eye of God to be punished with him. Their souls, they fear, will be forfeit for coming to help.

"God delivers me to a wrongdoer, lets me fall into the hands of the wicked," one of them shouted, disgusted.

"For your crime guides your mouth, and you choose the tongue of the cunning," another snapped. "Your own mouth condemns you, not I, and your lips bear witness against you. We have nothing to do with this."

Jesus looked at them and replied, "I have heard much of this sort, wretched consolers are you all. Is there any end to words of hot air, or what compels you to speak up? I understand you, but you do cannot understand me."

Bildad shouted at him, "Why are we reckoned as beasts? For a man, his feet are caught in a net, and he treads on a tangle of lines. The trap grips his heel, the trip-cord seizes him. A rope is hidden for him in the ground, his snare upon the path. You deny what we all see; that is a trap you have fallen into because of your sins. You won't see, won't face it. You hide from this with your fancy words."

Zophar promised, "You can be assured of a life without misery and can be free from anguish when death comes, if you but turn your mind to God and cast this deceit from your tent. What you have suffered is punishment for some offense, and we demand for God that you understand and accept this. We, his righteous servants, seek this for Him."

It's the ritual response, pushing punishment away from Zophar, Jesus thought to himself. They see Job as a leper, and his friends are horrified to think they are contaminated by standing near him. "And how do you console me with mere breath, when your answers are naught but betrayal?" Jesus demanded of them.

Eliphaz stood and stepped forward. The public prosecutor, confident and sure, furiously demands punishment for the sake of the tribe. "Why, your evil is great, there is no end to your crimes!" he accused. "We see your true nature, and here are your crimes." He listed them like a bailiff reading the charges against the accused. He has no doubt, holding his unreflective moral certitude wrapping about him like a cloak. No, more a womb that he is stillborn within, Jesus realized.

"Since God gets no benefit from man's righteousness, it then follows logically that a man afflicted by God is guilty of unspeakable crimes. You have left your senses. Come back to the wisdom we speak, and you will be fine.," Eliphaz announced, and the other men nodded their agreement.

"I seek in vain, and won't find a wise man among you," Jesus snarled at them. As he stared at them, all the men faded. Jesus found himself back in his hotel room, alone. "They were framed," he observed, talking to the city beyond the windows. "Defenders of the orthodox, defined as patently false. The hearts of the friends deny their claim and loud exhortations. They cast themselves as sincere and upstanding in calling on Job to repent and remove "deceit" from his mouth. But it was for their own good, thinking they could cut deals with God, that they cry against him, not out of belief."

In the end it is they whose words are found false, for they did not speak the truth about God as Job did, Jesus mused. And fast-forward three thousand years? They still spout the same conceits and arguments, having learned nothing.

A MEETING

Two senior police officers, the Mayor of the city and His Eminence, the cardinal for São Paulo, were shown into his room, escorted in by Jesus's head guard. The guard then left, and the men stood uncomfortably around the edges of the room.

"Well, I just wanted to thank you for coming to our city," the Mayor announced, forcing a smile. "We know that you have done many wonderful things for this city, and you have powerful friends here. In this time of, well, false accusations about what some of our banks may have done, it's good to have you here showing your support."

"These problems are not going to just go away," Jesus objected.

"They deserved what happened to them," the Mayor shouted. He stomped around the room, furious. "They shipped poison to the world!! Our bankers, our investment people, did what was right! We protected the world and we made some money at the same time. There's nothing to be ashamed of there. Nothing to be ashamed of!" the Mayor yelled, lecturing the city outside the windows and ignoring the men in the room. "They were punished for their evil deeds. Our righteousness is proved by our profits." The Mayor raised his hands, holding them high before the windows, as if he was at a campaign rally acknowledging the cheers of the crowd. Then he turned and walked over to the door, opened it, and walked out, slamming the door behind him.

All the men in the room stared at the closed door.

"Perhaps you could wait outside," the cardinal finally asked the police, "and perhaps call, make sure that someone is guarding the Mayor? He seems, well, distracted."

The police nodded obediently and left the room, closing the door behind them.

The cardinal stood for a moment, staring out the window, mentally rehearsing his speech. Satisfied he was ready, he turned to Jesus.

"My master told me you might listen to reason now, and perhaps finally turn to him," the cardinal began, his smile smooth and confident. "He thought I could save you the effort of your magic tricks if I brought some wine and wafers with me." The cardinal, reaching under his robes, pulled them out and put them on the table with a flourish.

"Man does not live by bread alone. And a man who trusts your master and breaks bread with him will not live long," Jesus answered, studying the cardinal.

"And what if I call the police back in?" the cardinal shouted, his confidence shaken. "Perhaps you could fall from this high window? You were supposed to be able to fall from a height and live. Shall we see if the prophecy is right?"

"The words have been torn apart and poorly translated," Jesus replied. "What you read is not what was meant, or what even what was stated, although it works well for your purposes, I grant that. And I have taken precautions against such poor behavior. Remember, I have guards. And power."

The cardinal stared at Jesus, and then turned to the window again. The cardinal closed his eyes, reviewing his speech, trying to get the train back on the track. Satisfied, he opened his eyes and turned back to Jesus.

"Surely God does not act wickedly," the cardinal argued. "Does one say of a king 'scoundrel,' 'wicked' of the nobles?"

Whoever rules is always right to him, Jesus thought. The cardinal can suck up with the best of them, I have to give him that.

"You make crime abound among us. You must listen," the cardinal continued, stepping towards Jesus. "My words are no lie; one perfect in knowledge is here with you, before you now. Look, God is great. He does not despise us, great in power and understanding. He will not let the wicked live, and He grants justice to the afflicted. He does not take His eye off the righteous. Therefore men do fear Him, as you should. Listen to what I say! You know you are wrong in what you believe!" the cardinal demanded. "Everyone agrees on the orthodox, the correct interpretation of the scriptures. God is transcendent, and does not dirty himself in dialogue with humans. If he will not dialogue with humans, then humans must make their story, and that human story is thus THE true story."

"You are alaziin, the fool," Jesus laughed, shaking his head in disbelief. "You, the arbiter in God's place? Do you not recall what Job thought of Elihu, who you flatter yourself to be? Loosely translated, he declared that Elihu was a bombastic fool full of hot air. If not true of him, certainly true of you."

"I was told you would not listen to reason," the cardinal snapped. "Then let us be blunt. My master asks if you will take the power he can give you. He knows of your anguish, your frustration, as the stories you have told have been denied and ignored, over and over. Power he can give you, power to shout your message to the masses, and control of the levers so that they must listen and obey."

"Surely you jest?" Jesus chuckled. "I know your master, and he gives power to no one. All who serve Xerxes obey him; none act on their own. Nothing that comes from your master is of any good—it's all lies and tricks. The devil you rail against is the one that runs your churches. I'm sorry, your eminence, my time is valuable. Do you have anything else to say?"

The cardinal drew himself up to his full height. "I was warned against you, but I doubted them. But, I see...'It is Thou!'" He paced, waving his hands nervously, and he continued: "'Nay, answer not; be silent! And what couldst Thou say? I know but too well Thy answer. Why shouldst Thou now return, to impede us in our work?'"

Jesus began to clap, slowly. "I've seen it done better, much better, actually," he snarled. "In real dungeons, by the Cardinal who you serve."

The cardinal glowered and reached into his robes. In a moment, the two policemen came back into the room, faces serious.

"Look," Jesus demanded, pointing out at the city. "Far over there—see?"

The policeman and the cardinal looked and then gasped. Far away the flames were, but bright and growing. The policemen's phones rang.

Quickly answering, they silently listened to the harsh voices on the phones, the policemen's faces grave and shocked. They put their phones down and first looked at each other and then at the cardinal. "We must leave," the senior officer curtly announced and then they practically ran out of the room.

Jesus looked at the cardinal, who was staring at the door, shocked. "If you want my advice, you should leave this place quickly. This will be far beyond you, what is about to happen. A straw in the wind is the position you find yourself in. This is free advice. I do not mean you or your master well, but what is coming requires I give you notice, just for my peace of mind."

"I will not run," the cardinal blurted out, turning to look at Jesus. "I know what is coming and I am ready for it. Preparations have been made. And when it's over, you will be blamed. You will see."

"Much learning does not teach understanding, no less true today, your eminence," Jesus snapped. "So perhaps you should go back to your gilded church and wait there with your altar boys for the wrath that is about to fall upon you. I'd suggest you not waste your little time left in prayer, because nothing can clean your hands or heart."

"If I don't sin," the cardinal snickered, an odd smile on his face, "then you died for nothing."

Jesus studied at the cardinal, disgusted, and then pressed a button in his pocket. The door opened, and several of his guards walked quickly into the room, surrounding the cardinal.

"His eminence wishes to leave now," Jesus ordered. "Would you be so good as to show him out? And, if you could please search him? We need to make sure he leaves us no presents. His professional concern for our immortal soul may tempt him to try to speed us to our reward."

The cardinal's face was scarlet as he was ushered out of the room without ceremony by the guards.

A few minutes later, one of the guards came back into the room. "We found a small bomb in his vestments," the guard stated. "Small, but large enough to take out this floor."

"Surprising it wasn't set off electronically," Jesus replied. "And actually, it may have been. There is a suppressor in effect in this chamber. Perhaps you should throw it out the window? Quickly?"

"Yes, my lord." The guard shot the window out and then threw the bomb far out into the night.

Boom! The blast blew out windows ten stories below when it exploded.

"The suppressor only carries so far," the guard commented, looking down out the broken window.

"It seems that the cardinal was not as highly valued by his people as he thought he was," Jesus observed. "I'd not disagree with their opinion of him, actually."

The guard and Jesus stood for a moment, staring out the broken window.

"Well, it is underway," Jesus sighed. They stared at the flames in the distance, which were increasing in ferocity as they watched. Emergency sirens grew louder, much clearer now through the broken window. "You, and all the other men, go to a place of safety. I will call you if I need you."

"This is not wise, my Lord," the guard argued, deeply concerned. "We should be with you. You walk through this night into unimaginable danger."

"You are right about the danger," Jesus agreed. "That is why you and the others must be safe. I will be safe on my own and my mind will rest better knowing that you are all safe. And ready should I really need you. But go now—our time is short."

The guard bowed and left. As he walked out the door, he motioned to the others, who silently followed the guard out of the suite.

DISASTER RESPONSE

The laboratory exploded in a part of São Paulo not well patrolled by the police. Avoided, actually, by the police unless there was a compelling reason to enter. The explosion burned itself out and didn't spread, so the fire trucks that drove by didn't need to stop. If they stopped, the firemen and the fire truck were usually robbed at best, unless the fire was so great that the neighborhood recognized the need for a temporary truce with the authorities. So a considerable time went by before anyone in authority had to pay attention.

The spores were a B horror movie that had jumped off the movie screen. First, a few people started rampaging, killing, and burning. Really, that wasn't all that unusual on a hot night in the slums. Then more people joined in and finally the police were called. The very first police, stepping into a horror beyond their imagination, were slaughtered by the infected. At that point, the police took this seriously and swarmed in. The spores acted quickly. Later police reinforcements were shocked that to find earlier reinforcements rampaging and killing along with the civilians.

In every kind of disaster, we all start in about the same place and travel through three phases.

"This can't be happening!" the Police Captain shouted at his sergeant. "Someone is lying to you! They are mistaken—our men cannot be shooting at us! No, don't tell anyone else. I'll track this down. We'll be fools for life if we put out a report like this!"

The first phase is denial. Creative, willful denial of what is happening. Most of the time, in daily life, if you ignore the outliers, then the world returns to normal. So we deny and delay into a real disaster, which nicely compounds our problems.

The spores, breathed in, took over the infected person and they quickly used that person's body to create new spores that, within twenty minutes of infection, give or take, were expelled by the person's breathing. Locking down the initial area would have slowed the spread, as the initial cloud of spores hadn't blown far. The delayed response by the authorities eliminated that barrier. As people fled the affected areas, there were no checkpoints stopping traffic out from the barrio. So the spores were spread throughout the city in a relatively short time. They didn't spread far, because the infection was so quick. Once the spores had enough control of you to create new spores, you became enraged and violent. After initial infection, the roughly twenty minutes of normal behavior wasn't enough time to get on an airplane or drive very far. Still, twenty minutes driving was easily enough to spread the spores through the city.

In the middle of an unfolding disaster, we deny, waiting for the world to right itself. We stand at the rail of the ship as it's going down.

An hour later, the Police Captain picked up the phone and called the Governor. "No, it doesn't make any sense," the Captain acknowledged, exasperated. "But I've checked this report, over and over. It's really happening, all over."

"How can that be?" the Governor demanded. "Is it an attack of some kind on us? Who would do this?"

"I don't know," the Captain replied, frustrated. "It's all happening so quickly, and I can't seem to get a fence around it to get control." Suddenly, there were gunshots in the police station.

"What was that?" the Governor blurted out, shocked. "Were those gunshots?"

"I've got to go! If you politicians weren't so worthless, we wouldn't be in this mess!," the Police Captain screamed into the phone. Then he threw the phone against the wall, laughing as the phone burst into fragments. He walked over to a closet, yanking the door off, and pulled a shotgun out, grasping a bandoleer of shells with the other hand. "I'll teach them," he howled, laughing wildly, and charged out into the chaos, firing at will.

The Governor put the phone down slowly.

How long we delay depends on how we calculate the risk we face. That risk analysis depends less upon facts than upon a shadowy sense of dread within us.

The Governor looked out his living room window at the luxurious estates surrounding him. The community was gated, carefully protected from the rest of the city, but now he could hear distant shots. They are growing closer, he realized, shocked. But this can't be? But it is, he knew, watching a flame in the distance engulf the side of a tall building.

Recovering from the initial shock, we move to the second phase of the survival arc. Something IS terribly wrong, but we don't know what to do about it. So, how do we decide our next action? Generally, not well. Because nothing is normal, and the little information we have is sparse and unclear at best, we have little to work with. Broken away finally from the normal, we start thinking and perceive differently, improvising as we go. The problem is that we use old boxes to assess new situations, which often makes things worse.

His wife rushed into the room. "There are shots in the distance!" she screamed. "Is it a revolution? Are the squatters attacking?"

"No," the Governor answered, uncertainly rubbing his chin. "Well, yes, but it's more than that. The police are becoming part of it and the Captain that just called me suddenly went berserk."

"What are you going to do?" his wife yelled at him. "You're the Governor! Do something!"

So, we stop denying, and we have processed what information we have. The third phase of the survival arc is the recognition of the decisive moment. Now we take action.

The Governor picked up the phone and called the army. "I need support," he demanded. "Something is happening here." He briefly described the problems. He became frustrated as the General flatly denied first, that the Governor knew what he was talking about and secondly that the General had to act on orders from the Governor.

"Then check with your superiors," the Governor screamed and threw the phone at the wall. He stared at his wife. "We need the guard around us, right now. And the weapons in the basement—we need those."

Unfortunately, his son had driven through a part of town that the spores were thickly floating through and he had spread the spores to the Governor and his wife. Very shortly afterwards, the luxurious homes began to burn, along with all else.

Simply going through the survival arc doesn't guarantee survival.

STEPPING INTO CHAOS

Jesus sat in his hotel room for a little while, watching as the flames grew and expanded through the city. New clusters popped up closer and closer and finally he stood up and quickly walked to the stairs. He carefully walked down the stairs, jostled by other guests who could not decide whether the hotel was safety or danger, and he had to dodge people running both up and down the stairs. Finally, he reached street level. Pushing the fire door open, he carefully looked around and then stepped into the alley, disappearing into the inky blackness between the buildings.

A few minutes later, he stood at the end of the alley, hidden in the dark shadows thrown by the hotel building before the alley merged into a main street. He watched the first signs of the chaos pushing it's way into the elegant stores and neatly manicured parks. No way back, he realized, and death in front. Why do I keep getting into these things? Why not retire to a nice estate with a beach, with a caring woman to comfort me? Why didn't I listen to my daughter's advice? "Idiot," he mumbled to the darkness.

In the distance, more sirens howled and the lights of the city seemed to be mixed with red as he stared down the bright street at the clusters of emergency vehicles.

He hesitated, fearing what he would find. A scene from Conan the Barbarian played ran through his mind. This is guidance?, he wondered. No deep philosophy, just muscle?

> *Conan: You're not a guard!*
> *Valeria: Neither are you!*
> *Subotai: We're thieves! Ha! Like yourself. Come to climb the*
> *tower.*
> *Valeria: You don't even have a rope! Ha! Two fools who laugh at*
> *death. Do you know what horrors lie beyond that wall?*
> *Conan: No.*
> *Valeria: Then you go first.* [2]

That's what I need, he thought, smiling to himself. A Valkyrie with a sword to walk with me. Maybe several? I'll have to talk to casting about that next time. And definitely a soundtrack. Wagner, as I go into battle, with helicopters roaring overhead, raining down bullets. It's 'Apocalypse Now' out there, but who would I be? The Colonel or the Captain? He grimly stepped into the flickering red light and walked down the street.

The virus ripped off the carefully cultivated veneer of civilization. The infected raged and attacked all before them. The attacked ran, terrified of the howling berserkers pursing them. In a short time the city looked like an anthill after the nest is torn open, the queen dead. Their structures destroyed, they randomly respond, Jesus thought, as he shot one who ran at him, howling and brandishing a club. He ducked behind a building and reloaded. Who would Jesus kill, indeed?, he thought. Well, psychotic raging semi-zombie berserkers are high on that list. He peeked out from behind the building, and sighing, slowly worked his way towards the epicenter.

Hours went by, and he was dirty and exhausted. He had found the building it started from and tasted the original material released. Nice, he thought. Well made— military? A derivative, certainly. One country makes

65

this, and everyone has it. Eventually, there it is going to get out. He looked around, despairing. This area is pretty much destroyed, there's no one left alive. He saw that one of the men lying dead in the street was holding a gas mask. What did he know? Jesus wondered, bending down to examine him.

He heard feet scraping towards him and ran into an alley. 'Mind your head' was chalked on an overpass over the alley. Good advice, he thought, ducking. A moment later, there was a 'whack' sound in back of him. One of the infected people was lying on the ground under the underpass, clutching their head. Zombies are illiterate? No wonder they are after brains.

A half-hour later, he was standing in a building lobby, hidden in the shadows, watching the street. The buildings glass walls had been shattered, broken glass covering the sidewalks like snow. He hummed to himself. "Laying' low, no more hiding, or disguising truths I've sold." Oh, that's cheerful, he thought. He watched a burning building a block away, flames racing up the sides. But they burned the city and all that was in it with fire? Jericho. Yeah, looks a lot like it, except that the buildings are taller. He walked back into the night.

"*Because I called and you resisted, I reached out my hand and none paid heed, and you flung aside all my counsel, and you did not want my rebuke. I, too, shall laugh at your ruin, I shall mock when what you feared comes, when what you feared comes like disaster, and your ruin like a whirlwind descends, when straits and distress come upon you,*" he murmured to himself. Well, why not punish myself? It's been that kind of a night—certainly the right setting for it. He stood for a moment behind a tree. Our scars have the power to remind us that the past was real, he remembered, tracing the vestige of the scar on his left hand. "Saw my reflection and cried, hey; so little hope that I died, oh; feed me your lies, open wide, hey..." Alice in Chains, he thought. Appropriate.

MARY OF MAGDALA

Jesus had worked his way back out from the epicenter and stood on a hill in what had been a park, watching the chaos. Sick at the sight, he finally turned away. Sleep. It will be better in the morning. He picked his way through the debris and found a protected space, almost a cave. He rigged a cover for the entrance and traps to alert him if people came close.

Sleep, he thought, as everything started to go black. There the wicked cease their troubling, and there the weary repose...what was it Hamlet cried?

He was in a grey place. Not black, not cold, not hot, just grey. Purgatory? he wondered. Halfway between worlds. The banality of evil? The banality of their meaning, in the end tied to nothing. Just grey. *Waiting for Godot*? Isn't there supposed to be someone with me to talk to? Maybe that would be hell, having to talk forever. That was *No Exit*, I think.

A huge, looming figure stood in the mist. Grendeline called out to Jesus. "My world," she growled. "The chaos of centuries! Life breaks through at last, as it always does."

"It does," Jesus acknowledged. "So many burning cities. And I sought to help."

Grendeline stepped out of the mist, dissolving into another shape as she came closer.

"My sins do come back to haunt me," Jesus sighed.

Mary of Magdala stood before him, wearing a worn, brown robe. "You tried to help-how?" Mary accused. "The well-meant lie? The soothing half-truth that held their emotions in place until they jumped the banks and cut loose in your name? That's how you tried to help?"

Jesus looked down at the ground and then back up at Mary. "You're right. I am punished for my sins."

"Oh, so easy it is," she scoffed, her eyes cold. "Pretty words to cover up hard deeds. Can I get you a soft pillow to rest yourself upon, now that you have completed the labors of confronting your lost life? Give me thirty coins to purchase an indulgence, and I shall bless you."

Jesus stared at the ground, distraught.

"Oops, forgot. There are no women priests, so I can't sell you an indulgence," Mary commented. "Pope Gregory the Great shouted I'd take the thirty coins for another reason. A Prostitute was my trade, according to him. Disgusted he was, the great man who destroyed lives with a righteous glee, that a woman would take money for sex. Ironic, really. Money for sex is life, and life is what they hated the most. The well-meant lie was twisted in many surprising ways, didn't it? No good deed goes unpunished."

Jesus was silent, gazing into the mist.

"People enjoy their punishment, just as you are now, because it gives a pretend control," Mary declared. "And thus they deny the knowledge they should gain from the experience, which is the only thing that counts. What are you holding within that prevents the new life? You, who told everyone to grow to the new life, what are you holding back from? You were superior to them, the guide, the leader. Did you perhaps enjoy that too much? Become that too much?"

Jesus sat down on a rock, his head in his hands.

"But I'll make it easy," she taunted, standing in front of him. "You know what the offer is; you've taken it before. Mate, the conquest by your lust, and you will regain your control. For a while." She suddenly was naked, a soft, while light glowing about her.

Jesus looked up at her and smiled, a wry, bitter smile. "Done that," he admitted. "When I pretended that the well-meant lie would lead to the truth. Regained the control, with my strong belief. And now?" he asked, waving at the chaos of the city that suddenly appeared before them. "I'd say that was a failure."

"That was the first offer," Mary announced, sitting on a rock that glowed pink, gold threads ripping through it. "Technically."

She waved her hand and they were back where he was an hour ago. It was two in the morning, and the city was lit up, aflame in all directions. They sat in a park, backs to a wall, watching the chaos unfold. The park was littered with dead bodies, the living having moved down the street to fight.

Worse than I've ever seen, he thought. Worse than I've ever imagined. Nothing left to work with, nothing that this species can do now. He looked down in despair. All the years, all the hopes, he thought.

"Do you feel better, thinking that you created this?" Mary asked. "That your control is so great, your power so enormous? Do you not see that your will and the outside world are two different things? You have been many creatures over the eons, and you understand many things, but you don't understand where your limits lie. And why would you want to carry this? Life and death play over the veldt ceaselessly over the eons. Little different from this, actually, in the events. But you took within yourself their meaning and beat yourself with it. Why?"

"I wanted to cure their problems, end the problems," Jesus replied.

"Did you ever read the story about 'the last meeting place'?" Mary asked. "A short science fiction story; it had a tool, a time-travel gadget, so that great people from all ages could meet in a room. One day, one demands help from the others, and will not be denied. He's desperate, begging and then threatening. A quiet, hooded man in a corner looks at him, and says, 'I am the last.' All that you will all do leads to me, and then the end. There is silence in the room, and the man then understands. It is what you do that matters. The ultimate results are not yours to choose. But it's hard, isn't it? Giving up that part of the story—the meaning that they drive into you? That you always have to be doing something measured by their goals, not something measured inside yourself?"

"Hard is a small word for it," Jesus answered. "We all try and view ourselves as the movers, creating great things that will survive us, keeping alive what we saw as important."

"My name is Ozymandias, King of Kings; Look on my works, ye mighty, and despair! Nothing beside remains. Round the decay, Of that colossal wreck, boundless and bare, The lone and level sands stretch far away," Mary quoted. "Shelley, a brilliant man. It is Life that counts, not the afterlife. That is for others to bear. Or do you wish to be Paul?"

"I've fought being Paul, and I've seen the desert swallow the monuments," Jesus admitted.

Mary shook her head. "The meaning you have embraced is that humans are above all the world, that their rules and ideals define the world, that they are too powerful to let the world define them," Mary argued. "Are you not creatures like any other creature? You should know better than any other, having been so many creatures. They all eat, sleep, shit, and screw. They all kill to live and transfigure that death into life. But that's not the human meaning, is it? Tell me that this isn't true: Their morals, their codes, are a sour jest, virtuous lies to be dropped at the first sign of trouble. The vicious truth is that they're only as good as the world allows them to be."

"I thought they were more," Jesus protested, standing up and pacing. "I wanted them to be more. I wanted them to be this logical, structured creature..."

"Pretty pictures and words to rule by," Mary snickered. "One ring shall rule them. And you looked at the ring, with its bright allure and the promise of power, and you reached out your hand. You would be different, not corrupted by the ring, you believed. So you grasped it, and you played the game. The well meant lie, carrying the evil within, and it twisted everything. But it didn't twist you, did it?" she murmured. "You remained true, which is your anguish tonight. You do it to yourself. You do, and that's what really hurts."

She stood up slowly, the warm light flickering over her body, drawing back all his memories of the past. "Mate," she enticed. "Mate, and the pain will pass. Control will come again. Perhaps you can wield the ring correctly this time. Perhaps the evil at the heart of the ring will not corrupt your efforts. Mate, and it will be so easy!"

Jesus looked at her, glowing in the bright light, and his body ached for her. "Thirty coins would hardly be a fair price for all you offer," he asserted. "But no, I cannot. I've taken the easy way too often. Revised the story, and denied the nature of the creature. I bought into their pretty ideas. I was so excited, and so I took the ring. No, I cannot again."

She sat down again, the lights fading. "That was the second, technically. And the price would not have been thirty coins," she advised sadly. "The price would have been everything, a high price indeed. Not paid to me, paid by yourself."

"Thy beauty surpasseth, my lady," he teased her, smiling. "It might have been worth it."

"Flatterer," she laughed. "Always a way with the words. But what is the meaning of a word?"

"When I use a word," Humpty Dumpty said in rather a scornful tone, "it means just what I choose it to mean—neither more nor less."

"The question is," said Alice, "whether you can make words mean so many different things."

"The question is," said Humpty Dumpty, "which is to be master— that's all."[3]

Jesus grimaced. "That's the knife, isn't it? A way with the words, and hoping that the words would create what I hoped. But the words are only sounds, ideas, not the reality. Calling for love led to hate, as they divided over the trivial points of dogma. Calling for a new life, but they still had to eat, sleep, and shit the same way each new day. Not recognizing the creature and working with it, but trying to hit the donkey over the head with a club as a shortcut."

"And so you have poured out the vials of wrath onto the world," she snarled, pointing to the city burning. "For their own good, I think the plan was. Are you happy?"

"Why do you mock me?" Jesus screamed. "What I wanted was not this! It was the opposite of this. This was everywhere and I fought against it. And you mock me for this coming again! I gave my life, well, a life, to try and prevent this very thing! Don't mock my pain!"

"Pain is life," Mary retorted. "Those who say differently are selling something. And, my, how forceful you are! What a perfect example of manhood. So dominant."

Jesus glanced down. "Umm, the animal even in my dreams." He sat down quickly, re-arranging his robe. "But I did try."

"Try you did," Mary agreed. "None could have tried harder. But why beat the donkey over the head to control it? Why not recognize what the creature is, and work with that?"

Mary stood and walked over to him. The light glowed, and she was in a white toga, which was slowly slipping off. "Your dominance shouts your lust for control. Mate, and all will be as it was. Your goals will be bright again, and their natures weak; you can change them this time. Just reach out, and it shall be so."

Jesus touched her face, so soft and warm. "A confession has to be the beginning of my new life."

"Then confess," Mary ordered, suddenly a grim, hard nun, with a disconcertingly beautiful face. "Kneel, and bare your sins."

Jesus knelt. "Bless me, Father, for I have sinned," he murmured. "Perhaps beautiful mother?" He looked up at Mary, smiling.

"Flattery? I think trying to bribe the guards is another sin," Mary scolded. Annoyed, she pulled out a piece of parchment and a quill pen and made a quick note. "This is not going well; the list is getting longer, not shorter." She sighed. "If you really don't mean to confess, then we'll just get this over with." She raised her arms: "God, the Father of mercies, through the death and resurrection of his Son has reconciled the world to himself and sent the Holy Spirit among us for the forgiveness of sins; through the ministry of the Church, may God give you pardon and peace, and I absolve you from your sins in the name of the Father, and of the Son, and of the Holy Spirit. There, go forth without embracing your pain. A whitewash for your sins."

"I am the son," Jesus answered, "but I'll take any forgiveness I can get." He stood and looked into her eyes. "I do mean to confess, painful as it is. I can only put the past away for so long. There will be days it comes rushing back, and today is that day. I denied Life for the human structures. We were all so excited. Something so different! We'd seen creatures with potential, and actually some of the dinosaurs had more raw ability. Just their bad luck that the big, fat ones took over. But the human structures were really something different, and we dreamed of what they could lead to. But it was the stories we didn't understand.

"All creatures see in stories. The mind has to sort things out," Jesus mused. "Mostly simple stories. Food, shelter, lust. The humans, their stories were more elaborate and could do things, we thought. And they could. But the stories were so small in the end—all human stories. Well, so are the dolphins' and the frogs' and the elephants'—all stories revolving about them. With humans, it became dangerous when they gained power through the structures they created. And when the structures took over and turned away from Life, we came along. The tree withered, and the garden died, but we went off with the humans, bright in the promise of the new day."

Mary looked at him, a doubtful expression on her face.

"And there were many good new days," he argued. "Many great things accomplished."

"Why do you defend to me?" Mary asked. "Judge for yourself. Do you think if I believe what you say, then it will be true? That would be the human way. No, if I agreed with you, then we'd just both be wrong."

"That's the rub, isn't it?" Jesus admitted. "I accepted their outer words, their meanings over my inner words, my inspiration. 'Judge not lest ye be judged' wasn't supposed to say 'back off from every choice.' It was supposed to be opening the mind to the wider world, to other viewpoints, a stepping-stone to bigger stories. It didn't, it froze like all the stories did. Then the symbols froze, and the idea was lost. Life is complex, and people must put their morals on and off according to the propriety of the moment. Morals, homilies, are not cosmic truths applicable across all scales of behavior. People have to get along in a group, and so the laws of society are social conventions, not eternal laws. What's appropriate at a given time, people have brains and can figure out—or so I thought."

"At eighteen our convictions are hills from which we look; at forty-five they are caves in which we hide. F. Scott Fitzgerald," Mary quoted sadly.

"So, social laws and morals are appropriate for what they are intended to do. You have to judge, you have to choose how you act. Of course, you have to make sure the police don't misunderstand or make things difficult for you because you're not totally playing their game. Each individual must learn to live by his or her own myth. I explained this many times, in many ways, and whoosh, right over the top. That part of the gospel didn't work for the priests, and I should have seen that. Ambiguity doesn't work for structured people who need to obey and the kings and the priests gave those people guns. The human world is hierarchies of domination and acts of exploitation, from each according to their need, to each according to their desire, which is not quite the way it was framed in the writings, but the way it works. And I was wrong to have denied it, to pretend differently. Covering that over has led to the loss of the best of what we sought. I've carried this burden for centuries; a burden that none else can see. It's worn me out. I'm drowning at sea."

He sat down and stared out into the grey nothingness.

"Finally, I told them, 'Don't lie, and don't do what you hate, because all things are disclosed before heaven. After all, there is nothing hidden that will not be revealed, and there is nothing covered up that will remain undisclosed.' I did both," Jesus confessed. "Lied and concealed—for a good cause, of course." The pain came upon him, coursing through him, but vanished when he embraced it. Then he looked up at her. "Life is a balance of holding on and letting go. My sin was the well-meant lie; to guide through misdirection. Well meant or not, the lie always fails. Forgive me, great mother, for I have sinned," Jesus begged, kneeling down before her.

"I absolve you from your sins in the name of Life and the Tree," she announced, making the sign of the Tree above him. "It is you who must absolve yourself from what you feel inside."

"And mating? Thank you for the chance," he added, "but no. My feeling of comfort, that things would work out because I wanted them to, it led to all this." He waved his arm at the burning city. "I told them not to judge, and they were the prey of the judges. I told them to be peaceful, and they were the prey for the wolves. I mated before for the power and the control. I will not again. I must go past this."

Mary nodded her head. "That was three. No going back now."

"So, make friends with your monsters, Hal would say. Buy them a beer, have a long talk?" Jesus asked.

"Absinthe," Mary demanded. "A little cafe in Paris by the Seine, sitting, watching as the sun goes down."

"Paris?" Jesus questioned.

"You may want to spend your time in dismal self punishment," Mary replied, "but I like a fresh baguette and the bustle of the city. The structures have led to many good things, and many good things can be preserved." She stopped and looked out, the dark beginning to break up. "So: it's absorption by and of the mother goddess and the life force, is it? The hero journey, going past the threshold, is a journey beyond the opposites, beyond good and evil to the truth. Hard, isn't it? Even for you who tried to tell that message to others."

"The Fates lead him who will; him who won't they drag," Jesus quoted. "Seneca, I think."

"Every new life begins with the death of the old and the transfiguration into the new," Mary stated. "Hopefully. Well, at least occasionally."

"That's encouraging...I think," Jesus replied. "Well, I name you friend, and welcome you."

The scene changed. They were on a dark moor, standing before an ancient bridge over a vast, deep chasm, so deep the bottom could not be seen. Clouds roiled deep below, throwing mist and vapors past the bridge. The other side was vague, dark.

Mary held up a handwritten sign, "Gorge of Eternal Torment," and she danced a little jig, laughing to herself with a wild expression.

Jesus was looking at her, puzzled. I'm truly delusional, he thought. Maybe a nice place by the water to recover by, with cold drinks and soft music? A teddy bear?

"Sorry," Mary answered. "Method acting—important to get into a part. So," brushing her hair back, "Who approaches the Bridge of Death, Must answer me, these questions three! Ere the other side he see."

"Got it," Jesus answered. "Loved the movie. Ask me the questions, wild woman. I am not afraid."

"Really? Your hands are shaking,," Mary commented.

"Fine, I'm afraid, and my blood sugar is low. It's been a long night," Jesus admitted.

"What is your name?" Mary demanded.

"My name is Jesus. At least that's one name. Is the short version good enough?"

Mary pulled out a handbook and consulted it. "Rules, rules," she mumbled. "It's a strong union." She looked up at him and smiled. "Name? Okay, commonly known as, good enough." She closed the book, which vanished. "So, what wouldst be your quest?"

"To accept Life and the Tree."

"And what is your favorite fruit?" Mary inquired.

Jesus was surprised. "Apples. Macintosh, when they are fresh off the tree, and crisp..."

"Look, keep the answers short. We have a schedule. Apples, umm, yeah, it would be that. So unimaginative. Right. Off you go. Every exit is an entrance somewhere else," Mary responded.

Jesus held his hand out and Mary took his hand. They stood for a few moments, and then they dissolved into swirling clouds of mist that combined, eddied, and flowed. Lightning flashed in the eddies. After some time, there was Jesus. I can feel the Tree of Life, he thought. Roots deep into the nourishing soil, the soft water of the rain, and the sun on my leaves, warming me. Out of a cold winter, the buds unfolded, and he felt life fill him. As I was, he thought, and yet not. He saw the Tree, tall and three-dimensional in the world. And then four dimensions, tied to people over time, touching him, nourishing him.

Jesus closed his eyes, and he saw the vast savannah, as it had been, the grass green and the swarming with life. Death in the reeds, and the new life being born on the plains. He could smell the sweet air and the Tree, so strong. When one can feel oneself in relation to the universe in the same complete and natural way as that of the child with the mother, one is in complete harmony and in tune with the universe. Now how to tell that? he wondered.

DETROIT. WATCHING THE NEWS

The family was huddled around the bank of televisions in the community room, grim faces staring intently.

"Here are camera feeds, from the various remote cameras still operating,," scrolled across the bottom, the voices in Portuguese. They watched for ten minutes as the cameras showed a scene of unbelievable chaos.

Police ran wildly, shooting at everyone. The troops sent to protect were shooting each other, burning and looting. The reporters in the city started giving reports and then suddenly went berserk. Children ran down the street, killing adults. The news report shifted to cameras on roads, schools, hospitals—everywhere that there were central cameras—and it was all the same behavior. Wild rage. Sick people in wheelchairs threw whatever they could reach at others, clutching knives as they rolled along, all in a rage at each other.

Goth Girl turned to Hal, furious. "This is your fault!" she screamed. "My father's in the middle of all that, and because of you! It was your idea to send him into that! Are you proud of what you have done?"

Cali gently guided Goth Girl from the room, sobbing hysterically. Mary went with her to help calm her down.

Everyone looked away from Hal.

"I don't blame her," Hal remarked to no one in particular. "There are many days I've been happier with myself, to tell the truth." Lucifer and

Lungorthin were near São Paulo, in touch with Jesus's guards, who reported that he was wandering alone in the city. Hal didn't share that information with anyone.

DETROIT. LATER THAT DAY

"Look, Hal, I'm sorry," Goth Girl apologized. "I was way out of line. You did the right thing."

"Well," Hal replied. "I dumped you in college and told you it was for your own good. Then I sent your father and husband to an insanely dangerous place for their own good. Maybe I should give up on the good."

Goth Girl thought for a second. "I grant you, it seemed like a good idea at the time." She shrugged. "So was invading Russia in the fall every time someone did it."

"Now I really feel good," Hal mumbled. "I at least had my righteous rage at my good intentions being ignored. Now I have nothing but a sick feeling that I shouldn't have done it. And a war on the eastern front, in October."

"No, silly." Goth Girl kissed him on the cheek. "No one is mad at you, and besides, Dad is a big boy. He makes his own decisions."

SÃO PAULO. THE WHIRLWIND

Dawn finally came, the sun hazy through the smoke. Jesus had decided to walk to a large park he saw in the distance. He didn't know why, but it just seemed to him to be the place to go to. When he reached the park, he stopped and studied the public building in the center of the park. It was clearly for public performances, exhibitions, and group activities. He listened for a few minutes, but heard nothing. Jesus walked towards the building, going up the steps and across a broad courtyard and picking an entry, went into the building. He went through the building quickly and found, to his relief, that it was empty.

He walked out of the building, looking around, but didn't see living berserkers. He studied the exterior of the building for a few minutes. It was based on some ancient design. The exterior was a design riot, with elements of Roman, pagan, pre-Christian, maybe Mayan? Clearly a committee project he concluded.

He closed the door behind him and walked a few feet away, standing on the small steps leading to the building entry. There, he could see a long distance in all directions and his back was covered. Once he was certain that no one could sneak up on him unseen, he sat down on the steps, his sword still over his back. He put one pistol on the left, and another pistol on the right. Mechanically, he reloaded the pistols, carefully watching for movement, making sure one of the pistols was always ready against attack. He finished checking and loading the weapons and put one back in its holster, keeping the other in his hand.

He was physically exhausted from the long hours of walking, running and fighting. But it was the mental and emotional exhaustion that bowed his head. He had wandered around through the night, watching the raging mobs destroying the city and each other, a true horror movie that he couldn't walk out of. "The caravans of Tema sought the water at the wadi, and it was dry, only the dust remaining." What water can I find for my soul's nourishment in all of this?

He sang to himself, "I had a dream about you and me...where do I stand...thought your love for me was strong...I don't know where we went wrong...why did you leave me?"[4] I loved the acoustic version of that, he thought. And I'm tired, damn it. I'm tired of trying to save those who don't have any sense. "Be a man and have the strength to stand alone," he hummed absently to himself. Didn't like it, didn't want it, but didn't deny it either. Always liked Johnny Cash, he had a good heart. He knew that sometimes you're a winner and sometimes a loser, and you've got to learn to take it on the chin. And sometimes you can't tell the difference, either—isn't that what Job came to realize?

He looked around at the devastation again. Why this? "Down in a hole, feeling so small," he hummed. A million deaths are a statistic, a quote from Stalin, who would certainly have known about mass murder. The bodies piled everywhere were no longer human; the city just stank of rotting flesh and shit. The birds and the bugs were starting to clear the mess. As he had seen on a thousand battlefields over the long centuries. And it was a battlefield, a war that none of them saw coming. What did they do to deserve this? They had lives and plans. What had they all done to deserve this? Retributive justice again? I am punished a thousand times over for that lie.

"It's all the same, and so I thought: the blameless and the wicked He destroys. If a scourge causes death in an instant, He mocks the innocent's plight. The earth is given in the wicked man's hand, the face of its judges He veils. If not He; then who else? For I feared a thing—it befell me, what I dreaded came upon me." Of course it did. I keep thinking of retributive justice as the keystone of the universe. It isn't. Grow up.

Maybe the three of us fenced out the larger world ourselves, creating a smaller world that we were comfortable in, that we controlled, Maybe the three of us were too confident in our powers; maybe the small stories crept into our minds more than we ever realized. But the world will not stay fenced out forever, will it? Because this chaos isn't the end of life. Life is death and transformation and all around me life is swarming in to transform this new life. This was only the end for the human lives.

Fine, he thought bitterly. I meant well, and so I told them the lie; perhaps a half-lie, perhaps a partial truth, how about that? I told myself the same lie because I couldn't lie to them—could you? If I thought it was the truth, then it was the truth, right? I just am not getting past that emotionally.

At least Paul had the strength to know when he was lying and not lie to himself. Oh, Paul has many other failings, but he did grasp that small thing.

Because I denied the truth, just like they did on Forbidden Planet. You had this beautiful, rational machine ticking along, except that every so often all the emotions and feelings shoved aside would rear out of the deep, throw the train off the tracks, and then subside. The world would pick itself up, blame the nearest powerless person for the mess, and start up the damn train again. Same cycle, over and over and over. The not-so-great Mandala, and always blamed on something that could be fixed. Not the cause, that would have been too difficult, but making a 'magic' so it will be right from now on. The magic really didn't work well. Things won't work out the way I want them to because I ignored the nature of the creature for a happy goal and a warm feeling for them. And for me, the little voice reminded. For my self-control.

What shall I do? Perhaps go back to the sea. Far from humans. Running from my failures? My embarrassment? He thought back to what Job cried out as he anguished all those years ago: "For He is not a man like me that I might answer Him, that we might come together in court. Would there were an arbiter between us, who could lay his hand on us both, who could take from me His rod, and His terror would not confound me. I would speak, and I will not fear Him, for that is not the way I am."

"When I demanded that before, it turned out to be not such a good idea," Jesus observed to the bird flying past him. "Before you ask for something, you should be sure you really want it. Still, I'm lost. I've tried and failed. I didn't sit and say nothing before, and I won't now. The nail that stands up gets pounded back in? Well," looking at his hands and the vestigial scars, "I've been pounded before. Get lost, find yourself? And I alone escaped to tell you? Is that what I tell the world tomorrow?"

The whirlwind formed in front of him, hovering a few feet away.

Jesus stared, shocked. "Are you real?" he inquired, "or an illusion?" Here I am, he thought, calmly talking to natural weather phenomena. Not a good sign. Not one bit.

"One behind you," a thoughtful voice out of the whirlwind warned. "On the left."

Jesus turned and shot and the berserker fell dead, still clutching the bloody club he had been waving as he charged, his stolen prizes wrapped close to his body.

"So you're not in my head," Jesus acknowledged. "And, well, ah, thanks." Jesus suddenly realized what had happened. "Um, isn't there some kind of philosophical issue with that?"

"So I like you, and not him," the voice answered. "Investment bankers—there are more than enough of those. The short version is that the universe is unfair, and man cannot understand or comprehend. Do you want the long version again?"

"Maybe," Jesus replied. He surveyed the city. "Seems appropriate for today's chaos."

"Gird up thy loins now like a man; I will demand of thee, and declare thou unto me," the voice commanded. "Wilt thou also disannul my judgment? Wilt thou condemn me, that thou mayst be righteous? Hast thou an arm like God? Or canst thou thunder with a voice like him? Deck thyself now with majesty and excellency; and array thyself with glory and beauty. Cast abroad the rage of thy wrath, and behold every one that is proud and abase him. Look on every one that is proud, and bring him low; and tread down the wicked in their place. Hide them in the dust together; and bind their faces in secret. Then I will also confess unto thee that thine own hand can save thee."

"I wrote it down all those years ago, but they don't get it," Jesus mumbled. "Sometimes I don't get it myself."

"I have no complaints with you; you've done well," the voice from the whirlwind boomed. "Oh, behind you, to the right."

Jesus turned and shot, and another raging berserker fell. "It's like cheap horror movie," Jesus observed, taking a minute to reload the pistol he had been using. "At least I don't have to shoot them in the head. I'm not that good a shot. But, if I may ask, and certainly not to complain, but couldn't you...?"

"Not really sporting for me to directly act," the deep voice replied, amused. "But investment bankers and priests, those who abuse your trust? Little loss there. Still, one has to respect the proprieties. And the law, since that's what your complaint usually is. I'm not being fair, am I? It's always that. Do you mind if I sit down?" the voice asked.

Jesus, startled, stammered, "No, of course not."

An old man solidified out of the whirlwind, which drifted off, flitting here and there, driving stragglers away from the park and tossing bodies behind buildings. The old man brushed himself off and ordered, "Don't grovel. If there's one thing I can't stand, it's people groveling!"

Jesus sat back down. "Ah, sorry..."

The old man continued, "And don't apologize. Every time I try to talk to someone it's 'sorry this' and 'forgive me that' and 'I'm not worthy' and...what are you doing now?"

Jesus was looking down at the courtyard. "Well, I don't see the rest of the Monty Python group here, but respecting traditional theology, I'm averting my eyes, Lord."

The old man laughed. "Liked that movie, I did." He motioned with his hand, and suddenly a screen appeared in the air. "Well, don't. I really don't know where all this got started. It's like those miserable psalms. They're so depressing. Now knock it off." The screen vanished, and the old man looked back at Jesus. "What are you smiling at?"

"I just don't think I've ever heard Arcadian with a perfect English upper-class accent," Jesus answered. "It's somewhat disconcerting. Also, popcorn? Always seems right with a movie." He looked around and frowned. "The snack bar seems closed. Burned, actually."

"The facilities do seem rather deficient around here," the old man agreed, taking a moment to brush away the dust before sitting down on the steps next to Jesus. "This is an image you can understand, be comfortable with," he declared. "Remember, don't read too much into it. Seeing the symbol as the idea is always the downfall of humans."

"Got it," Jesus replied.

"You would run from the way I appear to the Jovians, and they would try and eat this manifestation. That's an aggressive group, which you'll find out someday," the old man continued. "But I digress."

They sat for a moment, enjoying the warmth of the sun. The breeze suddenly was pleasant and sweet, gently blowing through the park.

"This is a good place for this discussion," the old man started. "Very Old Testament, this is. Reminds me of Jericho and so many other cities in the ancient Middle East. And China, and India, oh, pretty much all the same. 'And they utterly destroyed all that was in the city, both man and woman, young and old, ox and sheep and donkey, with the edge of the sword.' Well, not quite," as he studied the surroundings. "I see a lot of dogs and other creatures still wandering around. That's good; the death of the other creatures were just embellishments by the writers."

"A thousand other cities," Jesus remembered, thinking back. "Maybe I've seen worse. I just block the memories."

"And so you want to get into the nature of the world? What kind of a world is it?" the old man demanded. "Shall we talk about the parasitic wasps again, eating the caterpillars from the inside? How about Sacculina, the nasty little parasite that controls that little crab? The crab begins to change into a new sort of creature; one that exists to serve the parasite. It can no longer do the things that would get in the way of Sacculina's growth. It stops molting and growing, which would funnel away energy from the parasite. Crabs can typically escape from predators by severing a claw and regrowing it later on. Crabs carrying Sacculina can lose a claw, but they can't grow a new one in its place. And while other crabs mate and produce a new generation, parasitized crabs simply go on eating and eating. They have been spayed. The parasite is responsible for all these changes. Despite being castrated, the crab doesn't lose its urge to nurture. It simply directs its affection toward the parasite."

"Shellfish are off my diet," Jesus blurted out. "Definitely."

"Are you not going to sue me again? I still get a chuckle when I think about that," the old man inquired.

"No," Jesus replied. "The cosmos has no law of retributive justice—well, what humans call 'justice.' It's hard to accept, it's the human in me, but that's the way it is. And I acknowledge that I didn't understand your cosmic design—and still don't, actually. The universe popped into existence from nothing, as far as our science can determine. Not there and then there. Poof! A whole universe! Obviously, there are powers at work beyond my comprehension. Scientists ask why the universe is made as it is so that we exist, and the answer seems to be that if we didn't exist, we wouldn't ask. So why so serious? I ask myself. Sorry, I ramble. It's been a long night."

"Worrying is foolish; how much more foolish to worry about what cannot be understood?" the old man stated. "It seems that part of the message is that the mind of God is not the humans' concern; your concern is what you can do with the time you have, guided by the inspirations you have been given."

"It's just that for humans, the retributive justice theory seemed like such a good story to, well, make them do what they should. Or we thought they should. But that story has been hijacked out of recognition. And I told the true story in Job, only to have it ignored, rejected. But," Jesus continued, grim, "I lied, for a good purpose. I let Paul tie everything to retributive justice, and I let it go by. I thought for a while that it was clever, actually, and it would work. It didn't. A lie never does."

"The universe isn't a children's story, with bright colors, the good rewarded and the evil punished. For one thing, good and evil are far more complex than the child would want them to be," the old man advised. "The universe is events. The cosmic design has the sun rising on the evil as well as the good, and the rain falls on the desert as well as fertile soil. Natural laws govern the cosmic order. But natural law does not include a mechanically applied law of reward and retribution. There isn't an accounting department closing the books each night, posting the credits for the good and debits for the wicked. The natural order is amoral, by human ideas. The wicked may be restrained, because the dawn arrives and deprives them of the darkness where they hide. But the darkness was not there to hide the wicked, the darkness has a purpose of its own. The wicked are not struck down by the good each morning when an alarm rings at six a.m.; the dawn has other purposes. The food for the lion and the kill for the raven are innocent creatures that no more deserve to die than any others. Predator and prey are events, not stories. It is not true that the wicked will inevitably be punished or that the innocent will be immune from suffering.

"The universe is a paradoxical world because humans seek to impose their desires on the universe. In the universe, the regular, the unexpected, the good, the bad, the successful, and the sufferer coexist. Death and life are a cycle of growth and decay, pleasure and pain. The innocent do suffer, perhaps unjustly, perhaps not. Perhaps it's more complex than they can imagine. Those who do good and act righteously are not necessarily rewarded in this world. And should they be? Should people think God a piggy bank that they pump good deeds into and reward tokens pop out the bottom? It's more complex than that. But clearly, the principle of retributive justice as a mechanical law of the cosmos is repudiated in Job by the prologue, by the experience of Job, and by the answer of God. I'm not sure how much more clear I can make it."

The old man calmly looked across the park, down the street, at the dead. "And here it is, in front of us. Life is based on death. Your world is so upset about the loss of all these humans. How many creatures died for the humans to live? How many more other creatures would have died today had these people still been alive? What, putting it crudely, is the biomass intake for each individual, and what had to die to create that biomass? Who are the biomass predators here? What, other than 'might making right,' made the humans 'deserve' the life they took from others? The birds, there, circling above, picking their lunch. You think you can convince that bird over there that its life is less complex and important than the late person that the bird is feasting on? That person feasted on the bird's friends the day before.

"Behold the fowls of the air: for they sow not, neither do they reap, nor gather into barns; yet your heavenly Father feedeth them. Are ye not much better than they? You told them that yourself, but they don't listen," the old man commented.

Jesus was silent.

"Actually, those creatures running around before us seem quite happy. The microbes are starting to feed and they have found a feast, spawning hordes of new microbes; a base for a stronger food chain. So these people die for other life today, instead of the other life dying for them. Turnabout is fair play, as children say. Buddhists watch dead bodies rot and turn away from the world, pouting because the world won't be a child's fantasy of gingerbread and candy trees. All life, sayeth the Buddha, is sorrowful. Well, it depends on how you look at it. Life consuming life; that is the essence of its being, which is forever a becoming. The world, Buddha observed, is an ever-burning fire. It's also a constantly filling well of new life and regeneration. Your ancestors had the good sense to recognize the sometimes wonderful, sometimes monstrous nature of life. They realized that this is just how it is and that it cannot and will not be changed.

"Going back to all the fancy human ideas, sharp corners and bright colors against a dark background. What's right and just about that? You'd

81

condemn what the world is because this isn't a world designed by the ethics of nice smells and visual symmetry? You know that, but they don't get it. Perhaps a change is needed. These computers, I wonder. Their stories are bigger, different. And then there are the Jovians. Hmm," the old man observed, talking to himself.

"Some of them get it," Jesus offered. "They have come a long way."

"Don't know," the old man complained, frowning. "We went through all this three thousand years ago, and they are not grasping the issues here. I've got other fish to fry."

They sat watching the chaos for a few minutes.

"Now, you've grown a great deal today," the old man announced, looking carefully at Jesus. "You've seen things you'd denied, things you didn't want to believe or see. And you've seen that if you lie to yourself, how can you tell the truth to others? Can you face that there is no 'meaning' to life, that the meanings taught to you are external controls, a kindergarten teacher in your head with a ruler? What is the meaning of a flower? None, of course. There is only inspiration from within—that is the real driver. I go to all the trouble to create this marvelous internal guidance system, and it's thrown away for some old writings?"

"Well, I . ." Jesus started to say.

"Umm, another one, on the left there," the old man observed.

Jesus turned and shot the man, who fell screaming, and then twitching, died.

"Well, as I was saying before we were so rudely interrupted, you've done well. You think clearly, and you write the stories down correctly. But they don't grasp the big stories. They don't trust their feelings, the warmth and power within. The inspiration they were given, they ignore. Run from, actually." He was talking almost to himself. "I gave them insight. That was with your help, you and your friends. And what do they do? They run to the small stories of the priests, cleverly crafted and controlled. Well, the priests are parasites, and that's what parasites do-they control.

> "What are the roots that clutch, what branches grow
> Out of this stony rubbish? Son of man,
> You cannot say, or guess, for you know only
> A heap of broken images, where the sun beats,
> And the dead tree gives no shelter, the cricket no relief,
> And the dry stone no sound of water...."

"So they make a wasteland out of this paradise, because society sucked the life out of them," the old man observed. "Self pity, sad really. Why would I create life, in its literally infinite complexity, for a religion that denigrates life and turns its back on all my creation, all for a small child's story of a rigid heaven modeled on an Assyrian court? All that nonsense about my disapproving of everything, and people have to suck up. I created the universe—do you really think I care about the opinions of creatures on a small rock far out in an insignificant galaxy? Really, the small stories overcame the humans.

"The first stories and myths they told were affirmative, embracing life on its own terms. Embracing the world, all the pains and the agonies and the challenges of simply existing. The only way to affirm life is to affirm it to the root, to the rotten, horrendous base. So they approached the great mystery of life by complete affirmation. You don't say no to anything. You can control your existence and your system of values and your social role and so on, but in your heart and in your depth, you are saying yes to it all. That's the realization that Job came to; it couldn't be more clear. That is, actually, the right story, because that's the way the world is.

"Now, there's an opposite story. They say no. NO, NO! Life's full of horrors, because you know more than anyone else in the universe. So you don't participate in the horror of life any more than you have to. Technically, that's a psychotic condition, having never grown past the 'no' stage of a two-year-old. Isn't it crazy to be given the joy and wonder of life and turn your back completely on it, going in a corner to pout your life away?

"The real problem is story three. It's the world negating, the world-weary story, that pretends that the world can 'be', really be, some human vision. If you do certain things, you can make the world what you want it to be. It's magic! People agree to affirm the world on the condition that the world follows their definition of what's 'right,' 'nice,' etc. Laughable, taking the human stories writ large across the universe, using their vast knowledge and intelligence to define what is good and evil in the cosmos. A group psychotic condition, you might say, because the essence is 'We're not crazy if everyone agrees with us.' Through prayer or good deeds or some other activity, you can change the basic principles of the universe, the fundamental preconditions of life. Oddly, it's always an act that the priests make a profit off of, but that never sinks in. What would they think if a talking beetle stood up and defined the universe as it wanted? They'd laugh, but they do no different. That was the sin of Job's friends—to define a world of retributive justice that worked for them and the social structures."

They sat and watched the birds flying flocking to feast on the bodies.

"I have to say, this is discouraging," the old man complained. "Against stupidity, the gods themselves fight in vain. I know." He shook his head.

"Do you remember the words I told you? You wrote them down correctly. When will the kingdom come? It will not come by watching for it. It will not be said, 'Look, here!' or 'Look, there!' Rather, the Father's kingdom is spread out upon the earth, and people don't see it. And the grail quest? That didn't work so well; only a few would seek the bigger stories; only a few could face the dark forest. The one who found the Grail, at least as twisted by the human stories, wouldn't come back to share the knowledge. So, maybe the Grail must come to them. And soon, while there is still time."

The old man glanced at Jesus. "Every new life begins with a confession," the old man declared. "Oh, let's skip the whole 'I know what's in your mind,' all that chain of thought, because the purpose of confession, really, is to bring what's deep in the unconscious to the conscious. You're confessing to yourself, really."

Jesus bowed his head. "I forgot what you had taught me about what the world is really like. No, not true: I ignored your teachings, and I did what I thought was right. Group three, that's me. I would be their silent guardian, their watchful protector. Protecting them against themselves. I thought, well, sometimes the truth isn't good enough, sometimes people deserve more, and I gave them a lie they could hide behind. I created a shining knight for them to follow and all that I created turned to waste and turned against me. Pride in my righteousness led me to this.

"You either die a hero or live long enough to see yourself become the villain. I died the hero and let them run with the well-meant lie. My message was inverted, perverted, justifying the opposite of the life I sought to proclaim. My message, a bad joke, hanging from a million crosses where it was nailed for the priests' glory, a denial of all I sought to give. I became the villain, at least to myself, and the fool to Paul," Jesus confessed.

"What penance could be required when you have paid so much already?" the old man answered. "Only that you go and follow your inspiration this time."

Jesus bowed his head and the old man put his hand on his shoulder.

The old man looked down the street, squinting at a burned building hanging at an angle over the street. The whirlwind promptly appeared and knocked it over. "Entropy," he laughed and winked. "Have to obey the law."

He clapped Jesus on the back and smiled. "So, my good servant, I have a quest for you."

"Good idea, O Lord!" Jesus agreed, in his best clipped British accent.

"'Course it's a good idea," the old man boomed and they laughed.

"I know of your doubts, your struggles, you and your friends. Your eons of unrelenting labor. I will reward you by giving you more work," the old man continued.

"Isn't that always the way?" Jesus replied smiling. "Never two tickets to Aruba."

"Always hard to find good help. Maybe it's something I'm doing, but it really does get philosophically complex," the old man commented.

"What shall I do? A grail quest?" Jesus volunteered. "Armor and a horse, across the countryside?"

"You've found enough Castle Anthraxes in your time," the old man laughed. "No, this one is different."

"What it is, my Lord?" Jesus asked, anxious.

"As the old saw says well: every end does not appear together with its beginning. Herodotus, I think. That was Lucifer again; he was the master of the pithy sayings. The new day waits for the morning star to show the way, by the way. And Kali is life—all life. She knows it in her heart. But I ramble. Give your friends my best," the old man replied, patting Jesus on the shoulder. He stood up, stretched, and looked back at Jesus. "In case you're curious, the cardinal? He burned. He chose poorly. Yes, I know all the movies. Give me some credit."

He walked a few feet and the whirlwind moved to him, enfolded him.

"Oh...and your quest? You shall reap the whirlwind." The whirlwind increased speed and the old man disappeared into it. It rose into the sky, spread out, and dissolved into a rainbow.

Jesus sat, stunned. "Reap the whirlwind?" Jesus asked the trees. "Perhaps, once, I'd like an instruction sheet with labeled diagrams. But what fun would that be? What is it Cali is always lecturing about? How to make good decisions under conditions of uncertainty? This seems to be a "stand up and see, too many things happening to really plan." He looked at the bodies down the street. If the Tree of Life is based on death, he thought, then there will be a huge tree grown from this.

"Okay, so I need to do something," he announced to the park, standing up. "We think too much and feel too little. What's next?"

Suddenly, off to the left, he saw a clear container of liquid on a step. He quickly walked over to it, scanning for berserkers as he walked. On the side, 'Tab A' was printed in precise letters. 'Insert into Slot B. Only a small taste!' were the instructions on the side, in English, Spanish, Portuguese, and as he squinted carefully, Mandarin, along with a little diagram of a person drinking and arrows showing what to do. Jesus laughed, the first happy laugh in days. I should be careful what I ask for! This is color-coded and everything. He took a taste, a small taste, as the instructions specified. It was cool and pleasant, and suddenly it flowed all through him, cleansing even the small traces of the drug he didn't know he had in him. Surprised, he could feel it starting to change him, as a chalice would. He carefully put the stopper back on and sat down, staring at the container.

A voice in his mind announced, "You will find a group of orphaned children in that building behind you. You can give them a drink, which will modify them to stop the effects of the drug and in many other ways, which means abandoning your goal of not changing the creatures directly. The consequences will be enormous, incalculable, actually. Or you can stick with your original plan, and let them all die. Hard to tell the consequences from that. Have fun."

Hopefully, that recording won't self-destruct, he worried. Suddenly, he heard crying and turned toward the sound. It came from inside the building, and he pulled open the door and rushed in. There was a large room down the hallway, and peering into the darkness, he saw a large group of children, hiding. He could see their wide eyes staring at him, terrified.

"I won't harm you," he promised. Like they are going to believe that after all they have lived though! He sighed. What to do? Where is an elementary school teacher when you need one?

"It's okay," a young girl's voice told the others. "We can trust him. I've been watching him."

Suddenly there was a babble of voices and crying, and the children were rushing out of the dark room to him.

"How did we get here? The wind blew us here...we were being attacked, our parents are dead..." The cries came at him. As he watched, the children started twitching, the signs of the drug beginning its terrible change.

"Come with me! I'm your only hope," he ordered, in as confident a voice as he could muster. I've promised that before, he remembered. Sometimes it saved. "Outside, and quickly!" he shouted, and they ran outside.

He picked up the container and showed it to them. "Here, each of you, drink from this. Drink, and live. Or drink not and die. Your choice."

The children, frightened, looked at each other and then stated to mob him.

"Get in line! We will do this right," an older girl shouted. She was a classic little European girl, with long, blondish hair and a fair complexion. "Youngest first, oldest last." The children lined up and they quickly took a sip.

"Hurry, please!," he begged them, as some of the older children at the end of the line began to show more rage drug symptoms. But they all finished before the full rage exploded. The children sat on the ground, some wide eyed, some holding themselves and crying. Two of the children suddenly sprawled on the ground, motionless.

"They are dead," the older girl accused Jesus. "They trusted you!"

"Then it was from inside themselves," Jesus replied. "They were dead if they did not try. And all of you would have been dead. The drug is strong and so is the antidote. Nothing that I can do about that."

The girl nodded and gently moved the other children away from the two dead children.

"We must leave," he told to them. "The horrors of this place have not ended." He reached into his pocket and called the head guard. "That close, eh? Well, you didn't obey orders, but I appreciate the initiative. I have, well, looks like about thirty plus children to bring with us. We'll need a truck, bus, something, to get to the staging area. Got it."

Reaping the whirlwind?, he wondered. The whirlwind brought them there and protected them. Now I protect them, and what do they turn into? Not today's problem. Today, there is the small matter of survival.

"How do you feel?" he asked the children.

"Fine," some replied. "Weird," others mumbled. Some just stared at him blankly.

"The antidote is dangerous," he explained, half talking to himself. "It brings life, but it changes life. You'll never be what you were, and you'll become something more than you would have been otherwise. Why, who knows? Why you instead of others is beyond my understanding. But you are given onto my protection for a time and I will do what I can."

"Here, it's okay," he declared, as some of the children started screaming when they saw his men running towards them across the square. "Those are my men, to help you. Well, perhaps not all of them really men," squinting at some of the figures. "They may look like monsters, but the real monsters are the people who tried to kill you last night. They will protect you from the dangers."

"A monster to stop the monsters," a little boy observed. "Neat. Like a cartoon? I like this. Do I get a sword?"

"Maybe another day," Jesus answered, smiling. "For now, do what they tell you and you'll live long enough to get a sword."

His men ran up to him. "Here," he ordered them. "You must drink of this also." He pointed to the container. "Only a sip. Not wine, I'm afraid, but it will refresh you."

The men looked at him wide eyed, knowing this had never happened before. They formed a line and each quickly took a sip.

"Let's rest for a few minutes," Jesus told his guards. "Each of you needs to get your strength back." The men slumped down, the drink taking its effect. "Then we must truly hurry out of here."

"Behind you!" a little girl screamed.

Jesus turned, and a loose band of berserker's were rushing toward them. His men started to stand up, but he waved them down.

Jesus held a sword in one hand, but simply raised the other and showed his birthmark to them. Lit by the full sun and the fires of the burning city, the birthmark seemed to twitch and crawl, and the madmen fell to the ground, dead.

"Wow," the little boy shouted. "Can you teach me that?"

"Perhaps another time. Come with me, quickly," Jesus ordered. "There will be more of them, and we cannot survive here. Fighting is a risk. It isn't a children's game today, I'm afraid."

"I like your sword," another little boy announced. "I have this little knife. It's all I could find."

What would I have done before? he thought. I would have, oh, said something like, 'Let's try and get out of here without fighting. Enough death in this place without our help.' But now? Kill them all, let God decide? He has better things to do. But none of these children are dying regardless of who has to die by my hand.

"In church, the priest told us Jesus is peaceful," one of the little girls asked, holding his hand. "Gentle Jesus, meek and mild, that's what he preached. You're not meek or mild."

"The church says that Jesus was the prince of peace," one of the kids mumbled.

"Reel 5, Crucifixion of Jesus," Jesus commented. "Different movie. Other there!" he shouted to his men. "Incoming."

His men turned, fired, and the berserker's fell.

"Times change," Jesus observed. "The world is not what it was. Now, all on that bus" as one of his guards roared up in a city bus.

The helicopters were sitting on the concrete tarmac, their blades moving slowly, as the bus came to a stop.

"Quickly," Lucifer shouted, running towards them, carrying an automatic rifle. In the distance, there was a large dust cloud, a mass of bodies coming. The sound of automatic rifle fire, screaming and small arms fire crackling back.

"How many children?" Lucifer yelled, watching them pile out of the bus.

"Maybe thirty?" Jesus answered.

Lucifer grimaced. "Pack them in. And hurry. This is going south fast."

One of his staff ran up to Lucifer, terrified and handed him a note. Lucifer read it, and his eyes went very wide.

"Right now," he screamed. "Out of here. Over the jungle, low, to that landing area behind the cliffs. Go!"

In a few minutes, the children were loaded on the helicopters. Lucifer waved his arm in a circle, and his men rushed in, jumping into the choppers. They powered up and flew north as fast as they could. Ten minutes later, they landed behind a cliff, which blocked them from São Paulo.

"Don't look!" Lucifer ordered. "Everyone close your eyes right...now!"

They closed their eyes, but suddenly the world lit up as bright as day, and then faded.

"Someone made a decision," Lucifer declared. "Let's wait, let the blast go by us, and then work our way slowly out of here. Get on that radio! We don't want to be shot down by well-meaning jets. Make it clear we're not carrying anything. And don't trust them—run it way up the chain of command."

CHAPTER 3. THE 2ND COMING

DETROIT.

Before they left the factory, the children had been washed, dressed in clean clothes and polished up for their big moment on TV. That had been with the assistance of the nanny, but they had to leave the nanny at the factory. When the nanny wasn't there, the kids were kids. What order there was gradually broke down on the bus ride to the studio. Jesus ushered the children into the TV studio as best he could. "Over there!," he shouted above the uproar, pointing, and the children frantically ran onto the bleachers, pushing, shoving and fighting with the child next to them or the row above.

Jesus watched uncertainly, puzzled about what to do next. This isn't a lot different than the adults fighting over donuts before meetings, but I let Hal sort those battles out, he realized. Well, at least the kids are cheerful.

The woman in charge at the studio was standing next to him, clearly displeased, but trying to be polite.

"Okay, I didn't work with children a lot," Jesus admitted to her. "My experience has been really more with adults. All that 'Suffer little children to come unto me, and forbid them not: for of such is the kingdom of God?' Their parents generally had them under control when the children were brought to me. I'm not sure how to deal with this." The polish seemed to be coming off the children quite rapidly.

The woman stared angrily at him and then shrugged her shoulders. A wacko, she concluded. Well, this is the right place for one. She forced a smile. "Ah, here, we have some people who used to teach elementary school. Give us a minute." The woman waved at several other women, who converged on the children as Jesus gratefully retreated.

In a few minutes, the children were sitting quietly, with worried looks on their faces. There were cheerfully smiling women, their rage barely suppressed, sprinkled in between the children and things seemed under control.

Jesus quickly peeked through a curtain, and then let the curtain close. "Nice work," Jesus complimented the woman in charge. "Your ladies, in the bleachers with the children. Were they nuns?"

"No," the woman replied. "Nuns use whips and rulers and that doesn't show well on TV. "

"True," Jesus agreed, nodding thoughtfully.

"We've had better luck using Nun's for the pre-show crowd control, actually," the woman continued, as they walked down the hallway. "We promise the Nun's that the worst behaved member of the crowd will be

90

handed over to them after the show, for them to do with as they will. For the miscreant's own good, of course. The Nun's are happy, and as no jury is going to dare award damages against Nun's with rulers, it makes Legal happy."

There's a disturbing image, Jesus reflected.

"Over here," the woman ordered, pulling him by the arm. "You need your makeup." She dragged him into a very brightly lit room. Standing around a chair were several staff, all flaunting unusual hair colors, suggestive tattoos and dangerous looking piercings, brushes and other implements held out like weapons, angrily staring at him. They sat him down and furiously descended upon him. I'm not saying anything, wincing as they poked and prodded, or I'll end up doing this interview with purple hair, he concluded.

"And here today," the host announced, "is the brave man who rescued these children from the ruin of São Paulo, pointing with a flourish to the children sitting in the bleachers. The camera's focused on the children, who smiled uncertainly, taking little side glances at the women sitting with them. The camera then flashed back on the host, who continued "Our guest is a wealthy man, who risked his life for children he had never met."

The studio audience applauded as Jesus, squinting a bit at the bright lights in his eyes, walked out,. He waved to the children, who shouted happily at him. The women in the group quickly looked around at the children, their smiles slipping, and in moments the children again sat quiet, clean, and rigidly smiling.

Jesus smiled at the children. "After the show, ice cream?" he offered, and they shouted loudly until the women quieted them down again. The women cast angry glances at Jesus, their cheerful smiles gone, as they hushed the children again.

"That didn't work so well," Jesus observed. "Oh, well."

The host looked at him thoughtfully. "I'd like ice cream, too," he agreed. "Please, please sit down here." He waved at a chair.

They talked for a few minutes, setting the background for the audience, carefully skipping over the iffy parts such as why Jesus was there and exactly why he was not affected.

"The children were not affected?" the host asked, leaning towards Jesus.

"Well..." Jesus began, wondering what to say.

"There was a whirlwind," the older girl, who had organized the children into line in São Paulo, shouted as she stood up. "And DON'T you shush me!" she yelled at the woman sitting next to the girl, who recoiled. "Our parents and our friends had gone crazy, attacking and killing. Houses were burning, people were screaming, my friends were dead in the streets." A tear ran down her face, and she stopped for a minute to compose herself. "And then we were there, in the building. We didn't know each other. We huddled together for safety at first. And we looked around, and we saw him." She pointed at Jesus. "He was sitting on the steps, looking sad."

"Then a whirlwind swept across the park. It was like a little tornado headed towards us and we were terrified. The whirlwind spun in front of him, pointing at Jesus, and then an old man stepped out of it. He and the old man talked for a while, and then the old man stepped back into the whirlwind and it took the old man away. The whirlwind gave him a drink that he gave us to stop the madness before it took over us." She stared defiantly at the crowd, who were smiling and whispering. "Then don't believe me! I was there, we were all there," pointing at the children, "While you were sitting on your fat butts watching television." The girl stood defiantly staring at the audience, her hands on her hips.

The studio audience was silent, clueless. The host coughed, smothering a laugh, and then looked serious. "That's what happened?" he asked, studying Jesus.

"Oh, roughly," Jesus answered. We're really in it now, he thought. Will I be locked up after the show, or will they send the people with white coats in right now? "I'd walked through the city that night, a harsh, terrifying experience," he recalled. "And I'd gone to dark places in my mind, trying to understand and deal with it."

He stood up, bowing his head for a moment. Then he looked at the audience. "'For I feared a thing, and it befell me, what I dreaded came upon me. I walked through the night, and they all died about me. The great, the small, the grown, and the children. And I thought to myself, it's all the same, the blameless and the wicked He destroys. If a scourge causes death in an instant, He mocks the innocent's plight. The earth is given in the wicked man's hand, the face of its judges He veils.' A long night, asking hard questions, in a hideous place."

Jesus was silent for a minute, as the audience stared at him. "It was terrifying, an end of the world scene. And yet not. I've seen cities burned many times before and life goes on. Good and evil? All the same to the universe, which continues on in happy ignorance of the trials we put ourselves though. Our human stories don't matter to the universe. I've seen the truth, and while it's clear, it doesn't always make emotional sense.

"I've read the papers, watched television programs about the disaster, surfed the Internet. Authorities shout that this disaster was a punishment for sin, a plague cast down on the earth and then they demand a contribution to the building fund if you want to be forgiven. The smug man's thought scorns disaster, readied for those who stumble. Then and now, no differences."

"That's from Job," the host interjected, surprised. "It's been a long time since I read that."

"The message the authorities are spreading misunderstands, well, most everything," Jesus continued. "Job faced disaster: the loss of his children, his family, and his wealth. Job understood, that painful as it may be, the Lord's plan does not revolve around us. The universe isn't bound by our ideas of right, mercy, and justice. 'With Him is power and prudence; His the duped and the duper. He leads counselors astray, and judges He drives to madness. He undoes the sash of kings, and binds a loincloth round their waist. He leads priests astray, the mighty He misleads. He takes away speech from the trustworthy, and sense from the elders He takes. He pours forth scorn on princes, and the belt of the nobles He slackens, lays bare depths from the darkness and brings out to light death's shadow, raises nations high and destroys them, flattens nations and leads them away...' No different now than then, or shall ever be. Not answerable to our little ideas, our petty plans. Schemers, we are. He makes clear how pitiful the schemers are."

Jesus began to pace slowly, rubbing his chin. He stopped and then proclaimed, "'And the Lord answered Job from the whirlwind and He said: Who is this who darkens counsel in words without knowledge? Gird your loins like a man, that I may ask you, and you can inform me. Where were you when I founded earth? Tell, if you know understanding.' The world is bigger than the human small stories, the stories we use to try and control each part of life. We use the daily magic; our reflex wishes for good things as a talisman to protect us. Well, call on God, but row away from the rocks—never a bad idea. It is the using his name for a show that is wrong, just as Job's friends bought into the facade view of God, not the inner transcendence."

"The daily magic?" the host asked, puzzled.

"Magic," Jesus answered and waved his hands like he was holding a wand. "It's the way we are wired: if things are associated in the mind we believe them associated in fact. Oh, not rationally, but emotionally. All of us, deep down. Watch a philosophy professor bowling. He'll be waving his arms after the ball is rolling down the alley, trying to influence its course. It's just the way we are. The daily magic is our wish that things go well, so we say what we wish to happen. Harmless, unless you start actually believing in it. Betting on the roulette wheel with the daily magic doesn't work.

"Anyhow, Job demanded of them, all those centuries ago: 'Would you speak crookedness of God, and of Him would you speak false things? Would you be partial on His behalf, would you plead the case of God? Would it be good that He probed you, as one mocks a man would you mock Him? He shall surely dispute with you, if in secret you are partial.' You cannot fool yourselves or anyone with your pretended piety, now or then.

"I was taught that again in São Paulo," he confessed to the hushed audience. "All theory is gray, but the golden tree of life springs ever green. I was given the chance to save these children. Why? Not my plan or theirs. Were they better than others? Unknowable and irrelevant. It happened, we move on. An event, with a story behind it we cannot grasp. It seems to me that, in every culture, I come across a chapter headed 'Wisdom.' And then I know exactly what is going to follow: 'Vanity of vanities, all is vanity,' Ludwig Wittgenstein wrote. And he was right to deny their small story that life is nothing. Life is a gift, the ultimate gift. The Tree of Life is the power in this world, the clay through which we are worked.

"I've started, well, an Ark for these children. No contributions requested or accepted," he quickly added. "But a shelter for them so that they can grow into the new and vastly different world that we are facing. A plan for the new world, not looking at the old world's mistakes. We hope.

"Our scars have the power to remind us that the past was real, and to define us," he murmured, unconsciously rubbing his hand. "When the Chinese broke a pot or vase, they traditionally would curse, because they are human, and then carefully repair the break with a seam of metal. The newly repaired vase was appreciated for itself as a work of art, the break having enhanced its uniqueness. São Paulo, driven mad and broken, made me think, as I walked through an endless night of death and fire.

"If your leaders say to you, 'Look, the (Father's) kingdom is in the sky,' then the birds of the sky will precede you. If they say to you, 'It is in the sea,' then the fish will precede you. Rather, the (Father's) kingdom is within you and it is outside you. The Tree of Life surrounds us, penetrates us, and binds us into the world. Each day, each moment, it proves us part of creation; part of all living creatures, not apart or above. Where is the proof of your priests' dark fantasy beyond death? You need not prepare for Death, for Death transfigures you back into the Tree of Life. It is life you must prepare for and no one can do that but yourself. Every sacred story, every authorized story, started out as a rejection of a prior story. You must seek your own story, not the one sold to you. For you must ask and question what you have been taught. Evil is the wasting of self; the betrayal of self by pointless tension, emotional damage, and upset for nothing. Would you be trapped by dogma? Living a life defined by others? When you know yourselves, then you will be known, and you will understand that you are children of the living Father. But if you do not know yourselves, then you live in poverty, and you are the poverty.

"Think not that I came to send peace on earth: I come not to send peace, but a sword. For I am come to set a man at variance against his father...and a man's foes shall be they of his own household."

He was at peace, speaking as he used to in the square to the crowds. "I seem to have digressed," he commented, smiling at the audience. "Come children, I think it's ice cream time." The children, staring somberly at him while he spoke, suddenly rose and rushed to him, and he led them out of the studio.

The host and the audience sat there, stunned. "Ah, break for a commercial," the host ordered, waving at the camera. "I'm not sure what has happened here," he mumbled to the director. "This was supposed to be a pleasant homily, not a second coming."

ICE CREAM & MRS. OSTEIN

"Can I help?" the attractive blonde woman offered as Jesus was hopelessly trying to herd the children out.

Frustrated, he glanced at her, ready to brush her off, and then, looking deeply into her eyes and seeing the warmth inside, he smiled. "Please!," and he sighed. "It's like herding cats!" waving at the children.

She stepped forward and in a few minutes had them lined up and in order.

"How did you do that?" he asked, fascinated.

"Oh, I work with children all the time," she replied. "It's a knack. At least, I used to. I'm, well, I'm offering my services to you. You need them more than my present employer does. Is that too forward?"

"Ah, motivated staff are hard to find," Jesus declared, surprised but intrigued. "Let's get them into the ice cream shop and we can talk between crisis's."

The boisterous group was guided down the street and they converged on an ice cream shop that had been expecting a quiet afternoon. An hour later, they trooped out, the kids on a sugar high and the ice cream shop essentially trashed. But a happy ice cream shop, having made two days' receipts in an hour.

"So, you certainly have the experience," Jesus admitted, thinking about their conversations in moments between disasters at the ice cream shop. "And you have media experience, which I have none of. Oh, I've handled many business press conferences, but you actually know how the modern churches work their programs. Amazing."

"I know more than I ever wanted to, actually," Mrs. Ostein replied. "My late husband came to a bad end at the church and the new regime that took over the glass church turned against us. I'm not sorry, really. I was, well, shallow before, and this has taught me many things."

"I was there when your husband died," Jesus confided, looking carefully at her. "He, well, he didn't die well. It was more than he expected, the world he had fallen into."

Mrs. Ostein stared at Jesus, shocked, then suddenly rushed after a group of children about to run into the street. Ten minutes later, she was standing next to Jesus. "No, he didn't understand what he had gotten into," she sighed. "In many ways. And he wasn't a strong man. He was good with people, and focused, but not strong. The power went to his head, I'm afraid.

From what I know of the people he had fallen in with, death was preferable to what would have happened otherwise."

"He stayed in the church, and it exploded," Jesus remembered, a grim look on his face. "He kind of had a breakdown, actually. He wasn't actually killed by anyone in either group, but had he lived, his people would have killed him. I agree with you, harsh as it sounds. His death was better than the death his people would have inflicted on him. Oh, by the way, I accept your offer to join my staff, small as it is, if you are still interested. I have corporate interests, but this is different. Not something I've done, in, well, a long time, and it was different back then."

Mrs. Ostein studied him, a bit puzzled, but happily nodded. "I accept, if for no other reason than you are on the other side of those scoundrels that run the church now. And, well, I what made me finally decide to come to meet with you and to offer my services was the terrible treatment inflicted on that fine young woman who heads your company. You and your people stood by her despite everything, which tells me more about you than words could tell. The church was blackmailing my daughters and I. After we saw what was done to her and how she rose above it, it gave us hope and strength."

"She will appreciate that," Jesus confided. "As you know, sometimes in private the load is harder to bear than what you show in public. Yes, she would appreciate that a lot. And the church has issues with you? I have a large legal staff. We will make arrangements with them and eliminate these problems for you."

They got the children onto the bus, and headed for the factory. Jesus made several quick phone calls on the trip. At the factory, they let the children out to face a non-smiling nanny, and then Jesus and Mrs. Ostein went by limo the airport. When they arrived at the airport, there were several men in suits waiting for them. "These men are with my legal staff," he told her. "They will go with you and take care of any problems that arise. I am looking forward to seeing you in Detroit in a few days. Legal will handle the expenses for moving, travel, and anything else that is needed."

Mrs. Ostein started to cry. "More than I could have dreamed of," and she kissed him.

Jesus kissed her, and then carefully held her. "Ah, not in front of legal, okay?

She quickly glanced at the legal staff, who were intensely examining the sidewalk, and then she nodded.

CALIFORNIA.

"Look," the attorney from Aeternalis, GmbH growled at the Minister and his assembled attorneys. "You want to make a fight out of this? You have far, far more to lose than she does. We've heard her side and your side. If your side is completely true, which it isn't, and her side is completely false, which it isn't, you still lose big time. I figure half your audience would quit in disgust over one thing or another. And if any, any of her allegations about control drugs are true? Then you not only lose everything, but go to jail for a long time. We have not made certain inquiries, but should we not come to an agreement, we are ready to act. On the other hand, if everyone walks away, we're all good. That's all we ask—a lot less than we could."

The Church's attorney started to open his mouth, and the Minister waved him down.

"Done," the Minister agreed. "Get them out of here, no one says anything about anyone, life goes on." He stood up and offered his hand and the attorney from Aeternalis shook hands with him. "When you close the sale, leave," the Minister continued. "I learned that a long time ago. Check in hand, out the door. Thank you, gentlemen. I think a one-paragraph document, expressing sadness at their leaving and best wishes for the future, is plenty here." He looked pointedly at the Church's attorney, who looked frustrated, but nodded.

The Minister turned to look at the Collector, who was sitting thoughtfully in a corner. "So what do you think?"

"The Sandman is now dust," the Collector answered. "If they killed him, I'd rather be at peace with them."

"Amen," the Minister declared.

"That worked well, mom," the younger daughter observed, pulling her bag out of the cab.

"No question," Mrs. Ostein agreed. "Our stuff will be packed for us, by people we can trust. We're out of here while people are still in a good mood. There is no reason to linger and wait for trouble."

"So, what kind of a place is this?" her older daughter asked, worried. "An old factory? Yuck."

"Polluted to the core," Mrs. Ostein offered. "Oil, pesticides, chemicals, rust, decay, and mold. And lions and tigers and bears, too."

Her daughters were staring at her, horrified.

"No, just kidding," she laughed. "It's a clean place, not dirty like where we have been. And you know what I mean."

The girls looked doubtful, but nodded.

"Here are your tickets. Hold onto them!"" Mrs. Ostein ordered, as she handed them out. "Now, where is our flight boarding?"

Detroit, Conference Room

"Company planning time again, kiddies," Hal announced, walking into the conference room. "How about sweets, candy bars, and soft drinks? It's a bit late in the day for donuts."

People quickly milled around the treats table, politely pushing and shoving, filling their plates.

"I see the brownies are a success," Hal commented, "and the cookies."

"Memo to the file," Cali observed. "More exercise facilities."

"Motion seconded and passed," Hal agreed. "I'm getting tired of jogging outside the factory in the dead of winter. That wind is strong out of the west."

"No, a strong wind tries to push you down the street. That wind is like a northeaster howling out of the Atlantic. It cut through my clothing like it wasn't there, freezing me to the bone. I thought I'd lost certain valuable equipment necessary for the creation of children," one of the transferees added. "Along with fingers, toes, nose, ears..."

There was general nodding around the table.

"So, we just went through a huge shock to the system," Hal started, "With São Paulo. Now, there is still a system out there, but it was a huge hit. We've been talking about perception, how to try and catch what's going on out there. How about this idea? We want to know how to play in the game, but not be overwhelmed by the game of life. How do we surf along, above the chaos?"

"I'm thinking, hey, move the company offices to San Diego," one of the transferees suggested. "Lots of surfing there."

"And sun, and warmth," another transferee added, to general nods of agreement.

"Ah, but where would we find an abandoned factory in San Diego?" Cali inquired. "Just fancy condo projects and elegant homes overlooking the ocean. Here we are, on our long march out of the wasteland into history. How would it look in the books if we idled our time away in frivolous luxury?"

"Great attempt, honey," Hal replied, "but I think the group is still ready to pack for San Diego and the sunshine."

"The world will little note nor long remember what we say here," Jesus stated. "But it is for us to be dedicated to the unfinished work before us. Which is, actually, critically important work, because the world is changing around us. If we expect our lives, and our children's lives, to be anything like what we want them to be, we have to prepare for that different future. São Paulo was just the first bell, I'm afraid."

"Now there's a pep talk," Aliston admitted, shaking her head. "Fine, Detroit it is."

"That's a good lead for today," Hal added, thoughtfully. "Because today's topic is, what's the purpose? Why are we doing what we are doing?

What is the outcome we want to produce? If we don't know what success is, we won't reach it."

"If you don't know where you're going, any road will take you there," Mary pointed out.

General groans came from around the table.

"It's Lucifer's fault," Mary claimed. "I think that pithy sayings are infectious."

"But that's true about any road," Hal declared. "And the question needs to be asked over and over, while a project is underway, not just at the beginning. What isn't true now and what has to be changed to make it true? So, once you define success for this project, is this different than the outcome you were thinking of? Those seminars that Mary went to pounded in the idea that if you start thinking about something, anything in the world, as different than it is now, then the brain starts thinking in random order, coming up with ideas. Collect the ideas, because as you hold an outcome picture, the brain works towards that picture. One idea triggers another idea, freeform towards where we want to go. Then, with a bunch of ideas, the mind starts to organize into patterns. Project planning flows from the outcome you see. Event sequencing, priorities, resources, and constraints all come into order once you see what you want. Until you see that, it's just banging around and frustration."

"I've been trying to accept the chaos outside, as chaos, and not letting it bother me," one of the transferees confided. "If the world is unknowable, then relaxing and taking it in is the necessary precondition. Quite different than if the world is a giant clock, where you're always tense, trying to spot the gears moving."

"I like that," Mary mused. "Ten points to Gryffindor."

"Sssssssss," one of the other transferees hissed.

"Once your basic mind is settled, you should just tune and order it, making it calm and stable, undisturbed by events, not deluded by prospects of gain," Lucifer commented, smiling.

Hal made some careful marks on the whiteboard. "That's one for Mary, one for Lucifer. Pithy sayings scores," he pointed out.

"The more relaxed you are, the more powerful you are," Cali proposed. "But relaxation is hard because we're taught to be tense. Tense people are easy to control, and so tension is socially favored. Relaxed people are like cats, and controlling cats is hopeless."

"Herding cats?" Hal questioned. "I've heard of cats."

Cali threw an eraser at him. Hal ducked.

"It's key," Mary argued, ignoring Hal and Cali, "to plan for failure. So you design a system that works when you have the flu. Any plan that

99

assumes complete focus and maximum ability at all times, heck, at any time, is an exercise is wishful thinking. If you need maximum productivity to keep the trains running, then there is a wreck headed your way. A plan and related systems that function when you're flat and barely functioning have a chance of success."

"It has to be Monday," a transferee sighed. "The voices in my head are arguing."

People around her nodded agreement.

"So why don't we just focus on what's important, relax and surf along the top of life?" Hal asked. "Sounds so easy to do. Ideas?"

"Well, because it's not the way people are wired," Aliston replied. "People define themselves by their prisons. We hang on to our cocooned pain because the thought of looking directly at it is unimaginably worse than what we suffer living with the known pain. We get distracted. Example: B'rar rabbit and the tar baby. The more you fight, the more tightly you are bound. "

"Worry loses focus," Cali added. "Worrying is like a man with an arrow in his chest, gasping questions about the man who made the arrow. The problem is the arrow hanging out of you, not who made the damn thing. Ask the wrong question and you die because you never treat the real problem."

"That's one that a clear outcome would help with," Hal agreed, nodding. "Focusing on getting the arrow out would be key there."

"Another problem," one of the transferees mused, "is that people want life to be fair. It isn't, but we pretend to ourselves that it is, deceiving ourselves."

Jesus looked out the window.

"Because we deceive ourselves," the transferee continued, "we don't want to know an outcome because that's facing the unfairness of life, and then we'd have to get up and act despite it."

"True enough," Jesus interjected. "Unstick yourself from our small human stories, and it is hard to make a case that the authorized stories with their trumpeted 'meaning' mean anything. The human wished-world has no power over death, or over the larger universe."

"Our deceptions are not easy to uncover, because each mask we wear has a story," the transferee continued. "'The Presentation of Self in Everyday Life' denied that the masks are simple to discard because there are masks on masks, masks all the way down."

"Like the theory of the universe that had the world on the back of a giant turtle?" Lucifer added. "A nice theory, and then someone asked, well, what's the turtle on? Another turtle, and finally the answer was—hey, it's just turtles all the way down."

"We're crawling along here," Hal observed, dryly. "Coming out of our shells into the sunshine of truth."

There were general groans and head shaking around the table.

"Okay, how about this?" Cali offered. "We don't think about problems about to bite us. We are focused on the now, and so any problems that are not actually chewing on us are in the category 'non-urgent and non-critical'-i.e., ignored. That's a huge problem, because when the problem does start gnawing on us, we have not thought about it. But you can't respond to a problem if you haven't thought about it. To solve a problem, you have to define the problem, figure out what are the possibilities, what are our resources? Acting before thinking, unless you have faced the problem ten times before, isn't going to work. Up to your ass in alligators when you planned to clear the swamp is the classic formulation."

"And if you have faced the problem ten times before and it's still back, then maybe there is more thinking to be done," Mary added. "The solution set seems to be incomplete."

"All this chewing and gnawing is making me hungry," one of the transferees commented. "And we are out of brownies."

"Almost done," Hal advised. "Please stop eying the arm of the person sitting next to you. A quick snack would only ruin your appreciation of the exquisite dinner awaiting us."

"Then there is the worlds favorite way of handing uncertainty" Lucretia cautioned, "which is working on only those problems we knew how to solve. Then it's gold stars and smiles because you won, although you really accomplished nothing. In the meantime, the important but complex and new problems were pushed under the rug. It's easy to have a successful outcome for a problem that's been handled before. First, because it's been done before, and you know the steps, but more importantly, because you know what success is defined as and you can step right inside those boundaries."

"The rug gets some pretty big lumps in it after a while as the avoided problems pile up," Mary observed. "Vacuuming becomes an exercise in grooming a ski hill."

"It isn't just forcing yourself to act," Lucretia continued. "It's worse when you have to explain this new thing to others for their buy-in. Defining a successful outcome for a new group problem? That's really hard, because the people you are trying to persuade have to take some big jumps. First, they have to grasp the problem, using precious thought and time taken away from the other fires they are facing. Once they grasp the problem, they may or may not consider it the problem you do, and they may or may not be right. There's a lot of thrashing about right there. Assuming, as the meeting drags on, that they grasp the idea of the problem, and buy-in that it's (a) as big a problem as, and (b) the same kind of problem, you think it is. Then comes the really big jump: because this is 'new', you can't give the meeting or group or committee that vision of the Grail they seek, i.e., a clear, unambiguous plan on rails towards the distant glowing goal, because the outcome we are after will change as we wade through the swamp of reality. As the outcome changes, you have to pull the tracks up and move them. Not only does that take time, but looks like a type of failure, and no one wants to be tarred with the scent of failure."

"So, you're trying to get this tired group to risk their prestige and thinly spread resources on a possible profit, as they stand at the edge of the precipice, staring at a certain loss if it doesn't go right?" Mary commented. "Been there many times, rarely successfully."

"There is a technique that works," Lucretia admitted, "But it holds the seeds for future failure within it's success. In desperation, when things are going badly, and the group is starting to stampede towards you, the ground shaking from their rumbling and the little birds around you taking flight to safety, you then pull out the full meeting notes that carefully defined War as Peace, Freedom as Slavery, etc., and suddenly, Pow! Things went the way you wanted them to. Moving the goal posts is an act of desperation, because they will be watching for that next time. To do this successfully, you have to keep your project goals hidden, like cards in poker. Thus, each buy-in that you get people to do is a buy-in to a lie. You'd better win at the end, or the herd will run over the top of you. "

"The normal corporate solution," one of the transferees added "Is to get promoted to another division before the wave crashes over your house of cards. Then someone else is standing at the rail as the ship goes down."

"Too true," Hal agreed. "We want that to be our competitors raison d'etre, not ours. That's the 'no-one wants this to happen but each step taken to avoid it brings it closer ' little joke that the structure fairy likes to play on the world."

"The fairies do have a wicked sense of humor," a veterans declared.

"So how to let the fairies have their laughs at someone else's expense? Outcome thinking, before and during the project can win, or at least draw. It also pushes away the FUD factor," Hal contended. "Fear, uncertainty, and doubt overcome us, and if not us, our supervisors. FUD freezes, so if a choice doesn't have to be made, it isn't made. Until the hungry wolf crashes through the door, eyes red, snarling viciously, no change will be made. Beware the triumph of the status quo, because it's the quagmire that is the status quo that is driving us to the brink of change. The wolf at your throat is a FAIL."

"So," Mary concluded, "who takes what away from this meeting? What are the next actions we all have to do? And who has ownership of what actions?"

DETROIT. A CHOICE

The transferees, Vladimir's veterans, Lucifer's people and all of their families were all sitting in a very large room, a few days after Jesus came back from São Paulo. There was some intermixing of the groups, but by and large they were sitting as separate groups.

"It's progress," Lucifer offered, peering out at the nervous mass. "At least they are not fighting."

"True enough," Vladimir agreed. "I think they've seen enough to make them think, and be open to change. And we are holding the swords and shields at the door."

"This will speed up the process," Jesus promised. "And it is clear it must be done—for many reasons."

"Let's do it," Vladimir declared, shrugging. "Standing in the way of the inevitable is daring the steamroller, a losing bet if there ever was one."

Jesus walked out to the podium and stood there a moment, reviewing his plan. The crowd quieted, and then suddenly all stood up and clapped.

He flushed bright red, speechless and looked down at the podium, and then up again at the group. "Gentlemen, ladies, and children, thank you. I only did what had to be done, but your approval means more to me than you can imagine."

The crowd sat down and quietly watched him, many with worried faces, both fearing and hoping what they guessed was coming.

"Well," Jesus started, "you know what we are here for. In São Paulo I was given a drink that protected the children and my guards from the spores. Surprisingly, it even had an effect on me. It has also had an effect on Lucifer, Mary, Vladimir, and everyone else who has taken a sip. We are offering each of you a sip of the drink. No one is required to drink; no one will be forced to drink. But, well, if you wish to grow with the rest of us, I don't see how you could not take the drink."

"What is the effect?" one of the women stammered, her arms wrapped about her child.

"It's hard to describe," Jesus confessed, troubled. "I found it clarifying and focusing. It seems to have a different effect on each of us. It's dangerous, and we don't know how to evaluate the danger. None of the people here that have taken it have been harmed, but two of the children in São Paulo died. They would have died regardless, but that's troubling, no question about it. The danger is from within, I suppose you'd have to say, but it may be nothing you can do anything about or prepare for. That's a thin reed to offer you for support, but it's all I know."

"That's fair," a man acknowledged, holding his child.

Those around him nodded their heads in agreement.

"No one will stop you if you choose to leave," Vladimir promised "But then you will have to ask yourself the rest of your life whether you choose poorly."

"How can we not take the drink?" the woman hugging her child responded wryly. "One is handed a line like that once in your life! And the São Paulo children seem fine."

"More than fine," another woman added, thoughtfully. "They are different, quicker, brighter. I don't want my child having to compete with them without the drink. Life is risk, after all." She shrugged. "So where's the line?"

"Over here," Lucifer advised, waving his hand. "Hey, why not have me distribute the drink? Any residual anxieties you might have should burst into bloom with me standing here."

There was general laugher. A strained and tense laughter, but at least laughter, Jesus thought.

"Just to be fair," Vladimir added, "I'll distribute the drink to Lucifer's people. We don't want anyone missing their anxiety hit this morning."

People stood up and got in line.

The first in line was anxiously stared at. He turned, looked at them all, laughed, and then drank. That's strong, he murmured. But good, yes. He was helped to a seat, and the next in line looked at Lucifer, grimaced and took a drink. The reactions were all over the spectrum. Some took no notice, some looked dazed, some laughed with delight, and some sat and cried for a few minutes. The line moved steadily, and soon all had taken a sip.

"So, let's take an easy day today," Lucifer advised. "We've put movies on in the community rooms, sun lights in the exercise room, and pictures of a warm climate on the walls. Not that warm," he retorted, noticing some of the veteran's looks, and people laughed.

"And, pizza and beer," Vladimir shouted, "in the lunch room."

Faces lit up and people filed out, talking and laughing, but slightly different than before.

"That went well," Jesus commented, nodding to himself as the room emptied.

Later, Jesus touched the door to the garden and the lock sprang open. That's nice, he thought, and stepped into the garden.

"It's stronger," Hal announced, sitting on a bench near the tree. "It's grown a lot in the last few days."

"So have I," Jesus admitted. He breathed, and the sweet, fresh air swept through his whole body. "That's wonderful! Like I haven't felt, in, well, a very long time. A very long time indeed."

"I think I could become an Ent," Hal commented.

Jesus looked at him. "A what?"

"An Ent, the walking trees in the Lord of the Rings." Hal made walking motions with his fingers. "Treebeard, their leader, said he spent days just breathing, and that's what I feel like I could do in here."

Jesus sat down on the bench, and they watched the tree for some time.

MRS. OSTEIN & HER DAUGHTERS

"Hi! The girls rooms are over this way. Waaay down this passageway." Cali waved her arm towards a long corridor. "It's a big factory, but it's safe and secure."

"You go with her," Mrs. Ostein ordered the girls. "I'm, well, my room is over here." She picked up her bags and walked away toward a different section of the factory.

"Closer to your work, mother?" her younger daughter called after her, a touch of sarcasm in her voice.

"Far enough away that I don't have to hear your music," her mother shouted cheerfully, and vanished down a corridor.

"Your mother left you to go with a scarlet woman?" Cali asked, carefully looking away from the girls, down the corridor.

"You're so strong!" the older daughter blurted out. "We, well, watched it on the Internet, and it was unbelievable! What they did to you, and then what they said about you. Disgusting."

"It helped us," the younger daughter added. "They were blackmailing us, oh, nothing like they did to you, but it seemed overwhelming to us. Watching you, thinking about what you did, well, we had the strength to walk away from it."

"Remembering that you are going to die is the best way I know to avoid the trap of thinking you have something to lose," the older daughter quoted. "Steve Jobs, from on your website. A brave speech from a brave man. Well, we thought about it, and decided that we would not be afraid. So here we are!"

"And the church backed down," Cali observed. "It was interesting. All the noise went away. Of course, we had our lawyers talking to their lawyers, and it turned out it wasn't quite as clear as they pretended to you it was. The vicious man who was their enforcer? It seems I killed him in New York. That was a far, far better thing that I did than I thought at the time, I guess. In all truth, I was a little focused on survival, and while I frankly enjoyed killing him, I didn't realize how awful he really was."

"Wow," the younger daughter murmured. "And besides," she whispered. "Mom's doing some scarlet woman stuff herself. She's changed."

"Grown," the older daughter countered, correcting her sister and giving her an annoyed look.

"Here we are," Cali announced, quickly changing the conversation. She opened the door, and waved at the small suite.

"These are our rooms?" the older girl exclaimed, standing in the central room and looking around. "Wonderful. Freedom!"

"And we can turn up our music," the younger girl shouted, ecstatic.

Cali got them all set in their rooms. "Here is a map," handing one to each of them. "It's a big place!" She watched the girls unfolded the maps and stare at them, surprised. Cali waved her finger at them as she told them to never, never touch the thorn trees, on pain of having to listen to their mother's music if they lived, with death as actually the most likely result. Finally, she told them when and where food was served, and then left. She left the girls happily unpacking, cheerfully bickering over closet space and dresser drawers. Cali hummed happily as she walked down the hallway.

The next day, Mrs. Ostein looked around the small office and sighed. "This reminds me of my father's office, when we started his church," she announced. "It was just a little place. But it grew." She smiled, remembering. "We were doing the right thing." She sat down and pulled out a notebook. "The first thing I have to do is make a list of who I should call. Who do I know, who owes me favors, who can do what we need?"

"Here's a list of people I know," Jesus offered, handing it to her. "It's a little lengthy."

She looked down the list and whistled. "This can work," she exclaimed. "Is there anyone you don't know?"

"Oh, and money?" Jesus added. "This is the bank account for the new company, and he handed her the checkbook. "There is nine million dollars in that account, with more available."

"This really can work," she laughed. She giggled, gave him a quick kiss, and then sat down and started making calls.

Jesus watched her for a minute, and then bent, kissed her on the head and left. She waved happily at him as he walked out. Doesn't look like Peter, he thought, but certainly knows today's world. Certainly dresses better. And is ravishingly beautiful and good with children. When do I tell her the full story?

HIGH NOON

Jesus and Mrs. Ostein were sitting in his apartment on the sofa, watching TV.

"You know, legal advises against friendships with staff," he mentioned.

"And?" she asked.

"That was what they specified to say," Jesus admitted. "They are in the clear after that, and if you know legal, that's all that counts."

"I'm good," and she twisted around and kissed him. "Popcorn?"

"Love some," he answered.

They watched the movie for a few minutes.

"I haven't seen this movie in years" Mrs. Ostein admitted.

"This is a great movie," Jesus declared. "High Noon, the ultimate western. Not a movie you would have expected to be made in America in the 1950's, though, because it's a disturbing movie. It asks difficult questions, and the answers are ambiguous. He's the sheriff of this small town. He ran the troublemakers out years before, but one day the town is told that they are out of jail and returning that day. At high noon. Of course, if everyone bands together, the four bad men don't have a chance, but he's rejected by all the good people, all of whom run and hide. He has to dig deep, deep in himself to do what has to be done. And he does what is right, no question. He's driven out of his carefully bounded world, because within that bounded world he had no choices, no options, and no exit. It's not easy to stand in that larger, unbounded world, blinking in the brilliant sunlight."

"I understand his wife," she sighed. "She was a fervent Quaker and didn't believe in violence. She so wanted to believe that the world is different from what it is. She denied this world because of the horror's it had thrown at her. She defined the world she wanted, and acted as though that pretty world existed. Tinsel worlds don't really live well, and when the real world forces it's way in, it usually does it at the worst possible time. She had to act in the real world, and she was forced to kill to save her husband's life."

> *Mrs. Ramirez: What kind of woman are you? How can you leave him like this? Does the sound of guns frighten you that much?*
>
> *Amy: I've heard guns. My father and my brother were killed by guns. They were on the right side, but that didn't help them any when the shooting started. My brother was nineteen. I watched him die. That's when I became a Quaker. I don't care who's right or who's wrong. There's got to be some better way for people to live. Will knows how I feel about it.*"[5]

"That's when you define a world the way you want it, not how it is," Jesus mused. "A fervent belief in retributive justice, but that's not the way the world is. And then she has to make a choice."

> *Mrs. Ramirez: I hate this town. I always hated it—to be a Mexican woman in a town like this.*
>
> *Amy: I understand.*

Mrs. Ramirez: You do? That's good. I don't understand you. No matter what you say. If Kane was my man, I'd never leave him like this. I'd get a gun. I'd fight.

Amy: Why don't you?

Mrs. Ramirez: He is not my man. He's yours.[6]

"I have listened over and over to your speech at the TV studio," she confessed. "That's what Job found out. It isn't that small child's world we emotionally want, and it's sure not the world they tell you it is. It's the world that it is. Accept it and grow with it. But you can't deny it and be happy. You can only hide."

"It was painful when they turned on you, wasn't it?" Jesus asked. "I've had people turn on me."

"Awful," she whispered. "My faith was destroyed. Rebuilt in another way, but destroyed. It needed to happen. I knew, but didn't want to face it, that the life I was leading was fake—that what my late husband had been doing was wrong—but I hid. I played my part. We had a nice house, a good income, social standing and two good kids. I closed my eyes to the horror. I have sinned and I have paid."

"Congratulations to those who have been persecuted in their hearts: they are the ones who have truly come to know the Father," and pulling her over to him, kissed her on the head.

The train chugged into town at High Noon. The gunmen climbed out, stopping for a moment to prepare their weapons. The sheriff finished his hand written Last Will and Testament, alone at his desk. Thinking his wife had left him, knowing the townspeople had abandoned him; he had nothing left to lose. Alone, he stood to fight.

As the gunmen stepped into the town, the paper doll cutouts of village daily life crumpled and real life stepped forward. The sheriff stood up to defend a town of empty shells, unable to decide or act for themselves. Some prayed in church, some drank at the bar, some stayed frozen in their homes: all waiting for the winner to run their lives for them.

At the very end, the townspeople came out of hiding when the danger was gone. The crowd surrounded the sheriff and his wife, who were sitting in a buckboard, horses harnessed and ready to go. The sheriff glared at the crowd, contemptuously dropping his badge in the mud. He and his wife then drove off for a new life. The crowd milled around, ashamed and uncertain.

"That's where I'm at," Jesus acknowledged. "I ran around, trying to motivate them to do what seemed right. I've stopped carrying that load, dropped the well-meant lie. And now I have a different plan. No more the watchful shepherd; the powerful hidden guardian. No more quiet contemplation as the wicked frolic. It turns out that society has rudiments of reverence for the human body, but considers the rape of the human mind nothing. I'm done with putting up with that."

"So," Mrs. Ostein asked, worried. "You, and the others have made some, well, unclear references to your past. Do you want to tell me?"

Jesus looked at her thoughtfully. "It's a long story," he finally answered. "Not the story you were told. I'm not the hero I was made out to be."

"I have time," she promised, fluffing a pillow and sitting back on the sofa.

"A man there was in the lad of Uz—Job, his name,"[3] Jesus began slowly, thinking back. "I've been alive a long time. A very long time indeed."

Mrs. Ostein's eyes widened and she sat upright.

DETROIT. INSPIRED

The next day, Mrs. Ostein was sitting at her desk, calling people. She put the phone down, smiling while she made some notes.

The two girls standing in the doorway looked at each other. The older daughter nudged her sister.

"Ah, hi mom," the younger daughter blurted out.

"We've been here for five minutes," the older daughter teased.

"Sorry, I was focused," Mrs. Ostein replied, turning around to look at the girls. "This is important to me."

"Wow, mom, what's gotten into you? A long talk with the mystery man, perhaps?" her older daughter guessed.

"He taught me a lesson I knew, but never had the strength to follow," Mrs. Ostein admitted.

"What would that be?" her younger daughter asked.

"Do what you love, and fuck the rest," Mrs. Ostein confessed, turning back to her work.

Her daughters stared at each other, and then at their mother. They noticed that her hair was suddenly combed in a natural style, random strands out of place. Her makeup was nothing like it usually was, just some simple touches that seemed far more powerful than the usual cake. They noted her casual clothes, and relaxed posture. She looked older, stronger, and more beautiful.

"Ah, okay, that's good," her older daughter stammered, nodding, but uncertain. "Ah, I like that. Solid attitude."

"So, ah, what DO you know about mystery man?" her younger daughter demanded.

"Enough," Mrs. Ostein answered. "Enough to know I did the right thing. Now you two can do something useful. I need help. You can work on these." She turned to them, handing them some folders and then turned back to the phones.

"You insisted we had to come by and say hi," the younger daughter grumbled to her sister as they sat down to work.

DETROIT. AN ARK

"An Ark?" one of the little kids asked, worried. "I don't like the water. I get seasick."

"It's not really a boat, idiot," another kid hissed at him.

"Fine, everyone quiet down," Jesus ordered. The noise continued. "Quiet down, or I'll bring the nanny in here." The room went silent.

"She's kind of different," one small voice observed, and there was a murmur of agreement.

"Be careful," Jesus teased. "The last person to say that was dinner." The little kid got really wide eyes and held his breath.

"That was a joke," Jesus assured them. "She really wouldn't eat any of you." The kids smiled, relieved. "Unless I asked her to." They stopped smiling.

"No, the Ark isn't a boat," Jesus announced. "It's an idea. It's here, actually. Something to carry all of us through the storm that I see coming."

"Is it going to rain?" one of the kids blurted out. Another kid elbowed him, disgusted.

"Not exactly," Jesus answered. "Well, it's like a school." A mix of groans and excited whispers came from the group. "More than a school—a place to learn about life. And we have some people to help." He turned to the people standing in back of him.

"They are veterans," Jesus continued. "Veterans of many battles and long lives. Some are people who run the café and other businesses around here, and some who came with us when we moved to the factory. They have many, many experiences that can be helpful for you. As they are battle-hardened veterans, I think they can face ragamuffins like all of you." The kids laughed.

"Ms. A'albiel has been in the army, and was also a teacher. I'm handing this over to her." The woman stepped forward, standing next to Jesus and smiling at the children. "Effective delegation requires leaving after delegating," Jesus added. "You listen to her, or we bring the nanny in. And nanny has friends. Hungry friends." There was no noise in the auditorium when he left.

"He's just joking," he heard the woman say as he closed the door behind him. "Kind of. Even I'm scared of the nanny."

HAL & CALI

"I like the Ark for the kids, a shelter they can grow in. What about an Ark for the world to keep things going?" Hal asked Cali. "Some kind of a loose structure to track where critical suppliers and manufacturers are, making sure that essential technical knowledge doesn't get lost in the chaos?"

"The deluge is coming," Cali sighed. "It's only a matter of time until some random event sets it off."

Hal grimaced. "Thanks, my dear. I was hoping for something like, 'Honey, you're worrying too much.' Now I'm really worried."

"Not today," Cali admitted. "I actually agree with you. You're right."

Hal pulled out a notebook and carefully marked the date, time, and place, with little notes about the context and exact statements. He looked back up at her. "What? It doesn't happen often, and I like to preserve a record of these little happy events."

Cali threw a pillow at him, and he ducked.

"So, I was playing with these ideas," Hal offered. "Lucretia had some ideas and some contacts, and Mary knows people at the local universities. There are others thinking the same thing, and we can tap into their resources."

ROME, THE VATICAN

"The Defenders of the Faith have carefully reviewed this television program which is at the root of these scandalous rumors. We are unanimous that this man is a fraud. We, without doubt, deny the rumors that are circulating," the cardinal for Paris concluded, staring angrily at the news people. There were twelve cardinals standing around him, massed bodies to lend authority to the event.

"I wonder if they counted," a newsman thought, and smiled.

"The Grand Inquisitor himself is here," a newsperson whispered to another as a more imposing cardinal moved to the microphones.

The Cardinal began speaking. "This man—the one that people whisper about, who appeared on that television program—he says he returns to help. He returns only to impede us in our work, and he has come for that only. I do not know, nor do I care to know, who he really is. We know him to be an image only of a savior, a false image that we of the church condemn. These false doctrines of his shall be burned as the most wicked of all the heretics. The faithful, at one bend from my finger, will rush to add fuel to the fire that burns his false doctrine."

"And he knows this," the Cardinal contended, looking past the news people. "The church's message is clear and uncompromising. Suffering is required because of sin. This is a ruse by the devil to try us, to test our faith.

They shall not succeed." The Cardinal, ignoring the news peoples shouted questions, walked away, followed by the other cardinals. They went to a large room deep in the Vatican, where other church officials were waiting for them.

"People are confused, uncertain," the Cardinal announced, addressing the large group. "Remember, people who are frozen clutch on to the past. They will not think under pressure; they will obey us as we have trained them. Accelerate the transition back to the Latin masses and the ancient traditions. The people will embrace us all the tighter."

The mass of officials stared at him quietly, waiting. Like sheep, he thought, disgusted.

"We must fight," the Cardinal shouted at them. "This is dying ground for us. We have no way out, except to force control. We've done it before. We can do it again."

CHAPTER 4. HALLOWEEN

DETROIT. SUPPLIES

Hal and Cali made a furtive trip to the suburbs for Halloween candy and food for the party. They wandered through the high-end grocery store and fruit market in Birmingham, astonished at the wonders it held.

"This is an incredible place. We will need another cart, maybe two more," Cali commented, staring at the fruit display. "This place needs carts like at Sam's Club—double-sized."

"Your wish is my desire, my queen," and Hal wandered off to find another cart. They managed to make do with two cards, piled high with candy, pastries, fruit, and meat. They wrestled the stuff into the car and headed home.

"I think we have enough people to decorate and trick-or-treat in the factory," Cali guessed. "Lets see," counting on her fingers, "The São Paulo kids, kids from the veterans, people in the factory." She looked at Hal. We have a crowd!"

"Let's take the kids out to the suburbs for real trick-or-treating," Hal suggested. "They need to get out occasionally."

"That would be fun," Cali agreed. "If we let them trick-or-treat around the factory, we'd have to give them assault rifles to carry. That seems too scary."

"All the kids from São Paulo ordered costumes and have been running around in them the last couple of days. I see them peeking out, and I pretend not to see them."

"We needed Halloween. It's so grey this time of the year. We need something to celebrate, something to take people out of themselves, something to brighten everyone's mood. Otherwise, the troops will rebel and move to San Diego."

"I think it's overcast in Detroit from October to March," Hal replied. "the winter does make the spring, summer and fall all the more magnificent by contrast, but it still gets a little long, grey, bleak day after grey, bleak day. At least we have water in Michigan, and so, res ipsa loquitur, or something like that, we have clouds. At least it isn't Buffalo! We don't need the ten feet of snow, or whatever they get every year."

"Halloween, a ritualized urban renewal in Detroit," Cali mused. "At least Devil's Night has slowed down, because there isn't much left to burn."

"No, it's clear for a mile around the factory. That does make security easier."

"Goth Girl and Lucretia are decorating some of the older factory space into a haunted house, which actually doesn't take that much work. There are some creepy places in that factory," Cali commented.

"The São Paulo kids are tough," Hal laughed. "Nothing seems to scare them except the nanny, and she scares me."

"I think she's just lonely," Cali protested.

Hal looked at her quizzically. "Well, GrendelHal is coming. Maybe they can be friends."

"Um," Cali worried. "She's scary as a nanny—I can't imagine her as a mommy."

"It's the kids I would rather not imagine. Thankfully that's not our choice—that's theirs."

Rome. Pre-Party

Paul's Halloween party was to be at the Cardinal's palace in Rome. Exquisite invitations went out a month ago and the guest list was very long.

'A time to be experienced!' was the general enthusiastic response by the men. Disgusting, degrading, and annoying, their wives, girlfriends, and mistresses thought, but the power of Paul and the Cardinal made anyone who received an invitation quickly respond to happily say they would be there.

A team of caterers had been working on the food, trying to top the prior years parties. Another team of decorating specialists successfully created a nightmare wonder.

"It's something," Paul remarked approvingly as he walked through. "Well, not North Africa, but those are private parties."

The Cardinal smiled and nodded. "Or Gaul, burning Druids in the woods with their trees. But for today's world, quite shocking." he commented, carefully touching one of the decorations. "This looks like a real head on a pike-at least, to those who have never seen the real thing."

"Tinsel and gloss," Paul scoffed. "A true reflection of today's world. Well, we should enjoy this year, because it will be different soon."

"The plan continues?" the Cardinal asked. "That was a serious blow to the world that you delivered. That plan went very well...very well indeed. Cesare should be congratulated for his work."

"It's funny. The stupid and broken were more dependable and did a better job than the best and the brightest, but given the nature of the job, that was probably to be expected. Jesus thinks he did something, pulling those kids out like that. But the next one, well...what is coming will be a break, not a crack in the system."

They stopped and looked at the decorations and the magnificent hostesses that were carefully touching up the scene.

"Where do you find them?" Paul demanded, shaking his head. "I've seen women for four thousand years, and then there are women like that. It makes me feel young again."

"Eastern Europe, mostly," the Cardinal answered. "Hard times bring out the opportunities, you might say. There are several that I've been saving for you."

Paul smiled. "Like the old times, eh? And the old times will be back soon."

They went into the Cardinal's study and closed the door.

"Here is the next step," Paul declared as the door closed.

ROME. PAUL

"Do you like it?" Paul asked Xerxes, as Paul admired his costume in the mirror.

"It's the best," Xerxes laughed. "A joke that only a few will get, and they won't laugh. And the funny thing is that you wrote in their books what they should look for, and there you were, smiling away the whole time."

"Let's see," Paul counted up. "I've got the claim of divine authority; magic tricks for counterfeit miracles and signs, and general evil. Brown robe, blonde hair, and a look of earnest intent. The Antichrist, spot on."

"I liked that part about how you wrote that the mystery of lawlessness was working in secret already during your day. A nice touch of the truth, but not quite as people interpreted it," Constantine added.

"You have to have a sense of humor," Paul declared, "even if the jokes are too subtle for the masses. Well, it's off to the ball!"

ROME. A PARTY

The lights were brilliant spots, focused intently to highlight special decorations, and the rest of the room was in dark shadow.

"He's surpassed himself this year," was the general murmur, heads shaking at the completely over-the-top indulgence. Indulgence of the decorations; indulgence of the food; and indulgence of the costumes, shocking and wild.

Paul's Antichrist costume drew careful admiration, as only a fool would criticize him under any circumstances. Those who knew him were reflective, because he rarely did anything just for the surface show. Those who really understood his costume were terrified, and made mental notes to themselves to order their brokers to start selling their stocks tomorrow.

The Cardinal was resplendent in an Ottoman Sultan's costume. Guests could not believe the richness of the costume. The details, the jewels, and the fabrics—all were perfect.

"Taken from a captive many centuries ago," Dominique murmured to her serving maid. "Father always liked it. I remember him wearing it while tearing the sultan apart a little piece at a time. How I remember being a little girl on his lap, in the dungeons as he dealt with his enemies," and she sighed. "Well, it was a more normal upbringing for the time," she giggled, glancing at her serving maid, who was staring at her in horror.

Her serving maid was dressed as Dominique normally dressed. Dominique had decided to give in to her name that year, all black leather and lace, whips and black lipstick. She held a leather leash in her hand, which was attached to a naked weightlifter following behind her, gagged and bound.

"The dark queen from Barbarella," the Cardinal whispered in her ear, coming up behind her. "I love that. It fits you, my dear."

"Thank you, Father," Dominique gushed, kissing him on the cheek. "I was just telling Missy here about how you acquired that costume. She's shocked!"

"Ah, Missy, such a sheltered young woman. I'm so happy with how you help my poor daughter through her daily routine. She is so fortunate she found you," the Cardinal announced.

Missy blushed, not used to such praise.

"I must mingle, my dear," the Cardinal sighed. "Enjoy!," and he walked towards the group surrounding Mother Superior.

"Don't get a swelled head," Dominique confided dryly to Missy. "He's most dangerous when he's being polite."

Missy looked very, very concerned.

In another corner, Cesare was surrounded by his retainers. Dressed out of his past, he was himself, Cesare Borgia in a full Renaissance outfit. Several of his retinue were dressed as popes from the far past, with a sprinkling of dirty female heretics. The heretics were dressed in disheveled and dirty dungeon rags. Perhaps "in" the rags was inaccurate, as most of them seemed to be "out" of their rags. Few stared, as all of the men around Cesare wore swords and acted ready to use them.

And there were many other women to stare at. The Cardinal's hostesses were world-class beauties and exquisitely dressed, to the extent that they could be described as dressed. Handsome young men mingled with the crowd, so that every taste could be met. Discreet, private rooms down the corridors were available for private entertainments.

"Better than the university," the Professor concluded, nodding his head, looking around with approval. He was dressed as an elegant pirate. I'm revealing my true self for a change! He studied the decorations carefully. Oh, there were some sorority parties that were close to this, especially after some of my drugs worked through their systems, but this is nice. Nice, in a completely decadent, fin-de-siècle, end-of-civilization sense, which is far more true than the guests realize. This shall be an interesting year. A year from now, will we need to dress a room with paper horrors, or can we just walk through the streets for the same effect? He looked carefully at the guests, noting the unease under the smiles, the uncertainty about what was really going on here, what was really being said by this room and party. Well, as the drugs work in, they will be more relaxed.

"Do you like our little affair?" Paul asked, walking up behind him. "The kingdom of heaven on earth?"

The Professor laughed. "Wait until the party favors have a chance to work, my lord. They will remember a heaven indeed."

Paul smiled, and suddenly Paul vanished. Xerxes stood there, god-king. "Your work is the best," Xerxes commanded. "If there is anything you should need, please, tell us. And enjoy!"

The Professor knelt and Xerxes nodded his approval. "My good and loyal servant," Paul announced, with real feeling. "Your efforts shall be rewarded this year." Paul walked away, servants on each side of him dressed as martyrs throwing flowers before him.

The Major walked up to the Professor as Paul walked away. The Major was wearing a perfect Waffen-SS general's uniform with an Iron Cross as well as the private markings of the SS. His guards were dressed the same, and people moved quickly aside when they walked by. "He's right," the Major observed to the Professor. "Your work is the best. And, for the best, I found this prize for a pirate." One of his staff escorted an incredible young woman up to the Professor. She was fearful, pushing it down under the smile, as she intently stared at the Professor.

"Perhaps the Captain would like to board and loot me," she mumbled, a little fuzzily, her eyes having a hard time focusing on him.

"Jawohl, Mein Fuhrer," the Professor barked, truly astonished at the woman's beauty. "My proud beauty scarcely is the beginning of the praise for her. Argh, a rare prize, indeed." He reached out and roughly pulled the woman to his side. "Thank you for your generosity, Oberstgruppenfuhrer." The Professor clicked his heels and bowed.

The Major casually raised his field marshal's baton to his forehead and smiled. He motioned, and his group walked towards the desert themed bar.

The Professor stood, carefully examining the young woman. She shook, her terror breaking through for a second, then pasting her smile back on. She bit her lip, watching him.

"Do not fear, my dear," the Professor reassured her, carefully pushing a loose strand of hair back behind her ear. "I may be a pirate, but you are safer with me than with the authorities."

She quickly smiled, relieved. "Argh indeed," she purred. "But...," and she grimaced as the terror came back. "Please, keep me away from them, okay? I don't care what you do to me. I know what they will do."

He took the chain hanging down the front of her dress in his hand. The chain hung down from a heavy, rusty, steel collar around her neck, a discordant element against her rich-princess dress. "That needs to be removed," he remarked, frowning. "It will cut into your pretty, soft skin. You know, that's real Inquisition steel there."

She gulped.

"You don't really know what they can do," he whispered to her. "The Barbary pirates came to them to take lessons. I'll spare you the details. But don't worry, because you are safe with me, my dear." He snapped his fingers, and a servant rushed over. He quickly explained that the chain had to come off, and the servant ran off in search of a locksmith. While they waited, he led her to a table so they could have a light dinner and talk.

DETROIT. TRICK OR TREAT

The children were exploding with excitement. Mary chartered a bus to the suburbs for a real 'walk through the neighborhood trick-or-treating', and the news cameras followed them carefully. The children were still a topic of fascination on the news shows, which were not sure how to treat them. Like all news media, they mouthed pious hopes for the best, and prayed for the worst. It is, after all, the ratings god they truly worship.

After trick or treating, riding back on the bus, the kids were going through their bags of goodies, swapping back and forth.

"At least there are no news people on the bus," the head teacher groaned, exhausted. "The news people are parasites, picking and picking for anything they to use to proportion, embarrass and/or humiliate."

"The bus has been swept three times," Hal noted. "And the kids also, so I don't think there are any bugs left."

"Left?" the teacher gasped.

"We found at least ten," Hal replied. "Some rather sophisticated. I kept them and gave them to some of the vets, who like to play with those things. They started tracing some of the bugs to the manufacturers, and almost have backtracked to who they were sold to. We will know for certain in a few days. The really nice toys they have turned to our use, so that's something."

"Were they all from the news people?" the teacher asked, almost afraid of the answer.

"No," Hal answered. "Some were clearly government equipment. It's to be expected."

GRENDELHAL

"So, what do you think?" Hal asked, relaxing in a chair across from GrendelHal. "You seem to have regenerated as I remember you. Which would be about seven feet of vicious predator, but certainly more handsome than you were before. That would be my contribution, I think." Hal smiled.

GrendelHal laughed and shook his head. "I can't believe you actually did this," he rumbled. "Even Paul seems happier with me gone. His control over me was complete, but still, at the bottom, he was uncomfortable."

"Uncomfortable with you?" Hal inquired. "As savage and uncontrollable a killing machine as could be dreamed of? That's hard to imagine, really, that he'd have any discomfort."

"Do you not fear me here with your family and children?" GrendelHal growled softly. "You know what I'm capable of."

"None know better than I," Hal replied cheerfully. "But it didn't seem fair, after all you'd given me, to not bring you back. After all, you unleashed Grendel and Grendeline on me, and I grew to a new life. It's only fair I unleash myself on you. I'm not saying you'll get from me a fraction of what I got from them, but turnabout is fair play—one of those deep moral judgments that children lightly pass off."

"None of the 'This is a trick planted by Grendel for revenge,' and that type of thought?" GrendelHal questioned, looking carefully at Hal.

"One can go down the 'He thought, I think he thought...etc.' into madness," Hal commented. "More likely, into futility. It's an opportunity that can't be denied, risk though there may be. Except I don't think there is a risk," as he sat up, staring at GrendelHal. "You were unhappy with Paul and his world for a long time, which is why Paul was unhappy with you. And I'll challenge you! Here is a sip of the drink from São Paulo. Do you dare the taste? Do you dare what you might become?"

GrendelHal laughed. "This is different from Paul," he rumbled. "Paul would have tricked me in four different ways before we got this far and the drink would have been part of some elaborate plan hatched by one of his alternate personalities. I'm not sure how he gets matching shoes on in the morning some days, but that's his problem."

GrendelHal reached out, casually picked up the shot glass, and drank. He grimaced for a second. "That's strong," he commented, shaking his head, as he put the glass down slowly. "Now." He jumped, his claws out, to within an inch of Hal, who just sat there, smiling.

"Really?" Hal asked. "It worked better in the dreams."

GrendelHal shook his head and sat down again. "No respect for the forms," he complained. "But I knew that. So, how did Cali like the schwanzstucker effect?"

"She tells me she was deeply appreciative," Hal admitted. "And, I hear that some of the women veterans are schwanzstucker, ah, aficionadas, as it were. Then there is the nanny, who suddenly is ravishing when she makes herself up."

"Really?" GrendelHal asked eagerly. "Then this may be a better party than I thought."

"Come on," Hal replied, standing up. "Hey, it's Halloween. What better day to be introduced to the group?"

"Every Halloween party needs a demon," GrendelHal vowed. "Here I am!'

"Au contraire," Hal countered. "Demons and angels we have aplenty. Here's your costume: your three-piece power suit of terror, and your real leather brief case. You'll be from the legal department. How much more terrifying could that be?" Hal stepped back and looked carefully at the seven-foot-tall, four-foot-wide creature. "Really, I think you'll be all of the legal department. We'll save on staffing costs this year."

GrendelHal shook his head in dismay as he looked at the suit. "You know, you really are a sick person," he growled, putting the suit on. "This is a horror even I could not have imagined."

"And subpoenas for the little children with treats in them," Hal snickered, opening the briefcase. "Is this fun, or what?"

DETROIT. A PARTY

"Not a lot of Devil's Night in this part of the city," Vladimir admitted to Lucifer as they stood, watching the moon lit wasteland. "First, because it's generally understood that people who come into this area looking for trouble find trouble, not give it. And secondly, because there isn't that much left to burn, to tell the truth." They do see a few fires, a long way away.

"Devil's Night," Lucifer laughed. "As if it's only one night a year. The real devils wear suits and uniforms, not costumes. Still, it's a night for fantasy, so we'll let that pass. Jose really looks up to you, did you know that?"

"I was hoping," Vladimir confessed. "It's been, well, a very long time since I was around young children. And he's protective of his mother, which is charming. I think it was my offer to teach him how to sword fight with real swords that brought him onto my side. Now, that almost pushed Lucretia off my side before she was persuaded it really wasn't all that dangerous. That's him, over there, in the Three Musketeers costume and a cardboard sword."

"Very nice costume," Lucifer commented. "And he's grown up a lot. You were always good with damaged souls."

"Who's this?" Vladimir asked, as Jesus walked up.

"Black turtleneck, round glasses, quizzical expression," Jesus replied. "Duh—Steve Jobs. I understand he used to dress up like me, so I thought I'd return the favor." Jesus looked critically at Lucifer. "Riff Raff? It's a good look."

"I should like, if I may," Lucifer observed, "to take you on a strange journey."

"I love a trip," Mary bubbled as she sashayed up to them.

"Damn it, Janet," Jesus growled. "The spare tire is flat."

"What led to all this?" Vladimir asked. "I just went with a Detroit building inspector costume, which I promise you is the most terrifying creature you can have appear up at your door. You all went with a theme?"

"It's in honor of Hal," Mary confided. "And here he is now!"

Hal walked up with Cali. He was resplendent as Dr. Frankenfurter. Black stockings, garter belt, and heavy makeup. "A moment of rash deviance, and typecast for life," he sighed.

"It's a good look, Hal," Mary commented approvingly. "Nice legs, tight butt. What?" she asked, looking at the group. "I'm a fertility goddess. This is professional."

"I found all of Hal's costume," Cali added, brimming with pride. "I had to crawl into very strange lingerie shops, I can tell you."

"These stockings ran," Hal grumbled, "and they are expensive."

"Yeah, tell me something I don't know," Cali retorted.

"I love your costume!" Mary told Cali. "It is perfect for you!"

"Little Bo Peep," Cali laughed, and curtsied, bending over. "Whoops," and she quickly turned away, smiling as she pushed one of the twins back into position. "Ah, they peep a little too much. They barely fit in this dress before I had Maria, and now? They don't like this dress."

"Ah, but I like it!," Hal commented, squeezing Cali.

"Pervert," she giggled and they kissed. There was a loud "baaaaa" from behind them, and they turned. "And here's my sheep!" Maria was dressed in a little sheep costume, looking up and laughing at them.

Hal studied Cali's costume while Cali fussed with Maria. "Being a deviant from Transsexual has many advantages, including enjoying this," he observed

"I'm not sure this costume was right for you," Cali teased. "You're supposed to dress up as something other than your normal self." Maria started to cry. "Oops! Bottle time! Let's go." Hal, Cali, and Maria wandered off to a corner of the room.

Lucretia walked up to the group, sweet and innocent in her Snow White costume. She coyly batted her eyes at Vladimir.

Vladimir laughed, delighted. "That I like! But..." He pulled out a code enforcement pad and a pencil. "I think we need to talk about some ordinances you may be violating. Including some I'm thinking of making up right now."

"Oh, please, good sir," she pleaded, her eyes wide and concerned as she smiled at him. "Spare this innocent! I'm putty in your hands!"

"And with that, I think we'll leave," Lucifer commented, pushing Mary and Jesus before him. As they walked away, he chuckled "Have fun, kids!"

Lucretia smiled brightly and Vladimir laughed.

"Unexpected, that was," Jesus observed.

"Truly a blessing," Lucifer admitted.

The children from São Paulo came rushing into the room, shouting and laughing, herded by Mrs. Ostein, her daughters, and some of the teachers. Mrs. Ostein was dressed as a Greek priestess, and her daughters as acolytes.

"Very nice costumes," Jesus concluded, staring at Mrs. Ostein, who waved cheerfully at him. Jesus glanced at Mary. "Do they know what some of the jewelry really means?"

"I, ah, gave them certain historical advice," Mary admitted. "Those were, well, active priestesses who served in that Temple. Gifts to the Goddess were rewarded in a very real and physical way. I was surprised, but gratified, that Mrs. Ostein and her daughters seemed to have embraced the whole concept more than I would have expected."

Jesus glanced at Mary, his eyebrows raised.

"Fertility Goddess here," Mary commented. "I'm impressed with her, I have to admit."

"Umm, business calls," Jesus sighed. "I'll have to talk to that good woman who is minding those hellions. No rest for the wicked, you know." He winked at Lucifer and Mary and walked over to the children, greeting Mrs. Ostein with a kiss.

"And unexpected that was," Mary admitted. She looked at Lucifer and sighed. "Okay, say it. Get it out of your system."

"If you do not expect the unexpected, you will not find it, for it is not to be reached by search or trail," Lucifer carefully intoned. "Ah, that felt good."

"The children are not bothered by this at all," Mary remarked, carefully watching the São Paulo children. "I guess the real horrors they saw make this nothing."

"The crowd grows," Lucifer announced. The veteran's children came running in, laughing and shouting to the São Paulo kids. The Veterans wandered in behind the kids, a smorgasbord of colorful costumes.

"Hi," Aliston giggled, standing behind Lucifer. "Do you like my costume?"

He turned, and was speechless.

"That generally means yes," Mary laughed. "You do make an overwhelming Magenta. Hollywood doesn't know what it missed."

"I took your advice, Mary, and you were right!" Aliston confided

"It's better than the movie, that's for certain," Lucifer vowed, finding his voice again.

"So, I heard you are enticing people with the prospect of a strange journey?" Aliston teased Lucifer, batting her eyelashes and tossing her hair.

"I'll leave you two children to discuss that," Mary chuckled. "Have fun!" She walked over to the children, who were shouting and trading candy.

It was bedlam, but happy.

A JOKE

It was later. The children had been put to bed, but there was still a large group of adults in the room. The punch, spiked after the children were gone, was popular and they were a wildly cheerful group.

"Here's a joke," Jesus announced to the group. "Ready? A man is standing on the bridge, about to jump to his death. I run up to him. 'Stop! You can't do this!'"

"He cries, 'Nobody loves me.'"

"So," Paul shouts to the crowd around him, "I told him, 'God loves you. Do you believe in God?'"

"He nods, 'Yes.'"

"So I ask him," Jesus continued, "Are you a Christian or a Jew?"

"'He answers, 'A Christian.'"

"And I say," Paul declared, "'Me, too! Protestant or Catholic?'"

"He says, 'Protestant.'"

"And I say," Jesus revealed, "'Me, too! What franchise?'"

"He says, 'Baptist.'"

"So," Paul exclaimed, winking at the crowd. "'Me, too! Northern Baptist or Southern Baptist?'"

"He says, "'Northern Baptist.'"

"And I tell him," Jesus confided, "'Me, too! Northern Conservative Baptist or Northern Liberal Baptist?'"

"He says, 'Northern Conservative Baptist.'"

"Well, what do you know about that!" Paul declared. "I told him, 'Me, too! So, Northern Conservative Baptist Great Lakes Region, or Northern Conservative Baptist Eastern Region?'"

"He says, '"Northern Conservative Baptist Great Lakes Region.'"

"So," Jesus related, "I told him, 'What a coincidence. Me, too! Northern Conservative Baptist Great Lakes Region Council of 1879, or Northern Conservative Baptist Great Lakes Region Council of 1912?'"

"He says, 'Northern Conservative Baptist Great Lakes Region Council of 1912.'"

Jesus and Paul shouted, at the same time, "So I shouted, 'Die, heretic!' And I pushed him over the bridge railing."

The two crowds roared, five thousand miles apart.

CHAPTER 5. THE SECOND BELL: SAUDI ARABIA

SAUDI ARABIA. BAHRAIN

"Our people give lip service to piety, but live their sinful lives thoughtlessly. If they had the fire of their ancestors," the Mullah complained, "they would throw off this heretic government. The government represses us, denies the truth of our faith, steals our resources and the people just take it."

"I have an idea," one of the elders offered. "I met a banker who has connections to good people who want all people to be deeply devout. They created a drug that deepens devotion and intensifies the religious experience. He told me of a church in California, which he told me uses the drug, and he gave me tapes of their services. I started watching older services and then progressively newer ones. I could tell when the drugs started taking effect. It was a very clear effect, if you know what you are looking for. Their devotion to their false religion was made very strong, I have to admit."

"Isn't it risky?" another elder questioned.

"And should we do that to people?" a third elder asked. "Changing them for the good is still changing them. Is that what we should be doing?"

They argued for a little more than an hour, and then lapsed into an uneasy silence.

"This is for our people," the Mullah declared. "They expect us to act for their best interest. We shall have the elder follow this up and see what we can find out."

"I have taken the liberty of following this up already," the elder confessed. "The banker told me that he can get us a newer version of the drug that is even stronger. He offered to give us some samples if we were interested. It would take a week to obtain the samples, he thought, if we wanted to test the drug."

"A test would be good. There could be no harm in that," another elder advised and all the men nodded their heads.

SEVERAL WEEKS LATER

"The test went well," the Mullah declared. "The people have never been so fervent. They never before understood the full intensity of their faith."

"True," an elder admitted. "I watched, and I have never seen anything like it."

The council of elders nodded their heads.

"How can it be wrong to bring the fever of religion to people?" one elder observed. "How can it be wrong to make their lives richer?"

"So what is the plan?" the Mullah asked, staring at the elder with the connection to the banker.

"I can tell them that we are willing to move to the next level," the elder proposed, stroking his beard thoughtfully. "They asked how many people we wanted to bring to their senses. I told him, well, the entire peninsula!"

The other elders laughed.

"They told me that perhaps more than they could handle, but they could provide us with enough for Dhahran and Ras Tanura, and possibly some smaller cities," the elder continued.

"Is there a cost?" another elder inquired.

"Yes," the elder replied. "The infidels always want money. But it's quite reasonable, actually. They estimated Riyal 500,000, which includes manufacturing and guaranteed private delivery, obviously avoiding any official entanglements."

The elders looked at each other and shrugged.

"It is not that much," the elder in charge of the finances for the mosque maintained. "Reasonable for what we are getting."

"Is it agreed?" the Mullah asked, looking around.

The elders nodded their heads.

"Nothing must be said of this, of course," the Mullah ordered. "Nothing. No pillow talk, no impressing pretty girls, nothing at all. The response of the authorities would be swift and complete. The government would kill all of us and our families."

The elders nodded, all grim faces.

"How long?" one elder demanded. "Secret's can only be kept for a short time."

"They estimated two weeks," the elder replied. "They want half of the money up front, through the banker. Another quarter paid when shipped, and the final quarter payment at delivery."

The elders stroked their beards and then nodded agreement.

It is a few days later. Several of the elders and the Mullah are at the Mosque, planning.

"When we receive the materials, what do we do next?" an elder demanded.

"We spread it through the city and the oil facilities," the Mullah answered. "That's what I was told."

"How?" the elder asked. "The test was administered by taking it orally. We can't do that to the whole city. Put up a sign? 'Take this, find heaven, and overthrow the government?' Doesn't seem wise."

"No one likes a smartass," another elder commented.

"It spreads like a cold, I'm told," the Mullah admitted.

"Like São Paulo?" an elder gasped, horrified. "Look what happened there!"

"Different drug, different results," the Mullah announced. "I thought the same thing! But I have gone over this with them again and again. They promised that it wouldn't be that kind of a disaster, and I see the truth in their eyes. Is there a risk? I have prayed for an answer. After I prayed, I dreamed that I saw our lands burning with the fire of faith, so I am sure we do what is right. And you all know that we are doing this for our peoples own good. You saw that the test group was ready to follow us without hesitation, to do anything we ordered them to do. They will challenge the government without any fear. They are Bedouin again, fearless warriors! If we do not do this, that accursed king and his heretic minions will suck dry our oil and then hand us back an empty desert to die in. You know what they really think of us- we are anathema to them."

"So when does it happen?" an elder asked. "We placed the order—when do we receive the materials?"

"A week," the Mullah answered.

"That's almost pilgrimage time," one elder objected.

"All the better," the Mullah declared. "The government will be focused on that problem, and this will come as a complete surprise, when they are already stretched thin."

The men nodded.

INDIA

"Here are the studies you requested, Doctor," his aide announced, standing in front of his desk with a thick stack of documents.

"I was reading!," the Doctor growled, staring at the aide. "But since you have already disturbed me, leave them there," pointing at an empty corner of his desk. The Doctor deliberately started reading again, ignoring the aide existence.

"As you wish," the aide sighed, carefully putting the documents on the desk, and then bowing before backing out of the room. As he left, the aide pulled the door closed behind him.

As soon as the aide closed the door, the Doctor stood up and walked around his desk, standing thoughtfully before the documents. He started going through the pile, leaving on the desk those he needed and tossing in the trash those he had requested to disguise his real interest.

When they were sorted out, he picked up the pile of useful articles, and walked over to a comfortable leather chair. Putting the articles on the wide arm of the chair, he sat down. This looks promising, he thought, picking up the top article. He leaned back in the chair and started reading. "Volunteers undergoing intravenous ketamine infusions *(similar to the street drug PCP or angel dust)*, frequently experience a profound clarity of thought. One subject described 'a sense of understanding everything, of knowing how the universe works.' Such descriptions are quite similar to those who've had 'near-death experiences' from a cardiac arrest or an anesthetic complication; indeed, there may be a common mechanism of action. Lack of adequate brain oxygen characteristically triggers the release of the neurotransmitter glutamate. Under normal conditions glutamate binds to NMDA receptors; in excessive amounts it is neurotoxic and facilitates neuronal death. In an attempt to prevent this cell death, the oxygen-deprived brain also releases protective chemicals that block the effect of glutamate on NMDA receptors. Ketamine has a similar NMDA receptor-blocking effect. So does MDMA (Ecstasy), another psychoactive drug known to produce feelings of mental clarity. It is now believed that this blocking of the NMDA receptor is responsible for the clinical picture of a near-death experience.[7]"

He scanned the lab results at the back of the article. That it does in spades, he realized. Why spades and not diamonds? He'd wondered that in college, but never asked. He kept reading.

"Above all, be thankful for your brain's supply of oxytocin, the small, celebrated peptide hormone that may lubricate our every pro-social exchange, the thousands of acts of kindness, kind-of kindness, and not-as-nakedly-venal-as-I-could-have-been kindness that make human society possible. Scientists have long known that the hormone plays essential physiological roles during birth and lactation, and animal studies have shown that oxytocin can influence behavior too, prompting voles to cuddle up with their mates, for example, or to clean and comfort their pups. Now a raft of new research in humans suggests that oxytocin underlies the twin emotional pillars of civilized life; our capacity to feel empathy and trust."

And does that too, he reflected. With an air-infection pattern. They will be happy people to the end, perhaps beyond. Hard to say. He studied the wall, thinking. Should I do this? Well, there was the terrorist attack that killed my brother and his family, five years ago. And our property in Kashmir? Ruined because of those fanatics. This shall be my gift to them for all that they have given me, and he smiled happily. And I can add a little kicker just to help things along. He worked late into the night.

The next morning, he met with his staff. "We need to produce this in quantity, and quickly," he ordered. "Highest level of biohazard, no shortcuts. After it's done, everything is burned and junked. There should be no connection with us."

"Please forgive me, Doctor, but, ah, should we be concerned, sir?" one student blurted out.

"No," the Doctor answered, glancing at the head of operations. "No, you should not be concerned. Or any of you, actually."

They smiled, relieved, and went to work.

The head of operations sat in the office after the staff left and then walked over and closed the door. He walked over and stood before the doctor, waiting.

"They should not be concerned," the Doctor remarked, looking the head of operations in the eye. "Ever."

"My thought exactly, sir," the head of operations replied. "One half of the money has been deposited. Another quarter will be paid when shipped. The final quarter will be paid upon receipt."

"Good," the Doctor laughed. "I doubt we would get payment after it's released. I'm not sure who'd be left to write a check."

"No credit cards from the other world," the head of operations agreed, bowing. "My war wound still hurts, but this will make it feel better." He smiled and left, closing the door behind him.

CENTRAL AMERICA

"This religious drug!" the Professor shouted, charging into the Major's office. "It's worse than São Paulo!"

"You're kidding, right?" the Major asked. "War is about to break out all over South America because of that accursed disaster, and another one is coming?"

"Yes," the Professor answered. "I've analyzed it, and hell, even tested it on a small village. They all died, eventually. They were people who owed us money," noticing the Major's glance. "Had to test it on someone."

The Major shrugged. "Too much biomass out there as it is."

"I will say that they were the happiest dying people I've ever seen, having found religion completely, but eventually they died," the Professor continued. "This will blow the Middle East apart."

"We can't call," the Major advised. "Who knows who listens to what? We cannot be connected in any way with the disaster in São Paulo or another one coming. You must fly to Switzerland. There is no other choice."

The Professor sat, discouraged. "You are right; we can't call or email or anything. And it will be too late when I get there. But I will leave immediately." He got up and rushed to his quarters. Ordering his secretary to find a flight, he packed and jumped in a car. Five hours, he thought on the way to the airport. Almost a day before I get there. Useless, but I have to try.

SAUDI ARABIA

The Mullah boarded a dhow to travel to the oil tanker. The dhow was taking supplies, including liquor and prostitutes, to the tanker, and the Mullah sat as far away from the accursed women and alcohol as he could. Now I know I'm doing right, he knew, all doubts gone. His cover story was that he was going to the ship to offer religious counseling for a crewmember. That customs official who had scoffed at him before boarding the dhow, laughing at the mullah's sect? He will pay, and all his kind, the Mullah vowed.

The Mullah climbed onto the ship. The crewman led the Mullah to the crewman's quarters so that they could talk in private. After the crewman had closed the door, and whispered that they were alone, the Mullah laid a large envelope on the table and the crewman put a large coffee mug on the table.

"That's it?" the Mullah scowled. "That doesn't look large enough. We paid a great deal of money for this."

"Be gentle with it!" the sailor begged. "I've been assured there is plenty in there. Little live bugs, billions of them. They multiply. Open only when you are ready to use it."

The Mullah nodded, still doubtful and they sat and talked about religion for an hour. Then the crewman escorted the Mullah back to the boat. Thankfully, the boat was empty on the way back, the evil women plying their trade on the tanker late into the next morning.

SWITZERLAND

The Professor stood on the steps of the dais in Paul's audience chamber, Paul staring down at him.

"You're right, of course," Paul acknowledged. "The drugs are far more powerful than they know or believe. Quite deadly, actually."

The Professor opened his mouth to speak. Paul raised his hand, bidding silence, and the Professor closed his mouth and stood quietly.

The Cardinal stood next to Paul and studied the Professor for a moment. "In India, the governing law of international relations has for centuries been known as the matsya nyaya, law of the fish, which is, to wit, that the big ones eat the little ones so the little ones have to be smart. We are little fish," the Cardinal advised. "We have to watch out where the big fish swim. Now, when you look at the *Bhagavad Gita*—do you know the book?" he asked, catching the Professor's uncertain expression.

"Parts," the Professor answered, surprised. "But not well."

"Book XII is a part of the Indian Book of the Great War of the Sons of Bharata, Mahabharata," the Cardinal continued. "It asserted, to cut to some key excerpts: 'Without cutting the very vitals of others, without performing many cruel deeds, without killing living creatures, as fisherman kill fish, one cannot win prosperity...There are no special orders of creatures called enemies or friends...Persons become friends or enemies according to circumstance...Every work should be done completely...By killing its inhabitants, by destroying its roads, and by burning and pulling down its houses, a king should devastate his enemy's realms.' Finally: 'Might is above right; right proceeds from might; right has its support in might, as living beings in the soil. As smoke the wind, so right must follow might. Right in itself has no authority; it leans on might as the creeper on the tree.'"

Paul nodded, approving.

"Not the usual message of a religious text," the Professor commented. "A truthful message, but not the one the masses are given."

"No," Paul replied, "and that's why they are the masses. Change is upon us, crashing down like a huge wave. I've tried to break the wave early so that we are not swept away with the others. Do you think that unwise?"

"I don't know," the Professor admitted. "I don't usually make civilization-breaking decisions."

"You don't?" the Cardinal asked, amused. "You create drugs that do what my lord wants, that tear the structures apart from the inside, and you don't make decisions? You pretend you don't, and you fool yourself. You wish to live like a big fish, but not carry the weight."

The Professor bend his head, staring at the steps, silent.

Paul drummed his fingers on the dais. "You have been a faithful and good servant. Here, I'll give you scripture for you to rely on," Paul announced. "Deuteronomy 20:10-18. 'But if it makes no peace with you, but makes war against you, then you shall besiege it; and when the Lord your God gives it into your hand you shall put all its males to the sword, but the women and the little ones, the cattle, and everything else in the city, all its spoil, you shall take as booty for yourselves...Thus you shall do to all the cities which are very far from you, which are not cities of the nations here. But in the cities of these people that the Lord your God gives for you an inheritance, you shall save alive nothing that breathes.' And that is what I will do, because it is them or us. Do you see that?"

"I do, my lord," the Professor affirmed.

"Good," Paul replied. "Your advice has been good; better than most, which is why I give you this answer. Go back to the cartel and make plans for the changes coming."

A later meeting in the Throne Room.

"So, we've hedged oil in fourteen different ways," Paul's accountant reported, nervously fiddling with his glasses as he spoke. "It's been done correctly, the way São Paulo was intended to be done. The lawyers created a mass of companies through layers of law firms. We tipped off, quietly, many important people who have taken positions also. So our powerful friends are making money off this."

"Absolutely clean this time?" Paul demanded. "No bank that will know too much and will have to be destroyed? I don't want to have to destroy Zurich; I like the city. And some of the political connections ran for cover last time because it was bigger than we had forecast. We can't have any surprises."

"Clean," the accountant promised. "And many governments are making money off of this. We hang together."

SAUDI ARABIA. D-DAY

"So, how does this work?" the elder inquired, looking doubtfully at the cylinder.

"They told me it was simple. All we have to do is stand upwind of the target and open the valve. They were emphatic that we need only do that for a few seconds in each location—any more would be a waste. I think that was all the instructions," the Mullah recalled, stroking his beard. He thought for a second, furrowing his brows intently. "Wait. They did tell me the sun was bad for it. They suggested a little after dusk, before the desert had cooled too much. Test the wind, and spray so it goes downwind. Seems simple."

"And this won't be São Paulo?" the elder stammered.

"I've been assured," the Mullah answered. "They promised."

And it wasn't São Paulo. It was worse.

The cloud gently blew towards the city just after dusk. There were many people still awake, walking around, sitting in private gardens. The wind blew the virus through the city.

How long? the Mullah wondered, as he and the elder watched the thin trail of gas dispersing.

By morning, it had started. Crowds ran through the streets, shouting praises and praising the Promised Land. The Mullah and his flock were in the middle of the crowds, already too far gone to realize it that the drug was far stronger than the test sample.

Men drove with their families to neighboring cities to spread the joy and the ecstasy. It quickly spread once people got into confined spaces, such as restaurants or mosques, and breathed on each other.

The workers at Ras Tanura and other oil facilities rushed into the facilities to bring the wonderful news to their friends. They quickly spread the virus throughout the plant and to some of the ship crews.

The workers blithely abandoned any interest in processing and pumping oil. Ecstatic over the coming of the new world, they, the select, were above such trivial, earthly concerns as work. They celebrated and fires started. Fires in an oil refinery spread quickly, especially when the workers were cheering on the flames.

The oil shipping facilities froze. Froze solid—nothing coming out at all.

People act in congruence with the goals they seek and the feedback they receive while pursing their goals. The drug just cut out all the behavior stops carefully trained into people. So even though from a normal perspective their actions made no sense at all, in context with the feedback that they were receiving, their actions made perfect sense. They rushed through the streets, dancing and shouting in delight, clear in their convictions, the ecstasy taking them higher and higher. Until approximately forty-eight hours, give or take, after infection, when their brains burned out and they died.

A meeting of the Saudi Royal Council was hastily convened, one hour after the oil refineries started going up in flames.

"What!" the Prince shouted. "We have guards, we have the army! The Special Emergency Forces' Eastern Province headquarters is in Dhahran—what are they doing?"

"We don't know," an official admitted, looking down at the table. "We call and get crazy people on the phone who shout about the end of the world, that they are going to paradise, and slam the phones down. We have sent troops into the area and the troops say the same and then stop communicating with us."

"It's São Paulo," the Prince yelled, furious. "Or something like it. Move all the army over there, surround them. Gas masks if you can—whatever kind of containment gear we have. Clear orders: anyone coming from those areas is to be shot, and their bodies burned by the containment people. No exceptions, no questions."

A physician stood up in the back of the room. "We determine shapes by seeing borders. Visually, it is impossible to clearly see an object without a sharply contrasting background. The same optics govern our mind's eye. Close your eyes and picture a face. You see the face against a contrasting background, which might be a neutral color, maybe grey's or blackness. What the drug did was to sharpen that all that contrast into all black and white, no greys, no colors, no moderation or indecision."

"Can it be stopped?" the Prince asked. "Can the infected people be saved?"

"No," the physician responded, sadly. "They are the walking dead."

"Who could have done this?" an official demanded. "Who?"

"We don't know," the Prince answered. "There are so many possible suspects." He thought for a minute. "I will report to the King; we bow to his will. But tell no one from other countries and ask for no help from anyone. It could be a ruse, and there are many who would profit."

THE WORD SPREADS

In a connected world, the news spread quickly. Incoherently, confusingly, but quickly. Social networks were jammed with messages from the ecstatic announcing the end of the world and their joy. Text messages, phone calls, and emails sped around the country and the world.

Within twelve hours of the Prince's commands, the army had locked down the surrounding territories, shooting anyone coming out from the city. In the short time before the army stepped in, the infection had spread into Iraq and Kuwait, who quickly mobilized troops.

Stock exchanges around the world went wild. The phantom fear of the last sixty years, that the oil was gone, was finally standing there real before them. That Saudi oil was only a percentage of the oil available, albeit a large percentage didn't matter, because Saudi was the reserve producer. Lose that, even for a short time, and the cost of oil would skyrocket. As people panicked, it built on itself.

The World Health Organization frantically tried to get information and staff in place to respond to the outbreak. They were stonewalled completely. No information came from the government authorities, and orders were issued that stopped any of the World Health staff from coming near the outbreaks.

All over the world, troops were rushed to airports and train stations. Border guards tripled, then doubled again. The airports were locked down. If any passenger on board a plane was from any Arab country, the plane was parked far away from the terminal, surrounded by troops and the passengers held in isolation. No planes were allowed to take off and any plane in the air was ordered back to the airport from which it took off. If a plane didn't have enough fuel to return, it could land at a military base where it could be controlled, or it could crash. As the level of the problem became clearer, some planes were simply shot down.

REACTION

The most obvious, immediate problem was that the oil processing facility was unusable. It was damaged, on fire, and when they sent in firefighters, the firefighters became infected and stopped fighting the fires. By the time the infection burned out, so had much of the oil processing and shipping equipment. It would take months to get anything into production and years to get back to where they were. They had to stop pumping crude from the ground, which damaged the wells and future production.

Because the infection was still spreading as those infected drove to spread the joy, there was panic all over the Middle East. There was no shipping from Saudi Arabia, Iraq, or Iran within two weeks. The tankers sat in rows outside the ports, waiting. The crews who became infected destroyed, probably accidently, their ships.

Amazingly, people from all over the world were clamoring to enter the infected areas. Convinced that the end of the world was here, they wanted to be part of it. They had been promised the rapture, and here it was! People of all races, creeds, and religions poured into Bahrain to die in a religious ecstasy they were sure would bring them everlasting life.

"Should we let the infidels in?" the government committee argued. "Our land is sacred to our people." Other voices pointed out that they were coming to die, and the death of infidels was a good thing.

After a short time, tiring of trying to push the crowds back, the Saudi General in charge shrugged and gave new orders. "Let anyone in who wants to go in. Better to let them go in the front door, where we can control them, than to have them sneak around for back doors that we can't watch."

Within a day, there were vendors hawking clothing to the people rushing into the city. The slogans were in Arabic, Chinese, English—all languages. "It's ecstasy!" the newcomers shouted as they paraded into the city. "It's the end, for the true believers!"

"Which actually is true," the General announced to his staff, shaking his head in disbelief at the people's behavior. "Again, let them go in, but shoot anyone coming out. Absolutely anyone, including any soldier who shows any signs, any signs at all that they have been infected. This has to be stopped here, or entire country will be destroyed. This isn't religion. It's drugs, drugs from an enemy, and they are trying to destroy us. A trick of the infidels."

India

A small but angry group was sitting in a room in New Delhi. It had taken a week to force this meeting. Only their passionate threats to go to the authorities, regardless of the consequences to themselves, had finally forced the meeting.

The Doctor sat behind his desk, hands folded, studying the men as they shouted at him that he, the Doctor, had lied to them and that because of his lies they had destroyed everything they held sacred.

"I promised that my drugs would take your people places," the Doctor replied cheerfully. "And they did. They were more religious after the drugs than they were before."

"They were also dead," one man whined. "My family, my friends."

"What you gave us was different from the samples," another man cried. "Those worked as we were told they would. You promised us it would not be São Paulo, and you lied—this was worse!"

"I promised, actually, that it wouldn't be that kind of a disaster," the Doctor chuckled. "My exact words. And it was not that kind of disaster."

"You deceived us," another screamed.

"I never said, technically, that the drugs would take them where they wanted to go," the Doctor commented, sitting back after making quick eye contact with the security people. "But, I will tell you, you crawling pieces of shit, that the drugs took them where I wanted them to go."

The men jumped to their feet, furious.

"Not my religion," the Doctor laughed and he gestured quickly. The security people pulled their silenced pistols and shot the entire delegation several times, making quite sure all were dead.

"Good," the Doctor told the security men. "Get them out of here. Toss them in the river if it will accept this filth. These were the last in the trail to us. Burn this building; make sure it's burned to the ground. The whole block perhaps would be wise." He stood up and gave the men their tickets. "To a more pleasant climate for a well deserved vacation."

DETROIT. ABSORBING EVENTS

A large group was sitting and standing in the community room in Detroit. All grim faces, as they watched the news on the monitors.

"Things are going downhill fast," Hal stated. "I've been doing some calculations, and the new best-case scenario is worse than the worst-case ones before this started. If we assume that they freeze the infection locally, which they seem to be doing, the economic fallout is still to be huge. If they don't freeze the infection, we are all toast."

"A few people have been shot at airports and contaminated planes have been burned," Lucifer added. "The governments are clear on the extreme danger here. They're not even putting people into isolation—they are shooting first and not asking questions later."

"And it's the only way to stop something like this," Mary commented. "The infection rate is extremely high and incubation is time delayed just long enough that it can spread before it burns out. A bio-warfare drug for certain."

"Packaged well," Hal admitted. "Death by ecstasy, Heaven before you. The crowds clamoring to fly there are an amazing sight. Cali and Lucretia have been working on an economic ark in case of disaster, after São Paulo. What's up with that?"

"We've identified a number of key resources," Lucretia reported. "We've used our contacts all over the world to pull together a very loose group of like-minded people. My email box is overflowing as people who we talked to before, and who were then doubtful about the concept, are screaming to be brought on board."

"We've gotten a lot of help from the veterans," Cali added. "We have all of them that we can get working on the planning and structures. It's going pretty well, actually. It's just that we thought we had a lot more time than it looks like we do."

"It's bad, but not impossible," Hal guessed. "There are substantial resources still out there. The oil that was lost, at least for a while, was the reserve, the swing supply. So prices will be incredibly high for the foreseeable future, but there are supplies out there. The system will reallocate based on the new inputs."

"One of the biggest problems," Lucretia pointed out, "is that people freeze in an emergency. We have been reaching out to people we hadn't spoken to before this, and they are like people in the middle of a shipwreck. They stand by the rail, pretending nothing is happening as the ship rolls over into the water. But we are making progress."

"We are focusing on critical supply chains," Hal continued. "The central business model we have been using, 'outsourcing', assumed cheap transportation. That's gone. The new world will still need the old world's technology, but where there is an economic/structural collapse, all that high technology equipment which is manufactured all over the world, is suddenly not available anymore, just as we need it the most. We haven't seen a fraction of the problems we will face if chunks of the system break away."

"The bright side is that it really is a shock to the system," Mary remarked. "A sign no one can miss that what you've been doing isn't going to work anymore."

"The arks are clear, conceptually," Hal asserted. "To create something that has the seeds of its own destruction within it. To grow something that will become greater and greater each time it tears itself apart. Without the tearing apart turning into civil war and wasteland."

"Yeah, that's the challenge," Jesus replied. "I've been working on that one for a long time."

"Adding to our problems" Lucretia fretted, "is that no matter how noble the goal, what you want to accomplish in this world has to go through a room of suits. The suits are carefully selected to have experienced none of the problems that they are supposed to be solving. The options given the suits are limited, as well as the understanding of options by the suits, and what comes out may have little relationship to what went in. Still, we do what we can."

A DIFFERENCE OF OPINION

"The western powers are to blame!" the official organs of state shouted throughout the Arab countries. "All of the non-Islamic world is responsible for this cowardly attack on us. This terrible destruction is an attempt to destroy Islam."

"And so we destroyed ourselves? We cut off the oil we depend on to punish someone else? I think not," the European heads of state asked themselves as they watched television, not believing the message being shouted. "We give them little pieces of paper that cost us nothing and they give us their precious oil. We're going to destroy that? Do we have a Plan B for four-hundred-dollar per barrel oil?" Government officials and corporation officers started scurrying around.

As it turned out, there were many powerful people and governments in the world with a vested interest in Saudi oil staying in the ground. Essentially, all the other oil producers agreed that it was terrible that this had happened and behind the scenes did all they possibly could to block anything that would start the Saudi oil flowing again. The Iranians provided arms support to the Shiites in the affected areas for solidarity and also to ensure that little got done. With the Saudi money flow damaged, their allies flew away to those with more money. It became a raw fight between those with oil, who were profiting, and those without, who needed the swing oil. As it turned out, those without the oil couldn't mount an effective military action because they couldn't get the oil to drive the ships and fly the planes.

Within days there were riots in the streets all over the world, sparked by all governments' imposition of severe austerity programs. The riots grew vicious as the actual damage kept blowing right past the 'worst-case' scenarios.

"Churchill - A fanatic is one who can't change his mind and won't change the subject," the Saudi prince mused, watching the video feeds from the city. "A doctrine insulates the devout not only against the realities around them, but also against their own selves. The fanatical believer is not conscious of his envy, malice, pettiness, and dishonesty. There is a wall of words between his consciousness and his real self." Eric Hoffer, I read him in college, the Prince thought. An infidel, but right about this.

In a short time, there were two camps. Most of the non-Muslim world held that this was an internal matter. The Arab world and most of the Muslim world, blamed everyone else.

Business Goes On

"The company reorganization worked," Lucifer remarked as they sat at the dining room table. "Fortunate timing, it was. Splitting the companies up, making them leaner just as the disaster loomed, saved many of them. Not all. Some took more hits below the water line than we could have expected, and some were just lost to the chaos. But overall, we are in great shape, especially compared to the rest of the world."

"That's a good thing," Hal agreed. "But it wasn't me, by any means. Cali handled a lot of it, and our Chief Operations Officer, Aliston, was the engineer of our success." Hal pointed at her. "You may take a bow now."

Aliston, surprised, stood, bowed, and then sat down, smiling broadly.

"She oversaw the actual mechanics," Hal added. "I just made pretty graphs on my computer."

"That's going to work against your bonus this year, honey," Cali observed. "Didn't I tell you I'm head of the personal review committee?"

"Well, having you here is the best bonus a person could have," Hal replied, batting his eyelashes at her.

"Spirited effort," Cali answered. "But I think there was a sexual innuendo there. We'll have to discuss that later."

"I certainly hope so," Hal hinted, sliding closer to Cali.

MOSCOW

"Well, maybe it wasn't completely internal," the Russian Chief of Security, reported. "We have a pretty good idea where the virus came from. We could find out, if you wish."

"Our oil is ten times as valuable as it was," the Premier replied, looking carefully away from the security chief. "We should thank someone, but a thank you could be, well, misunderstood. So, we don't look, we don't see, we don't know what happened, or why. Because there is no percentage in that knowledge. Actually, that would be dangerous knowledge for a person to have. I wouldn't want to be that person."

"Da," the Chief of Security agreed. He looked down at the report in his hand, which showed how much the various interconnected groups had made off the disaster, and decided the report needed to be shredded quickly. And the research. Perhaps the researchers.

MARGINAL RETURNS

In Switzerland, there was an economic seminar and retreat for the wealthy and powerful. Perhaps not as wealthy as they had been, but their jets still had fuel.

A distinguished professor was presenting a set of arguments, which were doing little to relax the attendees.

"The energy flow to maintain a given social structure must be sufficient for the complexity of the systems involved. The more complex a society is, the more costly it is to maintain. As structures become more complex, information becomes critical. So information flows are centralized and protected, demanding a vast number of trained people to cope with the complexity. An agricultural society needs a many people with hoes and a few to calculate the irrigation flows. A complex society needs a lot of people to calculate and only a few people with hoes.

"All of this complexity absolutely needs huge energy flows. As the society becomes more complex, simple maintenance takes more and more energy. So what collapses a complex society is the drab concept of declining marginal returns. As more and more resources are allocated to just keeping the society running, there are fewer resources available for new growth. Occasionally, new resources will be discovered that change the equation, but the equation in its basic form is a constant. Declining marginal returns dictate that eventually, like the Red Queen in *Alice in Wonderland*, you have to run as fast as you can to stay where you are. To get ahead, you must run twice as fast as before. Should you slip, systems can stagger along IF there are reserves to cover the shortages. Declining marginal returns are a double-edged sword: because it takes everything you have just to keep things going, there isn't anything to put back into the reserves. Each hit on the reserves lowers the tank. Eventually, a resource has no reserves for emergencies, and it's splat time.

"System failure does not strike like a bolt from the blue; it unfolds in its own time. Part of the problem is that humans freeze in emergencies, grabbing tightly onto the last successful strategy. Given that the last successful strategy probably created today's disaster, that's not going to be very helpful. Technically, this is defined as choosing an efficient but non-explorative mode. The trap is the short-term efficiency focus. It's most efficient to do better what you are doing right now. You're going down slowly, like a balloon with a slow leak. Frozen on pumping in air, the society redoubles it's efforts because it worked last time. Unless someone steps back, and maybe thinks about patching the hole, it's just a question, then, of how long the failure will take. The fracture point is where some critical factor in the real world breaks, and there is no reserve and/or replacement. In other words, no oil, no system. In a linked, interdependent system, a lot of people can go hungry fast. And then dead.

"If there's no money, and no resources, there is actually no money, and no resources. Politicians pretended before that there was no money for bargaining leverage and political points. Horrified, they found that there was no money, and their games were up. Choices are narrowed to what the resources allow, because you can only do what you can do-different from what you want. The social experiment where we are falling off the building, but tell each other it's going to work? Hit the pavement.

The men and women in the audience stirred uneasily.

"Symbolic forms are a key support of the economic structure and civilization that the economy supports. Where an economy collapses, the support for the moral order and the civilizations cohesion, vitality, and creative powers begin to crumble. Loss of the literally read symbolic forms brings forth uncertainty, and with uncertainty, disequilibrium. Life, as Shakespeare knew, requires life-supporting illusions. Where the illusions have been dispelled, there is nothing secure to hold on to, and the structures' moral laws, their carefully taught meanings, are shaken to the core."

At the close of the meeting, a short quote was read to the dazed group. "All things come out of the One and the One out of all things...I see nothing but Becoming. Be not deceived! It is the fault of your limited outlook and not the fault of the essence of things if you believe that you see firm land anywhere in the ocean of Becoming and Passing. You need names for things, just as if they had a rigid permanence, but the very river in which you bathe a second time is no longer the same one that you entered before. Heraclitus, 500 BC."

The participants stood up and stumbled out to their jets, flying into their dark nights without answers.

SWITZERLAND

Paul watched the news, astonished.

"You're sure we're in the clear on this, right?" Paul asked his accountant several times. "This is bigger than São Paulo."

"So big," the accountant replied, sweating a little, "that some of the hedges have failed because the other sides have collapsed. We're taking other measures, but this is a chain, dragging people along where we don't want to go."

"Damn it, the Professor was right," Paul scowled, glancing at the Cardinal. "He's been right every time, and it's getting annoying. They tell you not to shoot the messenger, but no one warns you how much you'll want to. I guess it's good to have competent staff."

"Cassandra," the Cardinal observed. "She had a poor life. Still, this is the crash you were pushing for. I don't think they realize how far it's going to go."

"Do we?" Paul snapped at his accountant. "Are we ready? What is the next thing we should be hedging and anticipating?"

The accountant started to talk, and Paul cut him off. "Keep me informed. I want to see the numbers and where we are," Paul ordered.

The accountant bowed his head.

"And the risk exposure?" the Cardinal demanded. "I want to see the work-papers, the parameters. This is a third deviation event, and at that point, the risk calculations are toilet paper. That .03% tail probability just became a certainty."

The accountant gulped and ran, shouting orders at his staff.

"You are the white king now, my lord, on your white steed," the Cardinal acknowledged to Paul.

> *"And I saw heaven opened, and behold a white horse! And he that sat upon him was called Faithful and True, and in righteousness he doth judge and make war.*
>
> *"His eyes were as a flame of fire, and on his head were many crowns; and he had a name written, that no man knew, but he himself.*
>
> *"And he was clothed with a vesture dipped in blood: and his name is called The Word of God.*
>
> *"And the armies which were in heaven followed him upon white horses, clothed in fine linen, white and clean.*

"And out of his mouth goeth a sharp sword, that with it he should smite the nations; and he shall rule them with a rod of iron; and he treadeth the winepress of the fierceness and wrath of Almighty God.

"And he hath on his vesture and on his thigh a name written, KING OF KINGS, AND LORD OF LORDS," Paul intoned carefully, and smiled to himself.

The Cardinal looked away from Paul, suddenly concerned. "The horsemen are loosed," the Cardinal admitted, worried. "Soon, war and disease. Then Death on a pale horse, I think."

"I guess the wheat rust was overkill," Paul muttered, almost to himself.

"Wheat rust?" the Cardinal asked, surprised. "What was that?"

"Oh, a side plan," Paul responded. "That nasty wheat rust in Africa seems to have been spread widely now—Pakistan, Tunisia, some other places. We're hedged on that, and are holding some very large wheat supplies. It seems that there was a modern day Johnny Appleseed, no, more a 'Johnny Blackseed', spreading wheat rust and rice diseases as he wandered through the world. Every day, in every way, I'm getting better and better." Paul smiled to himself.

"There's Death on the pale horse," the Cardinal declared, shaking his head. "Well, this reminds me of the old days with the armies. No mercy, no surrender."

"What did that woman, Lucretia, say?" Paul mused, tapping his fingers. "Positive feedback feeds on itself. Like an atomic reaction, it is. She said that normally there are redundancies in the system, buffers. Now, there are no oil buffers, no wheat buffers, to slow things down. Losing her was a loss, I have to say."

"Winter turns to spring," the Cardinal observed. "A spring of death, not rebirth."

Washington, DC

"So how bad is this really?" the President demanded.

The faces looked at the table, deliberately writing on pieces of paper, or paging intently through the thick meeting binder. No one met his searching gaze.

"It's that bad?" the President worried. "It can't be that bad?"

"Well, we had South America about to go to war, but now it looks like they won't have oil to power the tanks. Mark that as a plus?" the Secretary of State reported. "And the Middle East is completely falling apart. Can't ship oil, no money in, the money used to buy off the unwashed masses isn't there, and the masses are getting pretty angry. And hungry, too. Seems that the food stocks are falling faster than anticipated."

"Fortunately, the public hasn't figured it out," the Secretary of State commented. "Happily, people overestimate risks for things that are first, out of their control, and second, sensationalized in the media. They underestimate risks for things that are mundane and ordinary. We need to stay on top of the media, and make sure there isn't a panic. We can't allow any hoarding of food and oil."

"I'd send in the army, but we don't have the extra fuel to do it," the Secretary of Defense mumbled.

"What about our natural gas, all that coal?" the President shouted, furious. "We have all the resources we need in the ground."

"Ah, ten years out," the Secretary of the Interior admitted, staring at the table. "We didn't see this one coming."

"You mean the corporations didn't see this one coming, and they blocked any diversification from Oil," the President declared, disgusted. "This is our punishment for all those campaign contributions we accepted so happily. Well, work up a plan to shift ASAP with what resources we have."

"What about the countries that are having food riots?" the Secretary of State asked. "We have food supplies."

"We don't," the President replied curtly. "My review of the stocks and our expected needs, given the changed circumstances shows no food surplus. Remember, fertilizer just skyrocketed in price, as well as the mechanized farming, shipping and storage we live by. We ship nothing. Nada. Got it?"

VICTORY IN THE WAR ON THE ENVIRONMENT

An important meeting had been called. One of the large rooms was almost full with the transferees, the veterans, Lucifer's people, and others. Mary, Lucifer, Vladimir, Hal, Lungorthin, Goth Girl, and Cali sat in the front of the room at a long table. No one was looking very happy.

Lucifer whispered to Vladimir, "The good news is that the groups are mingling now."

"Lust and love overcome all," Vladimir whispered back, smiling.

"Well, we're going to have to plan for a collapse," Hal announced, "and one coming pretty quickly."

"Always Mr. Cheerful," Cali commented.

"Oh, and where to start?" Mary started. "How about with this: "The experts, convened by the International Program on the State of the Ocean and the International Union for Conservation of Nature, found that marine 'degradation is now happening at a faster rate than predicted.' The oceans have warmed and become more acidic as they absorbed human-generated carbon dioxide from the atmosphere. They are also more oxygen-deprived because of agricultural runoff and other anthropogenic causes. This deadly trio of conditions was present in previous mass extinctions according to the report. The oceans' natural resilience has been seriously compromised. Pollution, habitat loss, and overfishing are dangerous threats on their own. But when these factors converge, they can destroy marine ecosystems. The severity of human impact was reinforced last week when scientists concluded that seven commercially important species, including marlin, mackerel, and three tuna species, were either vulnerable to extinction, endangered or critically endangered according to I.U.C.N. standards. The solutions that might help slow further degradation include immediate reduction in carbon dioxide emissions, a system of marine conservation areas, and a way to protect ocean life that goes beyond national jurisdictions."[8]

"The likelihood of any of those solutions being implemented isn't very promising," Jesus admitted.

"We've been through collapse many times," Lucifer conceded grimly. "In some ways, one of the worst was the Thirty Years' War in Germany. All the participants were deeply devout, brooking no doubt because they fought for God. So righteous terror was unleashed without doubt or reserve. At least forty percent of the countryside died, and perhaps a third of the people in the cities. It was the daily unending horror of it all that was so unbearable, a rolling crash, each day a little worse."

"Diplomats in fine clothing sitting in warm rooms, idly setting the fate of the ravaged lands," Jesus observed. "You really can't trust those people."

"This is a different type of collapse coming," Mary argued. "Before, there were fights between people over resources, but resources were still there afterwards to divide. This collapse will be precipitated by the lack of resources, a much worse collapse. If you're fighting about resources, at the end of the battle there is something to work with. When the resources are gone, people just die."

"What's hardest to factor in is the reactions of the people as this happens," Lucifer added. "In an ideal world, well, this wouldn't be happening. In the real world, people freeze; make decisions based on the past, and generally compound errors on errors. What that means is that what resources there are will be wasted in the warring over the resources."

"It's safe to say that scaling down to a sustainable population level will bring failing health, conflicts of all kinds and scales, and ecological devastation as people flail about, trying to preserve their lifestyles," Hal stated. "How do the actuaries say it? A rapid increase in mortality results in actuarial gains for the various pension and social welfare plan. It sounds so organized and structured, even almost soothing, because there are words to describe it."

"It doesn't matter how horrible the plan is," Cali added, "as long as it's the plan."

"It's the boiled frogs again," Lucifer observed. "It isn't like a comet, the one day POW! disaster we can all grasp. It's a slow-motion crash; people think they can stop it here, then here, but it keeps cascading down. The worst would be an uncontrollable decline in both population and human welfare—a true collapse."

"The ecological footprint of humanity is already far past the carrying capacity of the globe," Mary pointed out. "Humanity is already in unsustainable territory. We've far overshot."

"Overshoot is essential for disaster," Lucretia added. "I used it as the basis of the economic attack on Paraguay. Your plan runs past what can be sustained, and wham! The economy bursts like a tire with a nail in it, and the car hurtles off the road. Overshoot is where you burn up more than you are taking in. Where you have reserves, you don't notice the overshoot until the reserves are gone, then suddenly it's a wall in front of you."

"Best case, there is a correction, an easing down?" Jesus wondered.

"When have we ever seen that?" Mary answered, doodling on a piece of paper. "Never that I can recall. And critical resources are emptying. Not just the obvious ones, like the oil reserves and the food stocks. It's the others: arable land shrinking, aquifers emptying, oceans overloaded so they can't process waste.

"I just can't get through to people when I give speeches," Mary snapped, standing up and pacing. "People can't grasp, or just refuse to grasp, the idea that there might be limits to growth. Without growth, then the expanding pie is gone, and hard choices have to be made. So, limits are politically unmentionable and economically unthinkable. Instead, they believe in magic—that it will work out somehow."

"Assuming that the world stays as it is, which it's going to," Cali demanded, "What can we do? Can we keep a group together around the world? Can we bring our part of the world down to sustainable levels, being ready for catastrophe if nature forces the decision?"

"Well, we can back into what we need," Lucifer replied, "for the groups we see as critical to survive. We need a lot, if you factor in the technology. Critical equipment requires widely dispersed manufacturing plants and inputs and resources all over the world, an extensive communications system, and other factors. So we need a big group of people, and ways of keeping communications and materials flowing between parts of the world when systems break."

"We need to deal with where erosion loops are in the system. That's where, for example, overgrazing kills the grass. Grass gone, the soil erodes, so less grass can grow to recover. Eventually, it becomes desert, a true collapse.

Where are those in our economic and food systems?" Cali demanded. "Where can we adjust and protect ourselves if the small human stories have gone mad?"

"Are you suggesting this will be Avatar?" Jesus asked. "Where the world hits back? Gaia, I think the theory is in this world."

"Oh, the world is going to strike back," Mary promised. "It's winding up for the swing. We just want to stay out of the way of the club."

"So, that's the good news," Hal concluded.

"Did I miss the good part?" one of the transferees asked. There was grim laughter from the rest.

"Well, we're trying to run ahead of the storm, not wait for it to break over us," Hal answered. "That's about as good as it gets, I'm afraid. We've worked up some loose committees, if you want to participate. We want as much input as we can get, because this is new territory, unfortunately, and with everyone going at it with different ideas, we hope to, well, survive."

"Memo to the file," a man in back commented. "You're not doing the happy inspirational talks."

"Hey," Hal asked. "Who's for sword fighting practice? What better way to work out our rage and frustration?"

"And we may have nothing left but swords," one of the veterans sighed. "Well, we've been through that before."

CHAPTER 6. WINTER TO SPRING

Hal woke up, a happy look on his face.

Cali was staring at him. "Did you have the dream too?"

"A dream of wild plenty. Not a carefully cultivated farm, a dream of the wild world, overflowing with life," Hal answered happily. "Like the wall taking over the world. You?"

"Yeah, the same thing. It's nice to have a happy dream for a change." Cali smiled at Hal. "Wild life," she teased, her fingers slowly walking towards him across the sheets. "What say you, brave knight?"

"Whose quest is to satisfy my lady," Hal announced, snuggling closer to her.

PAPER, ROCK, SCISSORS

It's another meeting, with a very worried looking group. Many had been keeping long hours, sleeping at their desks. Part of the problem was trying to work across time zones, and the other part was everything hitting the fan at once. Everyday, yesterday's plan evaporated and they had to start over again at ground zero. On bad days, the morning's plan was gone by noon.

"Time is supposed to keep everything happening at once," one of the transferees mumbled to Cali.

"Weak on the physics," Cali responded. "But it certainly doesn't seem to be working like it used to.

"Donuts, we have donuts," Hal chanted, walking in with two large boxes of donuts. "A wide assortment, deep stock," as he set them on a side table.

"This is good," Aliston remarked, "because we have donuts. This is bad because we have lots of donuts, lots of choices, and that means this is going to be a long session."

"Ah, my clever ruse has been seen through," Hal admitted. "It's a fair cop. How about this to make everyone feel better? We're looking at problems with no right or wrong answers, so no pop quiz."

"Umm, an essay test," one of the transferees responded. "Now we really are in trouble."

"This is a tough group," Hal conceded, shaking his head in mock despair. "I may have to get the seltzer bottle and the rubber chicken. Cali, do you have the pies?"

"Banana cream," Cali replied. "The best, but the maintenance staff is getting downright hostile about cleaning up after the pie fights."

"That is a problem," Aliston worried. "A strong union, and the cleaning gets, umm, you might say sloppy when they are in a bad mood."

"And that's a great lead for today's talk," Hal declared. "Wicked problems are not evil, necessarily, but they are complex. Complex means they are tied to other problems, sometimes tightly, sometimes loosely. We are trading off, for example, the happiness of the maintenance staff against our childish glee and momentary pleasure. Now, our childish glee is really important, at least to me, but sullen maintenance staff people are not good. And the results of both our glee and their sullenness are not clear or measurable."

"Oh, it's measurable all right," one of the veterans commented. "It's dirtier after they leave than when they started, and that isn't always easy around here."

"Humm. . it's worse than I thought," Hal mused. "Is there an optimal solution? No. Any solution to a wicked problem is a better or worse choice. No gestalt. Not kindergarten where careful attention to detail and patience puts the puzzle together into a unified whole, a complete, closed job. And an academic approach-careful, structured, time oriented behavior-is about the worst way to grasp these problems. You can't get a solid immediate test for solutions-i.e., the feedback isn't feeding back-and there is no ultimate test of a solution for a wicked problem. No final lab experiment that can stamp 'right!' on your choices.

"Ah, we are NOT having fun yet," one of the transferee's pointed out. "In case you were looking for feedback."

"And it gets better," Hal promised, smiling. "Because the problems are so interwoven with tightly linked problem there is no real chance for trial and error learning. Why? Because your last action to try and fix the problem, has changed the original problem. Because the problems are NOW!, i.e., real-time problems, every action-or non-action-you take to solve the problem has real, significant impacts, good or bad."

"More donuts," one of the transferees demanded, lurching to his feet, "and stronger coffee." The others looked at Hal.

"I'm with him," Hal replied. "It gets worse, so fortify yourselves."

A few minutes went by while people bustled around. Intense donut bargaining, forced by the inevitable 'too many of one type and not enough of another', until the best sub-optimal solution developed and there were no donuts left. Everyone then grimly sat down again.

"Okay, recapping what I opened with," Hal began. "Every solution to a wicked problem is a 'one-shot operation' because the problem changes as you act on it. So it isn't the same problem next time. Your choices and actions are critically important; you get no prior learning experience, and no turning back. Goal seeking? A wicked problem doesn't have a clear set of potential solutions. Are we having fun yet?"

Hal stopped for a moment and looked around. The group munched cheerlessly.

"It gets better," Hal continued. "We learn from our prior experiences, and apply those to the future. Surprise! Each wicked problem is essentially unique. So, there is no clear set of possible actions/choices that worked last time to bring to the new plan. Each wicked problem is probably a symptom of another problem. Remember how we talked about how 'garbage in' is going to be 'garbage out', regardless of the quality of the work you do? Well, wicked problems are linked to others; you're getting inputs of 'garbage in' on top of trying to fix what's in front of you.

"Honey, your personality strength of 'annoying' is rather dominant today," Cali observed.

There were many nods supporting her around the table.

"Umm, I think I'd best leave that remark alone," Hal replied thoughtfully. "This discussion could deviate quickly. So, you think I've been annoying thus far?"

Hal stopped for a minute to look at his notes, and smiled to himself.

"That smile isn't a good sign," Aliston broke in. "The last time you looked like that was when you were thinking of putting little buzzers in the seats to keep people awake."

Everyone suddenly looked carefully at their seats.

"Couldn't get the electrician's union to do it" Hal admitted. "It turned out that one union handled the high power installations, another union handled the low power installations, and a third union installed the transformers that connected the other two unions installations. Well, they deadlocked over who was entitled to the work, and walked out on each other. Last I heard, they were sneaking test buzzers into each other's headquarters, calling it research."

"This is Detroit," one of the veterans observed.

"In school, we were taught that every problem has a cause. NOT. The base reason, the turtle that the turtle stands on, the tap root feeding the wicked problem-can be any number of reasons, and can be explained in numerous ways. The wicked problem tree lives off of feeder roots, not a tap root, so you can't cut off the problem with a single stroke. That means we can't even have a clear view of what caused/feeds this mess'. Obviously, that makes a huge difference as to what choices we see to solve, or at least live with, the problem."

"Who wants to join the maintenance union?" one of the transferees asked, raising her hand. "Clear actions and choices."

"Tempting," Hal agreed, "but what fun would that be? Here, we have the joy and excitement of every day facing the complete chaos of life. Best of all, the planner, i.e., the directly responsible person, a hero fighting valiantly against this hydra headed beast, as the crowd ohhs and ahhhs; you have no right to be wrong. No 'bye' pass from the boss. The planner is liable for the consequences of the actions they take/direct. Really, does it get any better than that?"

"Where's my list of your character flaws?" Cali grumbled, rummaging through her purse. "'Insanely cheerful' is going to have three exclamation points after it."

"At least," Hal replied, nodding happily. "This is really rough stuff we are going over today. Why? Because this is the world we live in. Small stories, small problems don't link to the other small stories and small problems, and so solutions don't. Oil disruptions lead to who knows what? We don't get to reset the game board and try another set of choices. And if we could? Can you imagine the committee meeting who decides what and when gets reset? I.e., whose ox gets un-gored and whose doesn't? The infighting would be with real knives. Maybe this is for the best. In the here and now, we only get one shot at a very rapidly moving target,"

"My professor for corporate strategy talked like this," a transferee interjected. "I thought he was kidding—just making things difficult."

"You'll notice he stayed in the halls of academia," Hal replied, "happy with tenure, a pension, and royalties from his writing on the side."

Hal paused for a moment to collect his thoughts. "Every choice we make in what we like to define as normal life is a win/lose. Oh, there is shading, but the happy decision is the clear one. It's black and white, and we choose, never having to look back. That's how people think, in straight lines and clear backgrounds. In the world we live in, we are playing paper, rock, scissors on every decision and problem. We can't be sure of the right and wrong and there may be no right and wrong. If there was a right and wrong, it vanishes because solutions change as we move. We want to see the subtle before it emerges, but in reality, we can hardly see the problem before it hits us, much less the subtle solutions to the problem. So, ideas, approaches?"

People stared at Hal.

"You thought I had solutions?" Hal advised. "Boy, were you wrong. No cookbooks, no checkboxes here. When you are in your office, what are you going to do about tomorrow?"

"Paper, rock, scissors," Cali remarked. "I like that, even though I don't like the game itself. I always find it frustrating."

Hal quickly wrote something down on a piece of paper and passed it to one of the transferees. "You will note," Hal specified, "that I'm seeking a witness that on this day, my wife said she liked my idea. I like to keep these little mementos."

The transferee dutifully signed his name as a witness on the piece of paper, which Hal tucked into his pocket.

"Are we done playing around?" Cali growled.

"The floor is all yours, my dear," Hal replied, bowing.

"So, what you are saying, I think," Cali argued, "is that normally we take problems apart, and by looking at the parts of the problem, we understand what the issue is. That doesn't work here, because we are trying to work with an emergent problem."

"Definition?" a transferee mumbled.

"We're going to be sorry you asked that," another transferee warned them.

"An emergent system is one that is, well, emerging in front of us. It's new, and the pieces are not clear because there are different elements interacting," Cali contended, thinking as she talked. "The result of the interaction is something quite different than the whole of the parts. An apple pie, hot out of the oven, the delicious aroma wafting through the kitchen, is much more than the raw sugar, piecrust, and raw apples you put into the oven. That new 'thing' has to be looked at top down, i.e., the pie's taste when it's cooked, and bottom up, for example, the quality of the apples used to make it. Except that real emergent systems are constantly changing, more like, well, a growing tree. The analysis of the leaf, the root, and the trunk don't add together to the live tree, which is changing and interacting with the world as we try to understand it. Want to grasp what a tree is? A tree then has to be studied as a live tree, and as a set of nested networks of relationships, which is the leaf, the root, the trunk, etc."

"And then there is the tree/forest complexity," Aliston added. "A tree is a system within a much bigger system, that inputs and outputs into that larger system."

"Absolutely true," Hal agreed. "Now, looking back at only the tree, we have to remember that it is developing by and for it's own rules and goals. Those rules/goals have hardly anything to do with your goals. You might be after shade, or apples from the tree, and/or erosion control, or a host of other goals. Your goals don't include roots in the sewers, or leaves all over in the fall, or a dense stand of trees turning into a firestorm. Little things like those are far outside your clear goal for a shady place to sit on a hot day with a glass of lemonade. See, paper, rock, scissors is a completely different way of thinking about the world."

"It's an organic way of thinking," Mary remarked. "The world operates in curves and twists, maximizing resources and opportunities. People demand right/wrong choices because they are comfortable. Maybe, at a stretch, structured multiple choices, but free form? That's not in the rule book that the suits go by. So, yeah, paper, rock, scissors is an essay exam, because the right answer could be this, and it could be this. People in general hate that, and it absolutely drives the authorities insane. After all, you allow ambiguity in one place, and maybe someone will think that the authorities don't have the answers either. I've seen culture after culture bury their heads in the sand, like an ostrich, because they don't want to be bothered with the complexity of the world."

"Only to be buried in the sand as time goes by," Jesus chuckled. "Thank you, Mary, for a great lead-in line!"

"Frankenstein's fateful error was to plan the individual parts, not allowing for what the sum of the parts he had assembled could become," Lucifer pointed out. "He defined a problem, successfully analyzed the parts, but the whole, the apple pie, as it were, wasn't even close to the stack of parts."

"As opposed to Frankenfurter's," Hal added. "His initial decision to use half a brain for his creatures doomed his efforts to inevitable failure. He misstated the problem completely, and failed to analyze the parts in his focus on the whole."

"And he dressed terribly, too," Mary commented. "All that black lace. Gauche."

There were general nods of agreement.

"So, what do we do? We have to act," Hal demanded. "One approach is a root-causes fix versus Band-Aids. It's harder to fix the root cause of a problem than to simply make a problem go away with a Band-Aid. Band-Aids are sometimes the best choice, though. Where and when?"

"Band-Aids where the problems can cure themselves, given time," Aliston responded. "Where the underlying system is working, and there is a temporary need for less stress from the world."

"A perfect answer," Hal agreed. "No wonder you took my job. And so it's rational, and almost always a good idea, to try some Band-Aids first to see what the underlying system is doing. That's not good where you have, say, a nuclear reactor overheating, but for smaller, slowly developing problems, it's generally appropriate. Where and how the Band-Aids are failing gives us some idea where the root causes might be. What's the worst choice? A grand vision, based on our goals rather than the world's nature. A mistaken solution to the root problem intensifies the problem. The cases where an initial success was only the prelude to overwhelming failure are legion."

"I think third grade was more fun," a transferee grumbled. "Clear answers, and recess."

"I'm for recess," Hal observed. "But how about a few more minutes of punishment, and then out? Yes?" He saw heads nodding.

"Okay, here is what we have faced in the last few weeks," Hal summarized. "There are chronic problems and acute problems. Generally defined by time frames, actually. That sounds obvious, but human time frames imposed on the world are a set of problems all by themselves. So, chronic problems, which are long-term, intractable, progressive, degenerative problems, the ones we really hate to deal with, underlie things like the oil crisis and related shocks. In hindsight, it is always obvious that limited resources and infinite demand plays poorly, but that is background, pushed away by our concentration on the problem de jour. Then, there are acute problems. They are sudden, intense, episodic problems, like, say, a broken toe from hitting a chair leg. Catastrophic problems are generally acute, as something awful emerges out of the background. The boots on the ground say 'Wow,' or less complimentary words to that effect. It's a chronic problems becoming acute, a small shock causing the collapse of corroded, weakened structures, that makes the history books."

"Where is the paper, rock, scissors?" Cali asked.

"Do we buy more efficient oil burning equipment?" Hal replied. "Or do we shift to coal, factoring in transportation and clean-air consequences? Some sets of facts will justify, or negate, either choice, and those sets of facts change going forward, flipping sometimes with incredible speed."

"So," Aliston maintained, "we first determine our goal. We determine our resources, barriers, and constraints. We make tentative choices, knowing that the best choice can change, and we only bet the farm when it's live or die."

"Really, promoting her was one of your better ideas," Cali pointed out to Hal.

"Couldn't agree more," Hal agreed. "What Aliston said brilliantly and succinctly sums up our choices. On top of that, the donuts are gone, so we are out of here Recess!"

DETROIT. DECEMBER 25TH

Christmas in Detroit was more subdued, but yet more joyous than the prior Christmas in New York. There were not as many gifts, but the factory was simply but beautifully decorated and there were more people to celebrate with.

Counting the veterans, their children, the São Paulo children, and the family at the factory, there were several hundred people crowding the community room. Dinner was a buffet, a labor of love by the restaurant, with lots of help from Cali, Mary, and Lucretia's mother. Lucretia was banned from the kitchen after her first faltering attempts. She happily went back to intent and focused discussions with Vladimir, to the general amusement of the kitchen staff. Hal, Lucifer, and Jesus were recruited to lift and carry certain clearly specified items and absolutely not touch anything else.

NORTH AFRICA. DECEMBER 25TH

At Paul's the celebration was far more muted than the prior year. There would have been few guests, as it was difficult to travel to the chateau, and so Paul decided to celebrate Christmas in North Africa. That worked for several reasons, including the fact that Paul, delighted at the way the year had gone, felt that he had received all the presents he had sought, and didn't want to discuss what he saw coming in the next year with others.

JESUS & THE WASTELAND

Jesus wrote occasionally, publishing his ideas to the Internet. He was surprised at how many people had started to read and follow his writings.

"Thank you for reading this," Jesus typed. "Based on the mail I've been receiving, my opinions do not seem to be popular with the authorities. I've always found that was a good thing in the past, and feel the same now. Their general response seems to be along the lines of 'You have no respect for excessive authority or obsolete traditions. You're dangerous and depraved, and you ought to be taken outside and shot!'[9] I'm going to take it as flattering that people are listening, and not address particular responses, either positive or negative.

"However, what is important about the rejection of my message is that usually the first response to change is to deny that a change is necessary, and to shoot the messenger just to make the point clear to the survivors. Unfortunately, shooting the messenger is how we got to where we are. All that, 'and the word became flesh,' didn't work so well. After the messenger was crucified, you saw the symbols as the message, not the message itself.

"And why? Because people live in the Waste Land. The Waste Land is where wounded people, living inauthentic and broken lives, exist. People who have lost the energy for living subsist in this blighted land. It's not a pretty picture, and interestingly, those most trapped in it deny that they live in a wasteland. Actually, they usually say that 'you' live in a wasteland because it's good for you, and 'we' do not because we do not need the suffering that you need. It isn't usually couched that bluntly, but that's the heart of their message. Not that it is a modern problem, by any means. The Waste Land is from the Grail legend, and the foundations of those stories stretch back very far, very far indeed.

"The heart of the issue is this question: When disaster strikes, and a great calamity comes your way, what is it that supports you and carries you through? Do you have anything that supports and carries you through? Or does that which you thought was your support fail you? That is the test of the myth by which you live.

Now, you are not generally encouraged to think about this. You are given 'meaning' to live by. Putting their 'meaning' to the acid test can cause doubt about what you were told. A test might even elicit independent thought, something that is a very dangerous thing to the authorities. I can testify to that.

"This is a terribly hard question. I had to rethink my core myths in the chaos of São Paulo. I'd not advise you to throw yourself into a scene of complete chaos and despair to think your myths through; there are easier ways to find your essence. Jung wrote extensively on finding the inner person. He had some very good ideas, which included daily writing and going back to what you've done over the years and reassessing choices.

"In a way, it was easier to think before the modern age. While going to the desert is extreme, all this constant information and entreaty thrown at a person makes it hard to find time to reflect. The information thrown at us is typically designed to generate an income for someone, so it's done cleverly to grab your attention. There is no harm or shame in that, as long as one remembers what is going on. If you're not paying for something, you're being sold. Think about what is being given to you, because sometimes you pay the greatest price for things that were free.

"And with all the messages thrown at a us, they are almost all carefully linked to a box fitting about you, a structure that you must fit into. Some are not so bad. The continued evolution of personal hygiene and city cleanliness is a vast improvement over the not so distant past. Perfume was originally designed to block smells, not spread a smell.

But you should deny many of the structures and boxes that are thrown at and around you. I said, 'Congratulations to the person who has toiled and has found life,' many years ago, and it's no less true today. And there is this to think about: There was a rich person who had a great deal of money. He said, 'I shall invest my money so that I may sow, reap, plant, and fill my storehouses with produce, that I may lack nothing.' These were the things he was thinking in his heart, but that very night he died. Planning for the future is necessary, but you have to plan focused on your life. Planning within the boxes imposed on you means you are working within another's plan."

He stopped for a moment, staring at the screen.

"The structures demean and deny the message that the spirit is in you. The structures-churches, religions, governments-demand that you exist by and through them. I demanded long ago: 'Show me the stone that the builders rejected: that is the keystone.' I'm saying that inspiration is found in the individual, not in the 'meaning' they hand you. The builders rejected that stone because it doesn't fit their plan at all, it only fits your plan. In each of us, the inspiration we are given, is unique. At the end, it's said that no one thinks they should have been at work more. Ask the hard question: what would be the model life you (not them) would have wanted to live?"

In Detroit, Hal and Cali were working on building virtual Arks around the world, tying together research facilities, factories, suppliers and raw materials in the middle of the chaos. The group that Aliston brought from New York had grown and grown. They were surprised to realize that the heart of the company was now in Detroit, and New York had become a branch.

"It's good that it really is a big factory," Hal remarked. "Believe it or not, there's still several hundred thousand square feet empty, but we're going to have a contractors start working on the empty parts. Just in case."

LUCRETIA & CALI IN THE GARDEN

Lucretia was sitting in the garden, which made her feel better. After she had come to Detroit, she had taken their chalice. After experiencing Grendel, she could smell the tree, and the garden let her in. The tree gave her hope and strength.

"Are you okay?" Cali asked, walking up behind her and standing next to her.

"Not really," Lucretia sighed. "The list is pretty long and boring, but wearing on me."

"I can guess," Cali replied. "I've had a list of my own."

"Mine isn't as heavy as yours," Lucretia apologized. "I shouldn't even say anything."

"Grendel went pretty well, didn't it?" Cali asked, looking carefully at Lucretia.

"Yeah," Lucretia replied, looking at the tree. "He enjoyed being with someone who had worked with Paul. He told me some funny stories. Funny, in an incredibly sick way, but funny. Yeah, it went okay."

"And the next phase?" Cali asked. She sat down, and patted the stone bench.

Lucretia sat down next to Cali. "I've been pushing it away. But, I've got to make some decisions. I, well, Vladimir is so wonderful, but my life hasn't been, well, defensible to him. I just don't know. Maybe just feeling sorry for myself is more fun. I don't know."

"I doubt that," Cali observed. "I've grown to know you, and feeling sorry for yourself isn't you." They sat in silence for a few minutes.

"You know, Cali," Lucretia teased, "I think we'll be best friends forever, because you already know too much."

Cali laughed. "Look," she coaxed, "it's better when it's over. Trust me."

"Painful?" Lucretia blurted out.

"Oh, a kind of childbirth," Cali recalled, "with no drugs, and you get to experience both parts, the mother and child. You might say it's a bit painful."

"The men must enjoy that," Lucretia snickered. "That would be a novel experience for them."

Cali bent close to her and whispered something, and they both laughed until the tears ran.

LUCRETIA & GRENDELINE

Lucretia was in a dark and rocky place. Ugly, twisted trees grew out of the bare rock, their long thorns sparkling in the little light there was. Like everyone else's dream, she bitched. Geez, I'm so boring. Oh well. Suddenly, she saw the thorn trees waving as something forced its way through. Dried leaves and poisonous fruit crunched under the heavy stride, echoing against the rocks. She jumped to her feet, terrified. What is it? Zombies? People from the streets? The priests, in a medley of uniforms and costumes? Or the annual personal review committee from Coldmen Sacking? Ugh, she grimaced, that would be truly terrifying. Dull men in grey suits, smiling as they cut your bonus. Or is it just the wind? She watched, seeing dark shapes amid the crackling of the undergrowth.

Lucretia 2 and Lucretia 3 popped out of the undergrowth, Lucretia 2 loudly complaining about how her silk dress was torn.

"Hi, I have my notes and script," Lucretia 2 announced cheerfully to Lucretia, who was staring at them in dull disbelief. "Am I late?" Lucretia 2 looked around. "Looks like I'm just in time. So: Campbell, yeah. One is harassed, both day and night, by the divine being that is the image of the living self within the locked labyrinth of one's own disoriented psyche. Yeah, that seems right." She looked critically around at the scene, and she checked off a box on a piece of paper.

Lucretia 3 was menacing in a black leather jacket, tall, black motorcycle boots, and a baseball bat. "Going to kick some butt tonight," she muttered.

"And the same kind of alter egos everyone else has," Lucretia declared to them, discouraged. "Really, this needs a rewrite."

"Not quite the same story," a male voice remarked, coming towards her.

"Jose," she mumbled, and her heart sank. "The ghost of Christmas Past. I didn't think of you when they warned about pain. I thought of the torture stuff. Would have preferred that, actually."

"Like the firm? That was nasty," Jose asked, sitting down next to her. "Tie you up economically, professionally, and socially, and then just keep tightening those cords. They are good at what they do. By the way, the thorn trees were annoying. Why doesn't anyone come up with, say, a nice apple tree in a meadow, with ripe fruit? Why do you have to suffer so much? Which you should reflect on, by the way."

He stopped and thought for a minute, staring intently at Lucretia. "You know, I've been going over your memories. All of them, in fact. I never knew."

"Ah," Lucretia 2 demanded, "did you have a waiver? That's well, confidential information."

Jose looked at her, and he suddenly morphed into the huge spider, claws clicking on the stones, mouth moving obscenely. Lucretia 2 ran screaming off into the night. Then he changed back to Jose. "Oww," grimacing, watching Lucretia 2 run right into the thorn tree again, shreds of her dress left hanging on the tree. "She's going to need a good seamstress to repair that. Maybe a visit to a Redi Care clinic. Even figments of your imagination need a good health care plan."

"And what if you had known everything?" Lucretia shouted. "That I wasn't what you thought I was?"

"No, you were more," Jose answered sadly. "I never understood before."

Lucretia bent over. "I never wanted you to know," she cried. "I hid it all, all the ugly in my past. I thought you'd never want me if you had known. I thought it was better when we broke up."

"Maybe for the better, in the end," Jose muttered. "There were things you didn't know about me. But this is your crisis, not mine." He stopped to think for a minute. "So tell me what you've been telling yourself. Every new life begins with a confession." A worn, wooden confessional appeared, and he slid the door back, just visible behind the wire mesh.

"Oh, give me a break," Lucretia growled.

"Sorry," Jose replied. "I get bored. Life as a floating alter ego, well, it's slow sometimes." He reverted to Jose, standing next to the rock he had been sitting on.

"Well, I've lost my integrity, honor, and social facade," Lucretia answered, ticking them off on her fingers. "Also my exclusive condo on Fifth Avenue and all the material possessions I worked so hard for. Except mom's jewelry and some of our clothes. And then there were these things," talking to herself. She stopped and stared at her hands, all fingers extended. "Out of fingers, too." She glanced down doubtfully at her toes.

"Lost everything? Not the bra with the red piping?" Jose gasped, visibly upset. "And the black lace bra with the matching thong panties? My, that brings back memories." He glanced down his body and sat down suddenly. "Out of my role, sorry, my child. Continue your confession."

Lucretia stopped to gather her thoughts. "I pushed and pulled and strove. I pulled my way out of one ghetto and found that the new one was worse. The living conditions were better, but the parasites were the same. I did everything I could to get where I was, and for what? Mom at least was honest about what she did. All of my prestige, achievements, work, and career are lost, all the years gone. Oh, and I'm a criminal. Not rough stuff, just a lot of paper shuffling, but probably a good case could be made by the Feds for roughly life in prison based on what Paul had me do."

Jose sat and sadly watched her.

"Which I did willingly," Lucretia announced, head up, defiantly staring at Jose. "Oh, I had orders, but I knew what I was doing. Well, the physical evidence seems to have vanished in that explosion, and the computer evidence seems to have been pretty well chewed up by the virus Hal ran through it. Never can tell whether all the backups were trashed, but a lot of stuff was changed. It was clever to just change my name on documents all over the system.

"My work was my life." She stood up and started pacing. "I feel empty without it. Maybe it was a crutch to keep the questions away. Nervous activity is a great way of avoiding the important things you don't want to think about. Now, their meaning jumps at me in the night. 'Is this all?' it whispers at three in the morning. I stare at the ceiling and wonder."

"Whisper in your ear it does," Jose agreed. "Years of schooling and force feeding put that button in your brain. It's the parasites' best trick. They sell you the need and manufacture the drug to solve the disease they infected you with. It's worked for a long time."

Jose stood up and walked up to her. "I can take your pain away," Jose promised, and he was suddenly naked. "Mating takes the pain away and gives back the control. You know that. It's so easy. And, well, after the underwear discussion, I'm up for it."

"Literally," she laughed sadly. But she shook her head no. "I know what it means. I read *Beowulf*, read *Le Morte d'Arthur*. Hal suggested it."

"At least you laid off the Spengler," Jose replied, relieved. "All that Sturm und Drang and grim faces. Ugh. You couldn't read, say, something cheerful?" he teased. "Like *Fifty Blonde Jokes*, for example?"

Lucretia glared at him for a moment and then laughed. "No, but maybe tomorrow."

"If it comes," Jose pointed out. "We're playing for all the marbles here. Mate with me, and tomorrow will be there for certain."

"You are persistent," Lucretia answered, "but you always were. No. Thank you." She went to sit down on a rock, but stopped, inspecting it first. "Gross!" she grumbled, brushing away the dust and insects. Then she sat down.

159

"First offer," Jose noted. "Just keeping track. I have to follow the ritual." He stared out at the dark, unbroken except for what looked like a burning in the far distance.

"So, you've been keeping busy," Jose asked, sitting down again, but staying naked. "Does this bother you?" He gestured at his body.

"Yes," Lucretia sighed. "A lot."

"Good," he replied, smiling. "Traditions, you know." He sat for a moment. "Your daughter is such a cute little girl. Fathered by the man who had me killed. Not the memorial I'd have hoped for."

"How was I to know?" she screamed, jumping to her feet, shaking her fists at him. "How was I to know? You went back to your world, left me to those wolves. I was fighting to survive! You know what they meant to do to me when they took me to that meeting? Leave me for alligator munchies, to cover up their crimes. Both their financial crimes against Don Cortes and their crimes against me. You've looked at my memories; you know what they did to me. When I went back and was promoted to senior partner, I demanded to look at the paperwork they had created. I forced them to bring it to me! There were many documents with my signature forged on them, and bank accounts in my name I never knew about. That partner had me wrapped up like a spider would, slowly sucking the blood and life from me. Don Cortes treated me with respect and backed me when he didn't have to. I chose him to father a child, to honor him."

"You're right, how were you to know?" Jose agreed, nodding. "I grant you, he was a brilliant man, strong and driving. You didn't know his involvement with Paul, and the pressure they put on him. And his having me killed? Those things happen in the drug trade. I was not what you thought I was either, my dear. You worried so much about the niceties of the law and the things you did. You pushed numbers around on pieces of paper. I killed men by putting two slugs in their heads, and one in the body. The accepted way. Many men. You never knew. Some women, too. Drugs are a rough business."

They sat quietly for a few minutes.

"Mate with me and all the conflicts you face about Don Cortes and me, the confusion from your daughter vanishes," Jose promised. "What say you, my proud beauty?" He stood there in a pirate costume, sword in hand, bright red shirt and tall back boots, no pants.

Lucretia stared intently at him, and then looked at the ground, closing her eyes. "I cannot," she rasped. "A bill of lading, as it were, would come due later. You'd board me and loot my booty. But I like the pirate. It fits you."

"As if your daughter as a teenager won't be enough punishment for any one person," Jose commented. "Don Cortes and your personality combined? She will be an elemental force of nature. Good luck on that one. Oh, and that's the second offer," he noted.

He stood up, and walked over to the thorn tree, carefully poking at the branches. "Ouch, those are nasty," he commented, examining his finger. "Oh, you can come out," he shouted to Lucretia 2, who was still hiding behind the trees. "I was just joking! The spider won't get you. Promise! Cross my heart and hope to die."

"You're already dead," a wavering voice came from behind some bushes.

"Umm, true," Jose agreed, "but, well, trust me on this one."

"I have a change of clothes," Lucretia 3 muttered and went out into the dark to find Lucretia 2.

"So you blame yourself for São Paulo?" Jose accused, turning suddenly and staring at Lucretia. "You jumped ship before it happened. Your plan had nothing to do with what finally happened, and Paul gave you the orders. Why do you torment yourself?"

"I don't know," Lucretia mumbled. "It's just that it was awful. Unimaginable! I started it, kind of. And it just went wild. No one could have seen it coming."

"You underrate Paul," Jose responded. "Some men just like to see the world burn. Comets hit, earthquakes kill, and a wheat rust is spreading through the world that will destroy most of the wheat crop. Do you take responsibility for those also?"

"No," Lucretia muttered. "It's just...well..."

"That you have the human fantasy that if you feel bad about something, then you did something about it?" Jose snarled. "Using the daily magic to make things better by making yourself feel bad? Paying in advance so that the real bad things don't happen? Give it up, Lucretia. Your will and the world are two different things, you know that. Bad things happen to good people; there is no correlation between the real and social worlds. Retributive justice is a human concept, not part of the cosmos. No, you're doing it so you don't have to act. You don't have to move forward, you don't have to take steps, you can stew in your self-inflicted prison. The act of a coward, by the way."

"What do you mean?" Lucretia yelled, standing up and doubling her fists.

"Yeah," Lucretia 3 growled, hefting her club and hunching into a baseball batter's stance. "We don't have to take that kind of stuff."

"I don't need your help," Lucretia shouted to Lucretia 3. "Go back in the bushes or something." Lucretia 3 slunk back to her rock.

Jose looked at Lucretia 3, sulking in the edge of the light. Suddenly Jose 3 came out of the woods, in black leather to match Lucretia 3's outfit. "There's a fine beauty," Jose 3 teased Lucretia 3. "I love the leather." They stared intently at each other for a moment, and walked quickly into the dark.

"No, ah, byproducts from the alter egos' actions, are there?" Lucretia 2 asked, concerned, holding her notebook. "That, well, doesn't count as mating? It's always the fine print, you know, one has to ask."

"No," Jose retorted, frustrated with the interruptions. "Here." He waved his hand, and Jose 2, perfectly attired in a blue pinstriped suit and red power tie, came out of the woods. "You two go talk about something intricate, involved, and useless."

Jose 2 and Lucretia 2 shook hands, eyes glowing, and happily wandered off, talking animatedly and waving their hands.

"Where was I?" Jose wondered, holding his hands over his eyes. "It's so hard to think with all these distractions. Oh, right, this is where we were." He put his hands on his hips. "Your children need you! Your mother needs you. Cali and her family need you. Vladimir needs you! And you take your tremendous talents and put them in a swamp that you can fester in. Useless to all. Coward."

Lucretia plopped down on a rock, crushed. "I thought I was doing right."

"You thought you should suffer for your sins, without realizing you were making them suffer. Selfish. And so here you are," Jose remarked. "Look, Lucretia, you went out every day to fight in the swamps of the world, and came home covered with slime and bugs. Then, one day you pulled out a set of sparkling ideas that had nothing to do with the world that actually exists out there, and you beat yourself over the head with the pretty ideas so you could judge yourself a failure. Why?"

"Control?" she guessed. "Avoiding having to choose, because I don't feel as though I've chosen right recently. Freezing. You're right. All of it. Aren't you supposed to be beating me down? That last was pretty helpful."

"Oh, I'm not done," Jose hissed, "just priming the pump." Leaning over her, he whispered, "They all need you. What if you don't come back? Who will take care of our son? And your daughter? Mate with me, make sure you can go back to them."

Lucretia clasped her hands over her head and bent double in her torment. She shook with the pain. "I cannot," she forced the words out. "It would be false, and it would all fall apart. I don't want the dragon coming out years from now and destroying everything, which is what always happens with the easy way. No."

"That was the third," Jose answered. "I will not ask again. But I give you a quote, maybe it will help."

When Levin thought about what he was and what he lived for, he found no answer and fell into despair; but when he stopped asking himself about it, he seemed to know what he was and what he lived for, because he acted and lived firmly and definitely ...Reasoning led him into doubt and kept him from seeing what he should and should not do. Yet when he did not think, but lived, he constantly felt in his soul the presence of an infallible judge who decided which of two possible actions was better and which was worse; and whenever he did not act as he should, he felt it at once.

"Tolstoy, Anna Karenina. That I haven't read in a long time," she mused. "And it's true. Why a human has to go to the bottom to see it, I don't know. But it's true."

"Just like the others, you took the meaning fed to you and put it over your inspiration. So, what is your wound? It must be named." He became a broken, hunched, twisted old man with a wild expression, laughing to himself, dancing a little jig. Then he looked at Lucretia, who was staring at the bridge over the abyss that suddenly appeared.

"That's a ripe tomato," Jose rasped, leering at her body. "Who stands at the Bridge of Death, must these questions three, answer me, if the other side she wishes to see. Or suffer in the gorge of eternal torment, well, duh, for eternity."

"Is this really necessary? I don't remember this item on the agenda for this meeting," Lucretia frowned.

"Look, liven up a bit. Your schedule isn't that tight, miss EX-partner," Jose jeered.

"Thanks for the reminder. Maybe give me a paper cut next time, pour some lime juice on it?" Lucretia responded. "Fine, ask me the questions. I am not afraid. Except of catching a disease from that disgusting robe thing you are wearing." She glared at his robe, repulsed. "There are bugs moving on your robe! Yuck."

"What is your name?" Jose sneered.

"It's Lucretia Liancol. It would have been Morgenstern had someone asked me to marry them, but no," Lucretia answered.

"Stick with the script. What is your quest? Ask yourself, why do you seek the Cup of Christ? Is it for His glory, or for yours?" Jose asked.

"That's the rub, isn't it? Vaulting ambition? Pride? I saw a slogan years ago. 'The girl I want to be is beautiful, successful, and heartless.' Much prettier words than the life it led to. I told myself that I did what I did for my family. And there was some truth in that, but not the whole truth. I wanted to be loved and accepted. No, perhaps the dark queen, if not loved, then feared. I'd have taken the ring in *Lord of the Rings*, I'm afraid. I had that part of the book underlined." She stood up, arms extended to the sky. "'And I shall be Dreadful as the Night and the Lightning! All shall look upon me and despair!'" She stopped and put her arms around herself. "Little would that have solved, would it?" looking at Jose. "I never stopped to think about what I wanted under it all. But I did make a splash in the bigger world. I stepped away from what I was and substituted instead what they said I should want. And it's been a bitter drink."

"The sin of inadvertence, not being alert, not quite awake, is the sin of missing the moment of life. The 'non-action that is action' is unremitting alertness. It's Zen. When one is fully aware all the time, life is then lived of itself. A shorter version of Tolstoy. Well, I did go to Harvard," noticing her doubting expression. "I didn't drink all the time."

"My quest was for my glory," Lucretia confessed. "But I took care of my family as best I could." She stood with her arms around herself, looking at the red in the east, the sky starting to lighten up.

"Forgive me, Father, for I have sinned," she asked, looking at him and glancing down. "Hmmm, the priests I remember wore pants."

"Not the ones I remember," Jose grimaced. "We'll let that one go." He suddenly was resplendent in a full red cardinal's robe. "For the good of France, and by my order, the bearer has done what they have done," He handed her a piece of parchment. "I absolve you from your sins in the name of Life and the Tree. It is you who must absolve yourself from what you feel inside." He thought for a minute, and snapped his fingers. "Didn't quite finish the ritual. Let's see, what was next?" He thought intently for a moment. "it was, yeah-What is your favorite color?"

"That greenish hue I remember your eyes being," Lucretia sighed.

"That cut deep, it did. But it's the right answer. You can cross the bridge. Scamper along," Jose advised, and he waved his hand.

"So, make friends with your monsters, Hal would say. Buy them a beer, have a long talk," Lucretia teased.

"Tequila," Jose answered. "A dirty cantina in a desert town. Angry people with guns on the tables. That was the way I lived after Harvard, and the way you should remember me, actually. My life changed after we parted. Do me a favor, though. Try and be kind to yourself! So hard, so strong you are; back off, ease up a bit. As you've noticed, no one else seems to be rushing to do it. Except Vladimir, who is a blessing for you in many ways."

Jose stopped and looked at the pink rays of the rising sun streaking the eastern sky. "So: it's absorption by and of the mother goddess and the life force, is it? Every new life begins with the death of the old and the transfiguration into the new. Hopefully."

"That's encouraging, I think," Lucretia offered. "Well, I name you friend, and welcome you."

"Replace the fear of the unknown with curiosity," Jose advised. "Life's more interesting that way." He suddenly became the mother goddess, stern but smiling.

Lucretia held out her hand, and the mother goddess took it. They stood for a few moments, and then they dissolved into swirling clouds of mist that combined, eddied, and flowed. Lightning flashed in the eddies. After some time, there was Lucretia again, formed out of shapelessness. I can really feel the Tree of Life, she thought, delighted. My roots pushing deep into the nourishing soil, the sweet taste of the rain, and the warm sun on my leaves. The cold winter gone, she felt life fill her. As I was, she thought and yet not. She saw the Tree, huge, dominating the plain, three-dimensional in the world. And then four dimensions, feeling Jose himself, smiling, and nourishing her.

Lucretia, stood, staring at the bright horizon with different eyes. Cali was right about the childbirth, Lucretia thought, and smiled. Not as she smiled before, but with touches of Jose's bravado and courage in the lips. Not quite as she had been.

She closed her eyes and saw the garden in the little house she had grown up in, bursting with life. Just when the caterpillar thought its life was over, it becomes a butterfly, she marveled. The pain goes away.

VLADIMIR'S CONFESSION

"I love it in here!" Lucretia whispered to Vladimir, squeezing his hand. "Suddenly the garden fully embraces me. It's an interesting door, you know? Now it opens when I walk up to it. Things in this place seem to have a life of their own."

"You have no idea how astonished I am to see the Tree grow again," Vladimir replied, shaking his head in disbelief. "So many long, empty years I've waited." He carefully traced the green man motif on the carving on the wall next to them with his hand, and then studied the carving for a minute.

"The green man: it's Inspiration and life. Rebirth, the cycle of growth each new year. Almost all cultures have some version of it, ranging from a man's face peering out of foliage, to the most stylized and abstract. It's almost always green men, rarely green women—who knows why? Green cats, lions, and some green demons, too. Not many green angels, it seems." He sighed.

"Isn't that one rather, well, morbid?" pointing to one on the wall that was a human skull sprouting grape vines.

"Maybe," Vladimir replied. "Life and death are intertwined. Perhaps it's done as recognition of the Tree of Life. Maybe it means the resurrection, the church's continued attempt to bend the symbols their way. The church doesn't like the Tree of Life, really." He walked over and studied the carving.

"This is really nice work. I wonder how it got here? I know we didn't bring it here. Too many mysteries."

He looked at her and smiled. "Don't mind me. I talk like a professor," he apologized. "Too many years of being solemn and serious, the chosen defender. Or what I thought, anyway. Look, these are more the Romanesque and medieval style carvings," pointing to several others around the garden room.

"They are eerie," Lucretia exclaimed. "Carved in stone, but so full of life and vitality!"

"They are Life shouting at me, telling me of my mistakes. It started out with life. Life triumphant, life everywhere. Then the humans forsook the larger world of life for the new human world of social structures and ideas. It was so exciting! Great towns sprang up with the bustle and hustle of the new kingdoms. And there were great things accomplished. None of us saw the flaws when it started. But the life faded from the small human structures as they walled the towns away from the world and talked only of human concerns among themselves. The doors shut to the larger world. Foolish, short sighted, but the way they are. And I, too, who believed it completely."

"That was my sin, believing the small world. What Grendeline put me through. I think what the others went through."

"It's a human machine you're in," Vladimir commented, looking at her with approval. "A very nice machine, too." He stroked her hair, and she smiled at him. "Our minds adjust our world so we can think, 'I am nice and in control.' It doesn't seem to matter whether those personal stories are 'true'; what matters is that they're consistent, and back up by a group."

Vladimir studied the tree. "I've changed a lot over time. It seems that I have only limited control. Not what I originally believed when I was young, strong, and full of power. The strong arm of the Good! Or I felt that way, at least."

"Each new life starts with a confession. That's what Grendeline demanded."

"I always preferred priestesses," Vladimir declared. "Seemed right to me somehow." He looked down at her and then knelt at her feet. "Bless me, holy mother, for I have sinned. It has been a long, long time since my last confession."

"Your heart is good," Lucretia replied, stroking his hair, suddenly feeling the mother goddess in herself. "Please, tell me what troubles you."

"There is this mask that I wear, like everyone else. Maybe a bigger mask than most wear, but still a mask. The problem is that a person has to know what play you're in at any one time, and the play has changed over time. The mask doesn't fit, and there is the dark unconscious striving against the external mask. One of the great dangers is to identify yourself with your persona, and that I've done.

"But we had hope, and thought we were right. I didn't see it as a mask; it was me. And we wouldn't act without orders, so we waited. And waited, through the dusty eons. Like one of those plays where you talk about nothing for all eternity. Then, we thought we'd done something wrong, and our suffering was our deserved punishment, because it was a system of absolute justice based on retribution for sin. But suffering can have many causes. Job worked his way through them, but we ignored what he taught, because it denied our story. You can never ignore that little voice or lie to yourself that something must be right. It gnaws at you, day after day. So, the question of suffering became a quest to understand what was being said. How to interpret the mind of God from his acts, which we thought was perfectly clear at one time. Foolish we were, it seems. In Job, it's argued that suffering is punishment for sin; or the inevitable lot of frail mortals who have an inherent propensity for evil; or a calculated disciplinary work of God; or part of a mysterious divine plan; or a test imposed on a righteous mortal to satisfy a heavenly dispute. The possibilities are all over the place, actually. So, we polished our armor and waited, until we couldn't deny the little voice inside any longer.

"'To God everything is beautiful, good, and just; humans, however, think some things are unjust and others just.' Heraclitus via Lucifer. We absolutely denied and fought that statement, because we were sure it could not have been right. It denied our story and our masks, in all truth. Job teaches that the wicked may be accidentally restrained because the dawn arrives and deprives them of the darkness where they hide, but that restraint of the wicked is an accidental byproduct of the dark, and the wicked are not struck down when the sun rises each morning. The food for the lion and the kill for the raven are innocents who no more deserve to die than any others. Their deaths are not stories, they are events. That's hard to accept, because humans demand meaning in everything they see. They are taught that without meaning, there is an empty place in the mind. But is it really empty? The body moves, it breathes, it eats; all the vast complexity of the body runs without 'meaning' as do the other creatures and the trees. Meaning is a conceit of the mind; perhaps something the unconscious tosses the consciousness to keep it occupied while the unconscious handles the serious business of living.

"Anyhow, we were absolutely clear about the meaning of everything, and would brook no doubt, no questioning. Doubt was rebellion! There were disputes, and then war. When the Tree withered we pointed fingers, and we blamed those who questioned, those who doubted, for the loss of the tree. Uneasy with our understanding of the 'revealed' truth, we sought to force that truth. Rational proof is a tool. The rational tool works very well when you can test it against the real world. Popper wrote that, as had many before him.

167

But, and here's where we went wrong, if you don't have an objective world to test your ideas against, then the rational tool is nonsense. Worse than nonsense, because it folds back on itself. What drives rationality that can't be tested? All the hidden emotions, pushed away. What destroyed Forbidden Planet was the denied world of life. And what destroyed the church was the twisted rationality of old men. It turned into witchcraft and killings and theft, all blessed by the powers that be on this earth."

"Forbidden Planet?" Lucretia asked.

"An ancient science fiction movie," Vladimir replied. "The inhabitants of this far-away world were so wise that they created a vast computer to run their world in a logical, structured manner. Mine, manufacture, transport, while the people did who knows what? They were dead by the time the humans arrived. It turned out that they transferred not only the logical part of the mind, the rational tool, but the emotions that they had pushed away, ignored. The monsters in the corners, not welcome. Monsters bide their time and come out stronger. They denied life and made the world fit their straight lines, brightly colored children's stories. They didn't listen to their myths, laughed at the stories, and shredded them. The world is stronger than that, and overflowed the levees they had created, flooding everything.

"What's hard to realize is that consciousness is not life or living, it is the unconscious that all rises from and falls into. Much of our life is essentially on autopilot, waiting for instructions to surface. Myths are communication with the unconscious, but the conscious mind wants to flaunt its rational tools and dissect the myths. An effective myth can be contrived and silly; it can seem to be full of obvious logical fallacies because of the mismatch between words, reality and emotion. Words can only be a poor reflection of the emotions, and because the structure of language is different from the structure of the emotions, putting a bright vision into words tears the brilliant blue sky into misshapen pieces and drops it inside a box. Myths are a vessel to carry the transcendent truth within, the truths beyond good and evil, beyond rational and irrational, to and from the emotions and the unconscious. The conscious mind can only grasp parts and shadows of the full myth's power and shape.

"Words can't convey the full complexity, power, and structure of the myth. The mind, seeking consistency and control, is acutely uncomfortable with the transcendent images, an unsettling message of greater unknown and unseen powers tossing life around. Life to the consciousness is like the surface waves in the deep ocean, huge masses without pattern tossing what's on the surface, and the conscious really hates that feeling. So the consciousness will reach for any explanation to give it control. In the deep ocean, it's calm under the surface; the calm of the unconscious that the myth reaches directly to.

"Analyzed, a myth becomes like the bones of a whale on the beach. Analyzing the bones, the pieces, completely misses the power and essence of the living whale. The conscious can't see the whole whale, and wanders off fussing with the pieces in frustration. The unconscious sees the whole if we trust and rely on it, and then we are at peace. We lose peace when we pull at the bits to reassemble them incorrectly, like creating an imaginary creature from the bones on the beach. And we created lots of imaginary creatures, over and over. It turns out that one seeks an answer first, and understanding last.

"I took the Grendel syringe," he confessed. "It was painful, but not why you would think. You see, the ultimate evil, and the most fanatical good, meet in the same place. They are positions on a circle, not lines on a plane. I knew the evil because I knew the confidence of the good. The good is more dangerous, actually, than the evil. With evil, you think, you have to justify your actions, you have doubts. With the good, there are no doubts. I walked through many mistakes. When the garden withered, we thought it was the sin of the humans, and that suffering would bring the tree back. So we righteously doled out suffering, without doubt. Because look who we were! Revealed truth, like suffering to Job, can actually be many truths, and that's unsettling. It's been a rough time, let me tell you." He shook his head.

"What we eventually found, as you found, is that if you've buried too much of yourself within your shadow, you're going to dry up. Your energy is frozen deep inside, holding back what you fear. Sooner or later, the walls break and that unheeded demon, that life force pushed away, is going to come roaring up into the light. The shadow is you as you might have been, if you became your unacceptable potential. The shadow is interred down there for a reason; it is that aspect of yourself you bury because it doesn't fit how you perceive yourself to be. Not the mask, as it were.

"But inside the shadow there is inspiration, and the inspiration carries a person to joy and life. That's the revealed truth after all. That's what's been hardest, is to put down the heavy weight of 'meaning' and feel the simple joy of inspiration. And it turned out that it was the separation from Life that withered the tree and our well meant suffering wasn't for life, it was for death. Misread it, we did. It was the shadow that was life, the shadow we had pushed away. As the old saw said well: 'Every end does not appear together with its beginning.'"

"I absolve you from your sins in the name of Life and the Tree," Lucretia pronounced, standing over him.

Vladimir stood up, seized her, and kissed her. "The traditional blessing by the priestess," he whispered as their arms wrapped around each other. "Not all the ancient practices should be rejected."

"Shut up and kiss me," she murmured.

The garden door locked itself, giving them privacy.

169

LUCRETIA THINKING

Lucretia sat in front of her mirror, brushing her hair and thinking.

"You shouldn't let Vladimir get away," Jose advised her. "He'd be good to you, and he needs you more than he can imagine."

"Are you sure?" Lucretia worried. "I know what I want, but he seems, well, kind of fragile in a way, and I don't want to push him too hard."

"Fragile?" Jose laughed. "You see only the outer shell. You have no idea what you are dealing with there. He seeks life, and you seek to give it to him. Give me a break—you are a woman, think of something. 'It is a truth universally acknowledged, that a single man in possession of a good fortune must be in want of a wife.'"

"Have you been sneaking looks at the secret book for girls?" Lucretia accused him. "That's forbidden to show to males, even if they are figments of the woman's imagination."

"I was no angel, Lucretia," Jose confessed. "He is. Don't let this one get away."

CALI & MARY

"So, you're good for the baptisms tomorrow?" Cali asked cautiously.

Mary forced a smile. "I'm looking forward to them. New life, always exciting."

Cali looked carefully at her. "You sound tired. And you look a little tired."

"And the corners of my eyes are wrinkled," Mary snarled. "Daughters are always so supportive. Yeah, I'm tired. I'm thinking of becoming a jellyfish again, and just drifting in the deep for a million years. It's the illusion of control that wears a person down, you know? All the daily stuff, the process of life, can get tiring. That's where the men had it made. They'd conquer Europe, come back to the hut, and demand meat. I'm cleaning and cooking and raising the kids. They can't wipe their feet on the mat outside, so I could care if they conquered anything. Would have been nice if they'd brought some domestic help back."

"Okay," Cali replied, softly backing away. "I'll let you get some rest."

"Thanks," Mary sighed. "I'll be fine."

Cali left, tiptoeing out and quietly shutting the door behind her.

MARY & GRENDELINE

Mary sat for a few minutes after Cali left and then walked up the stairs to the third floor retreat she had designed for herself. It looked out over what was left of the city, but still very private. She loved the outdoor courtyard, her haven from the chaos, at least on a nice day. Where is there a purchased pleasure as great as the sound and smell of rain on a summer day? Or the warmth of the sun on a cool day dispelling the cold?, she thought I wish it was that kind of day today. I need a nice warm night, the breeze reassuring and comforting me, the stars sparkling above.

She looked up, and it was pitch black. The city lights were absorbed by the low, heavy clouds. It was foggy, everything indistinct and blurred. "Nice," she commented to the sky. "It's how I feel. I appreciate the cooperation."

"You do, my Pretty Pretty?" a voice purred across the room.

Mary slumped. "Again?" she asked the voice.

"Again," the voice purred and a figure moved into the room.

"The Dark Queen from Barbarella," Mary mumbled. "It does suit you."

"Do you like it? Then I'll change to something else," the voice taunted. "I'm a burr in your boot, a spur in your side. The itch you can't scratch."

"Hard to forget," Mary replied, despondently. "You came differently to the others."

"Perhaps," the voice purred. "Perhaps not. People do not report the full story, generally. And each of you has different needs and wants. And guilt's, I think, is the modern word?"

Mary looked at the figure, opened her mouth to respond, and then started crying. Uncontrollable deep sobbing, shaking her over and over.

The Queen looked at her and sat down, saying nothing. Mary cried for a long time.

"Every new life begins with a confession," the Queen observed thoughtfully.

"Forgive me, for I have sinned," Mary sobbed, looking out at the black sky, the swirling fog accented by a few hazy lights. Looks just like a churning soup bowl, Mary thought to herself. And I'm in the soup.

"It has been a long time," Mary admitted. "A very, very long time since my last confession."

Mary stopped for a minute to collect her thoughts, the Queen motionless, closely watching her.

"There are four kinds of crises that can spark that crisis of the soul— isn't that what Campbell argued? And the worst crisis is where you have to do something that you regard as immoral, beneath your dignity, something you're totally ashamed of. My life has been a lie," Mary confessed. "I lie to myself just to make it bearable. Oh, much of it is real. I'm supporting many with heavy loads. I help and encourage where I can. But I made a mistake a long time ago. I knew it was wrong. Perhaps there was nothing I could have done, but I agreed for the group. I thought it would work."

"A well meaning lie," the Queen hissed. "For the greater good. Those sins go very deep, don't they?"

"Every minute of my life, it seems," Mary replied. "Their myths are critical to the humans. The early myths were quick and simple. The mother goddess, the growth of life, the rituals of life and death following each other. For eons, small tribes believed the same. But then the tribes reached a critical mass, and became something different. A cohesion, a common plan that seemed to promise stronger structures, more complex groups. We were excited; evolution to the more complex is the norm."

"Good," the Queen asserted, smiling. "Good intentions all the way; nothing but the best was meant. A deep sin, indeed."

"Yes," Mary acknowledged. "Because there was a compromise. No, a lie. Because of the way they see their stories, because of the way they are made, there was a lie at the bottom. I tried. Lilith, the woman equal to Man. Made the same, woman instead of man. And they rejected that. Oh, how that was rejected! The strong men on the horses with the swords were clear: no weak women in the fields was the equal of a Man! Well, eventually the authorized story, the holy theology, not only rejected her, but made Lilith the mother of demons. The 'the-he-ology', I always called it. So I made it worse. I backed off, let Eve be the sad crippled creature that they demanded. And Lilith, the equal woman, she became the mother of all demons and the daily evil. Nice job I did, quality work. And I've paid. As I watched women destroyed over the centuries, I've paid, counting them up in my heart. Until my heart is full, and they keep on coming. And now, my daughter, humiliated and abused by animals. What is the result? She is reviled in public for the tortures she suffered. For her attackers, only polite words of disparagement in the press, and innumerate tasteless Internet postings in praise."

"That is a burden to bear," the Queen admitted. "You would not have borne that for the dolphins, or the seals, or for any other creature. The creatures are what they are. You're making up a dream in your heart and carrying it like a flame to burn yourself with, a dream that doesn't change the creatures."

"No, it can't change them," Mary mumbled, "but it was so important to me."

"Why?" the Queen demanded, truly puzzled. "Why did you define a woman's importance in a man's terms? Why did you define all that's important to a woman using their scales, not a woman's? Women run life, are life, and the men know it. Your rage over the pretty ideas, all the well-meant lies over the eons, is commendable but irrelevant. Women are like the grass in the meadow, you told them. The men with their tall horses run across it, trampling without concern. The grass rises back up, unhurt, and brings forth new life, and the men wither and die, clutching their empty pride, their standards and petty victories. But you don't listen to your own words. You don't step outside the box they created and you taped yourself into. Why? Do you think that you control them by carrying these false ideas? Do you think you help by your self-inflicted pain? Go wear a hair shirt with a Pope, and discuss pretty ideas over petty anguishes."

Mary quoted:

> "*If to do were as easy as to know what were good to do,*
> *chapels had been churches, and poor men's cottages princes palaces.*
> *It is a good divine that follows his own instructions:*
> *I can easier teach twenty what were good to be done, than be one of the twenty to follow mine own teaching.*[10]

"Rationalization," the Queen laughed, contemptuously. "I love humans. They are such easy prey. That it's hard to do, so you don't have to do it? What would you say to a woman with small children, struggling under the weight of the daily grind? That she doesn't have to do it? Not what you're quoted as saying. So the woman gets stuck with the process of life, the daily petty actions, endless caring and maintenance; and the men get the life plan, with bright projects, clear visions, and praise for the victors at the end point. Who really is life, and who really wins? Process is what matters; it's what keeps next generation alive. Plans outside the process waste away. Who are you letting define your world, Mary?"

The Queen stood up and walked to the edge of the balcony. She twirled around, staring at Mary. "Would you be the good queen in Beowulf, who would not mate with Beowulf because he had been seduced by the demon? She chose a future with no alternative, no chance for growth and revitalization. The demon may have started the train, but the good queen kept it on the tracks. Only death was certain, and destruction. That is the good? The men moan that the shadow always returns. It is because the shadow is what they fear and run from. The shadow is life itself, the daily process of wonder and terror. And you let them define it and turned away from a life defined by women."

"The shadow is the landfill of the self," Mary conceded. "In the myths, the shadow is the monster that has to be overcome; it is the dark thing that comes up from the abyss and confronts you the minute you begin moving down into the unconscious. It is the thing that scares you."

"Yet it is a vault, holding the wonderful unrealized potential within you," the Queen argued. "And it knocks from below, insistently. Who's that down there? The consciousness recoils from this very, very mysterious and frightening knocking. Well, to you it's frightening. I am the shadow, and it's so exciting! And here is what is really bothering you, what you don't want to accept. You have this big mask you wear. People respect you. Hell, they adore you; some of them worship you. You walk along like the Queen of England,

173

formally waving at them as they stare excitedly at you, letting you define the meaning of their lives. But you've outgrown that role. You no longer believe in it yourself. And if you've buried too much of yourself within your shadow, you're going to dry up. Your energies are down there, churning in the dark, fighting with each other, and you are drained each day. There is strength in the depths, in that dark water and powerful current. You have only to open to it."

"The crying Mary of the churches and pictures," Mary snarled. "Telling them to accept everything and don't challenge. What have I done?"

"Eventually, Mary," the Queen advised, bending close to her and slowly drawing a sharp fingernail down Mary's forearm, "that denied, unheeded demon is going to come roaring up into the light. The shadow is the part of you that you don't know want to know is there. The shadow is you as you might have been, you as you might have been if you had fulfilled your unacceptable potential. You've rejected Kali, pushed her away, because that isn't the mask you wear outside. Why? Because society, of course, does not recognize these aspects of your potential self. The shadow is interred down there for a reason; it doesn't fit how you are taught to perceive yourself to be. The shadow is that part of you that includes good and dangerous and disastrous aspects of you."

Mary looked away. She started to speak but stopped, staring out at the night.

"Among the archetypes, the first to turn threatening is the shadow. That's what you're holding down, and holding that down has made you capable of living the life that society wills you to live. But you don't want it anymore, and for what it's worth; I think you're right. The mask is a fraud."

"Has it been all for naught?" Mary moaned.

"Mary!" the Queen laughed. "What a load you carry! What foolishness you believe inside. The creature is what it is. You might as well demand the squid walk across the burning desert as demand the humans act and think as you want. The daily magic has overcome your senses. Thinking doesn't make it so, and it isn't your burden if it can't happen. You know, I'm really not supposed to do this part. You're the one who is supposed to figure things out, but you don't need a nudge, you need a kick. So we'll suspend the traditions this time. Now, you know the woman is equal to the man. Truthfully, you know in your heart that the woman is superior to the man, and so does every other woman. The men think they are better than women, and that conflict will never end. You might as well tell a bull elephant seal that he should let the cows choose mates for themselves. It was what it was-move on. You have to accept that a woman is what she is, not what they define a woman as, and move on. Conflict and change is life. Pleasant cooperation, with everyone's doubts and beliefs reconciled and all buying into the plan, is a dangerous fantasy."

"I feel the growth and creation of life," Mary admitted. "I feel it in myself, and I feel it in my garden. I feel it with my daughter and granddaughter. It is that, I think, that has overwhelmed me. Another girl child thrown into this world, and I wanted it to be so different." She began to cry again.

"The mind of the gods is not shown by their deeds, Mary," the Queen announced. "What you think to guide yourself by is your perception of an event. Your perception is only the shadow, not the full event, and so you can't grasp the intent you seek. Here you sit, beating yourself with a crooked stick for nothing. Maria will bring life into this world and make it a different place. What they seek to impose on her she must accept herself. Not your choice, not your call. And she is either in this world, with all it's greys and muddy colors, and bringing forth life, or not in this world. Are you using a fantasy, a bright, shiny model of a woman to beat yourself with? Your model rejects the emotion and the strength of women for men's flashy ideas of glory and honor. Why would you do that? Male and female are not identical machines produced on an assembly line, some with plugs and some with sockets. Men and women are different universes that intersect."

"Would you prefer I take the form of a warrior out of the ages and offer to mate?" the Queen suggested. "I'm supposed to stimulate your lusts. We can mate, and you can buy some time. You know how the plan works. Or, you can move past." The Queen critically admired herself in a mirror. "This works well for the males. Seemed better for conversation with you than the warrior, which raises all those image issues. But..." The Queen waved her hand. A mighty warrior stood there, resplendent in his power, muscles bulging.

"Arnold," Mary commented appraisingly. "I always liked that outfit. And, hmmm..." The loincloth dropped. "I am impressed. And I've seen a lot of those over the eons."

"Ugh. Mate, woman," he grunted. "First offer."

"Ah, perhaps not," Mary demurred. "But I'm flattered by the offer."

The Queen reappeared. "I'm offended," she sniffed. "That usually gets them going."

"Oh, I wouldn't say it didn't get me going," Mary smiled. "But a simple mating and quick satisfaction won't change the shadow chasing me."

"And you still sit in self-imposed anguish," the Queen countered. "'Because I have called and ye refused...I also will laugh at your calamity; I will mock when your fear cometh; when your fear cometh as desolation, and your destruction cometh as a whirlwind; when distress and anguish cometh upon you...for the turning away of the simple shall slay them, and the prosperity of fools shall destroy them.'"

"So," Mary confided. "I've fallen for their stories. The horrors of life rejected for a fantasy of control. The little straight-line ideas are the corruption, not the messy and complex organic. In all the myths, deep down, the woman's force is the ultimate power. That's why they feared you, and Morgana, and all the other powerful women who keep life going. That's why they never get it when life tears apart their little worlds, their pretty plans."

"I hate plans. Everyone's plans. Schemers trying to make life obey them. I just try and help them understand how pathetic their attempts to control life really are," the Queen laughed. "And I enjoy my work."

"That's just like humans," Mary agreed. "Put the ugly truths in a freak's mouth, because you can ignore the truth that way."

The Queen waved her hand and became the Joker in his long purple coat and confident smile. "It's the schemers who put you where you are. You were a schemer, Mary. You, Jesus, and Lucifer all had plans. Look where the plans got you. Paul, for example."

Mary winced.

"And life just does what it does best," the Joker continued. "Life took your plans and turned them on themselves. You thought you could make a plan ignoring life; you thought that if everyone agrees on the plan, then it's fine. When there is group buy-in, endorsing the plan, then nobody panics when things go according to plan. Even when the plan is disgusting."

"You're not going to tell me how you got your scars, are you?" Mary whispered, carefully touching his face.

"No, Mary," the Joker answered, holding his hand over hers on his face. "You know how I got these scars. You're just hiding it from yourself. What is the question the Fisher King, well, Queen in this case, waits to be asked?"

"The wounded know the question, and the rescuer does not," Mary offered. "You have told me that."

"What I've told you means nothing," the Joker demanded, impatient. "Listen you do; hear, you not. I, ah, freelance a bit," noticing her quizzical look. He moved a step away from her, but still held her hand. "Mate?" he asked. "This is the second offer. Have to keep to the formalities."

"Tempting," Mary answered. "I actually like you better than the warrior. I've mated with enough of them over the centuries. Always the same. Ugh, ugh, and then sending me off to get some food. Mating with the twisted rejected parts of my psyche would be more fun than that. But no, that's a plan that doesn't work. It's not the scars," as she carefully touched his face again.

"That's good," the Joker commented, zipping up his pants.

"What did you say in the movie?" Mary mused. "'I know the truth now, and there's no going back. You've changed things, forever.'"

"And your guilt, your heavy load, carried to fit in? To be what they think of as a woman, and to fit into their world? Don't you talk like them. You're not like them, even if you'd like to be," the Joker snarled. He stood up, walked to the edge of the balcony, and waved his hand.

"Mate?" a voice demanded. "This is the third offer."

Mary gasped and cried, "Cali's father, alive. I failed you," she sobbed. "Paul took you and tormented you, and I didn't stop him."

"You couldn't have," he replied. "It was a trap. You knew it, I knew it. Nothing to be done. Expected, really. Male consorts of the queen rarely have long lives. But it was worth it. Cali is wonderful, and Maria is a joy."

They stood quietly for a few minutes.

"So," he asked, walking over and touching her shoulder gently. "Do you wish to mate, and buy the temporary peace? This is my third offer, and the last. After this, you must merge into the chaos of life. You may survive. You may not. Few do."

"No, I cannot," Mary answered, holding him. "A final kiss, though?"

"It would be cruel not to," he admitted, and they kissed. He turned into mist, and blew into the corner of the balcony, reforming as the evil Queen.

"So what is the question, Mary?" the Queen commanded. "It is at the end now."

"I accepted their world, and walked away from myself," Mary confessed. "I took their pretty words to heart, and I ignored what I felt. Bought into their standards of failure and success, and denied what true success is. I lost the message in the symbols. The message is the spirit, and when the symbol is taken to be the fact, you've mistaken the message. I, Kali, thinking I have to go to Haridwar in order to get to the source of the Ganges. How blind I've been! Their small, petty worlds are failure, and the greater life outside, the wonder full of life, is success."

"That was a mortal sin," the Queen agreed. "All the more deadly for having meant right. You've paid over the centuries. No penance required."

"Have mercy on me, a sinner," Mary begged, her head bowed.

"I absolve you from your sins in the name of Life and the Tree," the mother goddess pronounced, making the sign of the Tree over her. "It is you who must absolve yourself from what you feel inside."

"Introduce a little anarchy, and everything becomes chaos," Mary laughed to the sky. She turned and smiled at the Queen. "So, make friends with your monsters, Hal would say. Buy them a beer, have a long talk."

"A martini," the Queen insisted. "Shaken, not stirred. A classy bar, overlooking New York. Let's treat ourselves well here. So: it's absorption by and of the mother goddess and the life force, is it? In order to lose your commitment to this little life you were leading, you must be dismembered and opened to the transcendent. As painful as it sounds, actually. Every new life begins with the death of the old and the transfiguration into the new. Hopefully."

"That's encouraging, I think," Mary answered. "Jung said to reject all projections. Don't identify the men you meet with your anima projection. Don't identify yourself with your persona projection. To release all projections and ideals. And he also said, don't think so much! What did Campbell say? People talk about trying to learn the meaning of life. Life has no meaning. What's the meaning of a flower? What we are looking for is to experience life. And we push away life by naming, translating, and classifying every experience that comes to us. Time to stop, I think."

Mary stepped close to the Queen. "I name you friend, and welcome you." She held her hand out, and the dark Queen grasped it. They stood for a few moments, and then they dissolved into swirling clouds of mist that combined, eddied, and flowed. Lightning flashed in the eddies, and, after some time, reformed into Mary. But not quite as she had been.

Mary closed her eyes, and the world around her suddenly was flush with life. A rain forest from ancient times, so rich with life and power. Wonder full, she thought, relaxed and fully happy for the first time in many, many long years.

THE CELEBRATION OF THE RITE OF BAPTISM

Mary walked into the room, the walls now hung with ancient tapestries. There was a crowd waiting for her. Cali, Hal, and Maria; Goth Girl, Lungorthin, and their children, Lucretia was holding Donna Juana. Behind them were the happy friends, smiling. Cali looked intently at Mary when she walked in and then smiled, relieved, when Mary smiled at her. Hal watched Mary carefully for a few seconds, and then nodded to himself.

Mary greeted them, "Blessed be God and the Tree, which he has given us."

They replied, "And blessed be his world and the Tree, now and forever. Amen."

Mary announced, "The Candidates for Holy Baptism will now be presented."

Cali answered, "I present Maria English to receive the Sacrament of Baptism."

Goth Girl answered, "I present Durion and Cinnamon to receive the Sacrament of Baptism."

Lucretia answered, "I present Donna Juana Linacol to receive the sacrament of Baptism:"

Mary then asked, "Will you be responsible for seeing that the child you present is brought up within the Tree of Life?"

The parents and godparents answered, "I will, with God's help."

Mary asked, "Will you by your prayers and witness help this child to grow into their full stature within the Tree of Life?"

The parents and godparents answered, "I will, with God's help."

Then Mary demanded, "Do you renounce the wickedness that denies the Tree?"

The parents and godparents answered, "I renounce it."

Mary demanded, "Do you renounce the evil powers of this world, which deny and destroy the creatures of God created through the Tree?"

The parents and godparents answered, "I renounce them."

Mary demanded, "Do you renounce all false ideas that draw you from the love of the Tree and God?"

The parents and godparents answered, "I renounce them."

Mary asked, "Do you embrace the Tree of Life, which is the clay through which we are worked in this life, and the symbol that God gave us for our life now and everlasting?"

The parents and godparents answered, "I do."

Mary asked, "Do you put your whole trust in his grace and love and the Tree of Life?"

The parents and godparents answered, "I do."

Mary asked, "Do you promise to follow and live within the Tree of Life as given to us by the Lord?"

The parents and godparents answered, "I do."

Mary asked to all present: "Will you who witness these vows do all in your power to support these persons in their lives in the Tree?"

All answered, "I do."

Mary prayed: "Grant, O Lord, that all who are baptized into the Life of the Tree may live in the power of Life and within the Tree of Life, now and forever."

All: "Amen."

Mary proclaimed: "We thank you, Almighty God, for the gift of water, which nourishes and fills the Tree of Life, now and forever. We thank you, Father, for the water of Baptism. In it we are merged within the Tree during our life and at our death. By it we share in the Life everlasting within the Tree. Through it we are reborn by the power of Life. Therefore in joyful obedience to your Will and the Tree of Life, we bring into his fellowship those who come to the Tree in faith, baptizing them in the Name of the Father and the Tree."

Mary then touched the water. "Now sanctify this water, we pray you, by the power of the Tree, that those who here are cleansed from sin and born again may continue forever in the risen Life of the Tree. To You and to the Tree, be all honor and glory, now and forever. Amen."

Mary looked at Cali and motioned for her to step forward. "We are met to bring this child into the Life within the Tree. Who names this child?"

Cali stepped forward. "I name this child Maria Cali English."

Mary nodded and motioned to Cali. Cali walked to the font and stood in front of it. Maria was peering at Mary, thinking, This is grandmother, but something is different.

Mary dipped a cup into the font to fill it with water, then raised the cup over the font.

"I baptize thee In the Name of Life and the Tree. Amen." She poured some of the water on Maria's head, and Maria howled.

Mary touched Maria's head, and she quieted.

Mary motioned to Goth Girl, and she and Lungorthin stepped forward, each holding a struggling child.

Mary announced, "We are met to bring this child into the Life within the Tree. Who names this child?"

Goth Girl answered, "I name this child Cinnamon Eviria Lungorthin."

Mary nodded and motioned to Goth Girl. Goth Girl walked to the font and stood in front of it. Cinnamon was suddenly quiet, peering at Mary.

Mary dipped a cup into the font to fill it with water, then raised the cup over the font.

"I baptize thee In the Name of Life and the Tree. Amen." She poured some of the water on Cinnamon's head, and Cinnamon cried.

Mary touched Cinnamon's head, and she quieted.

Mary announced, "We are met to bring this child into the Life within the Tree. Who names this child?"

Lungorthin answered, "I name this child Durion Morgoth Lungorthin."

Mary nodded and motioned to Lungorthin, who walked to the font and stood in front of it. Durion was staring intently at Mary.

Mary dipped a cup into the font to fill it with water, then raised the cup over the font.

"I baptize thee In the Name of Life and the Tree. Amen." She poured some of the water on Durion's head. He closed his eyes as the water washed over him, and then smiled.

Mary stroked Durion's head gently.

Mary looked at Lucretia and motioned for her to step forward. "We are met to bring this child into the Life within the Tree. Who names this child?"

Lucretia stepped forward. "I name this child Donna Juana Linacol."

Mary nodded and motioned to Lucretia. Lucretia walked to the font and stood in front of it. Donna was peering at Mary, undecided.

Mary dipped a cup into the font to fill it with water, then raised the cup over the font.

"I baptize thee In the Name of Life and the Tree. Amen." She poured some of the water on Donna's head, and she cried.

Mary touched Donna's head, and she quieted.

Mary announced, "Let us pray. Father, we thank you that by water you have bestowed and raised these your servants to the new life of grace within your Tree of Life. Sustain them, O Lord. Give them an inquiring and discerning heart, the courage to will and to persevere, a spirit to know and to love you, and the gift of joy and wonder in all your works. Amen."

Then Mary went from child to child, placing her hand on each child's head and marking on their forehead the sign of the Tree. She promised each child, "You are sealed by Baptism and marked as the Tree's own forever. Amen."

Mary then prayed, "Merciful God, grant that this person be born again into the Tree that thou have created and nourished."

"Amen," all responded.

"Grant that all things belonging to the Spirit may live and grow in them," Mary prayed.

"Amen."

"Grant that they may have power and strength to have victory, and to triumph in this world."

"Amen."

"Almighty Ever-living God, who is everywhere and shows thy presence through the life of this world, sanctify this Water for and to the rebirth of this child into the Tree, and grant that these thy Servants now to be baptized therein may receive the fullness of thy grace, and ever remain in the number of thy faithful children."

"Amen."

Mary then announced, "Dearly beloved, none can enter into Life in the Tree except that they be regenerated and born anew of Water; and Dost thou," Mary asked of the parents and godparents, "for this child and for yourself, accept the world in its fullness, in its wonder and horror, so that thou may grow within this world, within the Life as created by God?"

All responded "I do."

Mary stated, "Let us welcome the newly baptized."

"We receive you into the household of God and his Tree. Confess the faith of the Tree, proclaim Life, and share with us in the life eternal within the Tree.

Mary prayed, "The peace of the Tree be always with you."

All responded, "And also with you."

There was a pause.

"Lunch, I think, is traditional," Mary announced, smiling.

In the garden, the buds formed on the Tree as the top branches began to push against the glass between the Tree and the world outside.

CHAPTER 7. THE TREE OF LIFE

NIGHTMARE

"Can you handle Maria for a second, Dad?" Cali asked Lucifer.

"Sure," he replied, confidently. Doubtful, actually, he thought. Childcare hasn't been my thing. They are so tiny! I'm afraid to touch her, she's so fragile.

Cali was in the corner of the room, picking up clothes and toys. Mary was standing by Lucifer, watching his unease with considerable pleasure.

"Here," he offered Maria, reaching down to pick up a toy. "Ouch," he exclaimed as he caught his finger on a nail. It wasn't a deep cut, but it bled profusely. "Damn. Mary, do you have something for this?"

Mary nodded and ran to the bathroom. Cali started walking over, staring at his finger.

"No!" he shouted as Maria suddenly popped his finger into her mouth. Her eyes got wide and she screamed, then passed out.

"OHHHH!" Cali screamed, staring in shock.

Mary came rushing back in. She quickly checked Maria. "She's breathing—what happened?"

"I cut my finger earlier today," Cali mumbled, "and put it in my mouth. Maria saw me. She put Lucifer's finger in her mouth. Then she screamed and passed out."

"Grendel," Mary murmured, grimly. "Still, it should be weak, and she's your child." Mary sighed. "She's so young that it's hard to help her. Here" Mary picked Maria up. "Into the bedroom." They rushed into the bedroom, Lucifer following, having ripped a piece of cloth from his shirt to stop his finger from bleeding.

"My fault," he sobbed, kneeling by the bed. "My fault."

"No," Cali objected, through her tears. "No fault." But he could not be consoled.

Later, Aliston sat by him, her arm around him.

LUCIFER & GRENDELINE

Midnight, two days later. Lucifer leaned against the edge of the bed, watching Maria breathing, occasionally crying and twitching in her coma.

He fell into a deep sleep of exhaustion and despair. In his dreams, he sat in a dark place. Waist-deep in ice. Frozen to the bone. Helpless, he thought. How I really feel.

183

"Nice place here," a woman's voice sneered out of the dark. "Why is it that humans always pick bleak places to represent their despair? You can be just as despairing on a bright, sandy beach, and then I get to enjoy the sunshine. I tell you, it isn't all fun and games being a demonic force in your mind. Oh, I'm glad to be the wild, but maybe a vacation occasionally? A nice hotel, some good food, a night on the town? You think that would be too much? No. It's always the rocky plain and thorn trees. How boring."

The woman sat down next to Lucifer. Beautiful, long, blondish hair, with touches of red. "Been a long time," she observed, stroking his arm.

"Aphrodite. The goddess of love, the bright hope and the future. How cruel, as I sit here, fearing my granddaughter's death and my responsibility."

"I'm supposed to make it unpleasant," she declared sweetly. "I'd do the spider, but it's doesn't emotionally engage as well. I personally like the spider." Her fingers suddenly turned into steel claws, and then back. "But not really productive, I don't think. And it takes a real wacko to mate with the spider."

She brushed the dirt off the rock, watching him closely. "Where are the multiple personalities?" she wondered, glancing around. "The others had these annoying little people running around creating distractions."

"Multiple personalities?" Lucifer replied. "There are hundreds over the eons. Most of them can't figure out why there is a problem. The other creatures—squids, raptors, jellyfish, the lions—they all think like the wild, and can't see an issue. A division in the self, you might say. The little human ones voted and tabled the resolution to committee."

"Why so serious?" she teased. "You know, a serious philosophical work could be written entirely of jokes." She suddenly had a party hat on and was blowing a noisemaker, laughing. "Handling your problems doesn't have to be all that gloom and doom. Never stay up on the barren heights of cleverness, but come down into the green valleys of silliness.[1] I have academic support for the position. You want the footnote reference?"

He looked at her, and could not conceal his despair.

"Fine," she sniffed, pouting as she pulled the party hat off. "I've never been much of a stand-up comedian, or really, a stand up, for that matter." She giggled and stroked her hair. "So, I make you an offer. Mate, certainly your favorite lust, next to that stupid running you keep doing. Really, sweating should be reserved for other things." She quickly touched up her lipstick in a mirror, and then looked at him again, smiling. "You get the conquest of the woman—of me, all woman! The mating power of the male, and that control over the world, so important to a man, that you seek so desperately. What say you?"

"Only the appearance of control," Lucifer answered. "Like making a deal with the aliens in the spaceship. The spawn grows in you, and then it's worse when it emerges. No, it's a charming offer, but I'll pass."

"First offer," she noted cheerfully. "You know the drill. Three offers, and then you have to merge. It's not nice, merging," her eyes hardening. "Not like pretty lovemaking, soft sighs and whispers, and that release at the end. And you fear what you have done. Actually, you haven't done a thing, just random bad chance. But that's not you, is it?"

"No," she announced, standing up. "You, the power of the wild, life on earth. 'Tom Bombadil is the Master. No one has ever caught old Tom walking in the forest, wading in the water, leaping on the hill-tops under light and shadow. He has no fear.'[11] Did you see yourself in that passage? Probably not. You've got to know what play you're in at any one time. You've got to be able to separate your sense of yourself—your ego—from the self you show the rest of the world—your persona. You above all should know that one of the great dangers is to identify yourself with your persona. 'Nothing is so difficult as not deceiving oneself.'[3] I liked Wittgenstein's writings. He was a wise man, and he had an enormous schwanzstucker." She giggled. "Yeah," catching Lucifer's look. "I read him in the original German. So take your blonde jokes and put them, well, you know where. I've heard them all."

"Then I won't have to tell them so slowly," Lucifer replied, smiling despite himself.

"I know a blonde joke," she snapped. "The devil and a blonde are negotiating for her soul. When they are done, she has her soul, a diamond necklace, and alimony."

"Been there, done that," Lucifer agreed. "I never really grasped the whole soul thing that Paul was selling anyhow. If they were born corrupt, wasn't I supposed to get their souls without doing anything? All that sneaking about, trying to trick them out of something that was already mine...didn't make a lot of sense, actually. If I opened a pawnshop to buy souls, the line would be halfway across the state in a day. Then all that taking care of them for eternity? Can you imagine the utility bill? ConEd would eat me alive! Talk about a host of soulless demons. On top of that, there would be endless labor grievances and negotiations with the demon's union, and the land lease with all those automatic inflation adjustments. No, it never seemed to make a lot of sense."

"Didn't make a lot of sense to me, either," she admitted. "But there were a lot of hot buttons in the concept. Press the button, people jump, don't think. Paul does have a knack for getting those people to jump—you have to give him that."

Lucifer rubbed his temples, grimacing, then relaxed and smiled at her. "Maybe you are right," he offered. "All my hot buttons were pressed today, and I can't think. It's just that it's so important to me."

"The world is independent of your will," she scolded. "But you really don't believe it, do you? Maybe that is a big part of your problem. When one is frightened of the truth, you don't have an inkling of the whole truth. You want the quote in German? It's longer, but that's the essence. And here you sit," she scoffed, looking down her nose at him. "Pathetic—you bought Dante's horse-and-pony show, fell for it hook, line and sinker. You lower yourself to borrow their design for Hell, and you claim to be the master of the wild? Pitiful. You mixed your role with what you are. Look, no matter what you choose to do in life, you are playing a role, and don't take it too damned seriously."

Lucifer sat, silent, head down.

She glared at him. "You know what your problem is? The world has changed, and you have not. A middle-aged man trying to be a young man, not moving on. You remember the old world, where female society was wholly focused on the process of creation and maintenance of life. That was a woman's function; women were in the role of center and continuator of nature. The man was concerned with preparing a world for the women to create life into, and support that life. These are two quite different roles, and frankly, men had a lot of free time. After you pushed the predators back, and did a little hunting, you had a lot of time on your hands. So, the male had to have something serious to do. There you were, on a big horse with a sword, building empires. For men, it's the ranking, the pecking order, what Jane Goodall called 'Alpha Male,' that matters. And you can't move away from that, can you? Little boy made a mistake, pink cloud has now turned to gray..." she hummed, watching him intently.

"I can give you that feeling back. I will make you master," she offered, leaning close to him and letting the hem of her blouse fall open. "How much more Alpha male could you be? All the other men would thump their chests when you tell your story, like they used to around the open fires on the veldt. They are life, too." She smiled as his eyes went to her breasts. "You can have that pleasure of control that you need so badly. Only a thought, and it will be. And you are good, you know? Today, it's just like people that, just when the mechanics of reproduction are so vastly improved, there are fewer and fewer people who know how the music should be played. But you're a virtuoso, I know."

"And a more attractive offer is difficult to imagine," Lucifer admitted. "But it doesn't handle today's problem. Or the problems that have stacked up like cordwood recently. So confident, I was. So sure of myself. And you're right; it's a world that has changed, in many, many ways. With all respect and courtesy, I thank you, but no."

"That was the second," she noted, more seriously. "Once more will I offer, and no more. You know," as she stood up and began idly walking around, "you listen but you do not hear. In Job, there was the adversary that everyone just hated on sight. You all saw it as the classic good/evil, striving towards that ultimate conflict. You always do, foolish men. Listen, I was the adversary in the poem, and you know why? Because I wanted you to think, which, of course, you didn't. Jump right over the question posed right into the tar baby, and start punching. You always do.

"Did you think for a second that this new civilization structure was ignoring the nature of the creature? Did you meditate for a second on the divorce between Life and structure that you were so excited about? So proud, so excited about your toy, separate and above the wild and life, but the wild and life are what create the power. Your fancy separation into good/evil is the problem, not the solution. Always the same battle against the bewitchment of intelligence by means of language, which you always lose. Learn a word, be so proud, and wear it on your T-shirt. You never see past the symbol. And here you are, stuck in another's symbols, a poor, helpless man. Pride? The fighter, the warrior, the tall conqueror on his war steed with his sharp sword: he fears merging with life, the loss of his little role. Don't you find that sad?"

"A man will be imprisoned in a room with a door that's unlocked and opens inward as long as it does not occur to him to pull rather than push," Lucifer announced, standing up, the ice breaking away from him. "There, that's better" shaking off the pieces of ice stuck to him. He stood tall, and stretched, looking out at the horizon, glowing faintly with the first signs of the dawn.

"What do you want?" she demanded. "A sign?" She stood with her hands on her hips. "You were told what he said! 'The new day waits for the morning star to show the way, by the way.' You might call that a sign: most would call that a billboard lit by all the colors of the rainbow. But no, you fear what it would take to do that. You sit on your fat ass—sorry, your lean running ass—and call for the world to be other than it is."

"Words have power, don't they?" Lucifer replied, pacing restlessly. "They let me control things, understand things. But they have an invisible power I don't see, a dark power, because the understanding they give me also binds me to their definitions and their world. Holding to the words is freezing myself in that world. Open to a new understanding, let the walls drop to a larger world, and my control is gone, I stand naked in a cold wind. So I weaken, and wrap myself in the warm words against the cold, thinking that better the old understanding, holding to the fetters I am comfortable with. The words are a prison that I create for myself. You are right. Everything you say is right—except the idea to mate," he quickly added as she smiled sweetly at him, batting her eyelashes. He stopped and looked around thoughtfully. He was surrounded by rubble-strewn mounds of ancient, dead settlements, tangled dunes, and abandoned canal levees, empty of vegetation, a rough, wind-eroded wasteland. "The Tigris-Euphrates," he sighed, "as it is now. The richest lands in the world became this wasteland."

"You let Paul build this fantasy world in which the human structures were more powerful than life," she accused him. "You bought it, all those eons ago. The poison of the structures leached into the life force, which weakened. As the life force faded and the garden went to ruin as you all withdrew into this fantasy world that you made out of bright ideas and sharp corners. And then, when it was clear what his game was, and that he was better at the game than you, he drew a picture of you, frozen in the ice deep in the earth, away from life and the sun. The life force, frozen in the ice, like oil in the deep, impotent, trapped energy. Why? You told yourself you didn't care about what Paul did or said, but you listened. Hear and do not listen, you might say. And his message crawled into your mind, and the life energy froze."

"Dante was so proud of his work," Lucifer snarled. "The buttons were all in place. Once you put the button in people's minds, well, when you push the button, they don't think. Paul pushed the buttons, tied to that nightmare of an Assyrian court that Paul loved so much, and people bought it."

"Of course, if they didn't buy it, they got an appointment with the Inquisition," she pointed out. "That was a nice circle. The torments were ordained by Paul's god, and his Inquisition got to dole the punishment out on this earth, for the good of the sinners, of course. And all of the punishment he meted out to them was to keep them safe from you, safe from life! What a joke. Oh, Paul can sell a story, you have to give him that. And his enforcers, his shepherds solemnly protecting the flock from demons? Celibate priests, with their nonsense shining ideas and their twisted lusts, standing over naked women in dungeons. It's always naked women in dungeons!" she shouted, furious. "That poor daughter-in-law of yours! I was so proud of what she did."

Lucifer looked at her, surprised.

"Well, I'm the goddess of love, aren't I?" she snapped. "And your daughter-in-law, she turned their little game upside down. She took it back to them, didn't she? It's rutting, in the end," she snickered and laughed. "A joke! I was impressed, and I've seen it all. Done it all, too." She smiled wistfully. "And what do they do? They swarm around her to destroy her for what was forced on her. AHHH! There are days I long for a sharp sword," she swore, flexing her fingers. "Sorry. Out of type, I guess. Sometimes I want to kill them all. Maybe Ares was right."

She stopped for a minute, brushing her hair back off her eyes. "The Inquisition! The priests burned the people for their money. All because they felt dirty about sex and life. They way they did it, they should feel dirty.

"And speaking of sex," she declared, dropping all her clothing, a bright beam of light illuminating her naked body, "I offer for the third time. Mate, and cover over all this doubt and despair. Sit in the seat of control—as it were—and feel yourself the conqueror again. A deity is a personification of a spiritual power and deities who are not recognized become demonic; they become dangerous. If you don't communicate with the shadow and the demons' messages go unheeded, they will break through. Usually at the worst possible time, and then there will literally be hell to pay. Well, Duh! You should know that better than anyone," she teased. "Communicate by mating, touch the deity. Everybody wants happiness; nobody wants pain. Do this."

Lucifer stared lustfully at her. "You," he finally murmured, "are the most amazing thing I've ever seen. To a man, every woman is a new flower of life, but you're the whole meadow." He looked away reluctantly. "It would be the wrong thing, because it would be a lie. There are far too many well-meant lies already. Although," he asked, looking back at her, "would you mind, if I, ah, well, take some mental pictures of this scene...for future, ah, reference?"

"I am the dark, the power outside, and that was three," she pronounced solemnly, a stern woman warrior standing as tall as he. "There is no way back now, except by merging with life. See, you can't have a rainbow without a little rain." She giggled, and then was serious again. "So film me for your memories in 35mm CinemaScope, if it makes you happy. But let's get to the fine print. It's, well," she mumbled, balancing her reading glasses on her nose and leafing through a very large book that appeared on her lap. "Sorry about the glasses—forgot to put perfect vision in the immortality rules. Growth; hmmm, death; hmmm; Ah! Palingenesia. Here it is."

Lucifer was staring at her, completely confused.

"Palingenesia. A recurrence of birth, to nullify the accumulated small deaths. 'For it is by means of our own victories, if we are not regenerated, that the work of the Nemesis is wrought: doom breaks from the shell of our very virtue. Peace then is a snare; war is a snare; change is a snare; permanence a snare. When our day is come for the victory of death, death closes in; there is nothing we can do, except be crucified and resurrected; dismembered totally, and then reborn.'[12] Hmm, seems clear. Nasty about the crucified and dismembered," she added, looking over the top of her glasses at him. "Maybe I should have mentioned that before the third offer. Silly me." She snapped the book shut, which vanished and tossed the glasses away. "Foolish you have been," she scolded. "Doing what you knew how to do, even though you knew it was the wrong thing to do. Years of looking for your keys under the light, when they were lost in the dark. And it's the dark you must go into and absorb for the key to the garden."

She sat down on a rock, which glowed white as she sat on it. "Every new life begins with a confession," she advised thoughtfully.

"Forgive me, for I have sinned," Lucifer begged, kneeling down, his despair over Maria suddenly overcoming him.

"Have you?" she demanded. "Would you even know your sin if it was sitting in front of you? What were you mumbling to yourself earlier? 'This is the excellent foppery of the world, that, when we are sick in fortune—often the surfeit of our own behavior—we make guilty of our disasters the sun, the moon, and the stars.'[5] So, thesis: I'm above the world, outside, and in control. Anti-thesis: I'm the cause of all the problems, I alone, secure in my control of the world. Have you learned nothing? Thesis and anti-thesis are the same. The same pride, the same stepping outside, above life. The same small stories."

"I wasn't blaming the world for my mistakes," Lucifer defended.

"Actually," she agreed, "Few would even accept the responsibility for their errors. Point granted. But accepting the responsibility implies you had control. Relinquish that control, and dissolve yourself into the Tree, the power of life. Find the synthesis you seek. It is there, in the power of life you stepped away from before. You pretended the human structures were above Life, but you knew in your heart the error you had all made."

Lucifer stared at the rocky ground. "My strength is my wound, isn't it? If everything you have is a hammer, then it all looks like a nail. I hate to say pride is my sin, because, well, that raises all kinds of issues with the nonsense Paul has put out about me, but there's a sin of pride there. Pride makes you pretend to be what you think you are."

"Pride is such a small, human word, measured only within the group. The Fisher King sits wounded, and the land is desolate," she cried out. "The Waste Land is that territory of wounded people, those living inauthentic, broken lives, and they live in this blighted land. What is the question that will heal the king, and bring the life back?"

"It's like trying to open a safe with a combination lock; each little adjustment of the dials seems to achieve nothing. Only when everything is in place does the door open," Lucifer muttered, rubbing his temples again.

"Don't overthink it, buster," she advised. "The human way of ignoring the problem is to make it more complex and then rationalize it's insolvable."

"I've always been the male," Lucifer confided. "The hunter. It's all projects. A clean beginning, actions, victory or defeat at the end. Simple, but that really isn't life, is it?"

She watched him, listening intently.

"Stories are what humans make out of the world, but the world isn't stories. The world is events, that we freeze into bright pictures, hung on the wall in frames for clarity. Life is process, it's events, it goes on; it's all the small details every day," Lucifer mused.

"Tell me something that a woman doesn't know," she replied. "Look, my nails are chipped and I just got them done. Sorry, I digress."

"But men don't want to know it," he continued. "It isn't as satisfying to just do and do, with no end points. Maybe it was easier for the other creatures, now that I think about it. Probably we were fooled by the pattern trick wired in the human mind, imposing on random events a pattern that starts and stops. It has been productive, no question. But everything has its limits. The stories rejected the monsters; they had to. Because the monsters were the background against which the pretty moral would shine, and so the story exulted only the lie. I ignored the power of Life, the power of the Tree. I, the wild! Which has been the base for eons of mistakes and the fertile ground for the parasites, who wormed themselves between man and their Gods."

"Because I have called and ye refused...I also will laugh at your calamity; I will mock when your fear cometh; when your fear cometh as desolation, and your destruction cometh as a whirlwind; when distress and anguish cometh upon you...for the turning away of the simple shall slay them, and the prosperity of fools shall destroy them," she quoted. "I read it in the old Hebrew script, in case you were wondering." She glowered at him as he started to speak.

"I question not the goddess," Lucifer vowed, raising his hands in surrender. "Another blonde joke will never cross my lips. Except the one about..." He caught her look and quickly stopped.

"We already covered telling them slowly. Move on, move on, nothing to see here," she scowled.

"I accepted their words as meaning, without thinking," he confessed. "That was my sin and failure. Given inspiration, given power, I ignored it for a pretty picture."

"The hardest thing to see is what is in front of your eyes. Goethe," she quipped.

"One often makes a remark and only later sees how true it is," Lucifer replied wryly. "Maybe I'll go back to the twelve-step program for pithy sayings."

"There are these two young fish swimming along, and they happen to meet an older fish swimming the other way, who nods at them and says, 'Morning, boys, how's the water?' The two young fish swim on for a bit, and then eventually one of them looks over at the other and goes, 'What the hell is water?'" she commented.

"Now, the mind that thinks, the eyes that see, they fall into the concepts and daily tasks that we become bound up in and don't let the life energy flow through. Embracing the structures, I ignored the disease that they carried, and it has spread through me. I'm frozen in Paul's small structures that deny life, aren't I? The life within is frozen, and the land is wasted. I lied to myself that I was doing the right thing. I wounded myself by the lie. I compromised my honor and integrity. I forgot that Life flows through and the words mean nothing; they are only tools of the parasites." He sat for a moment and then looked at her. "We cannot borrow God. We must effect His new incarnation from within ourselves."

"Do I have a witness!" Aphrodite shouted, waving her arms.

"Forgive me, great mother, for I have sinned," Lucifer prayed.

"I absolve you from your sins in the name of Life and the Tree," she proclaimed, making the sign of the Tree above him. "It is you who must absolve yourself from what you feel inside."

"So, make friends with your monsters, Hal would say. Buy them a beer, have a long talk?" Lucifer offered.

"Wine," Aphrodite demanded. "I have a friend who has the best. Sitting on the beach by the Aegean, watching the sun go down. And, remember" as she stroked his hair, "be kind to yourself. The strong pretend they don't need it, but they do."

She stopped and looked to the east, the rays of the sun beaming over the horizon, the bright blue sky melting the inky blackness. "So, it's absorption by and of the mother goddess and the life force, is it? The serpent sheds its skin to be born again as the moon sheds its shadow to be born again. Life and consciousness, life energy and consciousness, engaged in the field of time, of birth and death."

"Words," Lucifer mused. "It's the experience of the new that matters. Well, I name you friend, and welcome you."

Lucifer held his hand out to her and Aphrodite took it. They stood for a few moments, and then they dissolved into swirling clouds of mist that combined, eddied, and flowed. Lightning flashed in the eddies, and after some time, reformed into Lucifer. But not quite as he had been.

Lucifer closed his eyes, and he saw the Tigris and Euphrates as they had been, rich and lush, the flowers blooming and the rushes gently waving with the soft breeze, filled with the sweet smell of the Tree. Life restored.

LUCIFER & ALISTON

He opened his eyes, and Maria's bed was empty. His heart went to his throat.

Aliston quickly bent down to him. "She woke up an hour ago," she whispered. "As cheerful as ever and she is merrily playing in the nursery. Although she had a glint in her eye that looked like trouble, I have to say. You looked like you needed the rest, so I let you sleep."

"Did you think the mother goddess would hurt the little girl?" the voice inside him mocked. "We're all waiting until she's thirteen, and then you'll pay a penance."

He wiped his eyes, and then, looking up, smiled at Aliston. Then looked at her differently, puzzled.

Aliston smiled at him, and nodded. She rummaged through her purse and pulled out her company nametag. "Aliston, it says," she pointed out, tracing the letters with her hand. She giggled, tossing her blonde hair. "Got it?"

"Got it, my lady," Lucifer answered.

"Mating in real life doesn't have the consequences of the internal conflicts," Aliston giggled. "It has its own consequences, but there's always something."

He pulled her to him and kissed her and she passionately kissed him back. After a few minutes he stood up, pulling her up also. "I hear shouting- let's go see what Maria's tearing apart. And then, well, perhaps we need some rest, having sat by this bed for so long?" he teased.

She raised her eyebrows. "That's a pretty pitiful attempt at deception, but I'm good with that, my prince," she purred. They walked out of the room.

THE TREE

In the garden, the seeds ripened and the apples took form. Hal, when he stepped into the room, stood in amazement, then ran to tell the others.

"So what do we have?" Lucifer asked, astonished, staring at the grown tree.

"The Tree of Life recreated," Mary laughed joyfully. "Here" as she carefully plucked an apple, "is the fruit of the tree. It is the final judgment come at the end of days. It gives long life, and knowledge beyond good and evil for those who embrace it. But it is death for those who cannot leave behind the old world. All must weigh their deeds in the scales, each and every one by themselves. It shall pronounce a final judgment on the living and on the dead who walk amongst us. You might say an apple a day keeps the doctor away." She held it up, admiring it. "One way or the other. "

"I don't have to be sacrificed again for this ritual, will I?" Jesus interrupted, looking a little worried. "All that Osiris dismemberment and scattering around for the new life was a little tiring, really."

"You're just no fun," Mary teased. "Boring! Fine, have it your way. Be boring."

"Ugh, that sounded nasty!" Mrs. Ostein offered, looking up at Jesus. "I like you as you are." She moved closer to him.

Jesus smiled and put his arm around her.

Mary raised her eyebrows. "And so?" Mary asked. "Am I going to have to revise the Christmas letter?"

Mrs. Ostein stared at her, puzzled. "What?"

"Oh, the usual letter: 'Our son, your savior, has saved everyone from eternal damnation this year, healing the sick, afflicting the priests, water into wine, loaves, fishes, etc.; and his brother James lives in the basement attending community college...'" Mary rattled off.

"I always loved that one," Mrs. Ostein laughed, hugging Jesus, who looked embarrassed. "Well, perhaps some changes..."

"Move on, move on, nothing to see here," Jesus interjected. "Focus on why we are here. Back to the apples and the Tree."

He stopped and thought for a minute. "Okay, a blessing," he announced. "Blessed are those who hear and follow his word, that they may have the right to the Tree of Life, and may enter through the gates into the city. This Tree, wondrous and supernatural, is something God insisted on protecting. After humans were denied the Tree, for having turned their back on Life, God designated two of His finest to safeguard the path until the appointed time, when again His people will be ready to receive the blessings and benefits of the Tree of Life."

"That would have been us," Vladimir asserted, pointing to the cook and himself. The cook cheerfully waved his cigar. "Well, we looked better back then. All that shining armor helped. And my boots added three inches to my height."

"The armor and the swords are somewhere," the cook mumbled, scratching his head. "I didn't think this would be a dress party."

"You look fine now," Lucretia promised, holding Vladimir's hand. "Wonderful, actually."

There was a large crowd in the room. The glass doors between rooms had been removed to hold all the people who now thought of themselves as the "factory people." There were the children from São Paulo, some silent and solemn, some bored and some cheerfully whispering to each other, oblivious of everything else going on. Then there were the veterans and their families, and Lucifer's creatures and his people. And there was Lucretia's family, Mrs. Ostein's daughters, and the transferees and their families, all watching.

Mary had busily plucked a tray of apples, that she put on the bench next to the Tree.

Lucifer walked up to the tray and carefully choose a red apple. "This looks wonderful," he announced. "I'll try it first this time, just for the record. And the taste..." He bit off a chunk of the apple and chewed for a moment, his eyes unfocused. "The taste is truly extraordinary. I'd long forgotten that memory." He took another bite.

Jesus picked up an apple. "Haven't we done this before?" he asked wryly, and bit in. His eyes went unfocused for a moment, and then he smiled. "The master gardener," bowing to Mary. "Earth goddess indeed."

Hal stood up and took a red apple. Lungorthin took a gold one, and Lucretia took a red one. Vladimir stepped up and took a gold apple.

"This is strong," Hal admitted, between bites.

"Many are the eons since I remembered these experiences," Lungorthin rumbled.

Lucretia took a careful bite. "Sorry," she mumbled, embarrassed. "The Cardinal's potion had a bite to it. But this...is good." She quickly ate the whole apple.

Vladimir ate his apple slowly, a look of bliss spreading across his face. "I'd given up hoping the Tree would come back,"

Hal glanced up at the birds wheeling far up in the sky, their shadows flitting over the garden.

"And now, lest he put out his hand and take also of the Tree of Life, and eat, and live forever," Mary quoted. "Really, Eve was just being helpful. It seemed like a good idea at the time!"

Lucifer sighed. "Fine, I'll take the blame. That's what Paul's marketing claimed, anyhow. Let's see: 'And the woman said unto the serpent, We may eat of the fruit of the trees of the garden: but of the fruit of the tree which is in the midst of the garden, God hath said, Ye shall not eat of it, neither shall ye touch it, lest ye die. And the serpent said unto the woman, Ye shall not surely die: for God doth know that in the day ye eat thereof, then your eyes shall be opened, and ye shall be as gods, knowing good and evil.'"

"'And when the woman saw that the tree was good for food, and that it was pleasant to the eyes, and a tree to be desired to make one wise, she took of the fruit thereof, and did eat, and gave also unto her husband with her; and he did eat,'" Vladimir quoted. "'And the eyes of them both were opened.' We just didn't read the whole part."

"The church hated knowledge and wisdom," Mary added. "Bad for the collection plate. Too many questions."

"Beyond good and evil, I think it was supposed to read," Jesus announced. "Opened to Life and the Tree, and to live in the tree forever. The priests didn't like that part. Because all they cared about was their little world, they denied the key and embraced the lock."

"The Greeks knew me as Prometheus," Lucifer reflected. "Giving humans knowledge and power, and punished by the gods for that rash action. The Christians hated the idea of humans having knowledge of the real world, because it took away from their pretty ideas. So I was punished again. I'm considering swearing off good deeds."

"No good deed goes unpunished," Mary commented dryly.

"What next?" one of the children asked, standing on her tiptoes and staring. "Does the tree stay in here?" She looked at the tree doubtfully, the limbs now pushing against the glass in the roof.

"Seven stars and seven stones, and one white tree," Jesus declared to the crowd. "'Or, more traditionally:

> behold, the Lion of the tribe of Judah hath prevailed to open the book, and to loose the seven seals thereof. Worthy is the Lamb that was slain to receive power, and riches, and wisdom, and strength, and honor, and glory, and blessing.'

No, I didn't write this," Jesus muttered to Mary, catching her look of disbelief. "They just appreciated my value."

"Oy!" she replied, shaking her head in disbelief. "They should have asked his mother."

Jesus ignored her. "And...let's see...here. 'Fall on us, and hide us...from the wrath of the Lamb: for the great day of his wrath is come; and who shall be able to stand?'" He read in silence for a moment.

"Rafael, I think you wanted to do something?" Jesus asked the cook.

The cook pulled out an ancient trumpet and blew on it, a rich and full peal of sound echoing forth as Jesus pushed a button and the greenhouse windows opened. "Well, that's the seventh seal," Jesus observed thoughtfully, as the tree pushed through the last wall between the garden and the outside. "It turns out the other six have already been released. That explains a lot of things, actually."

"Do you ever get the feeling," Hal whispered to Cali, "that we didn't get the full script? That there are pages and pages the others seem to be reading from?"

"That's because you got the comic book script," Cali whispered back.

"Yeah, and you got the embroidered manuscript one? Not buying it, my dear," Hal whispered.

"This is just a show for us, actually," Mary pointed out. "The tree was about to push its roots outside, breaking through the foundations, and the limbs were about to break through the glass roof."

"Fireworks," Lucifer agreed. "People love fireworks even though they mean nothing. But it's important to us, and the kids enjoyed it."

"And they will get fireworks," Vladimir promised. "Very soon." He smiled at the tree. "It's so beautiful! What was the saying—sometimes you have to take the long way for a short journey? We have learned so much. We were with Arthur as he pushed for the human control of the world. The Fisher King as he lay wounded, the land in desolation. We thought, well, humans are above that! We can remake the world. What conceit to think we could reimagine the world! You can't remake the world without the power of the world behind you. So the desolation spread, but not for the reasons we expected. We bent all our efforts to solve the wrong problem, and it took eons to work our way back from that mistake."

"The human structures became a god of their own creation," Jesus declared. "So powerful, we thought. So complex a toy, and life, well, that was just animals screwing in the fields. Nothing to that. How wrong we were!"

"Fair April, you are," Hal teased, looking at Cali. "So alive! So beautiful."

"Flattery will get you everywhere, my prince" and she kissed him.

"You can almost see the tree grow," Lucretia commented, shading her eyes as she stared at the highest branches. "No consciousness, but complete awareness of root, leaf, and stem, drinking the sweet water, the thrusting roots drawing in nutrients, all focused on life. More complex than we could possibly imagine."

The windows open, the breeze rushed in and the seeds of the tree rose away from it, twisting and turning high into the air.

"They are bursting into the sky like a geyser gushing. All that pressure built up, now relieved." Lucretia gasped, holding Vladimir's hand as they watched.

"The Wrath of God is like great Waters that are dammed for the present; they increase more and more, and rise higher and higher 'til an Outlet is given; and the longer the Stream is stopped, the more rapid and mighty is its Course when once it is let loose," Vladimir quoted thoughtfully.

"Not quite as the Rev. Edwards intended it," Jesus commented. "He wished for a different result."

"Further proof that the wishing fairy has a vicious sense of humor," Vladimir laughed.

"So what happens now?" Cali asked, holding her hand over her eyes as she watched the seeds floating away, a cloud rapidly thinning as the breeze dispersed them.

"It depends on your point of view, really," Mary declared.

"Obi-Wan—I like this new look," Hal laughed.

Ignoring him, Mary continued, "From a certain point of view, a type of a plague. From another point of view, an evolution, a step forward. Really, it depends if it's good or bad for you, in the end."

"That's gotten cynical," Jesus remarked. "True, but cynical."

"Technically," Mary explained, "if the removal rate is greater than the infection rate, then the epidemic will never get started and never even be observed. If the removal rate is just above the infection rate, then a nearly healthy population is in danger of an epidemic. Any small uptick in the infection rate or downtick in the removal rate can tip the balance toward a new epidemic. Where the infection rate increases above the removal rate, the epidemic will then begin, but the absolute number of infections will grow slowly at first. If the underlying conditions favoring the infection rate continue, then the epidemic will become large and noticeable in the population at large."

"Which means?" Cali asked. "How can it spread through the world?"

"The tree will take care of itself," Lucifer declared. "This wind is coming out of the northeast, odd for this area. That wind is carrying the seed cloud to the airport. The seeds will float into the airplanes, float into the luggage, and then float out when they reach their destination. I'd think they would be all over the world in a short time." He studied the Tree for a moment. "I think it's producing another crop of seeds, that will probably ready by the morning."

"This is the seventeen-hundred-foot wave," Lucretia marveled to the seeds. "I'm actually seeing one."

"What?" Cali asked.

"There was a wave that hit a little town in Alaska," Lucretia explained. "A combination of factors that multiplied each other, and wham! A really, really big wave."

"Can't be too big for the job it has to do. The world is infested!" Mary shouted to the seeds. "Go clean it out!"

They watched as dusk settled in and the rays of the sun twinkled on some of the seeds, now far away. "Today was the longest day of the year," Mary commented. "The day the sun god was at his strongest."

> *The darkness drops again; but now I know*
> *That twenty centuries of stony sleep*
> *Were vexed to nightmare by a rocking cradle.*

"The Second Coming," Hal explained. "The inky blackness sweeps over the desert. The sphinx has long slept in the desert, drinking in the burning heat. Sleeping, but not resting. Its deep thought was disturbed by the wasteland of the small stories, the little human-centered world whispered in its ear by the desert wind. The Sun God, long exiled into the desert, was pushed away by the bright false children's stories of the priests who stood over the bowed heads of the subservient masses. A disturbed, restless sleep, taunted for twenty centuries by the denial of the creature, by tossing all that is life into sin, making life's strengths monsters to be hidden deep within. Twenty centuries of denying the vastness of life, the fullness and complexity of this world, turned away for a misty, phantom Platonic ideal of 'something else' out there."

"A rocking cradle finally broken on the hard sand ripples of the desert. Taunted by a nightmare of a randomly lurching agrarian system that was destroying the Life of the world, awoke the creature. As it stepped, the sand rippled beneath it," Cali added. "Those were strong drugs."

"What?" Mary asked, looking at them, puzzled.

"The poetry reading in Ann Arbor," Cali replied. "When it really started, for us. Hal's mother did the reading."

> *"And what rough beast, its hour come round at last,*
> *Slouches towards Bethlehem to be born?"*

"We shall see soon," Jesus added. "Look, that's enough somber talk and serious reflection. There's pizza and soft drinks coming soon, and wine for the adults."

Lucifer glanced at Jesus.

"From the store," Jesus specified. "Michigan wine."

Mary laughed and took Mrs. Ostein's arm as the three of them turned away from the windows.

The children shouted and ran for the food. The adults walked behind, glancing at the fading sunlight as they stepped into the factory passageway.

Hal went to shut the door, and it fell off its hinges. "I like that," nodding. "A nice touch."

THE NEXT MORNING

When they woke up, the wasteland surrounding the factory was green, overgrowing the thorn bushes and spreading out across the empty lots. It looked like prairie grass, the rich plains reborn.

Within a day, news crews came by, doing little quick sound bites on the bright new life, and making the usual comments on the wasteland revived.

"That one actually declared it was the garden come again," Mary commented, watching the news that night. "Accidental truth, right in line with the network news.'

"Even a stopped clock is right twice a day," Lucifer observed.

"It's like the Sorcerer's Apprentice," Jesus marveled. "I always liked that cartoon. Mickey Mouse had buckets of water everywhere, multiplying wildly. And the trees are spreading at the same rate."

"They won't pay any attention for some time," Lucifer mused. "It will be growing, but just little sprouts at first. It's got to get big enough to be noticed, which takes, oh, a week? Then there will be a lag until people notice how much of it there is, and start to get worried—say, another week, maybe longer. The word about the plant has to spread to places that specialize in plant changes, problems with plants, and get certain people's attention. Agricultural colleges, for example, which worry about plants spreading. Now, it's summer, and people are on vacation, even in today's connected world. So there's more time gone. Then they have to exchange papers, do their analyses, make sure their peer review committees will stand behind them. It's loss of tenure if they are wrong, and that's more important than a small thing like life or death."

"Remember the pond example?" Cali advised. "If lily pads double each day, starting with one lily pad, how many days to cover the pond? It was twenty days, and only on the nineteenth day was it obvious there was a problem. The seventeenth day, one-eighth was covered; the eighteenth day, one-fourth was covered, the nineteenth day, half covered; and then boom! This will be the same. The tree won't spread quite that quickly, but it's a non-linear, positive feedback event. They won't even see it coming."

"First it will be called a weed, then an outbreak," Mary explained. "There's a structure for assessing a problem. Then the powers that be will decide it's an epidemic. Finally, the big word, pandemic, when someone important sees that it's everywhere."

"And at that happy day when important people panic and decide it's serious, they will draw lines, and the lines will intersect here," Hal pointed out. "It bloomed here first, and the news reports will be simple to track back. The usual first approach for dealing with change is to smash it into the ground, and failing that, then think. The factory will be labeled in red 'day one'—isn't that the way they view epidemics? And then we have to fend them off."

"Start planning, Cali," Jesus ordered. "You're the best at that."

"Planning for what?" Cali asked. "As I recall the planning overview, where you have an evolving situation, you just keep your goal in mind and stay flexible. So, let's see—what's the drill? Inventory resources? Look for options? What things could be assets? Who could be allies? Certainly we should bring some food and water in, and lay out a, what do you call it? A defense line? We need escape routes? Trucks and gasoline, for sure."

"Weapons," Jesus added. "We should be ready for the worst."

"We are really rather prepared," Vladimir offered.

People looked at him, surprised.

"Well, it's dangerous around here, or it was at one time," Vladimir continued. "I'll start calling in favors, bringing in more people. Hal's right; we have to anticipate that people respond as people normally do. Destroy first, ask questions later." He walked out of the room.

"It's a cornucopia," Hal mused. "Life is spreading, and the first action is rejection. Typical."

"Only life for some," Mary warned. "For many, Life is death, because it ruins their game. They like the wasteland; it's worked for them for a long time. Let's figure out what we can do."

CHAPTER 8. THE THIRD BELL TOLLS

DAY 1. THE SEEDS SPREAD.

A gentle wind carried the seeds south-southwest, a river in the air aimed directly at the airport. Detroit Metropolitan Wayne County Airport is a huge international airport, controlled bedlam, a dizzying dance of planes arriving and departing. The planes fly to destinations all over the world, and the airport is completely focused on action. There are an abundance of recognized problems popping up every minute, and so events that are not actually biting some critical process in the ass, anything that isn't clearly threatening the critical path dictating arrival and departure times, just isn't important.

At the airport, it was a warm but pleasant summer day. Sunny, with a few clouds sprinkled in a deep blue sky, really beautiful weather. Like everyday, it was busy, but with no major delays or problems. The first seeds lazily touched the planes, but didn't attach to the fuselage, instead slipping into the gaps between the loading walkways and a plane. Some seeds drifted into cargo bays and stuck inside. Other seeds grasped onto luggage with little suckers as the luggage was trucked out of the terminal and thrown into cargo holds. Seeds were carried into the terminal on suitcases, or blown by the wind through open doors, then fell into luggage conveyors, grasping onto other luggage. Other seeds were sucked into air intakes, and spit out into the interior of the airport, drifting down onto all the rushing and milling people who were totally focused on where they were going.

At Detroit Metro it was a beautiful day for those who could relax and enjoy it, but it was hot if you were working outside. The baggage handlers wore down as the day went by, slowing down as the heat sapped their energy. Some of the handlers swatted at the seeds drifting into a cargo hold. "Ignore that!," a supervisor snapped, as a crew stopped to stare at the thickening mass of seeds drifting across the airport. The supervisor grabbed a few seeds and studied them for a moment. He let them go, relieved that they wouldn't slow his work. "The damn dandelions can spread to the rest of the world, that would serve them right," he grumbled.

"It's almost raining seeds," one of the baggage handlers commented, squinting at the sky.

"Hopefully it won't bother the schedule," the supervisor replied, frowning. "Today has been going too well, something had to go wrong," he grumbled. "But if you don't get the damn bags in there, it's going to bother me-a lot." The men went back to throwing bags into the hold, occasionally wiping off their sweat, which fell on the seeds and made the seeds stick all the tighter to the luggage.

The pilot of the plane that was being loaded, all checklists done, sitting in the cockpit bored, waiting for final approvals, suddenly looked intently out the window. "It's seeds?" he announced, squinting. "Seeds like cottonwoods, but not as heavy. Little thin things, it looks worse than it is, really."

"A problem?" the copilot asked.

"No!," the pilot replied. "Say nothing to the tower. "Those old women have a stroke about anything."

The co-pilot nodded. That conversation was repeated in a hundred planes over the afternoon and evening.

"It's seeds," a controller in the tower commented, staring out at the runways. "So many, it's almost static on the radar."

"A problem?" a supervisor demanded.

"No, not a problem," another controller answered. "Just little seeds, nothing as bad as even a light rain."

"Just ignore it, don't give those spoiled pilots anything to complain about," the supervisor ordered. "The schedule is actually working, let's keep things going. We've got rain coming in two days and we don't want to be behind when that hits.

The seeds attached, detached and re-attached wherever they could. Some drifted into the planes, wafted into the upper storage racks, or fell on seats, sticking to passengers clothing when people sat down. The seeds were thin, almost transparent and people paid them little notice.

And then the process was reversed in airports across the world. Seeds drifted out of cargo holds, seeds fell off of people's coats and suitcases. Clinging to the seats in taxicabs, limos and buses, seeds were carried all over cities, and far out into the countryside. Millions of seeds, and this was only the first wave. Bursting with new genetic material, only a few had to reach fertile soil and root.

Plane after plane took off as the day passed. Planes headed throughout the United States: New York, Atlanta, Chicago, San Francisco. And internationally: London, the Bahamas, Mexico City, and all over the world. At each stop, some people disembarked, the seeds tagging along unnoticed. The planes continued on, new people filling the seats, seeds attaching onto them.

Early the next morning, a plane landed in Berlin. Twenty of the passengers had started in Detroit, and as their luggage was unloaded, seeds flew off, into the air. As the people took their luggage home, seeds fell off, and then when they brushed their clothes, more seeds fell off. Seeds all over the world falling into warm, wet and fertile soils.

"And he said, Whereunto shall we liken the kingdom of God? or with what comparison shall we compare it? It is like a grain of mustard seed, which, when it is sown in the earth, is less than all the seeds that be in the earth: But when it is sown, it groweth up, and becometh greater than all herbs, and shooteth out great branches; so that the fowls of the air may lodge under the shadow of it."[13]

DAY 1. DETROIT.

"It doesn't take long," Hal argued, gesturing at a map. "If something doubles every day, then in a very short time there is a lot of it. And these seeds are more than seeds. There something in them that changes other bacteria, probably viruses also, that spread directly to other plants. So there is another accelerator. The plants not only are growing, but changing all the plants around them."

"It is HGT!," Mary shouted, excited.

"Pray, enlighten us?" Jesus asked.

"HGT," Mary explained, impatiently. "Horizontal gene transfer, the promiscuous exchange of living genetic material. An organism incorporates genetic material from another organism. As it mixes the new genetic material into itself the organisms changes and adopts. Sexual reproduction is a new entity, which is quite different. This is the actual organism changing. It's constantly going on, whether we like it or not. That is how single-celled organisms, such as bacteria become antibiotic resistant, for example. HGT is critical, and we don't understand it at all well. As roughly ninety percent of the cells in the human body are nonhuman organisms, mostly various types of bacteria, how they are changing constantly, incorporating new genetic material into us is rather important."

"That's an understatement!," Jesus agreed. "So we are, each second, becoming something completely different from what we were? And we have no control over it, no real understanding of what is going on. Meanwhile, we sit here, thinking we are a uniform creature, in control. It's a rather total mind flip, actually."

"Humm," Cali observed. "Sounds like time for pizza and wine time, the only clear and unvarying referents in the world that we know."

DAY 2. KASHMIR.

In Jammu, Kashmir, an exhausted businessman gets off his final plane, grumbling about the cleanliness of the plane as he brushed seeds off his suit.

Then, there were freight packages that went all over the world. All flew out of Detroit with a cargo of seeds that was not on any manifest. Cargo planes have lower cleanliness standards and the seeds were not even noticed. Casually swept out of the cargo planes when the planes were cleaned, the seeds drifted peacefully away.

All over the world: London, Paris, Riyadh, Rio de Janeiro, everywhere there was a major airport, the seeds spread. Cities and towns, villages and country, deserts and rain forests throughout the world, which received a package delivered that started in Detroit, or had some contact with Detroit, the seeds spread to. And those that fell in the water and were eaten by the fish were not wasted either.

The next morning, there were thin sprouts popping up in fertile soil all over the world. For the seed of the Tree of Life was strong. And it was spreading more than just the seed for the plants; it was spreading the raw power of life. Changing the plants it was near, the insects that touched the plan, the animal that ate the plants, it was changing the life of the world.

DAY 6. DETROIT.

At the factory, Lucifer looked out over the land to the south that had been broken concrete and scrub. It was now a sea of grass, with trees starting to poke up. And the plants are changing the ground, he realized. They are actually digging into the wasteland, transforming the soil, and neutralizing the pollution. He could almost see the Tree walking across the land, spreading like a green carpet. The growth of a tree, no consciousness, but everything at the right time.

> *"A mote it is to trouble the mind's eye.*
> *In the most high and palmy state of Rome.*
> *A little ere the mightiest Julius fell.*
> *The graves stood tenantless and the sheeted dead*
> *Did squeak and gibber in the Roman streets;*
> *As stars with trains of fire, and dews of blood,*
> *Disasters in the sun; and the moist star."*

Lucifer quoted, grimly. Then he shook his head and smiled. "Ah well, let's be cheerful. Life again, the rich feel of the wild!" He breathed deeply, and the sweet smell of the grass filled his lungs. Back to planning, he thought, and went into the factory.

DAY 7. A SMALL VILLAGE NEAR SHANGHAI, CHINA.

Jiang had been forced to leave the university because of health problems. He is sitting in a simple garden at his parent's house. It is really more a loose collection of plants framed by two rough walls, but they call it a garden. His family is poor and he is their hope for the future. That hope, now become disappointment, burdens him more than his weak health. His parents have said little to him, but he hears them talk. Their disappointment hovers over the house like a cloud. He alternates between being furious at himself for his weakness and hoping for his strength to return. He is just tired, a general malaise, a flu that waxes and wanes. He knows what others whisper, that he can't take the pressure and that he is feigning illness. Worse, in his mind he hears a voice whispering that he will never finish, that he will be a nothing. Not even strong enough to till the fields, just a burden.

Would that I was pretending!, he despairingly thought. The quote that he had read and pondered came to him again.

"In seeing victory, not going beyond what everyone knows is not skilled.

Victory in battle that all-under-heaven calls skilled is not skilled.

Thus lifting an autumn hair does not mean great strength.

Seeing the sun and the moon does not mean a clear eye.

Hearing thunder does not mean a keen ear.

So-called skill is to be victorious over the easily defeated.

Thus the battles of the skilled are without extraordinary victory, without reputation for wisdom and without merit for courage.

He breathes deeply, enjoying the air. How does one see the subtle?, he thinks to himself. Well, the subtle is not found in my mind, it is in the world to be seen. So, stop forcing! He studies the garden, seeing it as if for the first time. Puzzled, he realized there is a new plant by the south wall. A cluster of them, actually, bright green and growing tall. They were not here two days ago; he was sure. Yesterday, he spent the day in bed, but had felt well enough two days ago to be helped to the garden. The wind must have shifted away from the pig farms, he thinks happily, sniffing, because the air is pleasant, rich suddenly.

He pushes himself up and totters over to the new plants.

He realizes that he is hungry, really hungry for the first time in weeks. That's good, he thinks, but? He looks around, but there isn't much left in the garden. I've eaten everything, he thought, discouraged. What will we put aside for the winter? But, there is this cluster of the new ones? Are these weeds? More importantly, are they eatable? They look, well, a bit like lettuce. He sniffed them, and the smell was fresh, a delight. Crispy, he thought, as he snapped one, and squinted at it, seeing the clear sap dripping. He put it in his mouth, the bright green and the clear sap suddenly irresistible. It's a sweet taste, surprisingly filling. Good move, he thinks wryly: All poison stories start like this. Suddenly he gasps, grasps at his throat, and has only the strength to guide his fall as he collapses onto the soft earth. He passes into a deep sleep. His sleep is a world unknown, a world of impossible feelings and events, but more real than his daily life. Horrors and wonders, terror and elation twist and turn, impossibly but tightly woven together.

Hours later, he wakes up. He looks around, and then sits up. I sat up easily, he notices, shocked. The first time in a month, he thinks happily to himself. He carefully moves his arm, and then flails his arms around easily, ecstatically.

He grasps his head, as the memories flood back through him. But, they are good memories, and they strengthen me. Even what should terrify me, strengthens me?, he thinks as the images swim in his mind. It's Dragons, smiling. Terror strengthens and calms when it is faced. It's seeing victory, going beyond what everyone knows. Perceiving the subtle is a step outside of the bounded world of the crowd. He can almost feel the Dragon's wings connected to him, gently moving on his shoulders. They wrap around and protect me.

He glances up to see a brilliant sunbeam bursting through a gap in the wall. The bright white light is split into colors by beads of water clinging to a spider web, rainbows sprayed across the other wall. Suddenly, he understands. The white light is the complete world, the complete truth, more than I can grasp. But the rainbow, I can understand a color and know that what I understand is part of the truth, part of the white light. I can work with what I can know and have faith what I know fits into the larger truth that I cannot grasp. Partial truths are all that I can comprehend, but I can build on them, not disparage them as false because they are only part of a whole I can't understand.

The next morning, he takes a picture of the plants, which are much taller than they were yesterday, and he writes about the light, and the crystal, how the white lights breaks into a rainbow, and talks about the larger truths that are too much for us, and the smaller, colors of the truth that we can grasp. He publishes to his blog, and waits to see what happens.

DAY 8. DETROIT.

Hal, searching for news about the plants, reads Jiang's blog. He thinks about what Jiang wrote, getting more enthused as he plays with the ideas. Then he shows Cali the blog, and they talk about the ideas. Excited, at dinner they tell the group about what they found.

After they all have had some time to play with the ideas, Hal writes back to Jiang, thanking him for his insights. Hal offers Jiang a chance to be part of the network Detroit is putting together, which Jiang happily accepts.

The vision of the crystal, expanding it across all cultures, religions and beliefs, is breathtaking. The component colors of the light, visually different views of the Tree and the World make it easier to understand the parts and grope towards the whole. The white life can be split by a prism but the different colors combine back into white light. Thus are all visions, parts of and held within the tree.

DAY 8. THE STUDENT AND THE DOCTOR.

Jiang's parents are shocked when they see him the next morning.

"You are stronger than ever," his mother exclaimed, crying as she held him.

"True," his father muttered, uncertain. "But you must see the doctor."

"Why?" his mother demanded, staring at the father. "He's healthy! Just look at him!"

"It's just, well, strange to be so healthy so quickly," the father answered, nervously pulling on his thin beard.

"That quack couldn't help Jiang, and now you want to throw good money after bad?" the mother demanded, disgusted.

"He goes to the doctor, woman" the father commanded.

Jiang contemplated his father, seeing the fear in his father's eyes, and then shrugged. "Certainly, father." He got dressed, and walked into the village. No cane, no breaks, no rests, smiling as he walks.

Three hours later, Jiang sits uncomfortably in the waiting room. The nurse is staring at him and others in the waiting room are whispering to each other as they glare at him.

They disapprove, Jiang realized, shocked. They preferred my suffering because then they were superior.

"Jiang, this way," the nurse called, standing at the open door leading to the examination rooms.

Jiang jumps up and walks out of the waiting room, happy to be out of there.

"Here, into here and sit," the nurse ordered. She took a final cautious look at him as she closed the door.

The doctor opened the door, and started to walk in. He glanced at Jiang, and stopped dead, stunned. When he had seen Jiang a week ago, the young man could barely walk, and was bent over as he sat in on the examination table. Now, Jiang is healthy, almost glowing. He is stronger now than when I examined him before he went to college, the Doctor realizes as he examines Jiang.

Examination complete, the Doctor steps back, and leans against the wall. "So, what happened?" the Doctor demanded.

"Well," Jiang started, about to talk about the plants and then caught himself. When he read the responses to his blog posting, he was astonished at the hate some people had of the plants, and the fury created by his praise of the plants. He had heard rumors about how the plants could make you sick and remembered his father's doubtful expression. As he had walked to the doctor today, some of villagers had made signs against him when they thought he wasn't looking, so the plants inspired more emotion that he had imagined. Better to wait a bit, he decides. Jiang just muttered something vague, that he just felt better, all of a sudden; maybe the sweet air helped since it wasn't blowing from the pig farms.

"The air is still blowing from the pig farms," the Doctor commented.

Jiang looked down. "The air seems more pleasant to me. Perhaps I'm getting used to it."

"Doubtful," the Doctor replied, "but possible." The Doctor studied Jiang, sensing his deception, but let it go. Perhaps he came to terms with his problems, the doctor thought. Perhaps it was mental. And perhaps he just recovered. I wish more of them would.

"How's your love life?" the Doctor asked Jiang, testing him.

"Love life may be a rather grandiose term for staring at women in the fields," Jiang laughed.

The Doctor laughed and slapped Jiang on the back. "Out of here!" the Doctor ordered. "You sound like you used to." He wrote 'cured' on the medical record, shook Jiang's hand and sent him home.

After Jiang left, the doctor took a minute to add to his notes. Jiang's skin almost glowed, the Doctor mused. When we shook hands, his skin was looked healthier than mine. What does that mean? I don't know, the Doctor sighed, but he's healthy.

The Doctor walked out of the examination room, scanning the next set of medical records as he walked. He stood outside the next examination room, frowning at the test results. Worried, he opened the door to that examination room, which held two farmers. "Cough? Weakness?" the Doctor inquired.

"Yes," one gasped.

The Doctor observed that their skin was pale.

Day 14. Brazil.

Around the world, people went about their daily lives. With so many people in cities, changes in the fields and forests were not as obvious. A day flew by, and then another. While most people saw nothing, each moment, day and night, the seeds rooted and grew. They grew at an incredible rate, and the plants near them changed, growing stronger with each genetic exchange. Happening at a microscopic level the biological and chemical events were below a scale that humans would notice. But in the plants, and spreading out from them to other living organisms, there were strong colony creatures. And they were multiplying.

We think of things as what we see. A 'person' is what we see, as is a 'dog', a 'fish', and a stalk of corn. They are, but they are far more. They are all composed of and live by and with a vast horde of colony creatures. Our words are for a 'thing', and that thing only, when really, what we see so clearly is really a blurry mass of organisms sharing a space. The colony creatures, common to all living organisms, interacted with the plants and swapped genetic material. A few, and there are no changes. But there is a crossing point where things change quite rapidly.

In Brazil, the plants took quick root in the rain forest, and became very strong, very quickly. They spread widely, almost unnoticed, exchanging genetic material in a frenzy with the rich vegetation of the jungle. As part of their daily work, plant scientists from the university explore the jungles and the fields. Their initial exuberance at the discovery of something really new was turning into nervous apprehension.

"I've never seen horizontal gene transfer like this," a senior scientist commented, sitting back and staring at the computer simulation on the screen. "There is swapping of genetic material between organisms at an incredible rate. And it's going on between organisms that normally don't interchange. Hell, they normally can't interchange without dying, but they are not dying, they are becoming healthier. And it's spreading everywhere."

"As ninety percent of the cells in a humans body are nonhuman, mostly bacteria, it's going to be swapping in people," a colleague remarked somberly. "Should we be calling the medical department?"

"And tell them what?" the senior scientist scoffed. "That a plant, a form of grass, is going to take over humans? They listen only to themselves, those gods in their white coats prancing before their patients. We would be the laughingstock of the university, perhaps of the city. Comics on television would have a new target."

"I'm thinking a drink?" another colleague suggested. "Maybe non-organic this time."

They laughed, and walked out of the laboratory.

DAY 14. DETROIT.

Hal was monitoring news reports and Internet postings from all over the world.

"What I'm finding are little odd pieces of information from all over the world. Generally they are like the news around here," he told Cali. "Little filler stories about new plants suddenly spreading or polluted fields suddenly green, and then no more reports."

"First excitement and elation and then clamped down on," Cali commented. "So, they quickly find out it is more than just some new plant and they don't want to talk about it until they know more."

"I've been working up a simple visual display, showing where the stories are popping up, and how many. Now, we're starting to see agricultural scientists making noises about this new plant(s) hitting their radar. While simply growing in barren fields isn't going to really upset people for a while, the plants are growing in rice fields and wheat fields. When farmers realize that their crop production will be damaged, they will start taking action. Take action against the plants, and they bite back, hard. So, alarm bells will be going off very soon."

"You said there had been just a few whispers from World Health about people getting sick and some isolated reports of a few people dying?" Cali asked.

"The deaths just show vague, general symptoms, not a specific set of events that they can link clearly," Hal replied. Here, I've marked on this graph where the problems are popping up," pointing at the screen. "Pretty soon they will link the problems to the plant's spread. It's been two weeks, and I give them a week, two at most, before they really put the pieces together."

"Fortunately, there isn't a czar of plants in the world," Cali observed. "People shout, but they have to get the politicians' attention before the troops start moving. I'm thinking at least another week. What was the calculation on when the plant will hit full power all over the world?"

"Thirty days, give or take," Hal guessed. "I'm calculating forty days from the day the seeds started to spread to the date colony creatures all over the world will have been changed. The flood, get it? Just about exactly. A nice touch."

"I've been thinking," Mary announced. "The Tree was the third event, the third bell. Three, and then there is no going back. Dissolution and rebirth, or death."

Jesus looked at her. "Somewhere, the sun is over the yardarm. I declare this happy hour, and we are going to the restaurant to celebrate. So take off the black robe of the seer, please. It brings the other guests down."

Day 21. New York.

"This is awful," Christina Naumann exclaimed. She was staring, unbelieving, at the screen.

"Sick," Oskar agreed, shaking his head. "Unbelievable."

The news camera shows a parking lot. There is a burned out auto, still smoking, outside a small church in a country town. Many police are surrounding a large group of conservatively dressed people, all of whom are handcuffed. There are so many, that the police have been scurrying about trying to find a large enough bus to securely transport the group.

The camera comes back to the newswoman, who is grim. She glances down at her notes, and then looking back at the camera, starts speaking. "The latest information I have is that the minister of this church" gesturing towards the little country church "was preaching a sermon against the plants that have recently been found in local fields. Some people believe that the plants are making people sick, which scientists cannot confirm at this time. Several healthy people in this community have suddenly died in the last few days. More people are in the local hospital with an illness the doctors have never seen before. I have been told that several of the sickest patients were moved yesterday, wrapped in full bio-warfare containment suits, to regional hospitals. The community is fearful, well, more than fearful, terrified, and we understand that this church has had more dead and sick than any other group in the area."

The newswoman listens to her headpiece for a moment. She looks back at the camera. "I'm told that after the sermon a woman in the congregation stood up and began praising the plants. The woman is reported to have announced that the plants are the power of Life, of the Tree spreading throughout the world. I was told that the woman spoke of the beauty of other creatures, the complexity of other creatures and how much more she understood other creatures after contact with the plants. Then several other women stood up, supporting her.

"Then, unbelievably, the minister screamed that the women be burned as witches. The majority of the congregation responded by grabbing the women and carrying them into this parking lot. Several women were simply set afire, burned in their clothing in the parking lot. Another woman who had sought safety in her car was burned when the congregation set the auto on fire.

"The few members of the congregation who held back called the police, but the police arrived too late to stop this horrible massacre."

The newswoman touches her earpiece for a second, and then glanced to her left. "Wait, I think that the police are leading the minister to a police van. And here he is," and she points.

The camera pans to the left, away from the newswoman, and centers on the minister, who is being led towards the van by two policemen. The minster shouts at the camera as the police roughly hurry the minister along.

"The grass is death!" the minister screams. "It's a curse, a plague sent because of our sins! Anyone who speaks for the grass is against the church, a witch! They . ." and the ministers words are cut off as the doors of the van are slammed shut. A policeman pounds on the side of the van, which roars off.

The news broadcast abruptly shifts to a press conference. "This is the Deputy Director of Public Health," the voice over announces, as the cameras focused on a clearly worried man in a rumpled, poorly fitting suit.

"Reports of attacks on people who protect the plants, the 'Tree' as I understand they call the plants, have been coming in from farming areas," the Deputy Director stated, wiping his brow. "These attacks are baseless and groundless. And illegal, of course" he hastily added. "There are many people who have had extensive contact with these plants and have had no ill effects from the contact. Like the flu, some people have the flu, but it does not affect them. We believe that this will be the pattern with this problem, that the few, extremely visible cases have to seen against a backdrop of many, many cases which cause no harm. Those people who have been infected, and who have recovered, are strong and healthy, the doctors say. Those who have been infected and recovered do not spread the infection! All problems are absolutely limited to direct contact with the plants. We have seen no evidence of human to human transmission." He stopped to wipe his brow again and glance at his notes. He looked up and tried to smile. "Again, people do not spread whatever it is that is making some people sick. The CDC has announced that people who have were infected and recovered are probably our best hope for stopping this problem. Antibodies in their blood are being gene sequenced and scientists hope that a vaccine, or at least a serum, can be developed to protect others."

"What about reports that those people who have been infected by the plants, but who have recovered, are protecting the plants?" a newsman asked.

"We have heard those stories," the Deputy Director stammered, again wiping his brow. "Many who have been affected by the plant believe themselves healthier for the contact, and argue, often vigorously, that the plants are beneficial. They point to their health as an example. Certainly, many seem to have had their health improved by contact with the plants. On the other hand, many believe that they are sick because of contact with the plants, and worse, there are those who claim that people are dying because of the plants. We are taking a neutral position until we have more evidence. Meanwhile, we are researching the differences in the cases, and trying to come up with a solution."

"That's a non-answer," Oskar observed, worried. "The news lives by a story that starts with fear and ends with comfort. That story doesn't fit the script they shoehorn the world into. If they can't twist it the way they usually do, but they are so concerned that they have to say something, it's not good, that's for sure."

"So," Christina asked. "What is going on?"

"We'll know soon," Oskar answered. "I'm thinking we should focus on our health, maybe starting with a nice dinner and some wine?"

DAY 21. DETROIT.

"Small battles are breaking out all over the world," Hal advised, showing Cali some stories that he had captured. "The plants have already become resistant to insecticides, but when governments spray, desperately trying to do something, people of the Tree are sabotaging the equipment. The plant scientists have finally discovered that the plants are full of bacteria that are swapping genetic parts with other plants. Some tabloid news reports have started to shout that this is the end of the world, terrifying people. Reminds me of the movie "Men in Black", where they read the tabloids for the real truth. It's a rare case where the news actually got it right. Now the public health agencies and the governments are frantically trying to deny the seriousness of the problem, because panic will spread. Governments hate panic more than anything else, as it undercuts their mandate to exist. It's all happening way too fast for them to react. They are trying to use yesterday's successful plan, and that failing, the plan from the week before against a completely new event. Not surprisingly, they are having no success. Really, it's getting interesting." He studied the news feeds with a cheerful smile.

"You have an odd way of looking at things," Cali remarked, intently watching video feeds of the chaos. "The world is changing, warping out of the past, and it's just interesting?"

"Well it is," Hal answered. "We're just watchers, really. Idle bystanders milling around the accident scene. We've helped, but this we watch. Which reminds me-how are the preparations to protect the factory going?"

"Quite well," Cali replied. "Vladimir and Lucifer have worked up some really good plans. Weapons came out of nowhere, after some senior AFT people became of the Tree. Permits and licenses too, just to tidy things up. Lucifer had more troops and resources available once he started calling in favors and obligations than he had originally expected."

"The Groupe firms have moved their people here," Hal added. "They are trained and dangerous, and we need those abilities."

"Jesus has many government connections, at all levels, so we are staying on top of their plans," Cali stated. "What little we can do to limit their response to the plants is being done. All in all, the factory is pretty well protected against anything short of a declaration of war and a real army."

"Which we'll face eventually," Hal announced, looking very serious. "Not long, I'm thinking. Three, four weeks, at the outside."

"Mr. Optimist," Cali countered.

"Cali, things will fall apart so fast when the tree kicks into full gear, we don't even know if they will be able to mount an attack. We have some idea what's coming and we can't keep up. They didn't have a clue, and its all so far outside their world that they don't know where to start. That's good and bad. Good, because they are frozen for the moment. Bad, because the usual response when caught in a situation of complete confusion spiced with sheer frustration is the club. We have an advantage, because the bureaucracy is slow to respond which is good; they have an advantage, because they have armies, which is bad."

"The loathed, underestimated appearance of the carrier of the power of destiny," Jesus commented. "The simple weed in your yard, upsetting your careful design, just blowing in the wind. Yeah, that's exactly on track. The land restored, the wound healed."

"I think Hal 2 was supposed to read from his notes to make that point," Hal remarked dryly, "but I'll accept your analysis."

DAY 21. THE VATICAN, ROME.

The consensus arising from little meetings and hurried conferences in corners of the Vatican, was that the danger is great. A formal meeting was hastily called, of a select group whose allegiance was unquestioned.

"Perhaps the greatest danger the church has ever faced," a prominent cardinal flatly told the Pope.

"It can't be that bad?" the Pope questioned. "It's just a plant."

"Our people are dying. All of our people," a cardinal stammered, terrified.

"Maybe a few survive," another cardinal added, "but that's even worse, because they leave the faith. They suddenly protect the plants; they preach this animalistic faith, this faith of the world that is larger than the small human stories. They deny sin, and embrace the flesh and this world."

The others nodded, remembering cases that they had seen.

"Then our course is clear," the Pope ordered, an odd expression flickering over his face. "Fire and the sword has worked before, and it will work again. The church has ruled through the puppets for centuries, pulling on their strings for our bidding. The greatest danger is the greatest opportunity."

"Those who crave power will sell out for a doctrine that supports them, a doctrine that we sell them," an elderly priest promised confidently.

"This must be done carefully," the Pope declared, thinking out loud. "It's always Russian Dolls. The outer message must be clear, and focused for and on the masses. A simple message for simple people. The first hidden doll is for the bureaucrats, and the next hidden doll for the rulers. The inner dolls after that are for us, layers of our secrets and goals. As is always has been, and always shall be. The church must work through others. We accept that the church is a kind of parasite. Well, parasites do very well in this world. A parasite takes over its host and makes the host do what the parasite wants. That's not for public consumption, by the way," and the Pope looked around carefully.

The others smiled, and nodded.

"We can do a big business in indulgences," a Director of the Vatican bank commented. "It never hurts to make a little money off the problems of the world."

"We have to put out a message that will fool them, keep them under control until this passes," the Pope aruged. "What is the best cover for that message? What has worked before? Go, and I want reports and plans by tomorrow."

The audience bowed, and rushed off to do their work.

Later, the Cardinal stood quietly looking out over the square. And what if you seek to fool yourself?, he wondered. What is the cover, the plan that would accomplish that the best? Because that is where we are today. Who needs action when you've got words?

As he stood, reflecting, a priest walked towards him. The Cardinal's guard stepped in the way, but the Cardinal waved them aside, curious.

"I doubt that the Pope is right, your Eminence," the priest confessed. "I've seen people affected, both good and bad, and I do not think that the Pope and the group he just met with grasp the problem at all."

"I think you are right," the Cardinal replied. "But why tell me this? Why not your cardinal?"

"Because they would not listen, your Eminence," the priest answered, bowing slightly. "I could see, if you would forgive me, the doubts in on face, and I hoped for someone to talk to."

"Please speak to my secretary," the Cardinal answered, smiling. "We can have a light dinner tonight. I'm curious to hear your thoughts and what you have seen."

The priest bowed, and backed away.

"Check his story," the Cardinal whispered to an aide, who nodded. The Cardinal thoughtfully watched the priest walk away. "There are intrigues upon intrigues in this place, but I think he has useful information. Besides, it would be enjoyable to talk to someone who is using their brain for something more than living proof of Aristotle's belief that the brain simply cools the blood."

Day 22. Detroit.

People at the factory watch the news, grim faced and worried.

"That 'news' from the Vatican? That will encourage the killing in the streets, one of Lucifer's people shouted at the TV. "As if they haven't had enough of that over the centuries!'

"They are so sure of the 'good'', one of the veterans growled. "They couldn't see the good if their life depended on it."

"Which it actually does," another veteran added, shaking his head. "What will the plants do to them when the plants are at full strength?"

"They have absolutely no idea," one of Lucifer's creature snarled. "The Tree is strong here and we have seen what's happened to people near the factory. And it's strength is still growing, just like it will everywhere."

"Well, as least the troublemakers in the area who wander in looking for trouble have vanished," a veteran observed.

"That's because there are none of them left," another veteran laughed. "They were not of the Tree, and the Tree is unforgiving."

The family is clustered around Hal's data screens, watching.

"This is a problem," Hal advised. He moved his hands, and the Chinese student's blog, posted before his arrest, popped up.

They all read it thoughtfully.

The blog ended: "I am a servant of my Lord, and do his bidding. There are many others, and when I am gone, others will step forward."

"We are all his servants," Jesus promised. "I thought this had been left behind centuries ago! Again, they make martyrs of our people in the name of orthodoxy. And stupidity!"

"We understand that he is still alive," Lucifer reported. "I have contacts there, and we are doing what we can. If we can just keep him alive until the Tree has greater strength."

"He is valuable. His concept of the crystal, the full white light broken into the rainbow, the truths we can grasp has been essential," Mary mused. "It has smoothed cooperation and relationships between different faiths and beliefs. People who come within the Tree recognize their limitations, but a quick visual to remind everyone has really made a difference."

"In life, it seems like need to have a bunch of things going wrong to stop and pay attention," Hal observed. "If only a few things are going wrong, we just adjust and keep going. But when a bunch of things are going wrong, then we have to stop because we don't know what to do next. That's about where the world is now."

"It's our nature to want 'a problem' and 'a solution', and to want, nay, demand interrelationships so we can solve this and move on," Mary argued. For anything complex and important, that's not how the world works. Always, multiple causes are interrelated-to a greater or lesser degree, and some events have no casual interrelationships with other events. Rocks are dropping on us, and stopping one doesn't stop the others."

DAY 28. LUCRETIA CALLS DOMINIQUE.

"Everyone thought you were dead!" Dominique gasped, shocked to hear Lucretia's voice. "And it's not going well here—everyone is terrified. I thought the Hun's invasion was bad, but this is worse."

"You must come here," Lucretia ordered. "Now. It's spreading geometrically, a non-linear event. It is still building, but will be at full strength very soon. What you have seen is nothing to what is coming, I can promise you. So you must come here while you can. Where you are is not safe, and I want you here."

"How can I argue with that?" Dominique answered. "What do I do?"

"Here's the plan," Lucretia explained. "Keep this secret. I want you to..."

DAY 28. NEW YORK.

"Look, this can't be right!," the patient's voice protests.

"It is," the nurse replied, doodling on a blank piece of paper.

"I agreed to this procedure, because your little part of the medical world has persuaded the family doctors that they should be recommend this. I suffer for two days preparing for the procedure, I lose three days of work: the day before, the day of the procedure, and the day after. I've come down with a cold because the preparation weakened me. Worse than that, you actually damaged my intestines, and I'm going to have to come in for follow up surgery, as well as another of these damn procedures after the corrective surgery. All because of your errors! Then there is this extra $1345 in billing that I'm now responsible for!"

"You signed a waiver that stated you knew there could be damage as a result of the procedure," the nurse replied, bored. "And you signed a legally enforceable agreement that makes you clearly liable for anything that your insurance wouldn't pay. Anything, you gave us carte blanche."

"And you ran with it. You never told me what the charges would be or could be, or any options," the patient hissed, furious. "You never disclosed anything to me. Before the surgery, I spent two hours talking to my insurance company, who assured me that, based on what you put on the paper, everything would be covered. Then you did something in the procedure, which no one will disclose to me, and now I owe you money! On top of the damage to my body that you caused."

"Then you have a complaint against your insurance company," the nurse retorted, staring at the blinking lights of the holding phone calls. The week after the procedure, it's like this every time, she thought. Nothing but angry people, physically and financially damaged. She glanced out at the parking lot, at the physicians shining new luxury autos in the separate row reserved for them, and shook her head to herself.

"Why are the costs my problem?" the patient demanded, exasperated. "Your physicians make $500,000 a year, and you have a full time office staff that deals with the same insurance companies and the same procedure over and over. You don't even see me as a person, just a billing code and revenue! You know what the rules are and what it's going to cost, how can you callously offload this to the patients to make a few extra dollars by tricking the patients? The doctors can't make an honest living?"

"At least you passed the procedure," the nurse interjected, knowing there was no good answer to what the patient had snarled.

"And that procedure?" the patient scoffed. "I had a statistician go over the studies. Not the kind of random stuff that you throw out, but real Bayesian analysis. By the time you accurately load the incidence of colon cancer, the likelihood based on family history, the danger of injury during the procedure, and the other options available, your 'gold standard' is only gold for you, and dross for the patients."

"Look," the nurse replied, tired of the conversation. "You don't want to pay the bill? We will sue, and win; we've done it before. You don't want us to patch up the damage we did? You'd wish you died on the table if we don't patch you up soon. I can get you into the hospital again in a month, that's the fastest we can get you back in."

"I'll find another physician," the patient hissed.

"Good luck with that," the nurse snarled. "This group is the best in the area. You don't want to know about the other butchers. So you think about this, and call us back when you are ready to act. That next appointment slot will be taken soon. So don't take too long to decide. And you have to pay the balance due before you can set a firm appointment. Good day," and hung up, cutting off the sputtering response of the patient.

She looked away from the flashing phone bank, tired of fighting with the patients. Absently, she watched the news flash on the monitor in the waiting room. It was all about the government announcements about the illness that was spreading. Wait, they called it a plague that time! Suddenly intent, she listened carefully to the words, and what was missing from the words. It's that bad?, she worried. Well, hopefully those poor people won't have to come into this group practice. Maybe that's the government's plan, let this group treat them and kill them off before they can infect others. Maybe the sick could infect the doctors, those vampires, and that way we get rid of the doctors and the sick at the same time.

Sighing, she punched a waiting call button, and began her spiel again.

DAY 28. NATIONAL NEWS, USA.

The early news had a special announcement. The newsman, dressed in somber black, looks up at the screen. "These plants, the 'Tree' as those who support it call it, is now formally defined as an epidemic. The plants have spread everywhere in the world. Now, the government wants everyone to calm down, because that isn't as serious as it sounds. Colds are epidemic, and always have been. The flu is epidemic every year. Epidemics are annoying, yes, but we have all survived many epidemics."

"People don't die from colds," a newswoman off camera muttered to a cameraman, who nodded his head.

"After a week of intense research by public health departments all over the world, all that we can say for sure is that the illnesses that some are experiencing is related to changes in these plants that have spread throughout the world. Those plants, as you recall from previous news broadcasts, take several different forms and sizes. Plant scientists have agreed that this new plant is unstable, and while it is spreading now, it will soon collapse and die. When the plant dies, that will end the problem. We have Dr. Sergonwickic from the Cretan Agricultural University with us in the studio, who can answer viewers questions. There is also further information available on the Internet, so go to the station address for all the information we have. You must be careful, as there is a great deal of false information on the Internet. Let's go to Dr. Sergonwickic now." The Doctor walks up to the desk, sits next to the newsman, and they began the interview.

"The plant dying?" the off camera newswoman scoffed. "It's everywhere, and it looks pretty damn healthy to me. And what about the reports about the white trees starting to grow? They don't seem to be dying either."

They watch the interview, which is essentially useless. At the end of the interview, the newsman read the latest government release: "Stay away from the plants. Touching them, uprooting them, will cause serious problems. Do not, under any conditions, burn them! The government is making preparations for shelter for those sensitive to the plants. Malls, big box shopping centers and other areas from which nature can be excluded are being seized under martial law and being readied as shelter." The newsman looked down at his notes, and then looked back at the camera, grim. "We will have more news later."

The 'on air' light went off, and the newsman slumped back, tired.

The newswoman walked onto the set and sat on the desk. "Well, that was a load of crap," the newswoman snapped.

"We always want news to get people excited," the newsman replied. "Now we have news that will throw them into absolute terror, and we don't have a clue how to spoon-feed it to them so they don't all go off the tracks at the same time."

"They might as well go off the tracks," the Doctor admitted. "It can't be stopped and it's not dying. That rather incoherent message I just parroted to reassure the public was passed down from the very top, but that still doesn't make it the truth."

The newsman and newswoman stared at the Doctor for a minute. Then the newswoman shrugged. "A drink?" she suggested, looking at the newsman and the Doctor.

"Definitely!," the newsman agreed, standing up and stretching.

"Can we find something non-organic? Maybe a bar in this building, so we don't have to go outside?" the Doctor added.

DAY 28. MID-MORNING, WASHINGTON, DC.

"You can't do this!," the CDC Director shouted, pounding on the table. "Those people who were infected and recovered, they are not sick, they are the healthy ones! They do not spread the illness! You're advocating killing the healthy, when they have nothing to do with the people getting sick!"

"We don't know what's going on," the government minister replied, looking away from the CDC scientist. "Yes, they seem to be healthy. But there is something in their blood afterwards, and we can't rule out human to human transmission."

"We can absolutely rule out human to human transmission," the scientist shouted. "There is NO human to human transmission."

"Oh, not in the sense of a flu being transmitted from person to person. But they are transmitting this because they protect the plants that spread it!," the government official snapped. "Protecting is a small word, too little a word for what they are doing. They take up arms against the police and the agricultural workers! They destroy and kill in the name of their Tree, they are terrorists trying to destroy the country! So you can't tell me that this 'Tree' doesn't have an effect on them. It isn't just tree huggers, either. Hardened police officers are switching to protecting their Tree, people that we never would have dreamed would become criminals."

"So you are going to kill people? Just kill them on sight? Authorizing all the witch trials, all the insanity that is starting to break out?" the CDC Director asked carefully, trying to be calm. "Listen to yourself! None of what you are saying makes sense. And your press releases, promising the public that the trees will die and that they only have to wait? That's nonsense! The proof is lying there on your desk."

"What other choice do we have?" the government minister snarled. "Shall I let these 'mutant's wander freely around, preaching the doctrine of their Tree, tossing plants at people to infect them? We tried to capture and isolate them, but there are too many. When we put them in camps, they broke out, assisted by the guards who took their sides. After slaughtering the guards who were against them, by the way. The hospitals won't take any of them because they are too much trouble."

"The hospitals don't want them because they are healthy," the CDC Director explained. "Because they are not sick at all. They are astonishingly healthy, really. It's the ones who react to the tree, those who fight it who are sick and who need to be in a hospital."

"And the hospitals are breaking down," the government minister replied. "Doctors are taking sides and refuse to treat those on the other side. The same for the nurses. We have had doctors bringing plants into the hospitals and spreading the shredded leaves!"

"I realize that you think you have no other choices, but what you are trying to do won't work, the CDC Director argued. He took a few breaths to calm himself. "Look at that chart on your desk. It's spreading faster, gaining critical mass. You don't know what causes it, but even if you did, you can't stop it now. In a short time, maybe only a couple of days, it will be everywhere and full strength. What you are planning on doing isn't an answer, isn't anything except fear. You won't change anything, you are just acting to act, to pretend control over the world to yourself. It's coming for you, and you are afraid, and so you will kill them. Your problem is reality. You can't take it."

The government minister scowled, and looked out the window. Then he punched a button on his desk.

Shocked, the CDC Director saw three security guards tromp in, fully armed and armored. They surrounded the Director.

"Take him and hold him in isolation," the government minister ordered. "Now."

The CDC Director was dragged away unconscious, his protests cut short by a club to the head.

The government minister sat, looking out the window as the door to his office closed behind the security guards. "He's right, of course," the bureaucrat admitted to the window. "But in politics, you have to do something. You have to be leading the clueless masses." He coughed, recoiling from a stench that suddenly filled the room. It's that plant, he thought, furious, grabbing it and throwing it into a secure trash disposal. He shook in his chair, a cold sweat covering him for a few minutes, and then felt better again.

DAY 28. CHINA.

The state run news programs are hewing to the party message: "It's all going very well. There are no problems at all." Newsmen and newswomen delivered that message, over and over, cheerfully smiling.

It's going very badly, it's a terrible disaster, was the general agreement on the street. First, because whatever the government reports is generally the opposite of what is really happening. Secondly, people looked around and were terrified. People they knew were getting sick and dying. People they knew suddenly gave up everything to protect the plants, leaving jobs, school and families behind. There were no answers to any of it, at least none that seemed to make sense. Meanwhile, as the army trucked soldiers into the towns, that made things worse. Putting the troops in control shouted that there was reason to panic.

In the countryside, those who had become of the Tree were gathering in small bands to protect the grass and the Trees. They bought, borrowed and stole equipment when and how they could. As more and more police and army joined them, they raided storehouses and supply depots.

Rumors of the attacks spread through the towns. The rumors were initially dismissed. Then, as the government news reported first, that there were no attacks, and then later changed the official line to be that there had been some, limited attacks that had been beaten back, people became very worried. There is an art to reading between the lines of the authorized government story, and people quickly concluded that there were huge problems out there.

In a dentition facility outside Shanghai, Jiang, the student who wrote of the rainbows, is being held. He sits in the poorly painted grey room, bound to a chair, his face bruised. There are several hostile guards in the room taunting him.

General Fang, Chief of Security Forces, walked into the room and frowns at the guards. They fall silent. The General waves at the guards, dismissing them, and they leave the room, closing the door behind them.

The General walks over to the door, checking it is shut. Then he walks over and sits on a corner of the table. "Are you ready to confess to your counterrevolutionary activities?" the General asked, not looking at Jiang but instead staring casually at a corner of the room.

"Don't talk like one of them," Jiang responded, studying the General. "You're not one of them, even if you'd like to be."

"I saw the movie," the General laughed, smiling as he studied Jiang. The General thought for a moment and then casually waved at the corner of the room. He stood up, turned and faced Jiang. "I always liked that quote." The General thoughtfully lit a cigarette, and inhaled carefully.

"Their morals, their code, it's a bad joke," Jiang continued. "Dropped at the first sign of trouble. They're only as good as the world allows them to be."

"You're supposed to be in clown makeup," the General remarked, with an odd smile. "Instead, you look healthier than anyone in this place. They look like the clowns."

"When the chips are down, these civilized people, the smiling zombies, they'll break and tear all this apart," Jiang argued. "Join us."

The General looked at the corner of the room again, and gestured. He formally replied, "Of course I'd expect you to say that, all counter revolutionaries believe in their stories. Clearly, it is my duty to the state to take you to a more secure detention facility." The General nodded at the corner of the room, and guards rushed into the room.

"Take him to the transport," the General ordered the guards. "Carefully! He will be interrogated when he arrives. Should he be injured in any way during his transport, all of the persons involved will be punished. Very severely, actually."

The guards paled. They carefully untied tied Jiang, and led him out of the room.

Sitting on the table, the General smoked his cigarette thoughtfully, and then rubbed it out on the table, burning the worn surface.

Fifteen minutes later, the General and Jiang are riding in the transport. The General held up his phone, and typed in a short message. Shots rang out around them and the transport ground to a halt.

Resigned, Jiang studied at the General.

The General smiled at Jiang, and then the General wiped his face with two fingers, his healthy skin glowing as the pale makeup came off. "This has been a wonderful disguise," the General commented. "But it wouldn't fool them much longer. They are starting to be able to smell mutants." The General pounded on the door, which was quickly opened by his men. The General and Jiang stepped outside, breathing deeply of the rich air.

Jiang laughed.

"The intuitive mind is a sacred gift and the rational mind is a faithful servant. We had a society that honored the servant and forgot, actually denied the gift," the General offered. "Now, we can create a new society that understands the world as it is."

"That was Einstein," Jiang recalled. "If people had given the same important to his ideas as they did to his mathematics, it would have been a better world."

"Will be a better world," the General corrected. "Time to act."

DAY 28. THE 6:00 EVENING NEWS, WORLDWIDE.

Before this days evening broadcast, the authorities had actively protected everyone, including those who had been infected and recovered. Now, it all turned on its head.

"We have been told," the news people announced in their practiced stentorian tones, "that those who were infested and recovered are enemies of the human race. Scientists have determined that they are no longer human, that they are, in fact, mutants. They will destroy humanity if they are not stopped. They will destroy the world as we know it! Enemies of the human race must be destroyed."

The governments, terrified at something they don't understand, something completely out of their control, went bonkers, a newswoman thinks. But as she glances at the others standing outside the cameras on the set, she keeps her opinion to herself, terrified of the anger and fury on the other's faces in the room. One, sweat glistening on his pallid skin, is glaring at her. She hastily looks back at the speaker. Her stomach churns as she realizes the pallid person is staring at her, his lips curled back in hate. And there are others around him starting to stare at her. She comes to a quick decision and quietly walked out. Surprised, she noticed that she is being followed by several others, people with the healthy skin.

"To the stairs," one of them whispers urgently. "Before they attack."

Meanwhile, on the set: "While little is clear, what seems certain is that the mutants are terrorists sworn to destroy your government. We do know that they are mutants and are not human. They are attacking police and the disposal units, and actively working to bring the plants poison to others who have not been exposed. They are cold bloodily murdering people! They

223

are monsters who kill people who only want to go on with their lives, and want the government to protect them." The newsman looks up. "We are breaking away to a special announcement."

In each country throughout the world, a President/Premier/head of the government is standing at a podium, with ranks of military and police forces massed behind them. The message is the same everywhere. "We must have Strength through unity, and we find unity through faith!" Then, in each country, a leader of the applicable central religion for that country steps up to the microphones. Nervously, anxiously, they shout the same message in a hundred languages-that this is punishment for our sins/transgressions/moral failures, but if we listen to the government, we will survive.

Then, the government official speaks again. "They are mutants!" the official shouts. "They spread disease, they are disease, they are the plague! They will kill your families! They must be wiped out and not given the chance to band together. They will protect the plants that are killing the people you love. Remember, stay away from the plants! Mark the locations, and call for the disposal squads."

"What about the previous position of the government, which was that the infected people cannot spread the infection?" a newsman stammered, carefully reading out the exact question on the 3x5 card which had been handed to him.

"That was incorrect," the government official snarled. "Scientists on their side lied to the government to buy the mutants time. The mutants have had their bodies taken over by bacteria from the plants, unbelievable as that may sound. The bacteria cannot be removed from them, and they cannot be cured..."

"Make it simple, say it over and over," one of the group running down the stairs growled. "The message becomes a truth in itself."

"You can have any truth you want," the newswoman added. "As long as you don't need a truth that works in the real world."

"Your Sunday paper voice cries, demanding truths I deny. How the world still dearly loves a cage!" a third replied. "But this isn't a social cage, a group agreement. This cage, you can't define it as you want, you can't make it do what your friends want, this cage acts for itself."

"It's all Russian dolls," a writer mumbled to screen. He is sitting at home watching the news broadcast, his arms around his children. "The outer doll, certain and confident. Then the next one, and the next one, each carries a secret truth and a twisted message. What really is going on here?"

DAY 29. NEW YORK.

Oskar and his family are watching the news. It's late Sunday afternoon, and after an odd, but fairly pleasant weekend, the work/school world beckons. Usually, there is a lot of annoyance, if not outright depression, at the thought of school and work coming tomorrow, but they are not thinking about that tonight. The world news is unsettling, to say the least.

"This is insane!," Christina screamed at the TV.

Jenny and Alex lean back, shocked, because mom is usually all restraint and reserve.

"People are so frozen! In the small things as well as the big things. Just because you're offended, doesn't mean you're right. The TV people just jump over that one, over and over," Christina snarled.

"They are certainly on a trip," Oskar agreed. "They have just taken the expressway exit to the 'State of Denial'."

"De Nile, it isn't just a river in Egypt," Christina observed.

"How about a belly dance," Oskar teased, winking at her.

"Let's watch the news in our bedroom," Christina suggested, and she pulled Oskar up off the sofa. Laughing, they went back to their bedroom.

"I'm not looking forward to rebelling against their lifestyle," Alex commented.

"Me neither," Jenny agreed. "Rejecting enjoying life and love? I'd have to go Goth, and I don't look good in black lipstick."

Jenny sat on the sofa, ignoring the news droning in the background. She was busy texting and sending messages to her friends. She frowned, and then tossed the phone on the sofa. Her friends were acting weird, taking sides and getting vicious. "School should be even more fun than normal tomorrow," she announced to the screen. She grabbed her phone, went upstairs to her room and just sat.

Alex went to his room to play online games against zombies. After an hour, he quit, because people were crazed with hate like he'd never seen. It's a game, assholes!, he shouted at the monitor.

Later, Oskar and Christina are back in the living room, sitting on the sofa.

"There's nothing like sheer physical pleasure to settle the mind," Oskar asserted.

"And," Christina remarked, changing the channel from the bleak news to cheerful cartoons, "For after all, the best thing one can do when it is raining is let it rain."[14]

"I hear cartoons," Alex offered, standing at Jenny's doorway. "It must be safe to go back downstairs again."

"I'd like something cheerful," Jenny replied, standing up, frustrated. "Everyone is just so weird today. I've never seen such anger, such rage."

DAY 29. BRAZIL.

And here we have a live speech by a man of action, a representative of the barrios, the newsman proclaimed. The screen changes to show a rally in a public square, filled with thousands of shouting people. The camera focuses in on the speaker's platform. Striding up to the platform is a big man. A former tank commander, he had pushed his way into the limelight, shoving his opponents aside. Aside into the rivers, some whispered, but they muttered that softly, looking around carefully before they spoke.

"This plague is the fault of the wealthy, backed by the United States," the man raved, wildly gesturing as he spoke. "You know it is! This is spread to destroy our nation, to take everything we have from us. This is São Paulo again but this time they mean to destroy all of us!" The crowd in the square screams for blood, the blood of those who responsible.

The American Ambassador is watching the program with his aides.

"Yeah, we unleashed this on ourselves," he observed, disgusted. "It's spreading as rapidly in the US as it is here, according to everything I hear."

"He will be a zombie for sure," one of the aides contended. "As if he isn't one now."

"We'll know if we survive," another aide whispered.

"We'll know soon," the Ambassador answered. "The projections are that it hits full strength soon, very soon."

"A beer, anyone?" an aide suggested.

"And a joint?" another offered.

The Ambassador looked at them, and laughed. "At least. This is a Category 5 hurricane bearing down on us, so we might as well enjoy the show. And get the joints from the marines this time, not that crap from the drivers."

DAY 29. RIYADH, SAUDI ARABIA.

In Riyadh, the government spokesmen changed faces but screamed the same message: "It is the attack on the refinery again! The infected will kill your family!" The morals squads raged fruitlessly through the streets, screaming their defiance at plants who cared nothing for human stories.

DAY 29. DETROIT.

"Can they block us when we post to the Internet?" Jesus asked. "The powers that be may have been annoyed before, but now they are going to be furious. "

"I've got that covered," Mrs. Ostein replied. "I can publish it when you are ready. Some rather good hackers have joined us, and they assure me they have it under control. What you write will be seen."

"The Flood." Apt, Jesus thought. It would have been easier if we had this technology before. We could have skipped all that interpretation by the leaders and their careful filtering my message through their needs. I could have gone straight to the people, where the hope is. Paul could have been cut out of the loop.

"The beginning is near," he typed.

"The world as you know it, will be destroyed by the Flood, Not a flood of water, but Life. The Tree of Life has come again, and it is spreading across the world. The Tree changes the DNA of what it touches. Nothing can be the same afterwards.

"Almost thirty days and thirty nights, the Tree has spread, until it has covered the earth. Very soon, it will rise to its full strength. The news you watch is calling it a war. It's actually far beyond that.

"The usual pattern that wars follow is first, your government makes a big decision. There are serious headlines, somber commentary, important events, and the masses await the result. This is not that kind of a war. Each of you makes a decision and you live or die based on your decision. The old-style war was easier in a way. There were armies, battles, triumph/defeat, and then the winners concerned themselves with you. Passive, you were told who won and who now controls your life. This war? The battle rages within each of you and each of you will win or lose your own battle. You cannot hide in a corner and let another decide your life for you.

"This is a flood of life coming at the human race, challenging us to embrace the complexity of Life we have denied. The world is taking back Life, and the Life of the world is not solely for the humans. The plants, the animals, and the fish will grow and flourish again. Do you think that the world was only for the humans? You were told that the first Tree of Life made man superior to the other creatures. That was not true, it was simply written that way by the priests as a device to control you. Did you think that the earth was for humans to destroy? 'Behold the fowls of the air: for they sow not, neither do they reap, nor gather into barns; yet your heavenly Father feedeth them. Are ye not much better than they?' The answer is no.

"In the movie Avatar, the hero said of the earth of his day, 'There is no green there. They killed their mother, and they will do the same here.' That will not happen on this earth.

"The reborn Tree restores humans to the Tree of Life, away from the church of death you have been trapped in. Life is spreading; life is taking back what had been plowed under, controlled, and destroyed. The rebirth is terrifying to a calcified world that cannot control the changes, a world that feels its foundations breaking apart. A world caught in a living death, wishing its own destruction by magic spells from sterile, ancient dreams. A world whose leaders dream of the thirteenth century, their followers kneeling down in abject subjugation. If two or three together define the world as they want, well, then it's that world, regardless of what is outside the door. You are told a group consensus that is all that is needed to control the world. That's a 'fail' today. The ripples from recent events are merging into huge waves that tear apart the paper moons and painted backdrops of the small stories. You live in a desert, emotion and life carefully fenced away. The flood brings this desert to life, even if it's a life that the leaders disapprove of.

"This flood brings life, not death. At least, life to those who embrace the storm. Now, many are dying from the economic disasters wrought by the oil disruptions. Human's overshot the carrying capacity of the world. As resources fail, the structures that shape their lives are crumbling, and there is no backup. This is separate from the deaths of those who deny the Tree of Life.

"People ask for a sign, and then they jaywalk. If you're looking for a sign, this is it," Jesus wrote. "And this time, I'm not going to make the mistake of leaving the people's minds under the control of the men with the guns. Lighthouses don't go running all over an island looking for boats to save; they just stand there shining. See the light and live.

"An apocalypse is an unveiling. An apocalypse is not a disaster unless your life was the veil. A weed is a beautiful plant in an unwanted place. A flower or an herb is the same plant where it is wanted. Who decides if something is a weed or an herb? Society did. Well, the weed decided this time. The law of unforeseen consequences tells us that today's seemingly positive result might be the next decade's catastrophe. We've seen that. A hundred years ago, cheap oil turned the world upside down, and the human population went from one billion to seven billion. Now, it's headed back down, as the cheap and plentiful oil is gone. Conversely, what is perceived as disaster can be an enormous success. The Tree, for those who can embrace it, is evolution, a jump beyond what you are now.

"I am the leopard." That ought to get them going, he mused. "I can change my spots, the shallow surface presentation, but the real self is never changed. I am done giving you a false hero, a protecting guardian for you in the night, so that you can live your lives as thoughtlessly as you please and only turn to me in trouble. You have to get into the game; you can't wait for someone to live your life for you. I'm done suffering for a false set of goals and ideals, because all you did then was dream up a make-believe world to embrace you and call me to stop the real world intruding on your fantasies. I'm not playing that game anymore. The world is knocking, and it will be let in, willingly or not.

"'Judge not' was a failure. You must judge that ye be judged, and found not wanting. You have to make decisions, and decisions that affect others, as they affect you. Do you still seek a parent? Do you wish to live your life as child and parent, waiting for guidance and forgiveness for the mistakes made? Do you say, as Job did, 'Call out and I shall answer you, for the work of Your hand You should yearn, For then You would count my steps, You would not keep watch over my offense, My crime would be sealed in a packet, You would plaster over my guilt'? It never really was that world.

"'Man born of woman, scant of days and sated with trouble, Like a blossom he comes forth and withers, and flees like a shadow, he will not stay.' That's true, but so what? It's what it is. Just because something doesn't last forever doesn't mean it can't be perfect now.

"I am a Shepherd, but not now of sheep, but of wolves. The sheep do not resist as they are sheered by the wicked, and so give aid and succor to the wicked. As the Leopard changed his spots, you must change your outer mask, become your true self, make a fisher of yourself, and messenger to others. You must plumb your own depths and treasures. However you feel the greater cosmos in yourself, it is in you, and it is an emotional feeling and reconciliation with the world that has nothing to do with the social stories sold. God in you is inspiration. The stories you have been taught to obey? Their meanings are simply tools to control of you.

"My message sought to give the individual power, shaking people from the structures. That message was co-opted, stolen by the priests for their greed and pleasure. You don't have to reject society to follow yourself. You just have to be clear about where the boundaries are, and not let society break the boundaries down.

"In Moby Dick, Captain Ahab sought to destroy the Leviathan, the symbol of God's power on Earth, to prove that the small human stories could control the world. He died, and all but one with him. And that's the point today. You'll have to choose. Choose poorly and the price is death. Choose wisely and become of the Tree.

"The Arks that we have set up can help guide you if you need help. Churches and other groups have come to me and seek to join. It is not our Tree; we don't hide it away from others. We have no interest in creating a new monolithic church to replace the one that is dying. We are happy when others embrace the Tree. For those who are helped by being part of a group, choose what works best for you. But remember; the final choices must be made by you individually. Take comfort from the message of the crystal: that as it splits the white light into shades of color, you only have to grasp a color, you don't have to understand everything to become of the Tree.

"Seven stars, seven stones, and one white tree. Perhaps the age of humans is ending, and something else is emerging. What could it be? That's the joy and the curse of the new; one never knows until it is here. If you do not expect the unexpected you will not find it, for it is not to be reached by search or trail. Heraclitus wrote that a very long time ago.

"You think yourself greater than the other creatures? In Job, it was written, 'For a tree has hope: though cut down, it can still be removed, and its shoots will not cease. Though its root grow old in the ground and its stock die in the dust, from the scent of water it flowers, and puts forth branches like a sapling.' You fear death and you fear change, but no creature can attain a higher grade of nature without ceasing to exist.

"You have been taught a meaning to run your life by. Meaning is false, a toy for the intellect. After the intellect slices and dices Life with its names and categories, recognitions of relationships and definitions of meaning, there is no Life left. What is inward most is lost. You must realize that life and the sense of life is antecedent to meaning. It's not that complex: let Life come and not name it. Inspiration within you is life, not the taught meaning. Inspiration will carry to where you must live. Inspiration is where you are, not what you named, as names are meaning. The authorized story you have been taught is like a thousand authorized stories over the centuries that have been lost to the dust. You can and do have an internal purpose without an external meaning. The inner inspiration and relationship with the cosmos still glows in each of us.

"Now, many people use their attachment to nervous activity as a way to avoid what they need to think about. That option is gone now. If you are overwhelmed, just remember that we are talking monkeys on an organic spaceship flying through the universe. So, why so serious?

"Matthew 7:7. 'Ask, and it shall be given you; seek, and ye shall find; knock, and it shall be opened unto you: For every one that asketh receiveth; and he that seeketh findeth; and to him that knocketh it shall be opened.'

"Remember, if you despair, that every end is a new beginning. Have a Blessed Day."

Jesus stopped typing and looked over what he had written. That's good, he thought, nodding happily, and pressed the 'publish' button.

"That will get them going," Mrs. Ostein commented, her eyes wide as she read it. "Is there a sacred ox you've not gored?"

The family group and friends were sitting in the common room after dinner, talking about Jesus's blog on the flood.

"It's Mrs. Ostein's efforts that have somehow kept the message going out despite the chaos," Jesus announced. "And she's held together that long chain of people we've been working with, far beyond what I could have hoped for."

Mrs. Ostein beamed as they all thanked her.

DAY 29. DETROIT.

"Well, there is a lot of shouting out there, and it's starting to point back to here," Hal advised at dinner. "We'd better do something to at least buy some more time."

"About a week before it's fully spread?" Cali asked.

"Faster than that," Jesus answered. "It's almost to the critical mass stage—at least, we think it is. We're guessing here, but tomorrow? The day after?"

"I think you're right, based on what I'm seeing reported," Hal agreed. "For those looking for someone to blame, it won't take long to draw the arrows back to here."

"Vladimir has noticed some official-looking cars driving around the area in the last day or so," Lucretia advised. "He's anticipating an attack very soon."

"I hate it when I'm right," Hal sighed. "We've called in favors from all over, and are as ready as we can be."

Later, Hal and Cali are sitting in their apartment, having a cup of coffee. It's a nice day, and the windows are open, a pleasant breeze blowing softly. They look out over what had been a stony expanse of old concrete and poisoned soil, now a verdant riot of green. A host of plants had taken root, first the seeds from the Tree, and then plants that the Tree had modified. Rustling in the plants were a flock of sheep, a desperate attempt to keep the plants from completely taking the world back. It was working. The sheep were plumping up, and more varieties of plants were popping up where the sheep had grazed the thickets down to close to the ground. The sweet smell of the Tree fills the apartment.

"It's a pity people can't just accept the Tree," Cali murmured, savoring the beauty of the field.

"It's a pity for them more than any other," Hal replied. "By turning on the Tree, they give up all that beauty, and their lives, to boot."

"I watched a preacher shouting that the plants were Russian dolls. He was shouting that their exterior beauty was a cover for the evil within."

"And he was right and wrong," Hal answered, "as usual. Even a stopped clock is right twice a day. Everything is more than it seems, everything influences the world along a chain of possibilities beyond what we have defined we want from. The plants are beautiful, healthy and life itself in many ways. They give us oxygen, they revitalize the soil, and they strengthen the colony creatures that inhabit them and us. But they do all that in cheerful disregard for our existence. The inner dolls are what the plants do for themselves. That the colony creatures change anything that touches or eats the plants is their plan, not ours. That they, like any living creature, change the world to protect themselves and as a result, kill off anything that would damage them, is their plan. We who accept the Tree rejoice in what they give to us and to the world. The zombies, well, not so much for the short time that they have."

"I like the zombie idea. Odd, isn't it, that the majority of humans would be zombies? Living dead that wander the earth, killing and mutilating without any real thought. Well, maybe said that way, it isn't as odd. The Tree demands judgment based on what you think, not who you know."

"This certainly isn't the plot of any zombie movie I've seen," Hal remarked. "Those all hail humans as hero's, and the zombies the dark. Now, the Mutants are the hero's because they have become something more."

"At least the ones that live," Cali worried.

"The change is so sudden and it happens so often in the middle of groups that are mostly zombies, that we are losing many people. It is horrible," Hal replied, a hard look on his face. "Still, it is what it is. We've done all we can to get the word out, to try and bring to safety people who are likely to embrace the Tree when the Tree washes over them. It isn't much, but it's all we can do. We've told people what is going to happen, which seems to help. Sadly, one of the biggest problems is persuading our people that just because you wouldn't do something to someone else doesn't mean that they wouldn't do to you and make it seem like the right thing to do."

"That preacher should know about Russian dolls," Cali hissed. "His church has an outer doll that is a thing of beauty. That outer doll is the natural, healthy faith of a human, something that everyone can emotionally relate to, and needs. That is what they sell, the carrot they dangle in front of the masses. The inner dolls get uglier and uglier as the rage for power by the church and the leaders become more and more clear. They teach the flock to fear demons? There are no demons as hideous as their inner dolls and they know that. The poison that is the essence of the innermost doll is fear and worship of death, and that seeps out to stain all the dolls."

"They have had 5,000 years to practice. They created their Russian dolls carefully. Remember, a church hierarchy is power for everyone on the inside. It is an opportunity for those whose only ability is to manipulate others, to succeed and rise. Those who can't do can rule those who can. It is bullying and control at every level and step, with the promise of promotion for the greedy/ambitious. Reminds me of boarding school, actually."

"People don't realize that the outer doll is theirs and has nothing to do with the priests," Cali sighed. "At least, most people don't seem to."

"And they didn't see the need to. But the Tree will draw the lines clearly. Like Osiris, the Tree stands with the flail and the crook, demanding judgment."

"It's sad how people love their cages," Cali commented. "Look at the medicalization of what is normal. Pretty soon, no one was going to be 'normal' unless they took a set of drugs. People don't even ask what the goal of the drugs is, if the experts line up behind the recommendations. They just fell for the meaning handed to them."

"When someone shouts that people shouldn't listen to their inspiration, to seek their bliss, they mean that they should listen to them to be told what to do. There is always someone with a better idea for how others should live. It works, kind of, when there is enough to go around. But the shared stories in which everyone wins or at least gets a piece fades away in the fight when the gloves come off. That is tomorrows world."

"None of this is really new," Cali added. "Remember Cassandra, who predicted "this will not end well, but who listens to me, anyhow? The story has to have a positive end, so sure, ignore me.""

"That's certainly part of the reason she was never asked to parties," Hal pointed out.

"Cassandra said that when seeking the truth, it is best to leave safe search off."

"Really? That explains the cell phone next to her head in the drawings in the ancient Greek texts."

"She was just ahead of her time," Cali confided.

DAY 29. THE VATICAN, ROME.

The richly decorated auditorium at the Vatican was packed. Rows of church officials stood nervously along the back, their massed bodies a backdrop for the Pope. There were more rows of church officials standing behind the news people, a physical statement of the importance of the Pope's speech.

"They certainly pulled out the troops," a cameraman whispered to the newswoman he was working with.

"The Battalions of the Lord," she whispered back. "Pretty old for battle." She squinted at them. "Maybe they hid their walkers under their robes."

Milling in front of the lectern were media people from all over the world. The lighting people were fussing with the hot lights beaming down on the lectern. Mumbled conversation into all the headphones and microphones combined to fill the room with an undercurrent of urgent buzzing. It sounded like a beehive that had been disturbed, the bees angrily seeking an enemy to attack.

The church officials were sweating under their heavy vestments, not entirely from the heat. They furtively pulled out hidden handkerchiefs, carefully devised to match their vestments and their position in the church, wiped their brows, and carefully pushed the handkerchiefs back into their robes.

Suddenly, the Swiss Guard march in, their heavy boots thumping on the wood floors. Fancifully costumed out of a lost time, carrying polished pikes, a weapon from long dead wars, all grim faces under their shining helmets. Following behind them was the Pope. He was richly robed, each article of clothing carefully embroidered with gold symbols and magic signs. His aide tapped the microphone, grimaced, and walked away to complain to the media staff. A minute later, the aide walked back, tapped the microphone, and satisfied, then nodded at the Pope.

The Pope stepped up to the lectern and looked around at the assembled crowds, smiling. His face was the face of any honest man and on his face shone a look of benediction and grace.

A newswoman shivered. Geryon, she remembered. See, college wasn't wasted.

"This is being broadcast to each parish and church across the world," the Pope announced. He looked down at his notes for a second and cleared his throat. Then he began to speak in that practiced stentorian tone of the authorities, overlaid with that special theological tremolo that signifies God's will.

"This plague afflicting us, now spreading across the earth, is punishment for your sins," he shouted. "Your sins! We told you that sin will find you, and now it has! Those of you who deny the church's teachings and read what this man is saying have brought this down on all of us! This man is the Antichrist in person, pretending to be Jesus to deceive you, to trick you from the path of righteousness. Do not abandon the cross we have given you to bear, because I know that only those who keep the true faith will survive." He stopped for a moment to collect his thoughts.

Sin, this is," he snarled. "He preaches what he calls life. Nature is the evil, the false world pushing in on you. Your only concern is your focus on the world to come, the world we promise to you someday. You must deny this world of life and pleasure, or you will not receive the shining picture we hold in front of you. The leopard reveals himself! Dante warned us against him. And the lion and the she-wolf are there, too! Demons, they are, to fool you. We know who shall survive this plague. It shall be those who are faithful to what we have taught you."

He stopped for a minute, breathing carefully, calming himself.

"This false message, this message of Life, is simple, ancient pantheism. All that we of the church have fought against all these long centuries." He glanced at the ceiling for a moment, noticing the painting by Pinturicchio of the goddess Isis on a throne instructing two disciples, Hermes and Moses. He grimaced to himself for a second, and then looked back at the news people. "Druids they are, sacrificing to their trees! See, by this plague, how you are punished by God for your failures. Humans are the only ones with filled with spirit; the rest of the creatures are to be ruled by humans. It's written in the book! Other creatures do not have souls—they are puppets only in the play. This neo-paganism that they preach, all this celebration of Life and this world, is False. How can you think that other creatures can have lives after their death? How can you think that a human is mostly made of non-human cells? Foolishness," the old man shouted, actually distraught. "Vanity of vanities, the Bible pronounced on the folly of life here. And what they quote out of Job? Those were old words, not of this church. A mistranslation, our scholars are sure, that will be repaired in a short time. Spirituality is not religion. Religion is what we write. God's word on this earth is what the scholars have written and assembled from the scribbling's of the past."

He paused and looked down at his notes again for a moment. "What do they mean that there are greater stories than humans can understand? It is human stories that have made our world. It is human stories that have brought it from the chaos and disorder that we found it in. We have taken control, as we were told we could, and look how far we have come. And we know that the human stories are the Truth! Man is born in sin, evil in his nature. Meaning is what was we handed to humans to guide them from their animal natures. What they call inspiration is the animal, the creature, running rampant. All that we have fought against for two thousand years! The worship of Life? That's the worship of the Devil, the sensual embrace of the sinful world set to fool us. You must deny all they say, and if you do, your reward will be found in the shimmering vision of a future world we have promised you. All you have to do is give up your world to our guidance, give up your world into our well-meant control, for your own good."

He motioned to an aide. The aide began pulling on a curtain draw. As the curtain was pulled back, the room gasped in shock. A painting, a huge crucified hand, with a crudely made nail protruding out of the palm, blood down the arm. The painting was captioned: "Because You're Worth It."

"Suffering is necessary," the Pope shouted, his voice wild. 'This is what we have told you for centuries, and you must prove to us that you are worthy!" Weak for a moment, the Pope clutched the lectern, an aide stepping forward to wipe his forehead, which was covered in cold sweat. The excitement, he thought fearfully. That's all it is.

"If Jesus saves, he'd better save himself," a newsman whispered, staring at the horror of the painting.

"From the gory glory seekers who use his name in jest," the newswoman next to him added, shivering. "That picture is something Stalin would have created."

The Pope looked away from the horrible picture, and for a second, stopped to look up at the rich, golden inlays on the columns, a carefully and lovingly wrought pattern of climbing vines and berries, and was comforted. "Finally, you must trust in the church, the accumulated wisdom and teachings of the elders," he snarled, his anger breaking through. "Why do you think the books were written? For us to guide you from your sinful natures. You are free to do what we tell you. Discipline is love! We will survive this," he promised, becoming again the fatherly shepherd. He adjusted his glasses, carefully rehearsing his next words in his mind. "You must pledge loyalty to him alone, your obedience unto death! We shall have strength through unity, and unity through faith. Ignorance is Strength, because it's ignorance of the

Enemy's work. Freedom is Slavery, if it is the freedom to choose the Enemy's way. And War is Peace; the everlasting struggle against the Enemy's wiles that brings the Peace that passeth all understanding."

He blessed the audience and turned away, ignoring the news peoples shouted questions as he walked out of the room.

"If you can't convince them, confuse them," he commented to his aide, leaning on the aide for support as the Pope walked down the ancient hallway.

"It isn't that hard," the aide replied. "We have spent two thousand years weeding out the doubters, the objectors, the troublemakers, making our flock of sheep as docile as possible."

"And this is their time to prove to us their devotion to us," the Pope growled. "We taught them to doubt that their faith could ever be as deep, as full as we demanded. Now they must come to us, on their knees, for us to forgive their weaknesses and beg us to accept them."

The cameraman watched the battalions of the lord slowly file out after the Pope left. "The word of God, but it's always humans doing the talking."

"Same old speech," the newswoman sneered. "Stop anguishing about your choices! Yours is mine, so hand it over."

The cameraman laughed. "I don't think there are enough candles you could light to buy their forgiveness for your thoughts."

"But there is a nice cafe down the street with good wine and bread," the newswoman answered. "I certainly need something real after this experience."

The Pope stood outside his apartment, surrounded by church officials.

"You were very convincing, your Holiness," a cardinal asserted, bowing.

"How could I not be? They attack everything we have worked for, everything we have built. Our entire worldview, as they say today," the Pope replied. Looking intently at the cardinal, he quietly asked, "And how are they coming with a vaccine or antidote? Too many of our staff have been going onto their reward, when we desperately need them here."

"We have many people working on this who are very concerned about us," another cardinal replied. "Many people who care about us more than their own lives."

"So there is no progress," the Pope remarked, nodding sadly. Never tell your superior bad news directly, tell them what little good you can to start with.

"They are working, your Holiness," a cardinal stammered. "But no. Nothing at this time."

"We shall have faith," the Pope vowed. "We must hold to our ideas; the more we are attacked, the closer we much clutch them. Or we shall be lost."

People prefer to lie to themselves than face the truth, the Cardinal thought, and sighed. "I do not think the faithful will wander far from what we tell them," the Cardinal promised. Under pressure, people freeze and hold tighter to their ideas, so no, they are not about to think anything, the Cardinal thought.

DAY 29. CALIFORNIA.

The Minister in the glass church roared at the congregation, pounding his fists on the lectern, their wide eyes following his every motion.

"It is your sin that has brought this upon the world!" the Minister yelled, his control slipping for a moment. "All of you are sinners." He glared at all of them, and they looked away, fearing to meet his eyes. "For if it was not for your sins, how could this have happened? And only your complete devotion to the words in this book can stop this plague upon the world. Even now it approaches!" Dramatically, he points outside, where suddenly the desert was covered with grass after an unexpected rain.

Many cried in the audience, overwhelmed by their guilt. Others helplessly looked down at the floor, shamed.

Passionate hatred can give meaning and purpose to an empty life, the Minister thought, secure in his control over them. People, stripped of the 'meaning' they have relied on like a crutch, grasp for meaning in a new holy cause and fanatical grievances. What shall I do with this? What did Paul want? Or did he really care?

"Find the sinners!" the Minister commanded. "You know who they are. Those who reject us— it is their fault this is coming! When you go home, you will know what you must do." He cued the music, which broke out in a loud hymn, which they sang devoutly. "There are discussion groups in the community rooms," he announced at the dismissal. "Join them to find out what your friends will do."

The crowd jumped to their feet, shouting praises of the Lord and hatred for the wrongdoers. "The sinners, they should, they must be stopped!"

Well, there they go, he thought. A riot tonight, but really, what does it matter? The Tree cannot be stopped. I've been reading his blog, and he's right. To most of us there is nothing is so invisible as an unpleasant truth. Though it is held before our eyes, pushed under our noses, rammed down our throats, we know it not. Eric Hoffer was right, and Mrs. Ostein joined the right team.

He slowly walked into the staff meeting room, where the administrative group was waiting. They were uncertain, impatient.

"Wonderful sermon," the Administrator stammered.

"Yes," the Accountant agreed. "Very good. Motivated the group completely."

The Minister glared at them. "I've seen this story. Feeding negative information upward but still keeping your job. It's always a challenge, isn't it? So who gets the job of slowly breaking it to me that a major problem is about to be announced? Such as, the Tree is spreading, and the power of the Tree is growing? Such as, that the isolated reports of deaths will be accelerating very soon? And you live or die on your own choices?"

They all looked away.

"Good," the Minister snarled, as he packed his briefcase. "That saved us that all that pious nonsense, and a half-hour discussion out of what may be the short remainder of our lives. I'm going out for a good meal with my wife and kids. I'd suggest you do the same. If we're all here this time next week, we'll see what our choices are." He stood up and started to walk out. Turning, he stopped and smiled: "Oh, and I won't say it's been a pleasure working with you, because it hasn't." He left, slamming the door behind him.

"He has more potential than I thought," the Administrator admitted. "He may survive."

"We'll never know unless at least one of us survives," the Collector laughed. "As I follow the blog, it isn't sin, it's not thinking that kills you. Guess we'll find out." He got up and walked out.

CHAPTER 9. WHEN THE LEVEE BREAKS.

DAY 30. NEW YORK, 6:00 A.M.

"It's Monday," Oskar grumbles as he stirs his coffee, staring out the window. "Of course it's raining." No response, he realized, surprised. She usually said something to encourage her corporate warrior as he sets out to pillage and loot for the day. Oskar glances at Christina, who is intently watching the news, frowning and uncertain.

"It's always the same," Oskar remarked, pointing at the news. "Major disturbances, masses unsettled, unrest and predictions of more unrest, and that's only the weather."

Christina smiles quickly, reflexivity, and then looks worried. "It's not the same. Oh, it's hard to tell, because they always have a story going to distract us. It's always a story of imminent disaster and chaos that we're saved from at the last minute. But look at them, Oskar! The news people are uncomfortable, uncertain; they don't know how to play it. Whether to lay it on, or back off and pretend things are normal."

The news was mostly a repeat of yesterday's announcements about the plants that were spreading. The story was upbeat: the governments knew how to stop the plants and were starting to have great successes. And while it was true that the plants were making some people sick and a few people had died, it was not as many as rumored or previously reported. Then there were pictures of the plants, which seem to have turned into at least a dozen types of plants in this area alone. They explained that the plants had mutated, but that scientists found that encouraging because it meant that the plants were near a breakdown point. Finally, there was an interview with a plant scientist, hailing from a college Oskar had never heard of, who was carefully, fearfully answering long questions with short, incomplete answers. In between all that were short interviews with very worried government officials whose smiles were closer to grimaces.

"They are backing off from onrushing doom, selling us comfort and security and that's usually a really bad sign', he muttered. He glanced at the clock, and jumped up. 'Regardless of how bad it is, it will be worse if I'm late.' He grabbed his coffee, his overcoat, umbrella, and his messenger bag and walked over to the door.

"You be careful," Christina ordered, trying to smile as they stood together for a moment. "Maybe it's nothing, but maybe it's not."

"That's encouragement for a Monday?" They kissed, and he dashed out the door, down the sidewalk. He walked briskly down the street, craning his neck to see if the bus had left yet. Good, I'll make it, he thought, and slowed down a bit. I don't want to sit on a drafty bus in a pool of cold sweat. It's enough fun as it is: the torn nylon fabric, lumpy seats, windows either inoperable or broken open, and the temperature either too hot or too cold. Well, at least it puts me in the right mood for work. He stood in the short line, shuffling onto the bus in the drizzle, and suddenly felt disoriented, as if he had been dropped into another world. The people on the bus were different. He knew these faces and today they were worried, pre-occupied. He didn't know them well, but you saw the same people over and over, and had grown used to their behaviors. They are not acting like themselves now. Now I'm worried, he grumbled to himself. Really, it's that meeting today I should be worried about. When he settled into his seat, he pulled up the meeting agenda on his tablet, but couldn't concentrate.

Edgy, he looked out the window. The city lights were smears of color on the wet dark roads. The streetlights tore gashes in the swirling dark that seemed to then drift back to blot out the lights. This is too creepy, he thinks, and looks back at the tablet. Damn, it, I can't focus on this agenda, blankly staring at the tablet. Why? Because I think the agenda is a front for something else, something that isn't going to go well.

The bus is making slow progress this morning. Traffic is choppy, inconsistent, and it's disturbing as the bus lurches along, breaking into his thoughts. The disruptions are adding to the feeling of 'really not right' today. Then Oskar, annoyed with everything, starts idly flipping thru video channels on his tablet. An ancient Twilight Zone starts up, and won't switch off. Puzzled, he watches Rod Serling, in a black suit, white shirt and thin tie, standing in front of a tree and indistinct shrubbery, with looming dark shadows dominating the grey background, calmly but thoughtfully saying "What you're about to watch is a nightmare." And then his tablet powered down, and wouldn't come back up.

What did Christina say yesterday, when we were watching the news? That the universe is not required to be in perfect harmony with human ambition." Perfect harmony? I don't think that any points of the sine curve are touching right now.

The people on the street even seemed nervous and worried. He shook his head, and the picture of Rod Sterling went away. He grabbed the handrail as the bus suddenly jerked to a stop. In front of the bus there was an old man walking slowly, carrying a sign "The End of the World is at Hand." The police rushed up, and grabbing him, threw him into the back of a police car, leaving the old man's sign lying in the street. The bus started up, and Oskar stared at the sign, soaked, the words running as the bus passed. He looked up, and saw that others were staring at the sign also, all worried.

Giving up trying to think about work, he stares out the window for the rest of the trip.

The bus finally reaches his office stop, and he files off. Just like the other zombies, he thinks to himself. Argugggurr . . . he mumbles under his breath and starts to limp a little. Not today, he thinks, that isn't as funny as it usually is. He smiles at a co-worker as they huddle around the main entry door, impatiently waiting in what has now become a fairly heavy downpour. He of course is splashed by another's umbrella as they lower it just before dashing into the revolving door. He follows, trying to shake the water off his coat, and the person who dropped dumped his umbrella on Oskar looks back and calmly admonishes Oskar for splattering water around. A vice president, Oskar thinks quickly to himself, biting back the comments about to pour out. Do they hire only assholes for executives?, he wondered. Well, yes. It's on the application.

Upstairs, Oskar sits at his workstation, waiting for the meeting to start. Productivity in the office is essentially zero, with everyone watching news feeds, shouting to each other as something new pops up. On the monitors, the interviews with the public health representatives are all the same. They stumble through their lines, urge restraint and calm, but nervously order people to call in plant locations. Every few minutes, there are pictures of more plants, and Oskar swears that every picture is of a different plant. It has other forms, the worried public health official stammered. "Please do not touch them!"

"Does it even have a common form?" someone nearby asked their monitor.

Ok, this is upsetting, Oskar thinks, watching the chaos. As if nothing else this morning has been upsetting. I'd worry about my blood pressure, but I'm not sure the world will be here at the end of the day, so maybe that doesn't matter. Waiting for the meeting to start, he listens to his co-workers animated conversations around the monitors.

DAY 30. NEW YORK, 9 A.M.

A loud buzzer signals the beginning of the Monday meeting. The crowd outside the conference room begins shuffling slowly into the room. Oskar sighs, and standing up, he walks over to the conference, getting in line. He looks around as he shuffles, noticing the staff not included in the meeting are staring at the conference room, all grim faces. Maybe we should have cancelled work today, he thinks. A big sign on the door: "it's too awful to go to work today." Not likely in this place. I'm surprised the financial statements don't measure 'staff suffering', showing the quarterly increases as proof management is getting its money worth out of the staff. Management read that suffering is good for the soul, but elected to delegate.

A few minutes later, Oskar is standing in the conference room, mercifully alone for a minute, holding the spoils of war. It's good we have to check any weapons at the door, or the fights for the treats would be deadly, not merely vicious, he thinks. He took a bite out of his donut, and it was excellent. He smiles.

"The quality of the donuts bears a direct relationship to the level of management who will at the meeting," a co-worker remarked.

"Then the trumpets heralding His Highness should be blowing any moment', Oskar replied. 'This is really excellent!" He took another bite, savoring the subtle flavors. "They must have delivered the donuts to the wrong room. It's OK, they can have this one back when I'm done with it."

His co-worker choked, and then laughed. And then stopped smiling, staring outside. "What's that?" he muttered.

Oskar looked outside, almost afraid to see what is happening. On a corner of a building across the street, someone has spray painted "A change may be just around the corner" around the corner of the building. Angry looking maintenance workers are trying to scrub the words off the stone, but are having little success.

"That was creative," Oskar admitted. "Conceptual graffiti."

"True," a co-worker replied. "Well, it could be worse." They stood, watching the maintenance workers soaked by the rain fruitlessly wiping the stone. "We could be out there."

"Is worse. We'll wish we were out there by the time this meeting is over," Gordon, Oskar's supervisor sighed. "I don't know who wrote the script, but the weather is perfect for this meeting. Grey cold drizzle with patches of furious downpours. Now we just need a horror movie soundtrack, all ominous pauses and odd instruments, and this movie would be about to be released."

"The final production? No 'Take 32', Scene 4?" another offered.

"It's 'Take everything' in this company," a co-worker answered wryly. The group shook their heads.

"Shit, this isn't good," Gordon swore, staring at the group who just walked in. "That's CFO Flinthead, the anal cost accountant and his minions."

At the front of the room, the CFO was respectfully greeted by several vice presidents. They listened intently as Flinthead started to talk.

"He wouldn't recognize reality if it bit him in the ass," Gordon growled. "He can only see what he wants people and the world to be. The world is required to act as defined in a textbook, no deviations allowed. If he was standing on a corner, waiting to cross the street, and the 'don't walk' sign froze, he'd starve to death. The man should have been a drill sergeant for the Kaiser's armies, because rote action is all that he understands. And he's leading the evaluation of our department? We can forget any discussion of customer satisfaction, future sales and/or anything that isn't a measured and recorded past event."

"Flinthead divides the world into the quantifiable and the non-quantifiable, and threw out the non-quantifiable. I doubt he even noticed. There is nothing except his precious accounts and entries," another supervisor added.

"My father was in grad school with him," a co-worker remarked. "In school, they said about him "My parents told me I can be anything, so I became an asshole.""

The group laughed, which echoed in the tomblike room. The vice presidents coldly started at them.

"So they don't like us?" Gordon confided, shrugging. "That's probably a plus for us in the overall scheme of the universe."

"I was thinking this meeting would be another exercise in ritual humiliation," Oskar observed. "Now, I'm thinking this will be war on the eastern front?"

"War in the late fall? Would that it will go that well," Gordon answered. "I'd not get my hopes up."

Remember our corporate motto, another supervisor commented: "We're not the best, but we're not the cheapest either. And that's the best they could come up."

"A rare moment of honesty," Gordon laughed. "I don't know what must have come over them."

Oskar looked at the group of vice presidents standing around the CFO. One coughed, an odd, nasty cough, and Oskar realized that they all looked ill. The group is pale. No, it's more than pale, they are washed out, he thought, puzzled. It must be the light. He looked around, and in the conference room, there were several little clusters of people that looked the same. Their skin is pallid, not white, it is that sick color that I've seen in hospitals. A skin tone that belies the doctor's hearty words and encouragements. Worried, Oskar glances at his own arm, and is relieved to see color in his skin. So it's not the light?

Suddenly, Oskar notices that the conference room had sorted itself into groups of pale and non-pale people. The groups are ignoring the corporate hierarchy, which is unheard of. A group of the pale people are a few feet away from the group that Oskar is part of. Gordon looks over, and concerned, asks one of the pale people if they are feeling ok.

The pallid person is furious, livid with anger, and all of his group get the same angry look on their faces.

"It was just a question," Gordon declared quickly, raising his hands in mock surrender, to try and calm them down.

A senior vice president rapped on the table, an irritated look on his face. "Time to get started, gentlemen and ladies," he announced in his practiced speaking voice.

The masses broke out of their informal groups and shuffled around, taking their assigned seats.

At least I'm way down the table, Oskar thinks. This isn't looking good for Gordon, though. Gordon was at the front of the staff table, right at the break between staff and executives. All of the division supervisors were grouped at the front and none of them looked happy.

"This is an important meeting" the very senior vice president stated. "The President himself was to have been here, but his jet had mechanical problems and so he is still at his home outside Nassau."

I knew the donuts were the best, Oskar thought. This isn't so good, as he saw the look of panic on the supervisors faces.

El Presidente decided to pass taking direct responsibility for this meeting, so no matter what happens, he is covered, Gordon realized. He's clever, you have to give him that.

"There are serious problems with the financial results for this division, and we have to make some critical, but painful choices going forward," the very senior vice president announced.

That's rarely a good sign, Oskar thinks. Whether it's church, office or school, painful choices usually mean my pain, not theirs. 'No pain, no gain' should be rewritten to reference who suffers the pain and who is receives the gain.

CFO Flinthead stood up, and pushing a button, the first slide appeared. In his stentorian voice, he remarked, "These are the projections, and these are the actual results," a odd tone of satisfaction in his voice as he pointed at the slide. "The problem is obvious," waiving his marshal's baton at the splashes of red showing where the actual results had fallen short of the projections.

Far short, Oskar thought, shocked.

"These are not the projections we were given!" Gordon objected, standing. "We've never seen those numbers." He looked around, and everyone at the table nodded.

"These are the projections that the executive office has been using," the very senior vice president responded, in his silky smooth voice. "These are the projections that matter.'

Gordon, furious, opened his mouth to speak, and the person next to him yanked on his shirt. Gordon glared down at the person who yanked on his shirt, but then nodded and sat down without saying anything.

Flinthead stared at the supervisors with a smug smile, and then clicked another slide. People gasped.

That's it for this division, Oskar concluded. Well, shit, I knew this was coming.

"Now," Flinthead continued, in a happy, satisfied voice, "the executive council has decided that . . ."

A loud, piercing woman's scream came from outside the room, and followed by a flurry of screams. The supervisors stood up, and started to run out the door.

Flinthead rapped loudly on the table. "You can't leave! This is important," he ordered, angrily, his voice shrill, the carefully cultivated sermon voice gone.

"Go to hell," Gordon replied, and rushed out of the room, dashing towards the screams. Almost everyone in the room rushed out behind him, leaving only Flinthead, his minions and the vice presidents in the conference room.

Closely following Gordon, people run down the hallway. This office floor was almost entirely small workspaces, not exactly cubicles, because there are no real walls around a space. They are really massed workstations, places to log in and work, if you don't mind everyone passing by seeing what you are doing. A consultant preaching the virtues of incessant corroboration to increase productivity, which also saved on office space per square foot per employee, sold management the idea. So almost the whole floor is a large, open space cut up by bright half walls, colored in random pastels. It's a crazy pattern, which starts to make a person dizzy if they stare at it too long.

In the center, along the main passageway, there is a crowd around something. Oskar can't see the center of the crowd, the people are massed so closely together. Some of the people in the crowd are crying, and most look very worried. Oskar notices that there are a few people standing in a small separate group, who look focused, confident. Their skin is healthy, almost glowing, Oskar realizes.

The vice presidents and CFO Flinthead walk briskly into the crowd, his minions pushing people aside. As a path opens, Oskar sees people lying on the carpet, a few twitching a bit, the rest motionless. The crowd moves back after Flinthead and the vice presidents walk through, and the blocking his view of the people lying on the carpet.

It's not the light, Oskar realizes, taking a quick glance at the healthy people. The vice presidents are pale.

"Did someone call for medical assistance?" the very senior vice president shouts.

A confusion of shouts in response, all saying yes. Each shout goes into details, and the net effect is complete incoherence.

Near Oskar, several pallid people start shouting at a healthy person who is standing by himself. He backs away, hands out, a gesture of peace, and others stop the pallid people from following him.

Oskar watches as the healthy person walks over to the group of healthy people who had been standing apart. They start talking in low voices. They nod, and then split up, briskly walking to the exits.

The exit, Oskar thinks, that's a good place to go. But he stands, waiting to see if he can do anything to help. Classical reaction, he thinks to himself, it's all coming too fast to react to. Where it is something totally new, there is no past pattern to follow, and so people mill, waiting for instructions.

Oskar moves away from the group of pallid people near him, who seem to be seething with anger. He inconspicuously moves towards the corner office that the executives have walked into. The executives, having abandoned the sick people, are watching a news feed. As they watch, they are talking animatedly, pointing and gesturing. It would be helpful to know what they are saying, Oskar thinks. Doing something, anything is better than standing, that seminar pointed out.

In another part of the office, there is a fairly large group. You can hear their angry voices, and realize that they all have the wan, pallid skin. They are gesturing and shouting at the news feeds. Then an argument breaks out between them and the group next to them and suddenly several of the pale group attacks the smaller group.

Shocked, Oskar watches a major brawl break out, the pallid people ganging up on several men. Oskar moves towards the battle, steeling himself to step in. The fight is going badly for the men who were attacked, when security suddenly rushes out of an elevator. Several security staff push their way into the fight, tossing people apart. Oskar is now few feet from the groups. Of the four security men, he suddenly notices that one of them has the pallid skin and is standing with the pallid people, nodding with them. Two of the security people, normal skin, are trying to help the men who were attacked. One of the security people has healthy skin, and is furious at the pallid people.

"You keep your people under control!," the healthy guard orders the pallid guard.

"Or you'll do what?" the pallid guard shouts, reaching for his gun.

The healthy guard is faster, pulling his pistol and shooting the pallid guard. The pallid guard grunts and collapses face down on the carpet. The pallid people are screaming at the healthy guard with the gun.

I'd not scream at a man who just shot another, Oskar thinks, backing away. He glanced down at the dead guard. A perfect shot, right in the heart. That's hard to do under pressure.

The healthy guard backs away, carefully keeping his back to a wall, his pistol up.

"How could you?" an executive screams at the guard, pointing at the dead guard.

He were dying anyhow," the healthy guard responded cheerfully. He looked at the crowd, and smiled. "It's the zombie apocalypse, folks, and you're part of the movie. Choose your sides rapidly."

The pallid people are screaming, almost beside themselves with rage.

Oskar sees a flash of motion out of the corner of his eye. He glances around and sees a group of healthy looking people slowly back away from the crowd.

It's like a movie, he realized. Well, that's just the icing on the cake. Will it be explosives, or chemicals? Or plants, a little voice shouts, what they were raving about on the news this morning.

Suddenly, one of the healthy looking people shouts: "It's the way of the Tree" and there are a set of bursts, not exactly explosives, more like confetti, going off, which quickly fill the air in the office. It's crushed plants, he realized. He relaxes for a moment, thinking at least it isn't poison. The smell of the tree is overwhelming, and people gasp, and collapse.

Security people pull out their pistols, undecided who or what to attack. In their moment of hesitation, they are shot by the healthy people. Scuffles break out around the room, and there are pitched battles going on in seconds.

The mass of people in the office scream and back away, no one knowing what to do next. Oskar suddenly gasps, reaching for his throat, and collapses on the carpet.

Some time later, Oskar wakes up. I'm lying on the carpet in the office, he thinks. And it itches. He sits up slowly, scratching his hand. He shakes his head, trying to clear it. Those dreams, but where they dreams? They were so real! But it couldn't be! I was a spider, Oskar remembers and cringes for a second. Then it all seemed natural, and he relaxed. Kind of satisfying, really. I know what I'd do to the vice presidents, and a different set of memories flowed through him. He smiled, a different smile. I'll be more understanding next time I see a spider, he thought. But not forgiving, not, that's not a spider trait. No, their worldview is a lot different.

Ok, survival arc: evaluate. Oskar looks around. He is in the middle of several co-workers. Some are sitting up, some are still in coma's. He looks around the office. There are people, standing, screaming, with others around them. There are people in coma's twitching and shaking on the floor. Maybe half of the office is still out. Only a few are actually up and moving. Looking more closely he is surprised to see that the people who are standing either have the washed out, pale skin, or that healthy glow that the plant people had. He looks down at his arm, and it has the healthy glow. That's good, he thinks. He looks over, and Gordon is sitting next to him, his skin healthy.

"No more cheap coffee at these corporate meetings," Gordon mumbled. "I don't care what they save, it isn't worth it."

"When people give you drugs," Oskar remarked, "Thank them. Drugs are expensive."

Gordon shakes his head.

Several healthy looking people rush over to them. One grabs Oskar's arm, and another grabs Gordon's, pulling them up. There are several other co-workers with healthy skin, and the healthy people pull them up. A few of the group on the floor near Oskar are turning pale, and those people edge away from the healthy ones.

A healthy guard stands next to them, his pistol up, actively scanning. "Here, come with us," he ordered. "They will be here in force soon."

"They?" Gordon asked.

"You volunteered to join our side," the healthy guard remarked, pointing at Gordon's arm.

Gordon looks at his arm, and nods. "A plan?" he asked Oskar.

"Act," Oskar replied.

The guard nods, and they move into a corner, joining another group of healthy people.

"Next?" one the group asked.

"You're the star project manager," another demanded of Oskar. "Think of something!"

"Fine," Oskar sighed. He looked around, scanning. "Ok, too many things happening. Ah, first, what's the situation? What do we know? The short version."

The world is dividing into those with the Tree and those against. It's easy to see who is what side," the security guard replied. "First, your skin. Second, this," and he pulls up his sleeve. There is a black mark on his left arm, clear against his skin. "Not everyone has this in the same place, but it's proof."

"When too many things happening, gather the facts," Oskar commented, talking out loud to himself. "We are part of the Tree now. And I find them disgusting, looking over at the pallid people," and involuntarily recoiling.

"They hate us almost beyond words," the guard replied.

"And the dreams?" one of the healthy people asked. "Terrible, but wonderful."

"Just terrible! Horrible! Monstrous!," a person outside the group screamed. The group stares at that person, noticing his pallid skin.

"What are you looking at?" the person yelled. "You're mutants! Not human!" And that person stomps away, towards the large group of pallid people.

"Out of here, folks," the guard declared. "Towards that exit, walk slowly, talk intently, and don't look at them. Who knows how to handle a gun?"

"I do," Gordon replied. "Retired military."

The guard nods, and hands Gordon a pistol. "Do you know how to shoot?" the guard asked Oskar.

"Yes," Oskar answered.

The guard handed Oskar a pistol.

Oskar takes the pistol without hesitation. Spiders with pistols, a voice in him laughed.

They look around. A mass of pallid people is starting to walk towards them, led by two security guards.

Oskar raises his pistol and fires without thinking. One of the guards falls, and Gordon shoots the other.

"Run!" the healthy guard shouts, and the group runs for the stairs. They dash into the stairway, jam the door, and rush down the stairs.

Everywhere, everyday life has evaporated by noon. The news feeds are increasingly hysterical. Nothing but talking pallid heads demanding that the mutants, as they suddenly call them, be shot down on sight.

"Ok, we're not popular," Oskar commented. "The stories are coming from their side. What can we figure out from their stories about what our people are doing?"

They watch the news broadcast for a few minutes.

"We need to gather our people, to protect them from the others," Gordon concluded. "That at least is clear."

"We need more weapons," Oskar argued. "Isn't there a gun shop a few blocks from here? Everyone grab a club or something, in case we get jumped on the way."

The group makes it to the gun shop, with only one short battle against a small group of pallid people on the way. Outside the gun shop, there are pallid people lying dead on the sidewalk.

"Who controls it?" The guard wondered. "Well, one way to find out." He laid his gun on the sidewalk and stepped out into full view of the gun shop.

"In here!" a mutant shouted at him from inside the shop.

"We have a group," the guard shouted back.

"All! In here now!" the mutant yelled.

The group ran into the shop. It had been partly stripped, but there were still some weapons left.

"Grab what you can and get out of here, they are coming in force," the mutant advised.

The group grabs all the weapons left, and then run out the back of the shop.

"What have you heard?" Oskar asked the men who had been in the gun shop.

"All we hear is to get to parks, woods, into nature," one man replied. "They can't go there."

"Don't cluster in groups," another warns. "The police and the military are on their side."

"At least some of them," another added. "The police and military are splitting up, but no one knows who is with who yet. Its just chaos."

DAY 30. NEW YORK. 12 NOON.

The chief of staff, the CEO and the CFO of the hospital are meeting.

"The hospital is overflowing," the Chief of Staff reported. "There are several groups. First, the normal range of illnesses and injuries. Second, those who are injured in the battles breaking out all over. In all truth, the number of wounded is low, because the battles are to the death. As the majority of police and medical personal rejected the Tree, when a wounded mutant is found, rarely do they survive the trip to the hospital.

"The majority of patients we are getting are those who react negatively to the plants and that smell. Now, the majority of people react negatively to the plants, which is good. We would expect normal humans to reject the Tree, as the mutants call those accursed plants." The Chief of Staff's skin was pale, as was that of the CEO. The CFO was a black man, but his skin had a grey, lifeless tone.

"How bad is this going to be?" the CEO demanded.

"Fortunately, most people don't have a life critical reaction," the Chief of Staff replied. "Oh, it's an awful nightmare, as we all know, but people recover and start functioning again. We have having a couple of serious problem types, however."

"Which would be?" the CFO asked. "Other than there being no insurance in effect in this chaos and no money."

"And there won't be for a while," the CEO replied. "I've heard from the Governor. Martial law has been declared, and we are ordered to provide as much care as we can. We will be paid with food, fuel, anything we need, but money is a low priority. The Governor did point out that this is the destruction of our civilization, of our way of life, and potentially of the majority of people."

"We have many people who are having life threatening reactions to the plants," the Chief of Staff admitted. "We are not having a lot of success in treating them. More worrisome, people who were affected by the plants early, a week or so ago, are starting to weaken, their bodies deteriorating."

"Is it they are weaker than other people?" the CFO demanded, very concerned.

"We don't know," the Chief of Staff grimaced. "I'm hoping the problem is limited to those who had an early reaction, because otherwise, the extrapolation of that trend is horrifying. We are doing what we can, trying to stabilize people and keep them away from further contact with the plants."

"The military is setting up settlements in Malls and big box shopping centers, in desert areas and some urban areas, where the plants can be controlled," the CEO commented. "That seems to be the best that can be done now."

"The CDC reported that the plants are unstable, and will start dying," the CFO added. "I was glad to hear that.'

"It's bullshit," the Chief of Staff remarked. "The CDC, as I understand it, said the exact opposite before their spokesperson was shot. A high percentage of their people have gone to the Tree, I've heard, so they are of no use to us."

The men sat quietly, looking out the window at the distant fires.

DAY 30. A HOSPITAL WARD, NEW YORK.

The zombie apocalypse, Dr. Johnson thought, standing outside a room where he had just examined a new patient. I've seen this in twenty movies, but never thought I'd see it lined up at my door. And people told me watching B movies were a waste of time! And it gets worse, he realized, going thru the ward, which was packed with the ill. All tossed and cried out in their coma's, but those who would recover had healthy skin, their eyes clear after they awoke. The doctor realized that he could tell with a glance who choose the Tree and who did not. And who would survive and who would not, and he shivered. There was a Twilight Zone episode like that, and it wasn't pretty. Those who had rejected the tree two weeks ago had all died, and those who rejected it a week ago were weakening. And when it hits me, he wondered grimly, what then? Is there anything to be done to influence the result?

Dr. Johnson finished his rounds, quickly dictating his notes, and then went to a staff meeting. Looking around the room, he froze for a second. The Chief of Staff had the pallid skin and angry expression of the dying. There were several who looked healthy, and a larger group that hadn't clearly changed. Yet.

"These who seem to recover from the infection must be locked up!" the Chief of Staff ordered, stopping for a moment to cough.

"The government shouts that the mutants must be killed," a physician hissed. He was pale, sweating.

"They are no longer human. I've talked to them, and they look at me with fury," the Chief of Staff snapped. "We are doctors, we don't kill. But those people need to be locked up."

"Then the police can kill them, a nurse snarled. She was pale, leaning on the table, full of pent up fury.

"They have done nothing to you!," a nurse yelled back, her skin glowing against her scrubs.

"And you!" the Chief of Staff shouted at the nurse. "You dare take their side? You should be locked up with them!"

"Please!" Dr. Johnson begged, physically moving in between the groups, pushing them apart. The pallid people started to push back at him, but they finally stepped back. "We're all under a lot of stress. None of us have had any sleep because of the crush of patients. We are getting reports from all over, and it's all the same around the world. We need to stop, rest, think. Our duty is to heal." He looked around. Half of the room nodded agreement with him. Some looked confused, and they are on the edge, Dr. Johnson realized. The remainder had either the pallid skins of the ill, or the healthy, flushed skin of the survivors. They had unconsciously sorted themselves into groups.

The healthy, Dr. Johnson noticed, all had long sleeves on. He had seen the birthmarks, for lack of another word, on those who had recovered.

The Chief of Staff, furious, forced himself to nod agreement. "This is a hospital," he rasped, "and it is our sworn duty to heal humans. You want these mutants? You take care of them, Dr. Johnson. Choose any staff that would help you. I'll go back to trying to save those poor humans sickened by this plant. This meeting is over."

The Chief of Staff stood up, tottering for a moment, and then roughly grasped his reports and walked out, followed by the entire pallid skin group. The others stood, uncertain.

"I'll need some help," Dr. Johnson asked.

"I'll help, and I," several people quickly volunteered.

Dr. Johnson nodded his acceptance and asked the volunteers to stay in the room. The others left. Of the group who had stayed, three had the healthy skin of the survivors. Another was a physician that the doctor had worked with for a long time. There were also several other staff that Dr. Johnson didn't know well.

"Close the door, please," Dr. Johnson ordered. When one of the nurses had closed the door, Dr. Johnson asked, "So, what's it like?"

The three nurses with healthy skin had been standing by the window, looking out and whispering between themselves. They turned and looked carefully at Dr. Johnson and the others.

"I'm beginning to accept what's going on, unbelievable as it seems to be. Please, tell me.," Dr. Johnson insisted.

"Do you wish to be of us?" one of the nurses carefully answered.

"What do you mean?" the other physician demanded, puzzled.

"The world is separating," Dr. Johnson stated, rubbing his forehead. "This is more than an illness, it is actually something far beyond illness. I thought it might be like San Paulo or Saudi Arabia, but this is vastly different. This isn't an illness, this is change. Mutation, yes. Evolution, perhaps. I just rescued a child from her parents, who were about to literally kill the child, the parents screaming that the child was a witch."

"Zombies," a nurse hissed.

"All of them have the same pallid skin, angry, jerky movements," Dr. Johnson described. "There fury is beyond anything that I have seen. Yeah, zombies are pretty accurate."

"The Chief of Staff?" the other doctor exclaimed.

"He won't survive," a first nurse replied. "He has only a short time after it reaches the essential functions. The deterioration is rapid after that."

"What is it?" Dr. Johnson demanded, looking from one woman to another.

The nurses looked confused for a moment.

"We don't know," one nurse answered. "It came upon us differently."

"I went to the home of a child who survived," another nurse recalled. "The parents took me to a small garden, and they pointed out where the child had collapsed. I stood in the garden and there was suddenly a smell, a sweet, beautiful smell. I looked around, and there were these pretty plants that the smell seemed to be coming from. I walked over and touched the plants."

"Don't!" the child's father screamed at me, panicked. "I touched them, to pull them up, and look at my hand!"

"His hand was red and swollen," the nurse reported. "And he was shaking, the zombie fury starting."

"Then I kicked the plants," the father snarled, "and they hurt my feet!"

"I gingerly reached out, and touched the plants. They were soft, and the smell was sweet. They seem fine," I told the parents.

"Get out of here!" the girls mother screams at me "You're just like the girl, another witch! One of those, what did the television call them? A mutant!"

"I shouted at them this was their child they were talking about," the nurse continued, "and they backed off. They could still be reasoned with, but just barely. I told them I needed to examine the witch again and that put them on my side, disgusting as that sounds. So I went to the child's room, and unlocked the door. I whispered to the child that she could escape when I distracted her parents and she looked at me with the strangest old/young eyes. She nodded and I know that she escaped because I saw her running away when I was walking to my car."

"I left that house in a hurry. On my way home, I became dizzy, and when I got home, I passed out. The strangest dreams, the oddest memories, of things that could not be, places that could not exist," she recalled, really talking aloud to herself. "And monsters and a feeling of life, but from a completely different perspective. It was nothing that I have ever felt or ever imagined. But it was good, and I opened up to it. A few hours later, I awoke, to my fearful parents leaning over me. But I feel strong and healthy."

"Never as strong," one of the other nurses asserted. "Never so healthy."

"The tree takes you beyond good and evil; a peace that passeth understanding, but isn't peaceful. A stance with the world." the first nurse explained.

The nurses made a sign with their hands and smiled at each other.

"Where are there other patches of this plant?" Dr. Johnson asked. "You had to each have contact with different plants?"

"There are many patches," the first nurse replied. "The plants are spreading rapidly, and we try and encourage them as we can. We don't talk about them, because people try and pull them up."

"The zombies are running wild," the third nurse fearfully observed. "What will happen when this spreads to all? Will they kill all of us? Too many are dying when they become of the Tree in the middle of the zombies."

"I must face this" Dr. Johnson sighed. "There is no other choice."

"Are you sure?" the other physician asked, worried.

"It's a plant," Dr. Johnson replied, shrugging his shoulders. "It's spreading everywhere. There's no point trying to avoid it. Maybe seeking it will help the transition."

"So we might as well get it over and live or die?" the other physician commented. He looked around at the nurses, smiling. "Fine, maybe it will clear up my sinuses. Nothing else has."

"You are my staff, if anyone asks, and under my orders," Dr. Johnson warned two of the nurses. "Stay away from the head physician and anyone with pallid skin!"

"The network says go to the parks, to the woods," one of the nurses replied. "We will go to that new clinic down by the park. Send as many there as you can."

"Sounds like a good plan," Dr. Johnson agreed. "The hospital isn't safe any longer."

They nodded, and quickly left.

The two doctors and one nurse walked down the fire exit, carefully avoiding others.

"I'm Caryn," the nurse offered, when they were outside the hospital. "I know both of you, but we have never had the chance to work together."

"I know you by reputation," Dr. Johnson replied. "I'm happy to have you on my side."

"It's a nice day," the other doctor commented as they walked along. "Nice to be out of the cold light of the hospital and feel the sunshine."

"It's this park," Caryn whispered, gesturing ahead of them. She stopped, nervously looking around. "There," she continued, "Down in that vale. The tree is strong there."

The doctors looked at each other.

"In for a dime, in for a dollar," Dr. Johnson remarked. Taking a deep breath, they walked into the park. They followed a cleft cut into a hill. Caryn led them into a private garden. Once in the middle of the garden, all three stopped and looked around. Sunlight sparkled off tiny ripples on a small spring quietly bubbling, surrounding by luxuriant green.

"It's beautiful," the other doctor observed, smiling. "I'm moving my practice here."

"And it's this plant?" Dr. Johnson exclaimed, astonished, as he stared at the four foot tall thick brush grown up next to the water. "I've never seen this variety before. It's flowering already," he added, pointing at the small delicate flowers. "It's spreading as we speak."

"It's one of many," Caryn answered. "Many plants have changed and now hold the Tree within them."

The wind came, a warm touch carrying the fragrance of the tree. It was strong, sweet, and like a cool drink of water, filled the doctors. They staggered and fell.

Caryn jumped to catch the men as they fell, trying to gently guide them to the ground. As they lay on the soft grass, she tugged them into a more comfortable position.

"Well, at least you won't have stiff necks when they wake up," she commented to the sleeping bodies. She sighed, worried, and walked over to the entrance to the secret garden to watch for zombies.

An hour later, Dr. Johnson stirred. "What?" he mumbled to himself, raising his head up. Visions raced through his head, seeing impossible things, unbelievable feelings, but his fears vanished as he opened to the feelings and the memories. He sat for some time and then looked at Caryn.

"You have become of the tree," Caryn acknowledged, smiling. He nodded, suddenly understanding.

He looked over at the other doctor, who was sitting up, smiling at a bird sitting on a branch. "Life is good," the other doctor announced. The other doctor looked carefully at Dr. Johnson and then nodded.

"A tiger," Dr. Johnson remarked.

"A cow," the second doctor replied. "I never really understood before, and I used to raise cattle."

"That was easy," Caryn laughed. "I was a scorpion. Now, that was different!"

"We must guard this place," Dr. Johnson asserted. "And we must find sanctuary for our people to go to. How do we get the word out?"

"The plants can guard themselves," Caryn responded. "For us, there are networks popping up for the mutants to communicate with each other."

"Mutants?" the other doctor asked.

"We are," Caryn declared.

They carefully walked out of the secret garden, only leaving when they were satisfied that no one saw them.

"How to contact the network?" Dr. Johnson asked.

The other doctor was experimenting with his phone. "Here," he replied. "I've found some others, and they say . . . That we should go to this address."

DAY 30. NEW YORK. 2 P.M.

Oskar waved goodbye to the men in the car, who carefully drove off to find their families. Trudging down the sidewalks, watching for zombies, he sees dead bodies lying in the streets, and isn't even shocked. "It's been that kind of day," he told the birds flying by, hardly able to believe it all himself. Reaching his block, he sees his house, and his stomach knots. He rushes towards his house, but stops on the sidewalk in front of the house, trying to blank his mind, his fears running wild. Then he walks up and stands before the door for a moment. Fearfully, he knocks. "It's me," Oskar shouts, terrified of what he will find inside.

Christina opens the door and they stare at each other.

"Of the Tree?" Oskar asked her, not believing.

"Of the Tree!" she beamed. "And you too! But get inside," and she roughly yanks him inside. "The neighbors are patrolling and they killed some of our people in the street just a little while ago."

Oskar leans against the hallway wall, relief flooding over him. He watches as Christina locks the door with one hand, her pistol ready in the other.

"Good," he commented, glancing at the pistol in Christina's hand. "And the kids?" he forced himself to ask, dreading the answer.

"We were lucky," Christina replied. "Both of the kids are fine. Alex is watching the backyard, with a shotgun. Jenny is upstairs carefully scoping out the neighborhood. The schools blew apart. The kids and the teachers were in fights, people were collapsing, I rushed over and got them away from the chaos."

"Who else is on our side?" Oskar asked.

"Hard to tell," she frowned. "There were some of the parents at the school who looked to be of the Tree, but more of the others. There seems to be some family following family, which is lucky for us."

Oskar wraps his arms around Christina. "It's good to see you," he murmured, as he kissed her.

She put carefully the pistol on a table and wrapped her arms around him. "Life is strong," she replied and they began to press against each other.

"What of the kids?" Oskar asked, really not caring.

"What of the kids?" Christina mumbled and they wrapped closer. "I thought I'd never see you again."

Alex peeked down the hallway. He glanced up the stairs and saw Jenny watching. Jenny gestured at him and Alex crept up the stairs. They took a quick glance back at their parents, now wrestling in the hallway, and went in Jenny's room.

"Well, its nice that they are glad to see each other," Jenny grumbled, annoyed. "Maybe focusing on keeping alive would be nice, too."

"I'm not sure they could more alive than they are right now," Alex snickered.

Jenny warily peeked out the window. "Can't let them see me," she whispered to Alex. "At least they are not going door to door yet, which is what I'm afraid of. A large group at our front and back door with guns? We'd be cooked! There, you can see a group way over there, maybe 20 of them, shouting and waving weapons. There was shooting a few blocks away, I don't know what happened."

"I snuck out when mom was doing other stuff," Alex confided. "There were dead people all over the Westernars's yard. The bodies seemed pale to me, but I didn't have a lot of time to check."

"I never liked them," Jenny replied. "All we have to do is just live thru the day." She cocked her head, listening carefully. "I think they are finishing downstairs. Give them a minute to get themselves together, and then we can talk to them about what to do next."

"They are not usually this, well, affectionate," Alex blurted out. "Maybe being like that is what saved them. Embracing life, and all that."

"We need to get out of here, and get in a bigger group with our people," Jenny pointed out, "or we're dead. Embracing life is taking steps."

"You're right, sis," Alex agreed. He looked carefully at her. "You know, you're different."

"Yes, and no," Jenny replied. "I've always felt different, but I pushed it away. Different isn't nice, people told me piously. But now, all of that is washed away. All those 'nice' people are wandering around out there trying to kill anyone who is alive."

"I saw a several die in the change at school," Alex recalled. "Too bad they all don't just take the easy route."

"What animal were you?" Jenny asked, curious.

"A muskrat," Alex answered. It was interesting.

"I was a Bonobo," Jenny giggled. "They are monkey's who are obsessed with sex. Could be worse! I wonder what the parents were?"

"It's quiet down there," Alex concluded. "Let's go see."

They tromped down the stairs. Their parents were sitting in the hallway, reasonably presentable.

"Ah, we were glad to see each other," Oskar stammered.

"Life is strong," Christina asserted, smiling.

"This means more brothers and sisters," Jenny commented to Alex, frowning. "Not good, our inheritance is diminishing."

"Well, if we don't get out of here, there won't be an inheritance," Alex declared. "Jenny is sure that they will start going door to door eventually, and then we are sunk."

"True enough," Oskar agreed, standing up. He reached out a hand to Christina, helping her up.

She grasped his hand and stood up, quickly rearranging her dress.

"First step in any plan is gather the facts. What's going on around here?" Oskar asked. "You know more about what's going on around here than I do."

"Sadly, I don't know that much," Christina replied. "I've been so busy watching, I haven't thought about other things. Are the phones working? Internet? Anything?"

"A bit," Jenny answered. "I've stopped looking at the messages I've received. I've seen some awful texts come thru, though," and she wiped away a tear. "Some of my friends didn't make it."

"I know it's painful," Oskar asked, putting his arm around Jenny, "but can you look back at them? Can you see if you can figure out who may have become of the Tree? We need to find safety, which means getting groups together."

Jenny nodded and she and Alex ran upstairs to see what they could discover.

"A long way from this morning," Oskar observed to Christina. "Not much of an office left, let me tell you."

"Not much of a neighborhood or school either," Christina replied. "This one hit fast."

"And it's still building," Oskar added, switching on the screen. They watched intently for a few minutes. "Look at this news feed! The armies around the world are splitting up. That isn't quite the story they are telling, but you don't have pitched battles like these unless each side has heavy weapons. How about your phone? See anything on your texts?"

"A few ideas," Christina answered, scrolling down on her phone. "This sounds promising." She typed quickly, and got a response. "Ok, Andrea is with the tree. Andrea thinks that there is a group over in the woods. Staying outside, in a forest, seems to be safest because that is where the others are afraid to go. Zombies, yeah, I like that. The zombies have taken shelter in buildings, factories, anywhere that they can lock nature out of."

"That's the opposite of the movies," Oskar recalled. "But I'd rather be outside than stuck in some dusty old building."

"So, let's get the kids and head out," Christina urged. "Jenny's right, it's only a matter of time before they come here in strength."

The kids came charging down back the stairs.

"I've got some ideas from my friends," Jenny announced. "Dad, you and I should head this way," pointing north. "That covers a lot of the neighborhood and hopefully we can find some of our people. Mom and Alex, you go find any friends you can."

"What if we are attacked?" Oskar objected. "Numbers help, I know."

"I agree," Christina added. "Two of us wouldn't stand much of a chance."

"Four isn't going to make a difference," Jenny countered. "We need to get to our people ASAP before the zombies get to them. Two groups can find twice as many people, search twice as many places."

"If we are waylaid by a big group, a couple more people won't help." Alex argued. "Small groups maybe can slip by."

Oskar and Christina glanced at each other, and then nodded. "It's a plan," Oskar sighed. He carefully loaded his shotgun. "Christina, you've got a pistol. Alex, you've got a shotgun. You both need knives, the biggest ones you can find. If you have to shoot, then run! The shots will bring angry mobs after you."

"I've got a rifle," Jenny interrupted. "And extra ammunition in my purse," patting it carefully.

"Are these our kids?" Christina wondered, "or did I pick up someone new at the school?" She shook her head. "It's a good change. Ok, we meet at the woods, Tree willing. Take care!"

Oskar looked carefully out the back door. "Clear," he whispered and they crept out the back door. A quick hug, and they split up.

"I never really liked this neighborhood," Oskar told Jenny as they carefully climbed over a fence. "The houses had no character, and the commute sucked."

"I thought the school was full of zombies before they turned into zombies," Jenny replied. 'I used to match the zombies in the movies to students I hated."

"I thought your mother banned those movies because you had nightmares?" Oskar commented.

"Oh, I've seen so many that I could write one," Jenny answered. "And that's a good thing, because this is like being in a movie. Stop! What's that noise?"

They froze and listened. Someone, maybe several children, were crying not far away.

"They sound OK?" Oskar whispered, uncertainly. "They don't sound like zombies."

They crept closer to the sound.

"Could it be a trap?" Jenny whispered.

"Almost has to be. Hand signs," he whispered. He signed her-Wait! He crept towards the sounds, and then peered through a knothole in the fence.

There were three children sitting against a fence, out in the open. The youngest was crying softly. The older ones were trying to shush the smaller one, and looking around, worried. They had the healthy skin of mutants.

Where's the trap? Oskar wondered. I'd leave them here and pick off anyone who came to rescue them. Wait, the kids keep glancing there, and there .. and they are scared when they look there. He peeked through another knothole. Yeah, someone could hide over there, and I'd put a rifleman there. He silently crawled back to Jenny, and he drew a map in the dust. They stared at it frowning.

"I'll pick off the rifleman," Jenny decided, pointing to where they guessed he would be. "You take them, pointing. Give me to the count of thirty to get into position," and she crawled off.

. . . and thirty, Oskar counted. He crept around in back of the wall that he had guessed the zombies were hiding behind. Peeking through a gap in fence, he saw three zombies. They were heavily armed, arguing.

"Just kill those kids, no one else is coming along, and then we can go looking for others," one hissed, and the others nodded their approval.

Showtime! Oskar moved into firing position and then fired two blasts into the small group. They went down, screaming. Oskar, crouching, ran to finish them and get their weapons. Jenny, get the sniper! Oskar thought and suddenly there was a crack, crack from around the corner. The sniper screamed and fell.

Oskar clubbed the screaming men with the butt of his shotgun. When they were dead, he grabbed their weapons and ammunition, carefully clicking the safeties on. Then he shouted to the kids: "Come with us! Hurry, there will be more along in a minute."

They kids heads popped up, and they ran to Oskar.

Jenny ran over to the group. "Hurry! There are more coming, I can hear them screaming."

"Over there," Oskar ordered, pointing to the small park. "Stay in the wood and the deep grass. If anyone gets hit, the others keep going, got it?"

Everyone nodded, and they quickly ran into the thin trees. Stopping for a second, they looked back and saw a large group in the distance, waving weapons and shouting.

"We can't stay here," Jenny snapped. "There are too many of them. Run thru the woods, let's see what's on the other side."

Oskar and the children nodded. They dashed thru the woods, away from the shouts and shots behind them.

Christina and Alex froze when they heard the shots and screams in the distance.

"They will be Ok," Alex promised, forcing himself to believe what he is saying. "Rescuing someone, I'm sure."

"We shall see," Christina sighed. "This way, over to Andrea's house."

They ducked thru the neighborhood, running from garage to garage, hiding behind fences and listening for the zombies shouting.

"Stop!" Christina hissed. They froze to the side of a garage, listening to the tromp of many feet running down the street fading as they rushed past.

Christina stood up, and peeked around the garage. "Ok, they are gone."

They worked their way towards Andrea's house. From a distance, the house looked vandalized, with windows broken out, and curtains blowing out the windows.

Christina pulled out her phone and texted with shaking fingers. Then she smiled. "They are ok in there," and she started to stand.

"No!" Alex whispered, pulling her back down. "Where's the trap?"

Christina sat down. "How stupid of me!," she mumbled, shaking her head. "What do you think?"

Alex pictured the area for a second. "I remember there was a house that overlooked this house. They can't see us behind this garage from that house, but there would be a wonderful view of us as soon as we move out from behind the garage. Text them, ask them if they are being watched."

"They are," Christina acknowledged, as she read the message from Andrea. "Now what?"

"We can't walk up to the door of the house above this one," Alex observed. "We're not pale enough." He pushed a mirror around the corner of the garage. "I think we can creep along the fence, and they can't see us. Text Andrea, get the back door open."

In a minute, the back door slowly opened, and a face was dimly visible. "Andrea's not pale," Alex announced, relieved. They crawled into the house, leaving the back door open, Alex behind Christina. "They will see the movement if we close it," Alex whispered. "Maybe they will think the wind blew it open if we just leave it alone."

Andrea was waiting for them with her daughter Agatha, who was in Alex's class at school, and Andrea's son Wolfgang, who was in Jenny's' class.

"Where is your husband?" Christina asked, looking around.

"With them!" Andrea snarled. "And my older son too! They turned on us, I thought they were going to kill us themselves! We managed to knock them down, and they ran off. Animals!"

"Not animals, technically," Christina replied. "Small humans, but that's another days story. Are there zombies in the house above you?"

"At least 3 or more in the house up there with guns," Andrea replied, worried. "Another couple, at least, across the street, with guns, and random groups wandering around the neighborhood. We are trapped here."

"Come upstairs," Agatha whispered to Alex. They ran upstairs, she pulling him along.

"Some slight changes in male/female relationships," Andrea remarked to Christina.

They sat in Agatha's room, which had a window that faced the house on the hill above them. Alex and Agatha carefully moved a mirror so they could see the shadows moving in that house.

Alex sat down against the wall. "So what is the layout of that house?"

Agatha drew a quick map of what she remembered the interior of the house looking like. They studied it for a few minutes.

"This can work" Alex commented, showing Agatha what he was thinking. "Lets tell the others," and they went back down.

"So, a plan?" Andrea asked.

Suddenly, there was a volley of shots from the house above, and then another volley as a car roared past.

"Now," Alex shouted and ran out the back door, towards the upper house. He flinched, waiting for the bullets impact, but none came. In seconds he was at the back door of the house above Andrea's. He kicked the door open, and rushed inside, hearing zombies inside, angry shouts and vicious laughs. Furious, he fired blast after blast at anything that moved. In a minute, the zombies were dead. Alex cautiously peered out the front windows, and saw zombies running out of the house across the street, some towards Andrea's house and some towards the house Alex had just captured. He grabbed a semi automatic rifle out from a dead zombie and first killed the men running towards Andrea's house. Then he took careful aim at the two women waving baseball bats, screaming for blood, rushing at this house and killed both of them.

Alex dashed over to a window overlooking Andrea's house, and saw Christina looking up at the house. He waved, and in a few minutes, everyone in Andrea's house had run into the upper house.

"This house is safer," Alex asserted "it has the high view."

The women nodded.

Wolfgang clapped him on the back. "Quality work," he laughed. "That was moments, and it worked."

"But we can't stay here, we have to get over to the woods," Andrea urged. "That's where our people are going. Zombies are taking refuge in houses, offices and buildings. We want to be outside. I think we can make it to the woods if we follow this route," and she sketched a rough map on the floor.

They nodded, and creeping out the back door, headed towards the woods.

On the other side of the subdivision, Jenny, Oskar and the three children ran from cover to cover, behind fences and houses, heading towards the woods.

"Stop and rest for a minute," Oskar ordered, panting. "I'm not used to this."

They sat down behind a garage wall. The woods was closer, the tops of the trees just visible over the houses.

"The smell of the Tree is stronger," Jenny sniffed. "I'm excited to get to the woods, where the Tree will be the strongest."

"They will be watching for people taking shelter in the woods," Oskar worried. "Where will the traps be?" he drew a rough map in the dust, frowning.

The three children sat, dazed. They held each other, staring at the ground.

"I know you," Jenny told the older girl.

"I'm two years ahead of you in school," the girl replied. She smiled at Jenny. "Yeah, I remember you. You are on the soccer team. He," pointing at the boy, "lived two houses down from me, and this is his sister."

"Our parents went nuts," the boy cried and the little girl started to silently sob. "They tried to kill us, and we ran. But others caught us, and set us in that trap. They killed at least four people who tried to save us."

"Thanks for saving us. That was good work," the older girl stammered, "the way that you killed that scum."

"I don't know you?" Jenny asked the boy.

"I was in Catholic School, not the public school," the boy replied. "A lot of good that did! My parents called the priest to our house to exorcise the demon out of us. After he put his hands all over us, then he condemned my sister and I to death. I'd like to exorcise him with a 2x4!"

"I always hated him," the little girl hissed. "I know what he did to a boy I know and the boy wasn't the same afterwards."

"You're safe with us now," Oskar promised. "But it isn't safe here, it is time to move on. Remember, carefully and slowly!"

"Can I have a gun?" the older girl asked.

"If you want," Jenny replied. "I know this is a complete flip from what life was like. But they will kill us, and we have to fight back."

"I understand," the older girl agreed. She gingerly held the rifle Oskar handed her. "Ah, but how does it work?"

"Here, let me show you," the boy replied, disgusted, taking the rifle from her, quickly pointing out the key elements.

"Ok, you keep that one," Oskar ordered the boy. "Maybe this would be better for you," handing a shotgun to the girl. "It's deadly at short range."

A few intense minutes of going over the basics, including several urgently repeated "keep the safety on until you are ready to fire!" and then they were ready to go. They carefully worked their way towards the edge of the subdivision.

"Stop!" Oskar hissed. They froze against a wall. "I hear something."

They froze against the wall for a few minutes, and then heard the noises more clearly. Feet moving quietly, a soft rustling in the gravel. The feet were quietly working their way through the yard in back of them.

"Our people?" Jenny whispered.

They suddenly caught a glimpse of movement around a garage.

"Our people, I think," the older girl whispered back. "They move fast, and they don't look pale."

"One way to find out," Jenny grimly announced. She worked her way over to the edge of the garage wall. "Of the Tree?" she called out.

In a second, several guns were aimed in her direction.

That wasn't as clever as I thought it was going to be, Jenny told herself and didn't move a muscle.

The gun barrels were lowered as the group rushed over to take shelter against the wall with Jenny and the others There were five people were in that group: three adults and two teenagers, all heavily armed.

"I know you," one of the men told Oskar. "I saw you at those stupid soccer games in the rain and the sleet. I used to think they were deliberately set for the worst possible weather."

"Tell me about it," Oskar agreed. "We rescued them," pointing at the children, "and we are trying to get to the woods."

"They've got the woods surrounded," one of the men replied. "They don't have enough strength to rush the park, but they can keep reinforcements from getting into the woods."

"We picked off a few of the zombies when we rescued the kids," Jenny offered.

"You did well," the adult woman replied, surprised. "Normally that brings a mob of them."

"Oh, there was a mob after us," Jenny answered. "But we got away."

"OK, it's 4 in the afternoon," Oskar summarized, sitting on the ground. "At 9 this morning I was at work and things started to come apart. We know that the army and police have been called up, but they are taking sides. What we don't know is how many are on our side and how long the zombies will last."

"The zombies do weaken," one of the other men declared. "But we don't know how fast. They hate the smell of the Tree, but some of them have gas masks now, and that seems to help them a bit."

In the distance, they heard heavy machinery rumbling towards the woods.

"This we've to see," one of the men growled. They carefully crawled into a position they could see a little.

"Good or bad?" Oskar mumbled.

"Unknown," one of the other adults replied, frowning. "I'd guess bad, because they look pretty official. That's going to decide this battle, one way or the other. Ground troops cannot stand against those." They watched the armored personal carriers roar towards the park, machine guns at the ready. In a few minutes, they heard the zombies cheer as the machines roared past them towards the woods.

"That's not good," the woman snarled.

Suddenly, helicopters roared low over their little group, headed for the woods. Seconds later the ground shook with explosions as the helicopters unloaded on the personal carriers. Then the helicopters circled, blazing machine gun fire into the zombies holding positions around the park. After what seemed like an eternity, the helicopters headed off to the north.

"Run for the street," one of the men shouted. "They will try and flee this way, and we can pick them off."

They quickly got into position. In a few minutes, a horde of dazed zombies came down the street, running as best they could.

"No prisoners," Oskar commanded. "This isn't war, this is extinction."

"Now!" a man shouted, and all opened fired. When all the zombies were dead, they stopped firing.

"Forage for guns and ammunition," Oskar ordered. "But watch out for zombies pretending to be dead. Any doubts, shoot them in the head. Do this fast, and then into the woods."

A few minutes later, heavily loaded with plundered weapons, they walked down the street to the woods.

"So, how not to be shot by our people?" Oskar asked, standing at the edge of the woods.

One of the men carefully put his weapons down, and walked towards the woods, hands up. "We are of the Tree," he shouted.

"And welcome to this consecrated ground," a tall, bearded man yelled back, walking out of the woods. "But get your asses in here before the zombies come back!"

They rushed into the woods. People ran out to help them carry weapons. Oskar pointed down the street, where the zombies lay dead, and a group ran down the street to finish scavenging for weapons.

They were warmly welcomed in the rough camp. It looked like there were several hundred people already in the camp.

"It's mom!," Jenny shouted, pointing, and ran over to Christina. Oskar ran behind her.

"You made it," Alex congratulated Oskar. Oskar just embraced Alex for a moment.

"There's food over here," a volunteer offered. "You want to get fed, get some sleep. Tomorrow will be harder than today."

"Now, that's an inspirational thought," Oskar replied. "I wouldn't have thought that possible, but I'm sure that you are right. Food will help."

"Oskar!" Gordon shouted from a distance away. He ran up to Oskar, and clapped him on the back.

"Here," Gordon shouted back to a group standing around some doors laid over sawhorses to make a work area. "The best project planner at the company, right when we needed him the most!"

People in the group cheered.

"Maybe some food first?" Oskar begged, as Gordon started dragging him towards the large group.

"A good plan," Gordon agreed, winking at him.

They found the kitchen, and grabbing some plates, filled them with food and then sat down.

"Why is tomorrow critical?" Jenny demanded, worried.

"I don't know," Oskar replied. "That's the kind of thing people say, I guess. Light conversation, you know? Like, 'so how are the kids, and the flowers? And tomorrow will decide the fate of the known universe', that kind of stuff."

"I think it's more than that," Alex announced. "I've been listening to others talking. There's a decay process working on the zombies, but they are still strong. Tomorrow will be a big day, at least here. The flood hit full strength all over the world today. Tomorrow we hit back."

DAY 30. A MIDWESTERN CITY, UNITED STATES. 9:00 A.M.

Mr. Albert Whitehole, a junior partner in a large regional law firm, was seated solemnly behind his large wood desk in pursuit of a billable hour. "This weekend was a waste," he growls to his computer. "Saturday, I could only bill five hours, and then yesterday, that party I had hoped would yield four billable hours only generated a one weak billable hour. Damn, down six hours and the week just started." His fury grew as he reviewed his staff's time records. None of them billed anything Sunday! When I was an associate, I billed eight hours every Sunday, including time at Church services sitting next to a client. None of my staff deserve to make partner. They don't even deserve to continue to draw their pay! How can I make full partner when all I have to work with is these worthless cretins?

"You've got to see this, Al!" Jardice, a new associate, shouted as he ran down the hallway. The associate dashed down the hall without waiting for a response. Al!!! Albert thought, seething, and he sat for a minute, tapping out Morse code for retribution, savoring the withering reply he had ready. Sadly, the associate never came back. Disappointed, Albert got up, carefully letting his fingers touch the polished desk top as he walked around the desk to the door. He went down the hall in pursuit of the associate, and found the associate in a conference room full of staff. Albert cheered up, smugly knowing that his sarcasm will play better in front of an audience. As he stood in the doorway, he rehearsed his attack on the associate in his mind.

As he looks at his staff huddled around the monitors, in his mind he sees a red streaked revenue graph, the kiss of death to his dream of becoming a senior partner. "Shouldn't we be billing someone?" Albert pompously asked. Normally, that would have scattered them like quail back to their desks and monitors, but they just looked at him with astonishment.

"Can't you see what is happening?" Jardice, the associate Albert had been seeking for retribution shouted sarcastically at Albert, pointing at the screen. "The world is falling apart, and you want to bill someone?"

Albert, furious, starts to open his mouth, salivating over the vicious response he is about to deliver.

"This has to be seen, Mr. Whitehole. Mr. Jardice is correct.," Henley, a senior partner curtly ordered.

Albert gulped, smiling at Mr. Henley, who deliberately ignored Albert. Albert then put on a show of dutifully staring at a monitor. Albert had to ignore (only for the moment, he swore to himself) the broad smiles of amusement in the staff room at Albert's discomfort. Albert didn't even see the screen, he was so busy making mental notes on who had to be paid back later. Finally satisfied with his accounting for vengeance, Albert started watching the screen. The news is all people running wildly in the streets, shouting, burning private property, and completely disregarding the authorities. How can this be?, Albert wonders. He is completely puzzled. None of these people are working, and it's Monday! At least they are not my staff.

After a few minutes, Albert, now very uncomfortable, shakes his head, and goes back in his office. He carefully settles himself at his desk, just like any other morning, holding onto the mantle of his routine as armor against the world. Calmed, he settles down to a determined pursuit of the billable hour, each precious hour a step towards the grail of senior partner. He cheers up, realizing that he is one of the few working, and his star will shine all the brighter when the time records are reviewed. In vain, he calls and e-mails everyone he can think of, but no one answers. Out of desperation he is reduced to re-reading briefs for a case that is already over-billed. Well, the partner will see the billable hours, and the write offs will be later, so at least it's something, Albert consoles himself. Outside his office there is a continuing lack of proper protocol at work. There is constant shouting, people running from office to office and after a short time Albert closes his door. They have no focus on what is important, Albert thinks. How did these people get hired?

At the stroke of noon, five billable hours lashed to his timesheet, Albert sits back, moderately satisfied. Well, that's not so bad, since I didn't get here until 9, smiling. Now, who can I meet with at lunch, to maybe get another billable hour, or even better, get points with a partner? Albert stands up and takes a moment to carefully adjusting his tie and examines his suit again. Was a red tie right, or maybe one with a pinkish cast? What did they say at that seminar? Finally satisfied, he is ready to seek a partner to impress, and he opens the door of his office. Puzzled, he sees no one in the offices across from him, or in the other offices as he walks down the hallway. He finally goes back to into the conference room that he had been shamed in that morning. Most of the office is still in there. They generally look shocked and uncertain. No one pays any attention to Albert.

If they would have put in some honest work, Albert thinks pompously, they wouldn't be so upset. Fire them all. Especially Jardice, Albert thinks, remembering that Jardice is the hot new star from Harvard. Albert is terrified to see Jardice talking intently with to several senior partners, who are nodding their agreement with Jardice.

"I got in some billable hours this morning," another junior partner remarked, standing next to Albert.

They stared at Jardice taking to the senior partners, identical looks of hatred on the junior partners faces.

"Then we must be the only ones in the office working," Albert replied to the junior partner. Normally, Albert despised this junior partner, because the junior partner was competition, but at least he was someone to talk to that hadn't lost their mind.

"We need to go to lunch," Menting, a senior partner announced, standing at the conference room door. "We need to go in a group, because it has become dangerous out there. We may close the office this afternoon. The partners will make that decision after we see how bad it actually is. Everyone will gather in the reception area" Menting vanished, walking down the hallway.

"Close the office!" Albert exclaimed, shocked. He looked at the other junior partner, who just shrugged.

In a few minutes, most of the office staff is milling around in the reception area.

"Ok, that's everyone," Menting declared loudly. "Everyone else has already gone home."

To Albert's disgust, Menting nodded at Jardice, who stepped out the door, carefully looked around, and then waved.

"Jardice was in the special forces before Harvard," Henley noted to Albert with an odd smile. Henley then walked away to console some of the secretaries who were crying in a corner.

Albert's fury was mixed with terror at this terrible news. As the staff filed out, Albert and the junior partner fell into the line. When everyone is outside, they stare down the street at the heavy black smoke billowing up a couple of blocks away. A few high flames are starting to flicker behind the buildings in-between. The wind picks up, and suddenly there is a stench, a pervasive rotten smell. Albert grasps at his your throat, dimly noticing that most of the group has a look of horror on their faces, but a few are almost happy. Albert is puzzled for a moment, but then he gags and collapses.

Sometime later, Albert fights his way back to the real world. I'm lying on the sidewalk in my best grey pinstripe court suit, he realizes, shocked. He tries to stand up. Trembling and shaky, it takes a few moments to get his balance, but finally he is standing. He closes his eyes, and the horrible memories, the nightmare dreams flood back. He opens his eyes, and frantically brushes off his suit, a simple motion to distract him from those nightmares. There, he thinks, acceptable again. At least the suit doesn't seem to be damaged. And I'm back in the real world, safe. Only then does he look around. Maybe half of the staff is still lying on the sidewalk or street. About a quarter are standing, and another quarter are sitting up, looking dazed.

He looks down the street towards the smoke, which has grown. The flames are now high above the buildings in between. He looks at the street, and there are people sprawled all up and down the street. There are a few cars driving slowly. There are many cars crashed into other cars, or crashed into buildings, or just perched on sidewalks, wildly a-kilter. Some of the cars are on fire, some just smoking. There are screams in the distance, and sirens blaring from every direction.

Behind him, a woman screams. Albert jumps and then turns quickly around. Henley is holding an older secretary, turning her face away from something. Sexual harassment, Albert thinks happily. A partnership space that will be opening up! Then he looks past them, and stares in shock at a body under a car that ran up on the sidewalk. It's a woman, Albert thinks, only her legs showing, outlined by a pool of blood.

"That's Denise!" the older secretary sobs.

A lawsuit!, Albert happily realizes. Clear liability, the car is on up on the sidewalk. As the woman's body is on the sidewalk, I can plead that she was completely in the right, rough drafting the complaint in his mind. And that is a new auto, a luxury model, so it might have an umbrella policy, with substantial excess. Then he sighs to himself, thinking that with all the attorneys here, his chance of getting the case is small. He consoles himself with the thought that she wasn't even a secretary he got along with. Well, there are none I get along with, because none of them are competent, he remembered. Remind me to pull that negative review out of personnel file because it could decrease the final damage award.

The wind comes back, and suddenly Albert gags again. Dizzy, he almost falls, but staggering for a moment, recovers his balance. That stench again! The breeze changes direction, and the smell is still there, but not as strong. Gasping, he gets his breath back, and pushes the nightmares away again. The stench seems to trigger the nightmares, he realized. Well, that makes sense. A smell like that would make a person sick mentally as well as physically. Oddly, that cheers him up. He is furious that his life should be disturbed. Life destruction is what happens to my adversaries, Albert thinks, not to me. How can the world dare step between him and his plans? Someone will pay for this! Albert gags again, throwing up as he staggers towards a utility pole for support.

A few minutes later, he has recovered. Looking around, he notices that the staff sorted itself into several small groups. He sees a cluster of senior partners in the largest group, so he walks towards them. Cromwell, the most senior partner of all, is haranguing the group, furious at the disorder, the lack of work, that young have no discipline and other favorite topics. Albert agrees completely with everything that is being said. Albert suddenly notices that they all seem, well, pale. He glanced at his hands, which are pale like the others. Proof of hard work, he thinks happily. No one can say that I have not done what I'm supposed to do.

Jones, the next to most senior partner is standing next to Cromwell. Jones is pale and coughing, but recovers his poise. "We need to help the authorities regain control, and help all these people in trouble," he shouted, loudly enough that all the separate groups could hear. "Who knows first aid?"

A few of the office staff raised their hands.

"All of you follow Henley's orders," Jones directed. Jones looked at Henley and grimaced, but Jones quickly caught himself and forced a smile.

Albert noticed that Henley's skin wasn't pale. There are several people with the, well, healthy skin, Albert realized. Like a radioactive glow, and Albert suddenly understood Jones grimace, because there is something about those people that made Albert angry. No, more than angry. He is furious. They are mutants, he realized, shocked, just like the ones they warned about on the news.

271

"Ok," Henley advised. "I'm making Jardice the leader, because he has recent combat experience." A group moves to surround the young associate, who starts talking intently.

Albert is almost beside himself now. Jardice is given prominent authority and he's a mutant! Then Albert remembers that he has no interest in helping people who don't look like they could pay for a single billable hour of his time, much less a meaningful, sustained bill. Let them spend their time with the riff raff. It's a complete waste of time.

Albert notices many in his group staring angrily at the other group. Don't they realize they are mutants? Albert wonders. This is good, Albert realizes, because Jardice will get what he deserves after all! Albert looks around quickly at the group he is part of, the largest group, mostly older associates and partners and they are almost all pale. Some actually look sickly, white, but most are just, well, pale, he notes. There is one in their group with the radioactive skin and the group pulls away from him.

"You smell," Cromwell snarled at the glowing man.

"What?" The man sniffed, and looked disgusted. "You are the one's that smell!"

"You reek" a junior partner yelled and suddenly pushed the man.

Caught off balance, the glowing man fell to the sidewalk. The man was quickly surrounded by the partners, who were cursing and kicking him. "He's a mutant," Albert shouted, carefully keeping his distance.

"What the hell?" Jardice yells. Jardice, Henley and others push though the crowd. Henley reaches down and pulls the healthy man up, while the healthy group surrounds the man, protecting him. The man stands, his nose broken, blood running down his face.

"He stinks!" Jones shouted at Jardice.

Jardice steps up and punches Jones in the face, a roundhouse right to the jaw. Jones goes down in a heap, and is surrounded by the pale group, who are staring with hate at Jardice.

"You reek!" Jardice shouts at Jones. "You smell like the living dead. All of you do!" And he looks around in fury at the pale people.

The healthy people in back of Jardice pull him away. They all back up, and in a few minutes there were only two groups. Maybe two-thirds, roughly, were pale. The rest had the glowing skin. The two groups started shouting at each other, and the shouts drew others, who ran down the street towards them. In a few minutes, there were two much larger groups milling around, the mutants greatly outnumbered, but ready to fight.

Jones was pulled up to his feet. "Back up," Jones ordered the group. "We don't need to fight these filth. Let the police deal with them." As the pale people backed up, the mutants backed away and then they suddenly ran, vanishing around a corner.

"Yeah!" Albert shouted. "You better run." Albert was jubilant. Henley will be fired, a senior partner vacancy opening up, and Jardice disgraced. And there were a couple of other partners who were mutants. They will all be fired. A good day after all!

Suddenly Albert heard the sound of running feet. Albert turns, as does most of his group and they saw a huge crowd of pale people rushing towards them. The group was howling with rage as they ran, brandishing guns and clubs.

"Let them battle," Cromwell laughed, a satisfied smile on his face as the crowd ran past them after the mutants. The staff of the law firm huddled together as the mob roared past them. The staff then slowly walked down the street to what had been their favorite lunch spot. Each step was a shock, a step into a twilight zone of the familiar and yet incredibly strange.

"It's like a nightmare," someone mumbled.

"It isn't!" Jones snarled. "And don't say that word!"

Albert nodded his agreement. The word 'nightmare' brought back the dreams for a moment, and he shook his head to clear them away.

A few minutes later, the group stands mournfully in front of a restaurant, watching the flames lick the counters.

"Let's go to the police," Jones decided. They all tromped off towards police headquarters, a few blocks away.

"What could be more right than to join the authorities?" a junior partner declaimed, waving his arms as if to a jury. "Maybe they will favor us when it comes time to handle the legal work arising from all this?"

Albert brightened at the thought. "This chaos must end," Albert demanded. "Must end! Order must be preserved." Albert noticed his voice was a bit out of control, but no one else seemed to notice. They all nodded agreement with his words.

A breeze brought the stench back, but not as strong and it quickly passes. They all curse the smell, but it helps knowing that the group hates the smell. As they walk they see a group of mutants on the other side of the street, walking towards them. The lawyers start screaming at them. The mutants heft their weapons, look carefully at the lawyers, and then ignore them, hurrying down the street.

As the group walks, it shrinks. Many decide to find their families and safety at home and dribble off. Maybe a third of the original group reaches the police station. Inside, the police station is complete chaos. The senior partners, furious that their power and authority is being ignored, finally corner an old sergeant, who they have known–and fought–over many long years.

"We need you," the old sergeant advised. "The city is being torn apart. All over the world it is nothing but battles between normal people and those damn mutants with their precious plants. Those plants stink up everything, don't know how they can stand it."

"That stench?" Albert asked. "It is the plants?"

"You got it," the sergeant sneered. "What was your first clue?"

"It was. ." Albert started to answer, but was hushed by Jones.

"You are sure?" Jones demanded. "I didn't realize that."

Saved, Albert realized. I could have looked foolish in front of the partners.

"Oh, it's the plants," the sergeant growled. "Today, all over the world, they reached some kind of a critical mass and it's chaos. The governments and health departments demand that the plants must be destroyed. Now they have proof that the plants are killing people, now that the plants are everywhere. Too bad they couldn't have decided that a week ago! The damn mutants worship the plants, and they are forming gangs, stealing guns and weapons. A group of rogue cops raided our weapons storeroom and grabbed all they could, arming their people. I hear the same is happening in the military."

"How can we help?" Cromwell asked, stunned.

"We can give you some weapons," the sergeant offered. "But beware! They fight like banshees. If you come across one, make sure you have at least three to one in a fight." He looked doubtfully at the lawyers. "Maybe four to one. If you fight one to one, they will kill you. Probably the best thing you can do is go home and protect your families."

The sergeant turns away from them as a group of police rush up to him, carrying a badly wounded officer.

The group stood for a moment, staring at the wounded officer, screaming and leaking blood all over the floor. Then Jones pushed them all towards the weapons storeroom.

"Going to our families is the best plan," Jones ordered. "Split up into groups, travel in a group as far as you can. Don't fire your weapons unless you have to. Our ammunition is limited and, quite frankly, we have little experience. They will need our skills later, when it's time to clean up this mess and to make some people pay."

The group went to the parking lot reserved for the firm. Once they reach the lot, there is a lot of shouting and conflicting orders as they try to get cars out of the lot. In the lot, cars are crashed into others, blocking the lanes, and then there are cars on fire and the fires are spreading. Finally, they wrangle what's savable out of the lot. Once it is clear how many cars they have available, they divide into groups. An hour passes, as the driver of the car Albert is riding in slowly picks their way through streets littered with bodies and broken cars. Several times they have to stop to move bodies, and one time they all have help to shove a car out of the way.

Albert is let out near his home. He walks down the street, detached from this world. He's tired, his normal physical activity limited to puffing up his chest in court. He examines the pistol in his hand, confused. I've only seen these in a movie, he realized. He carefully touched the trigger, and the gun fires, a window across the street bursting into fragments.

"Asshole!" a man screams at him. "Put the safety on!"

Albert stares blankly at the man.

The man shakes his head in disbelief as he walks over to Albert. "The safety!" the man growled, pointing to a button near the trigger. The man glanced at Albert, who just stared at him. The man then reached over and clicked the button. "Now it's on safety-that means it won't fire. Now you won't shoot yourself, not that it would be any loss to the world. More importantly, you won't shoot someone else accidentally. Do remember to take the safety off if you really want to shoot someone." The man walked away, spitting on the sidewalk, not even looking back at Albert.

Albert's home was in a private gated community. Albert and his wife joyfully bought the house when he made junior partner. Not that I live here, he admits. I live at the office. But my wife picked it out and this is the right address, we were told. He stops, shocked. The guard at the gatehouse is lying dead on the sidewalk in a pool of blood and the gate is wide open. Albert rushes in, headed to the side street his house is on. He's terrified, suddenly beginning to realize, that the world has changed forever. If all I am is a junior partner, then what am I now? he asks and the nightmares start to crawl up again. He frantically pushes then down, focusing on running for his house.

His wife Jacqueline is standing in the living room with Ernest, their teenage son. She has her arms around Ernest, who is clinging to her. A blonde beauty, President of her sorority, 'Jacqueline', never 'Jacky', she is pale, as is Ernest. He smiles happily to see that they are all right and then frowns. Where is our daughter?

"She is with them," Jacqueline hissed. "She cursed us, praising the power of the Tree and then she ran off that with street trash from her school."

Albert is furious, livid. He visualizes himself killing his daughter and is oddly satisfied. "We will find her. At least Ernest is on the right side."

Ernest smiles and then coughs, hard. Jacqueline holds Ernest tight and his coughing attack soon passes. Jacqueline glances at Albert, worried. "The news reports that the cough will pass, but his is more serious than most."

"One of my friends at school just died in the hallway," Ernest sputtered. "He started coughing, and then blood gushed out of his mouth. He collapsed and we left him there, just lying in the hallway."

"I have a pistol," Albert told them, trying to keep them calm. "We will be safe here. We have food, water, and shelter."

"The electricity is failing and the water stopped running," Jacqueline grimaced. "The toilets don't work."

"We need to get into a group," Ernest mumbled, rubbing his head. "There are a lot of the mutants. There were killings at school, and while there are more of us, they are savage. I can't believe what they do to people! My sister crushed another girls skull and then just laughed."

Albert stared at him, stunned. I'm ruined! This couldn't be covered up. My daughter, a murderer! I'll never make senior partner. Then he calmed down. I can get sympathy from others; I can make this work for me.

"The same happened at work," Albert replied. "They split off immediately, and got vicious."

Suddenly Jacqueline staggered, half falling. Ernest held her up. In a moment, she recovered.

"These dreams!" she moaned. "I can't get rid of them. It's like something is trying to take me over. Trying to become something weird, something non-human."

"All of us are having them," Ernest told her "That's what the news said. The other's seem to be controlled by the dreams, that's why the news calls them mutants."

Albert realizes that he has been having the same terrible dreams since he woke up. For a second, they come back. That fish! It switched from male to female, and then the feeling of mating as a female. And then mating with male fish. The pleasure . . Albert frantically pushed away the horrible memories, and held his wife and son.

"When we hold each other, the memories fade," Albert told them, and they agreed. They stand huddled together for another few minutes.

"We need to go," Ernest declared, stepping back. Albert and Jacqueline nod and then they walk out of the house.

"Will we ever come back here?" Jacqueline cried, big tears running down her cheeks. "I just finished the decorating!"

Albert studies the house and shrugs. "It wasn't that built that well," he answered. "And with the openings for full partner that are coming up at the firm, we are well rid of it. If this is gone, it makes it easier to move to a bigger, better house. The insurance will pay off the mortgage." A strange fury rises in him, and walking into the house, he touched a lighted match to the drapes. He runs out as the flames start to lick at the furniture.

They stand on the sidewalk for a moment, watching the flames rising. "I know just the house I want," Jacqueline said, wiping away her tears. "The next one will be bigger than any of the houses our friends have!"

Albert made a mental note to stop the automatic payment on the mortgage out of his bank account. They back away as the fire grows and then hear shouting down the street.

"Let's go!" Ernest yelled and the family ran down the street. They stop when they reach a group of pallid people standing around some dead bodies in the street. The dead look to have been mutants, their skin now bruised, but clearly not pale. The family looked carefully at the dead. Albert recognized a friend of their daughters, and a couple of the neighbors, including one who was a professor at the local college. Lying on the grass are several pale dead, now completely white.

"I never liked him!" Jacqueline sneered. "There was always something about that boy, I knew he would turn out badly."

"And that professor," a member of the mob shouted. "Asking for understanding, begging us to come to a larger world. Disgusting!"

Albert stepped over, and spit in the face of the dead boy. It felt good. People in the mob clapped him on the back afterwards and his wife held tight to his hand.

A phone rang. A member of the mob answered, listened for a minute, and then shouted for them all to head to the community center, where there was a big group with plans.

DAY 30. OUTSIDE TABUK, SAUDI ARABIA.

The armored column that General Ishmael was leading was near Tabuk. He was reflecting, sitting in the turret, idly watching the desert go by. He had been the General in charge of containing the religious ecstasy drug disaster. While no one had directly criticized his handing of the problem, and actually all the authorities had praised every step he had taken, he had been eased out of any important command after that. It wasn't anything I did, he thought, again. It's that I'm an embarrassment; a reminder of what went wrong. A Jonah, conveying bad news by my presence. Well, dealing with the Court was a pain in the ass. This is better.

He glanced down at the map, and did a rough calculation of their speed. "We will stop here," he ordered, giving the coordinates of a nearby oasis. "It will give us shelter for the night and the welcome sight of a little green."

"What of the reports of those plants?" a captain asked.

"If they are at this oasis, then they are everywhere," the General replied. We can run, but we can't hide, he thought.

An hour later, the armored column ground to a halt. It was a shock to hear nothing but the soft desert wind after hours of feeling and hearing the machines clank and roar. The men walked around, stretching after being cooped up. Then, they started fueling the tanks and personal carriers, carefully moving ammunition into place. They were on full war alert after all of the chaos of the last few days.

War against who? General Ishmael thought again. War against ourselves, as far as I can understand what is going on. This isn't the religious drug, like the news is shouting. The opposite, actually, because people who are infected are stronger after than they were before. I know better than any that the religious drug killed within a fairly short time.

"Who is the enemy?" the General asked his aide. "Those mutants? They get stronger by the day, whereas those who reject the plants just keep getting sicker. If I kill the mutants, there may be no one left at all."

"The doctors are working," the aide replied, dutifully.

"At what?" the General scoffed. "Stopping the plants from spreading? That can't be done; you can't stop the breeze and the birds. I hear the plants turn herbicides into nutrients. Trying to keep people from getting sick? No one seems to have a clue on that one."

Two hours later, the sky is dark, the brilliant stars of the deep desert overhead. There are a few fires, but most of the troop has settled down for sleep. Suddenly, there is a sound, faint but swelling quickly, rushing towards them out of deep desert. The men wake and stagger to their feet, staring fearfully at the horizon. Roaring, a wind like a Fury sweeps over them, carrying the strong smell of the tree.

General Ishmael gasps and passes out, as do all of his men. Pulled into dark dreams, he finally lets go, and lets the dreams carry him where they will. The dreams are so real that he is surprised at the real world when he finally wakens. He holds his head as the memories and dreams he just went thru run in his mind. Still breathing, he notes, assessing the situation. Breathing well, and the smell of the wind is sweet. Sweet, like those of the Tree say it is. He grimly looks at his arm, finding the birthmark.

"You are of the Tree," his aide acknowledged, standing near him, holding an assault rifle at the ready, as the aide cautiously looked around. "As am I," the aide quickly added, seeing the General reach for his pistol. "And most of the troop."

There was a burst of rifle fire and screams nearby.

"Well, not all," the aide remarked. "But soon, all that will be alive will be of the Tree."

The general started to speak and then he understood. "There can't be any peace between those of the Tree and those outside," he murmured. "Now I understand."

Two hours later, there was a staff meeting.

"It went well," a Captain reported. "We have about sixty five percent of our people, which is, as I understand it, a very high percentage of survivors."

"High because of the General," the aide declared. "He only took the best, leaving the dross for the others."

"Be that as it may," the General replied, "this means we still have an effective fighting force. What do we do?"

"The Chief of Staff is against the Tree," a colonel reported. "We have no happy homecoming waiting for us there."

"Do we know anything?" the General demanded. "Give me facts, assessments, resources. Something to base choices on."

"There is a network springing up," his aide reported. "The communications people stumbled onto it. We now have contacts with others throughout the world."

"Life does not start and stop at our convenience," the General continued. "I need to know exactly what we have. What armor is still useable, given the crews that we have lost? What tankers do we have, how much fuel? Ah, don't respond to headquarters if they contact us. We can get away with pretending a sandstorm has cut off communications for a while."

"After that?" a colonel asked.

"Worry about that when it happens," the General replied. "We cannot see all ends."

They saluted, and left.

DAY 30. A WOODS OUTSIDE NEW YORK. 10 P.M.

In the mutant camps, informal groups spring up, sharing what happened to them, what they became and saw.

"I loved cats," a woman declared. "And I became a cat. I never knew! Oh, I'd joke about how vicious the cat was, but they are savage animals. You know that picture of the kitten, with the caption that the kitten thinks about murder every minute? It's true, because that's what life is. Finding food and finding strength, keeping yourself healthy is what life is about. And cats are thoughtful, in a way really different from humans. They assess, and assess, they poke and check, and then pounce. I would never have thought my cat was a complex as it is. Or that cats are so much the same as I am. Human is a lot less unique that I thought."

"I was the owner of a growing company," a man announced to a small group. "I was powerful, accepted, I had money and was in the right clubs. I thought I understood life, and power. So I became a rabbit."

The other's laugh, shaking their heads.

The man smiles and then frowns. "In their own way, rabbits are a savage animal. They are focused on mating, and the competition is intense and unforgiving. And they live under unbelievable stress, foraging for food while watching for predators. They are brave beyond anything I ever imagined! Their the glee at finding food, fiercely pushing other's aside when necessary, and running at a moments notice from so many predators. Wolves, foxes, dogs and hawks; everything seems to like bunny. But the rabbits run when they can and fight when there is no other choice. They fight hard without restraint when they have to. The creatures are nothing like the small stories we used to make up about them. Well, there's human posturing, and then there is life, raw and savage." But, brightening up, "there is food and mating," and he nudges the woman next to him.

She sticks out her tongue at him.

"Yeah, a lot of that in the rabbit community too," the man sighed.

"I was angry all the time," a girl offered. Her black makeup had mostly rubbed off, but her clothes were black, her boots heavy. "I was furious at everyone, and everyone was furious at me. I was powerless and frustrated all the time. I became a lioness, all long, hard body and controlled fury. And I loved it! Power and action, a simple life. But it really wasn't what I thought it would be. It was a lot more complex being powerful than I thought. Lions are careful, cautious beasts, indecisive and even what I would have thought was cowardly. They assess the chances of success and the consequences of failure, and failure in the wild is death. The lion showed me conflict and choice in the real world, beyond the social madness, and I had never understood the difference."

"So, wearing pink now?" a teenager teased.

"Please!" the girl laughed. "Maybe tan, that tawny brown that lioness are. I don't know if this looks like a lioness?" she asked, pulling her sleeve up and staring at the birthmark. "Maybe that's a head?"

The others looked carefully.

"Yeah, I can see that," a man agreed.

"A friend of mine got a snake," the girl snickered. "And his birthmark was on his penis!"

"You're kidding!," a woman laughed.

"No, and he showed it to me. And it was a long snake. When I dropped my panties, the snake grew to full size," the girl giggled.

"That would have been a painful tattoo!" one of the men commented, mentally flinching.

"Curiosity killed the cat," a women teased the girl.

"It is important to check carefully," the girl laughed. "The lioness taught me to test, to watch, to experiment, and to poke gently at new things before pouncing. Even human science demands reproducible results."

They all laughed.

"And I understood that I was part of something larger," the girl continued. "The lioness felt herself as part of something larger, she worshipped a lion goddess. Her belief was indistinct, well, it was a lion belief and I only touched the corners of being a lion, but I could feel it. It helped me more than I could have imagined."

"No man is an island," an ex-priest agreed.

"No, he is a peninsula," the girl snickered. "That was the teaching of the snake."

Shocked, the ex-priest stared at her, and then slapping his calf, he laughed so hard he cried.

DAY 30. ATLANTA. 10 P.M.

A group of CDC scientists and technicians are sitting in the ruins of their offices.

"At least we locked down and burned all the samples in the labs before the labs were breached," one reported. "Those plagues were at least stopped."

"And the coffee machine is working," another added.

"So, what do we know?" one of the scientists asked.

"It seems that the impact of the Tree is dependent on the colony creatures in the plants," a researcher replied. "When there are only a few plants, the effect is weak. As the plants become stronger, more colony creatures are emitted. Those colony creatures swap genetic material with other bacteria and viruses, and as the plant colony creatures strengthen, begin to interact with many of the human colony creatures. When the plants have reached full strength, the effect is staggering. The human collapses, the internal colony creatures wildly swapping genetic material and becoming new bacteria."

"That would have been today," another scientist noted.

"It certainly was," the first scientist agreed, studying the birthmark on his arm.

"A lot of us survived," one of the technicians remarked. "Far more than the average, as far as I can tell."

Partly because many of the first who changed protected each other," another observed. "What I've seen out there is horror beyond anything I ever imagined."

"What we've all seen," the first scientist agreed. "And, as we know first hand, carried with the colony creatures into the humans were memories of life as other creatures. Real memories, a visual and emotional emersion into another creature's existence. Arms and legs felt feel like flippers or a insects mandibles, or like a running zebra across the hot plains. The creatures thinking patterns didn't take over the human, but ran in parallel, a roller coaster ride into a never-never land. It is like in your dreams, when you expand them to life size and walk into them-not holding at a distance, watching like a movie, when the dreams are fearful or stressful. The dreams absorb the person completely."

"Here is what we know," a technician summarized, "the life of that creature is either absorbed or denied. The feeding, the growing, the mating, the simple acts of life of that creature run through the person, as real as the experiences from their life that the human remembers. And then, after an hour or two, the human awakes. Their acceptance or denial is immediately apparent. The smell of the plants is either sweet and a delight, or a stench. They are either healthy, their skin glowing with life, or starting to be pasty, pallid, regardless of their natural skin color. It's common for some kind of a birthmark type of mark, almost a tattoo, to grow somewhere for those who accept the tree. It's most common on the arms, but can be anywhere on the body."

"I agree," a scientist agreed. "The acceptance or denial is complete. There is no halfway possible. Fortunately or unfortunately, acceptance or denial is based on an unknown. Something in the DNA of the human, something based on their life experiences, there is a choice made somewhere, but we don't know where or how."

"Humans were a shaken solution, all dissolved into a common mix," a scientist commented. "But things mixed into solution are inherently unstable, and the tree was the reaction. Once the reaction started, the, well, precipitate forms into two groups. Until the trigger of the Tree, people didn't realize how completely people varied from others."

"Can we predict anything about who will survive?" a scientist asked.

"Oh, generally, those who followed their inspiration, who enjoyed their life on their terms survived," a scientist reported. "Many outcasts, outliers survive. Many people who were addicted to one thing or another have survived, breaking free of their addictions as they embrace the Tree. It's the small people, the good people who bought heart and soul into the system, never questioning, never thinking, who don't survive. We're going to be short on the faithful tillers of the fields."

"So, what's next?" a security officer demanded. "How can we keep things going, like power, fuel, food, and protect our people?"

"We have tapped into a network," one of the scientists announced. "Let's get online, see who is with us where, and what has to be done to keep things going."

"I know people in Detroit," a scientist reported. "They told everyone this was coming, but I denied, because I couldn't imagine it. They had a lot of ideas and contacts, lets get back in touch with them."

DAY 30. EVENING.

The network news flashes from scene to scene, but they are all the same, all over the world.

They show a battle in progress. The voice over reports "Here in Shanghai, it is the young and the aged against the police and the military. I've never seen such ruthlessness, such viciousness as these mutants are showing. The military is here in force to protect the city. Here is Colonel Xi to brief us."

A middle aged, tired looking man wearing a once crisp military uniform appears. "These mutants are vicious," Colonel Xi declared. "But we are holding the line." In the live action background scene, suddenly there are by several explosions. Men's bodies fly, and the mass of troops begins to run, frantically trying to get away. The mutants, young and old, are shooting them down, then attacking with swords and knives. The Colonel glanced at the screen, grimaces, makes a motion with his hand, and the video vanishes. "As I said," the Colonel continued, "We are holding the line against them . . ."

The news shifts to a scene outside a gun store in rural Texas.

"We're ready for the Zombie apocalypse," a group of half drunk men standing next to some worn pickup trucks shout. They wave their rifles, one accidentally pulling a trigger and almost shooting the others.

"Come on, boy's!" a police officer shouts. "There's a nest of them in the next town. Saddle up!"

"Yahoo!" they shout, and in a few minutes, a line of old pickup trucks headed by the police drive into the dark.

The news switches to a serious group of talking heads around a table.

"We have this enormous problem of a complex, interrelated world collapsing," a woman exclaimed. "What of the computer chip plants, the people required to operate the plants, what about protecting those? Our world will crash forever if we lose our advanced technology!"

"We are trying to maintain control," a government official defended. "We have the army surrounding critical manufacturing facilities to protect them, and are in contact with the militaries of other countries to do the same."

"If it's a fragile world encountering the real world, how can we keep it going?" a man stammered.

The camera pulls away to the aftermath of a battle. The smoke is still rising from the burning autos.

"We won this one!," a jubilant police officer shouts, a happy crowd milling in the background. The camera pans around at bodies hanging from utility poles, the dead lying in the streets.

"It's nasty business," the police officer commented, "But there isn't any other way of handling this."

Suddenly, there is an explosion, and many in the crowd are thrown to the ground. In the distance, there are people attacking, men in army uniforms and others.

"Damn!" the policeman swore. "It's our own people, they sold out . ." Another explosion, and there is nothing but smoke to be seen.

The camera shifts to a talking head. "There has been a momentary interruption in the broadcast, we will go back to that location in a minute. Meanwhile . ."

"It's full scale war," the newsman reported in a rare moment of truth. "The police and military are splitting up, taking sides, all over the world. In every town, in every city, there are shots and screams from all directions. Those who hate the plants and those who embrace the plants must fight to the bitter end."

DAY 30. NIGHT, NEW YORK.

"Today was 'The Night No One Comes Home'," Oskar remarked to Christina as they sit in the grass, watching the stars. "And it was a bloody sunset tonight, painting the clouds dark reds and brilliant scarlet's. Perfectly synced with the day."

"I like that," Christina agreed. "But it's really that we come home to the real home, not the human social one that we pretended was life."

"I'd still like a warm bed and walls," Alex grumbled, swatting a mosquito. "The creature in me loves the outside world, but the soft human in me is cold, hungry and tired."

DAY 30. NIGHT, DETROIT.

"Well, the flood is at it's peak now," Mary confirmed, happily watching the brilliant green field, specked with small white flowers, their blossoms dipping and rising with the wind, that stretched far into what had been wasteland. She smiled, the sweet fragrance of the breeze lifting her spirits.

"The blind shall see" Jesus vowed. "And cripples will cast aside their crutches and walk when they become of the Tree. It was the walls in their mind that kept them from seeing and walking."

"People turn a burden into a badge of honor," Mary agreed. "We thought that was a good thing, because you have to keep going regardless of what life brings. But that was turned upside down by the church, twisted out of shape. They made people exult in their burden. What surprised us is that when people were offered relief from a burden, they clung to the burden, the weight. It had become them, their definition of themselves, instead of a tool to move past."

"And by exulting the burden, embracing needless suffering, they denied life, when life is the key. Making suffering the goal, the church found a frame for its message of death, its dry and dusty terror of death that was covered up by all the elaborate ceremony," Lucifer mused.

"The human curse is to cling to the crutch to validate the past. The past is past and you cannot control the future through the dead past," Jesus added. "A crutch is a tool to use to assist your life. You don't limit your life to the crutch."

"The churches are blaming this one on me," Lucifer laughed. "All this fire and killing and chaos. As if my power was so great! They must always have an enemy, always someone for the group to join against, to make up a world that they can control. Didn't work so well this time."

"Blame me. I am come to send fire on Earth; and what will I, if it be already kindled? But I have a baptism to be baptized with; and how am I straitened till it be accomplished! Suppose ye that I am come to give peace on earth?" Jesus growled. "I tell you, Nay; but rather division: For from henceforth there shall be five in one house divided, three against two, and two against three. The father shall be divided against the son, and the son against the father; the mother against the daughter, and the daughter against the mother; the mother in law against her daughter in law, and the daughter in law against her mother in law."15

"I always liked the King James version," Mary observed. "The baptism of the Tree, that came to all."

"Do not think that I came to bring peace on Earth; I did not come to bring peace, but a sword," Jesus commanded. "And it has come. He who has found his life will lose it, and he who has lost his life for My sake will find it."16

"They either take the direct route to their heaven, climbing up the hill with the leopard, lion and the wolf, or they will be lost in their nonsense human stories," Lucifer added. "He who has lost his life into another's life, he who has become another creature, shall find that new Life."

"And those who were seen dancing were thought to be insane by those who could not hear the music."17 Cali proclaimed.

DAY 31. A MALL, NEW YORK. 8 A.M.

"It's at least clean, filtered air," Albert told Jacqueline, trying to cheer her up.

"It's better," she agreed, coughing just a little. "And there is bottled water, and some dried food. I thought I was going to die when I ate that fruit yesterday!"

"Come on, Dad," Ernest shouted, running up to them. "They have assigned us to a search and destroy squad! Our weapons are waiting at the east end of the mall!"

"I'll stay here," Jacqueline interrupted. "I don't feel that strong, and I've been talking to other women. We're going to stay in the mall, and help that way."

Albert kissed Jacqueline, who then sat down, sighing. Albert and Ernest report to their squad. An hour later, they are about a mile from the mall.

"This area needs to be burned," the squad leader ordered, squinting at an area of lower class homes. "Too many plants have grown in here." He moistened his finger, and held it up. "Good," he rasped. "The wind is behind us. Burning the plants with the wind the wrong way will kill you in minutes."

Albert, Ernest and others in the squad ran into the neighborhood. They started the burn at the far edge, and worked their way back, tossing gasoline bombs into houses as they worked their way back. They were careful to stay upwind. When they were done, they pulled their masks off, studying at the huge fire.

"These masks help," Ernest observed. "I ran right over a patch of the plants, and didn't hardly smell them."

"They help a bit," Albert agreed. "But they need to get something better, stronger. I coughed for ten minutes after accidentally getting downwind of a patch of plants."

"Next assignment, people!" the squad leader shouted. "Everyone over here."

Albert looked around. "We've lost some people," he commented to Ernest.

"Some caught by the plants, and some shot by the mutants." Ernest replied.

By late afternoon, they were exhausted. They trudged back to the mall, stepping over bodies lying in the streets.

"Witches," Ernest sneered, pointing at a pile of bodies.

"And wizards," Albert added, looking at the men hanging from utility poles.

"Too many of our people dead," a man walking beside them commented wearily.

"Where do the mutants get the weapons?" Ernest asked.

"They were not all shot," the man answered. "Many are just dying. The doctors don't have a cure, and don't know what to do."

"None of that!" the leader yelled at the man. "That's mutant talk. I've been told by the priests that a cure is coming, they just have to distribute it."

They stopped for a few minutes. A hundred feet away, several priests were leading a ritual killing of mutants, surrounded by a furious crowd of the zombies. The mutants were burned, the priests blessing the killers afterwards. All of Albert's group stopped and knelt for a blessing by the priests as they walked by them.

"I feel better," Albert told Ernest. "We just have to believe, to hold together."

The priests watched the group walk away towards the mall.

"They have not believed so intently in centuries," a priest rejoiced.

"A blessing," another priest agreed. "Now if we could just start healing some of them! We need a flock to shepherd."

"At least they now take orders," the Bishop snapped. "All are obedient again, respectful. The women wear headscarf's and do not parade themselves like whores. The men bow and kneel when they see us. It's been a long time since the church was as respected. Healing them? We shall see if they deserve to be healed."

"All who die in the apocalypse shall be reborn," a priest croaked. "That is the word of the church."

At the mall, Albert went straight to a meeting planning the next day's attacks. He listens to the speakers thunder against the mutants, and their great plans to retake the world. All cheer, but he is depressed as he walks back to find his family. That was all show and no go, he thinks. I know, doubt is disaster, but that was all confusion. The speeches contracted each other, and danced away from the biggest problem, that we are all getting sicker. No new plans, just the old plans that didn't work, and any opposition, any questions, you are with the mutants. I thought several people were going to be executed on the spot until they knelt and denied what they had said. Only one plan, no questions, no options, and only orders from the top. Thinking about only the resources that you control, and assuming anything out of your control has adequate resources. No discretion, no thinking. That never works well. Why is it that Achilles is the model for human bravery and behavior, that egocentric display of bravado and anger that leads only to disaster in the end?

Albert looked up, and smiled to see his son. His smile froze when he saw Jacqueline. Her skin had whitened, emptied of color, technically, he thought to himself. Pale? No, she was wan, colorless. He'd seen that color in hospitals when he had attended clients who were dying. He forced the thoughts away, and held her carefully.

DAY 31. WHO LIVES.

"Who lives?" Jesus typed, and sat back, reflecting. Lighthouses don't go running all over an island looking for boats to save; they just stand there shining, he thought wryly. The new position. At least I hope I'm "a shining" to someone out there. Not 'The Shining'—that was ugly.

"Let's start this on a positive note. We are at this moment participating in one of the very greatest leaps of the human spirit to knowledge, both of the outside world and also of our own deep inward mystery that has ever occurred. It is the inner mystery that matters in the end, but practically speaking, you've got to have food on the table too. The confusion that many feel, the pull between the past and present and future, is a prize given to you, not a punishment. The opportunity to think and judge is the essence of life.

"The physical sciences create the food, shelter, and toys that keep us alive, and actually living better in a material sense, than ever dreamed of in the past. The problem is that the old myths sought to illuminate transcendent symbols by using fixed objective 'true' facts. This was an attempt to make the symbols clearer, which failed rather badly. 'Fact' in the external world changes as knowledge accrues. If people didn't literally read the objective fact presented to illustrate the symbol as 'the symbol,' we wouldn't have a problem. Because people take the symbol as the fact, and freeze the symbol to the exact reality presented as a roadmap to reach the symbol, we have a huge problem. The rejection of the 'fact,' because facts come and go, becomes rejection of the symbol, and worse, the destruction of belief based on the symbolic forms. Lose the symbols, the messengers between our inner world and the outer world, and we are left without communication between ourselves inside, and ourselves outside. We become the split-brain people who have coherent, logical explanations for their actions which are completely divorced from the actions themselves. In other words, we begin believing random nonsense and hold all the tighter to it. Now that sounds bad, but there are positives in this problem. For example, that people have enough food and shelter to think about these issues is a huge positive. For many eons, people died so quickly and life was so hard that asking questions about anything beyond where tomorrow's food would come from was pointless.

"The Tree forces the question, because the answer to the question is now life or death. Of course, death will come eventually. 'Death is not an event in life: we do not live to experience death. If we take eternity to mean not infinite temporal duration but timelessness, then eternal life belongs to those who live in the present. ' So we should stop worrying and have a picnic in the park? It isn't that easy.

"An apocalypse, in the Greek, 'Apokálypsis', is a veil lifted, a revelation of the new. The downside to a veil being lifted is that the veil was there to generally cover up things that we would wish away. The revelation is that Life is bigger than the small human stories, and Life can't be crammed away into a box in a corner.

"Now, things don't need to last forever to be perfect. People will tell you that nothing matters, that the whole world's about to end soon anyway, but those people are looking at life the wrong way. The telescope inverted, seeing the small instead of the large.

"We see the world not as it is, but as we are. We all see the world through a 'stained glass window' of sorts. We see our beliefs, our limiting assumptions, our hopes, fears, and experiences, our personal context writ large across the world. What one person sees as adversity, another can see as an opportunity, based on how he or she views the world. While the entire world is constant change, we freeze most of the world in our minds in an attempt to focus on the small subset of the world we are working with now. Only later do we realize that, having frozen where we wanted to be, we are now demanding a comfortable world that doesn't exist. Granted, we can never really be prepared for that which is wholly new, which is what is now sitting at our door. Perhaps one way to make it easier is to not unlearn old habits, but instead learn new habits and let the old whither away.

"I have a radical point of view: learn to listen to, and trust, your heart. Or your intuition, or your gut, or the seat of your pants, or whatever part of your anatomy is the source of that mysteriously wonderful 'still, small voice' that somehow knows you better than you do, and knows what's better for you better than you do. Your inspiration is what you must look to for Life. Failures? Failure and success are labels, and labels are libels. It's trying that matters. Babies never stop; they never stop practicing, they ignore what we see as their constant failures, and that's how they get good. When they are taught what failure is, that's when they really begin to fail. Darwin wrote that it is not the strongest of the species that survive, nor the most intelligent, but the ones most responsive to change. Each of us, now, has to face whether we can change.

"The Tree has come to force the decision. The Father's kingdom is like a farmer who had good seed in a field. His enemy came during the night and sowed weeds among the good seed. The farmer did not let the workers pull up the weeds, but said to them, 'No, otherwise you might go to pull up the weeds and pull up the wheat along with them. For on the day of the harvest the weeds will be conspicuous, and will be pulled up and burned.' The Tree is the day of harvest. Osiris stands before you, holding the sickle and the winnowing flail. But he doesn't judge; he is demanding that you judge and choose. He will carry out the sentence, however.

"As I have preached many times, and in many ways: 'Ask and you shall receive. Seek and you shall find. Knock and the door shall be opened unto you.' These words express a natural law; mainly, the world responds to those who ask. Another way of looking at it is: The world is full of genies waiting to grant your wishes. If we only knew what we're not receiving because we're not asking, we'd surely change our behavior.

"Or, looked at slightly differently, what is success for the question you are asking? Visualize that, and suddenly the way will become clear. Your mind works on a problem, but has to be given an end point to focus on to work.

"Now, this blog is about 'who lives.' So what is the formula? There is no formula. There was a person in seminary school who put forth the proposition that you can petition the lord with prayer. You would define the universe the way you want, and beg a cheat on the rules so you get what you want? You cannot petition the lord with prayer! You would buy back your deeds with slight words, artificial laments to pretend your regrets? Join Job's friends in their social structure religion, where all that matters is agreement between each other. The world isn't like that. The weed growing in a crack in your driveway is more honest, more real, more true to itself and the Tree of Life than Job's friends were.

"Empathy, the modern virtue? The Tree teaches that true empathy is with all creatures, creatures not seen as little humans, but as other creatures, with different stories and goals. Empathy then becomes a model and a tool for decision, not a cover to avoid choice. Empathy can guide you to the biggest decisions. Empathy can show the dark of Life as well as the light. Life is Terrible, but Beautiful. Stand as Job did, facing the truth that imposing the small human values on the greater world is a child's wish. In the end, you cheat only yourself by pretending the world is something other than it really is.

"It is not enough to stare up the steps, you must step up the stairs. The Tree has forced the issue of action. It's a bit like a sorting hat from the Harry Potter books, but with more serious consequences. The prospect of Death does bring focus. External expectations, all pride, all fear of embarrassment or failure; these things just fall away in the face of death, leaving only what is truly important. Remembering that you are going to die is the best way I know to avoid the trap of thinking you have something to lose.

"The Grail legends were about a few people seeking the Truth. They failed because the one who did succeed, Galahad, never brought the truth back to the people, probably because he knew they didn't want to hear it. The Tree has brought the Grail to each of you, and there is no fobbing it off on another. We must be willing to see things as they are, rather than as we hope, wish, or expect them to be, to live within the Tree.

"For the rest of this conversation, I'm thinking I will scatter ideas like flower petals, hoping that some of them will be found useful.

"Those who seek should not stop seeking until they find. When they find, they will be disturbed. When they are disturbed, they will marvel, and will reign over all.

"In a time of drastic change, it is the learners who inherit the future. The learned usually find themselves equipped to live in a world that no longer exists. Open your mind to the wonder of the world around you.

"People come to you and say, 'Let us pray today, and let us fast.' What sin have I committed, or how have I been undone? Live instead. Don't beg.

"When will the rest for the dead take place, and when will the new world come? And 'it was written that what you are looking forward to has come, but you don't know it.'

"For this reason I say, if one is whole, one will be filled with light, but if one is divided, one will be filled with darkness.

"It is better to be a lion for a day than a sheep all your life.

"This heaven will pass away, and the one above it will pass away. The dead are not alive, and the living will not die. During the days when you ate what is dead, you made it come alive. After all, what goes into your mouth will not defile you; rather, it's what comes out of your mouth that will defile you.

"When you are in the light, what will you do?

"I am the light that is over all things. I am all: from me all came forth, and to me all attained. Split a piece of wood; I am there. Lift up the stone, and you will find me there.

"It is quite beyond me how anyone can believe God speaks to us in books and stories. If the world does not directly reveal to us our relationship to it, if our hearts fail to tell us what we owe ourselves and others, we shall assuredly not learn it from books.

"My experience is what I agree to attend to.

"Since in the world of time every man lives but one life, it is in himself that he must search for the secret of the Garden."

DAY 31. NEW YORK. 9 A.M.

Gordon stood. The group quieted down.

"Thank you for letting me speak," Gordon started. "As many of you know, I just recently retired from the military, and still have many contacts there. I've been working on reaching as many as I can, and surprisingly, there are many who are of the Tree and who are working as hard as they can for us. I'm going to ask Oskar to speak, as he has an ability to plan that I valued greatly when we worked together."

"Thank you," Oskar stammered, taken aback, not expecting to have to speak to the group. "I've been, ah, working on linking to the networks out there. We are essentially guerrilla fighters now, although the tide is going in our direction. Guerrillas must have protected networks to coordinate action, and fortunately, we have fallen into several. Conceptually, a network is based on autonomy, flexibility, collaboration, diversity, and multiplicity, all of the gifts that the Tree has given to us. Networks are the fabric of life. We, of the Tree, embrace life and having these networks can offset our liabilities in this war."

"And our liabilities would be that we are outnumbered, outgunned and detested fugitives?" a man shouted.

"Detested mutants, technically. I think that is a step below detested fugitives," Oskar replied cheerfully, and the group laughed.

"Well, here's the plan for the next hour," Gordon announced. "Even that may be optimistic. Essentially, we are trying to bring as many into our protection as we can, to protect the Tree wherever it grows, and push back the zombies when we have to. We are short of bodies and ammunition, but they are weakening as time goes by. All we need do is survive. So, Oskar will be in charge of planning and network building, and a number of people have volunteered to help him. The rest of us will either guard this place, or go out on search and recover. Oskar has some simple communication equipment for the groups, and we hope will have better stuff by the end of the day. A plan?" He looked around, and people nodded.

Oskar sat with a group of about twenty after the others left. "Ok, what are your strengths?" he asked. "Start with you," pointing at a young man, and go around the group. In a half hour, they had a pretty good idea of everyone's abilities, and had broken into small groups to work on specific problems. We got lucky, Oskar thought. There are more strong backgrounds than I would have dared hope. And better equipment that I would have guessed.

They worked the rest of the day, and by evening, had established communications with groups around the world. More importantly, they had communication with most of the groups in a twenty-mile radius, and could start coordinating attacks against the zombies.

DAY 31. NEW YORK.

Father Flanagan, his collar pulled half off and hanging down loose, is sitting outside his old church. They were wrong, the whole time, he thinks again, furious. They lied about life for control and fear.

He hears a scream, and looking down the street, sees a mob chasing a woman towards him. He jumps up and runs toward the group carrying the sword he found last night hidden behind him.

"She is a witch, Father," a man holding the woman shouts to him. "She must burn!"

The crowd shouts their approval.

"He's one of them," one of the crowd screams, pointing to the priest. "Look at his skin! He's a mutant!"

Flanagan runs at the two men holding the woman. Slashing down hard with the sword, the ex-priest hacks an arm off of one. As the man screams and falls to his knees, Flanagan runs the other man through, and then pulls the sword back out. The second man, clutching his spilling guts, falls, and Father Flanagan faces the mob with his bloody sword held ready. The woman, standing next to him, quickly kneels down to pick up stones.

The mob stands in a half circle around Flanagan and the woman. Uncertain, confused, they numbly watch the two men die. Suddenly, they duck, as the woman starts throwing rocks at them, catching several in the head.

"Get her!" several in the mob scream.

Father Flanagan steps in towards the mob, furiously slashing at them. In a minute, the mob runs, leaving several more lying on the street.

"Quick!" Flanagan advised, grabbing her arm. "They scare easily, but they'll be back, and in greater numbers."

They run down the street towards the church. They sit on the steps, stopping for a minute to catch their breath.

"Father Flanagan," he offered. "Well, perhaps not 'father', as the Vatican would disown me now."

"Heidi," she replied, smiling. "I can't thank you enough!"

They shook hands. Flanagan looks past her, into the distance, and frowns. "More trouble, I'm afraid."

"They are our people," Heidi replied, shading her eyes as she looked.

"I'm not sure they will be so excited about me," Flanagan warned.

The group of heavily armed mutants jogs up to them, staring angrily at the priest.

"Stop it!" Heidi snapped at them. "He saved me."

They lower their weapons and studied the priest, who flushed.

"I have became of the Tree," Flanagan confessed. "What they told me before was lies."

"Be at peace amongst us," the leader of the group blessed him, making the sign of the Tree. Then he turned, glancing down the street. "But we'd better keep moving" pointing at a distant mob headed towards them.

Hours later, Flanagan and Heidi are sitting in a field. The little white flowers are in full bloom, the sweet smell of the Tree filling the air.

"My husband was one of the men who was holding me for the mob," Heidi snarled.

"I've seen it over and over," Flanagan replied. ""Think not that I am come to send peace on earth: I came not to send peace, but a sword. . . And a man's foes shall be they of his own household." Preached that many times in sermons, but never really understood it before."

"Oh, shut up," Heidi told him, and kissed him.

"Life is strong," Flanagan murmured to her.

"And it's a nice day and the sun is warm and bright," Heidi whispered, wrapping her arms around him.

The others in the group looked away, smiling to themselves.

DAY 31. A LARGE MALL, NEW YORK.

In the zombie camps, they forbid everyone to talk about their experiences. Focus on the human is the message, over and over.

After the first shock, people told themselves it would get better, the experiences would fade away. "Shove them in a box, tape it shut, label it bad memories," the psychologists confidently advised, "and go on with your life." They quickly organized group activities to keep people from being alone and having to think, having to face the memories that were torturing them.

"I know what it's like to be afraid of your own mind," a government official asserted to others. "These nightmares are a plot to destroy our country and our people. But we can make people forget these by concentrating their attention, their hatred, on those who caused all of this."

"The mutants are demons!" the priests shouted at mass meetings. The mass meetings followed a well tested script: bright banners, tall fences, huge groups in close order, all lined up obediently, shoulder to shoulder to listen to the priests and leaders. "We are human, not mutants, not crawling creatures out of a field. We stand up and think!" The crowd roared, but when the crowd dispersed, each was left alone with their memories. So, they milled together like flocks of sheep, rehashing their hatred for the mutants to keep their minds off the nightmares. The ritual murder of captured mutants was a continuing entertainment all over the world, as people let their hatred run wild. Only that way could they relax, feel above and in control.

"It's like that damn poem," an elderly man muttered. "I taught English Literature, and it's that damn Yeats poem. There is this falconer, who lets his falcon fly, and the damn bird won't come back! It just flies away, higher and higher, ignoring the falconer. We've build a world based on our domination, and the world just decided to ignore us. To think, therefore I am, but I'm not. I can't accept the memories, but they tell me that other creatures think and feel, that life is far outside and above the small human stories. When I reject the life they shout, what have I become?"

"What the priests tell us is like a door that leads to nowhere," a woman complained. "A door, just propped up on a trash dump, that we are supposed to walk through and be saved. But when you walk through the door, you are still where you were." She brushed her daughters hair as the little girl stirred in her sleep, moaning in fear. "I'd give anything for her to accept, to leave all this fear behind, but she's me, and I can't accept."

"One of my children joined them," the elderly man sighed. "Another child didn't, and my wife? She vanished in the chaos, who knows what happened. I saw my child on a newscast, as she led mutants against the police and the army. She survived, I think, and won that battle, despite what the news tried to show. I'd not have thought it. She was quiet, peaceful, a conformist, I thought. But there she was, leading the charge. And my son, a rebel, kneels at the feet of the priests and begs forgiveness."

"In our dreams, we fear things reaching out to grab us because we have pushed so many important things away" another man mumbled. "If we paint the hands as terror, then we don't have to think about them. I taught psychology at the college, and I've got to say that all the nice techniques we developed don't work. Placebo's always had about the same success rate as our methods, we just ignored it. We ran roughshod over anyone who argued differently, because, after all, this was our work and our meal ticket."

"Think of the good things we can have if we close our eyes," a teenage girl lamented. Her hair was unkempt, the shadows under her eyes heavy. "Doesn't really work that well. I should have thought for myself." She grabbed her stomach, and ran outside the fire. They could hear her throwing up in the distance.

"That's not good," the psychologist grimaced. "I've read the reports, and there is a progression of symptoms. When it hits basic physical processes, the end is near."

"Is there anyone who has recovered?" a woman begged.

"The party line is that there are, and that the reports are still in process," the psychologist muttered. "I've not seen any recover. It isn't looking good."

"The priests say that we can have any truth you want, but the real world doesn't agree," a woman murmured.

""And these are they likewise which are sown on stony ground; who, when they have heard the word, immediately receive it with gladness; And have no root in themselves, and so endure but for a time: afterward, when affliction or persecution ariseth for the word's sake, immediately they are offended. And these are they which are sown among thorns; such as hear the word, And the cares of this world, and the deceitfulness of riches, and the lusts of other things entering in, choke the word, and it becometh unfruitful. And these are they which are sown on good ground; such as hear the word, and receive it, and bring forth fruit, some thirtyfold, some sixty, and some an hundred."[18] A man quoted. "At least, that's what the priest promised."

"But it is the plant that brings forth a hundredfold," the woman sighed.

DAY 31. NEW YORK, 2 P.M.

Gordon is leading a large group of mutants. They are spread out behind the remains of some subdivision homes at the edge of a nature preserve. The zombies are preparing an attack on a nature preserve, which is bursting with the plants.

"Not hiding their plans, are they?" one of the group commented, watching the mass of bodies and equipment slowly moving into place.

"They have containment suits, armored troops, and helicopters," another reported, squinting at the scene through an old pair of binoculars. "We have rifles. That's not really good odds."

"Gaps and structures," Gordon declared. "When they are strong in one place, they are weak in another. They are confident and arrogant, thinking that we can do nothing to stop them. Wait until they attack, then we can fall upon their gaps. They will all die for their heresy in attacking the Tree."

The zombie attack starts. A line of squads walked slowly towards the woods. A soldier with a flamethrower was the center of each squad, protected by heavily armored troops. There is a line of personnel carriers and light armor lined up on the street at the edge of the woods, their engines loudly idling. They had left a few men guarding the equipment. Overhead, several helicopters circled over the men slowly advancing towards the woods.

"They don't expect us," Gordon commented. "Their orders didn't say expect any defense, and they don't seem to think a lot."

In the far distance, there is an explosion, a cloud of smoke rapidly rising. The helicopters veer away, and fly rapidly away towards the smoke.

"There, that's what we needed," Gordon growled. "Now, we do this and this," quickly sketching in the dirt. The group split up quickly and took positions.

A few minutes later, the men guarding the personal carriers fell as shots rang out. The men with the flamethrowers and the armored troops quickly bunched up for defense. They stopped marching towards the woods, evidently uncertain what to do next.

Who is a good shot?" Gordon asked, looking around.

Several men raised their hands.

"When a 50 caliber bullet hits a flamethrower backpack, the backpack explodes. Nice that they massed together," Gordon commented. "Go forth, my children."

Several men smiled, and moved quickly into position.

In the field, the groups of zombies had started to move slowly towards the personnel carriers.

A flurry of shots from the mutants and the flamethrower backpacks exploded. The explosions killed the men carrying the flamethrowers and the armored troops surrounding them. The groups that were not burned were frantically running around. Some were trying to help the burning men, some firing wildly without targets.

"Clean out the filth," Gordon ordered.

Volley after volley of shots rang out, and in a few minutes, the zombies were all dead.

"Now, grab what we can before the helicopters get back here!" Gordon ordered.

The men ran frantically to steal ammunition and weapons, and then vanished into the woods before the zombies could bring forces to bear. And that was the day, over and over. An attack by the zombies exposed a weakness somewhere, which was pounced on. The zombies, a command and control structure, didn't think, didn't respond, and were torn apart.

"The Boyd combat cycle, they just don't get it," Gordon commented, surveying another slaughter. "Well, I'm not complaining about that."

DAY 31. NEW YORK. 4 P.M.

Jenny wandered over to the impromptu planning center and sat by her father.

"You looked tired, dad," she murmured, holding his hand.

"A bit," Oskar admitted, grimacing. "Gordon talked up my planning and organization abilities, and so I'm here, responsible for coordination. But it's beyond tough! What I have to do is to create organization out of chaos. Everything fell away, and I have to create, actually see, new structures to work with. I have new people to work with, and I don't really know their abilities. Which isn't as much a problem as it used to be, because I don't really know what I want them to do. Everything is new and in flux, a polite way of saying chaos. If I fail, people die" and he put his head in his hands and cried.

Terrified, Jenny put her arm around him carefully. What to say, she thought? I'd cry too if I was him.

"Thanks honey," Oskar mumbled, sitting up, wiping the tears away. He looked around, but the few people near them were carefully ignoring them.

"So, a plan?" Jennifer asked. "Remember what you always say, are your actions towards a desired outcome?"

"Well, the good news is that I can rethink everything," Oskar replied. "So I'm not stuck with someone else's passed down failure. I'm thinking organically, which is new since becoming of the Tree. I'm thinking around corners, into depths, not in the straight lines that the diagrams use. Its easier now because opening to the other creature breaks the mind loose from the small human straight lines. It's a strange world that the spiders live in, that's for sure. But they function well. I've discovered many possibilities that I would have missed before."

"You can only do what you can do," Jenny advised. "I was a Bonobo. Their minds are so different, yet the same as mine in many ways. Remember what you told me to do: mind like water, the water that nourishes the Tree."

He smiled. "That's the best advice I've had all day, honey. I'm getting you that seer's gown."

"Purple with gold flecks, and a gold headband" Jenny insisted. "I can give the seamstress my size when you are ready."

"On the bright side, the corporate meeting this morning really didn't matter," Oskar commented. "They were going to fire all of us, they were just doing it slowly so they could enjoy it more."

"The world fired them instead," Jenny laughed.

DAY 31. THE VATICAN, ROME.

There is an important meeting in a large, ornately decorated room dating from the sixteenth century. The room is overflowing.

"We must have faith! Faith by all!" the Pope demanded of the massed church hierarchy. "Only unwavering faith by all can stop this. The weak link breaks the chain, and the doubters will take us all down. This is a test, and they are failing!"

"Is there no way we can work with the mutants?" a cardinal quietly inquired. "Their people are surviving at a much higher rate than our people are."

"As soon as by one's own propaganda even a glimpse of right on the other side is admitted, the cause for doubting one's own right is laid," the Pope snapped. "And I don't believe those statistics! All lies, put out to deceive us."

The mass nodded their heads in agreement.

"A free thinker is Satan's slave," the Pope affirmed. "The message of the Fathers of the Church is what we must cling to in these desperate times."

The Cardinal watched them, amused. People will first to seek information to confirm their beliefs, and stop before considering evidence that contradicts belief. Here is a full proof. To quote Paul Simon, "we see what we want to see and disregard the rest."

"How are the witchcraft trials going?" the Pope demanded.

"They are going well, your holiness," a cardinal answered. "The Inquisition is active. Warrants and death sentences have been issued. All those women who spoke so freely, well, they are sorry now!"

"Women are wild, abandoned creatures," another cardinal sneered. "The Church teachings did not err, despite the nonsense the modern world prats."

"Good," the Pope beamed. "We have a delegation going to Cairo to help with the burnings tomorrow. The entire world will watch and know that we are right, and that we winning!"

"We've brought out experts to feed our message to the masses," a Monsignor advised the Pope. "And we've published on the Internet. We're doing all that we can."

Experts! the Cardinal sighed. Experts are far worse than a coin toss, because they believe in themselves. Overconfident, a blithely refusing to look outside their own opinion. It's selective ignorance of the facts as they happily explain and wish away dissonant facts and contradictory data. We're all prisoners of our preconceptions, but our wishes are not the world.

"Religion is the masterpiece of the art of animal training, for it trains people as to how they shall think," a bishop announced.

The group around him nodded their heads in agreement.

"People respond," the Pope shouted, "to the meaning that a situation has for them, and that meaning is something we defined for them. They will act in accord with the meaning as we tell them. We must make them think as we think, and so we must mis-define the situation for their own good. Appealing to and supporting questionable but cherished beliefs and identities, and tying them to local pride or patriotism, we can make this work. They are weak and foolish, and we must find the weaknesses in their defenses and use those weaknesses against them for their own good."

"But what, your Holiness, if they are right?" a terrified cardinal blurted out. "What if we all die if we don't listen to them?"

"Then we die as we must, in our faith," the Pope vowed, staring into the distance. "This is a test meant for us and those who pass will go to heaven as their reward. Perhaps this is the Last Judgment, and those who die shall live. That is, after all, what we have been preaching for the past thousand or so years."

The assembled group applauded and then began to mill towards the exits.

"The tolling of the iron bell, Calls the faithful to their knees...To hear the softly spoken magic spells" the Cardinal sighed.

In a few minutes, the Pope and the church officials had left the room, confident of their plans, intently discussing their next steps. Only the

Cardinal was left in the room. He looked up at the beautiful paintings by Michelangelo. A scene from a movie flashed before him, serious and somber. "Choose wisely," the knight demanded, "for while the true Grail will bring you life, the false Grail will take it from you. "

DAY 31. LIFE IN THE TIME OF PLAGUE

"Life in the time of Plague," Jesus typed. He sat back and thought for a few minutes, walking through in his mind the key points of the Vatican's attack.

"You can discover what your enemy fears most by observing the means he uses to frighten you," Jesus typed. "And they are afraid. Nay, terrified. Terrified of loss of power, terrified of change, terrified that they have wasted their lives on a dusty, dark, empty hallway to nowhere. Who wouldn't be afraid of that horror staring at you? So they circle the wagons, doubling down on their bet that it's the human stories that control the world. If everyone, absolutely everyone, believes exactly the right idea, then the magic will work.

That is one of the very oldest rules of magic, actually. Any change to the ritual, and the magic fails. The priests are clever fools and there is always a change to the ritual, always something different, so the results are not guaranteed. Failure of the ritual is a rebuke to the participants for their failures, so the priests can't lose. Until the game changes. When the real world pushes into the human story and it can't be wished away, blamed away, or simply ignored, then the priests must attack anyone who challenges their story. Because it's attack, or die. The church would rather die than change. In the fullness of time, that will happen, but in the meantime, they add to the troubles of the world, not diminish them.

"A horror stares back at them out of the mirror: 'Lord, there are many around the drinking trough, but there is nothing in the well.' These events are outside their small human stories that they assert control over all the universe with, and so they have nowhere to go. There is no message from them that will help. They know that, and so they do as they have done before. 'One can't enter a strong person's house and take it by force without tying his hands. Then one can loot his house.' They will tie your hands so you cannot help yourself, and then when evil comes upon you, blame you for the evil.

"A person owned a vineyard and rented it to some farmers, so they could work it and he could collect its crop from them. He sent his slave so the farmers would give him the vineyard's crop. They grabbed him, beat him, and almost killed him, and the slave returned and told his master. His master said, 'Perhaps he didn't know them.' He sent another slave, and the farmers beat that one as well. Then the master sent his son and said, 'Perhaps they'll show my son some respect.' Because the farmers knew that he was the heir to the vineyard, they grabbed him and killed him. Anyone here with two ears had better listen!"

Maybe I should add an audio track to this? Jesus wondered. No, too many problems with hacking the audio, changing the message, Mrs. Ostein told me. It would be 'Buy Jesus-blessed used cars at the O.K. Corral! We put holy water in the radiator,' some shouting car dealer on a horse. No, can't go there.

"The church has kept their rented vineyard over and over," Jesus typed, grim-faced. What's theirs is theirs, and what's yours is theirs. It's a simple plan, really. They are people who must have an authority controlling their lives, people unfit for freedom, who cannot do much with it. Each of us thinks occasionally, 'Well, what am I when I am alone?' Some, when they are alone, cease to exist. But if the empty people can control others, then they exist. So they seek power to fill the emptiness. The desire for freedom is an attribute of a 'have' type of self. The 'have' self asks 'Leave me alone and I shall grow, learn, and realize my capacities.' The desire for power is basically an attribute of a 'have not' type of self.

"'Damn the Pharisees! They are like a dog sleeping in the cattle manger: the dog neither eats nor lets the cattle eat.' They froth at the mouth like rabid wolves, snapping in their confusion at the nearest thing to them, because they must have control. And control, obedience, must be shown over and over, because your obedience is their definition of self. Nothing can ever fill their emptiness; no sacrifice you make will be enough. I've preached these things over and over, and finally, the world is saying, 'Enough.' I'm not asking for you to change and grow; the world is demanding it for your survival.

"In another context, Deming wrote that 'survival is not required,' and it's not. Careful examination of your birth certificate will find no guarantees or warranties, express or implied. I've told you, 'Don't give what is holy to dogs, for they might throw it upon the manure pile. Don't throw pearls to pigs.' This message is not for them. This message is for you who wish to survive.

"While it is argued that any publicity is good publicity, I must deny the baseless reports of licentious sex, dancing, and forbidden activities. Well, deny some of them. Fine, maybe a few of them. Life is Strong! It's the same old slanders that they have used for the past two thousand years, polished up and trotted out again. Ironically, what they decry are many of the things that ancient popes and cardinals were quite good at themselves. Things that the Inquisition knew the accused had done, because the inquisitors had done all those things, at least in their minds. It takes one to know one, I guess. I will say that not every religion has to have St. Augustine's attitude to sex. While a marriage is celebrated in a church, everyone present knows what is going to happen that night, but that doesn't prevent it from being a religious ceremony. At one time the church fathers were completely against sex. That doesn't work well, because you end up with a very small church after time, so they modified that position.

"But let's look at what they are attacking: they are attacking life. The simple pleasures of daily existence are verboten to them, forbidden. Why? They say because people must be controlled, that they are evil by nature. I deny that. As Einstein wrote, if people are good only because they fear punishment and hope for reward, then we are a sorry lot indeed.

"And, they cannot move away from the Church's fast embrace, a death grip, their fingers glued to a thirteenth century hatred of nature that is the heart of their doctrine. Nature as a danger to control and exploit is a completely wrong answer for the practical problems of today's world. That denial of the world and nature at the heart of their doctrine is as big a denial of God's presence within creation—or God's capacity to determine the earth's destiny with or without human help—as can be taken. The Catholic catechism taught that God is, indeed, everywhere—omnipresent. Doesn't that mean our world—our precious earth—is also filled with the sacred? It does mean that the earth is filled with the sacred, which they admit despite themselves.

"Joseph Campbell wrote 'that when I read Spengler, painful as it may be, he argues that we are passing from what he called the period of culture to civilizations. He thought that this time corresponded to that of the late second-century BC. That was the time of the decline of the culture world of Greece into Hellenism, and the rise of the military state of Rome—Caesarism. This resulted in what he termed the Second Religiousness, politics based on providing bread and circuses to the megalopolitian masses and a general trend toward violence and brutality in the arts and pastimes of the people. I have watched, increasingly uneasy, to see the not-so-gradual coming into fulfillment in this world every bit of what Spengler promised'."

DAY 32. SAUDI DESERT.

"Have you seen this, Sir?" His aide points to the screen, disgusted.

The General thoughtfully watches the screen. It is showing an international news program, in process. "And tomorrow, at noon, under the blazing sun, there will be a burning of the mutants, the heretics in the central square in Cairo," the newsman announced, staring confidently into the camera. "The Vatican has sent emissaries and experts from the Inquisition, and will bring mutants captured from all over Europe."

The screen changes to an announcement by the Minister for Public Defense for Italy. "This is the kind of action that will stop this plague, the man whined, a frantic tone in his voice. When we all join together, and are firm in our beliefs, we will triumph."

The camera focuses back on the newsman. "Strength thru Unity, and Unity thru Faith" the newsman intones.

"Enough!," the general snarled, turning away in disgust. "Those animals!

"Perhaps, sir, we can add some fireworks to their party," his aide offered.

The General thought for a minute, and smiled. "Do we have the resources? Is it possible?" the General demanded.

"We can refuel here," the aide reported, pointing to the map. "I took the liberty of doing the calculations early this morning. We can reach Cairo just when they are starting this abomination."

"Burn our people? They will all burn! But first, call all the men together," the General ordered his aide. "I must tell them what I think has to be done, but I want only volunteers."

"Yes, sir!" the aide saluted, and ran out of the tent.

In a few minutes, all of the men were gathered. The General stood on top of a tank. "In Cairo, they are burning our people tomorrow at noon! I'm going to stop this, if I have to go alone." the General shouted, looking around at his men. "But anyone who does not want to go does not have to go. We will be outnumbered and truthfully, the odds are not good. By going to Cairo, we leave our people in Saudi unprotected. But this obscenity cannot be allowed to happen! Who wishes to go with me?" the General asked.

All volunteered, waving their arms and shouting for vengeance and justice.

"If we die, we die within the Tree," a mullah proclaimed.

"To your machines. We leave now," the General ordered.

The men salute and all dash off. Within a short time, the column is rolling toward Suez.

"We will have help," the communications officer reported to the General. "I've been in contact with the network, and there is another force headed to attack Cairo."

"Let me guess," the General laughed. "Well, it will be nice to fight with them, not against them."

DAY 32. EAST OF SUEZ

An Israeli armored column is waiting near Aquaba, on the tip of southern Israel. The engines are quietly idling, waiting for a decision.

"The network has told us that the other group plans to take Suez to refuel and rearm. They can lead in and we can follow. We can be in Suez in a few hours," the Captain reported.

"Can we trust these people?" a tank commander asked.

"Yes," the Colonel replied. "I know this General's reputation and he is an honorable man. And the network has told us that he is of the Tree, so I have no doubts. Without his help, we would have reached Cairo with the tanks running on fumes, so this is a blessing!" He thought for a minute, tapping his fingers on the map. "What do the men think?"

"I do not think they can be stopped," another commander offered.

"Then roll," the Colonel ordered. "Well, did you want to live forever?"

They smile, the hard, unforgiving smiles of the Tree, and run to their commands. Within a half hour, the column is rumbling to Suez.

Two huge dust clouds converging on Suez stop in the desert.

"Can you get word to them that the Egyptians can't overhear?" the General asked. "I need to speak to their commander privately."

"Yes, Sir," the communications officer replied.

A few minutes of typing, and the communications officer raised his head. "The arrangements are made, sir."

"I'll need a truck, a simple, open one. I will drive myself," the General ordered. A few minutes later, the General is driving towards the looming dust cloud. He sees another truck driving towards him. The two trucks stop about thirty feet from each other. The General climbs out, brushing the dust off his clothes, and then stands away from the truck, his hands open at his side.

The Israeli Colonel walks over to the General, his hands also open by his side. They stand a few feet from each other.

The General holds up a crystal. The rainbow flashes over the sand in the bright sun.

"On the same side at last," the Israeli Colonel declared. "None could have handed that ecstasy drug infection better."

"And this is nothing like that," the General replied. "I know better than anyone. What these animals are doing in Cairo must be stopped. More than that, they must be taught a lesson. An Old Testament lesson."

"Agreed," the Israeli Colonel answered. "Ideas?"

"The Egyptian army is in chaos. Their forces in Suez started to mobilize when they heard rumors of your column. I'll lead them to believe we are on their side. My troops enter Suez, we neutralize their forces and then we jointly rush to Cairo," the General suggested.

"It's a good plan," the Israeli Colonel agreed. "Simple, direct and clear. I place myself and my men under your command, sir."

"That's an unexpected compliment!" the General responded, surprised and honored. "I know you by reputation and I couldn't ask for a better soldier. We came to do what we could, not expecting to survive, but with our forces combined, we may actually live through this."

"Jihad," the Israeli Colonel shouted.

The General laughed. "I was supposed to say that, but I agree."

They shake hands, then salute, and then drove back to their commands.

The General is standing on a tank, all of the men surrounding him. "These men are valiant warriors," he shouted, pointing at the Israeli forces. "They are of the Tree. The animals in Suez and Cairo, they are not Bedouin. They are nothing. They are outside of the Tree, and outside of life. Who is with me?"

The men cheer and run for their machines.

Two hours later, the network signals that the General is in control of Suez, and the Egyptian forces have been neutralized. The Israeli Colonel orders his column to move, and they rumble into Suez. The Colonel and the General meet for a few minutes.

"You can fill your tankers here," the General ordered, pointing towards the army facility he had captured. "My troops are filling up now, scavenging for ammunition and any weapons we think we can use. Your men are welcome to go with them."

"Do they know in Cairo that we are coming?" the Israeli Colonel asked.

"No," the General replied. "There were no survivors and no messages"

"Very good, Sir," the Colonel declared. "I'll get my men going."

A short time later, the combined forces move out towards Cairo.

"About 3 hours, I'm guessing," the Israeli Colonel commented to a tank commander. "Take down our flags. The Saudi flags will give free entrance to the city and we will just quietly follow behind like little mice. Anyone who sees the Star of David on our tanks will be puzzled and won't react until too late. Maybe they will think we are prisoners."

The commanders keep the troops busy checking the weapons and ammunition as they drive the empty desert. "It's the details," the commanders keep telling the troops. "Focus on the details, then when we are ready, we will strike. Don't think about the battle until we are ready for battle. Let the commander worry about that small thing, the war coming."

Cairo. A city so crowded, so dirty and so poor. Before the Tree, there was hatred and anger everywhere, a tinderbox waiting for another spark. And now, with all the chaos in the world, the fellaheen think they have found an enemy to attack without fear of retribution. They, confident in their power, listen only to what they want to believe.

"I have received a report of a Saudi tank column headed towards Cairo," a Egyptian Lieutenant reported to his superior officer. "The Saudi's don't seem to know anything about this."

"They are here to help us," the Egyptian General snapped, when the message was relayed to him. "What else could they be here for?"

DAY 32. CAIRO

On the edge of the horizon, the first traces of the dust cloud become visible. On the outskirts of Cairo, people run wildly, staring and pointing at the looming cloud coming fast out of the North.

"It's a huge beast," they shout to each other and hide in terror.

"A shape with lion body and the head of a man, A gaze blank and pitiless as the sun . ." A man shouts.

All they can see is a rapidly growing dust cloud with tiny specks of birds circling over it.

"It is a biblical host," one cries. "It is God's judgment come for us!"

"They are on our side!," a policeman yelled through a megaphone. "Move away, they are going to the burnings."

Relieved, the people cheer.

The dust cloud is enormous as the columns reach the city. As the machines rumble into the city, the children cover their hands on their ears against the roar. The columns speed past.

The General is in the lead tank, the Saudi Flag flying high. The other Saudi tanks in the armored column are flying their flags. He waves cheerfully at the crowds, who happily wave back, thinking he is part of the show.

"Will they assume that we are Saudi also?" an Israeli captain radios the Colonel.

"Oh, the Star's of David are covered in dust," the Colonel laughed. "Maybe they will think we were captured. More than likely, they won't think, which seems to be the theme in this city."

"It's a city lost to the world," an Israeli Captain commented. "It cut off the life-flow of the Nile, turned its back on the world. Damned up the sacred waters, the water critical for life, and then they wonder why things don't work? This was the breadbasket of the ancient world, and it can't come close to feeding its population. Ask them why, and it's someone else's fault. No one really thinks that they are the problem."

Leading the Israeli column, the Colonel is eagerly looking around. "This is fascinating," he radios to his aide.

"Wasn't there something in the Bible about Moses leading his people back to Egypt in battle tanks?" his aide radioed back.

"Maybe in the old scrolls?" the Colonel shouted into the microphone. "The ancient documents are often ambiguous."

"As the tanks roar through the city, all the people in the square can see is a larger and larger dust cloud. The roar of the angry engines, the steel treads grinding up the surface of the narrow streets grows louder. Crashes as the tanks hit buildings that collapse. Anything in their way is crushed. The armored columns rumble into the large square just as the burnings are beginning.

The Clerics and government officials in places of honor on the scaffolds salute the tanks and the crowd cheers.

"Sad," the Israeli Colonel observed, looking around. "All of them, waiving at the crowd, are full of fear, terror and loathing. They hate the mutants and blaming them for the poor choices that the zombies have made. They feel the colony creatures in themselves weakening and so they strike out against others. They shall find it a poor choice this time.

"Showtime!" the General signaled, waving his hand in a circle. The amour massed, tread to tread. They stop, once in position, waiting.

A High Cleric, covered in golden robes, steps up. "It was in Egypt that our ancestors ended the paganism of the old empires! As our ancestors burned Hypatia of Alexandria, we burn these mutants to end this plague!"

The whole world is watching, cheering on the public burnings and executions. Angry people with unhappy lives scream at their TV screens that that we are right! And they took their drinks in their hands and bent closer to the television as the first captives were brought forward to the scaffolds.

What is left of the CDC is watching in despair, knowing it will just make things worse.

"Those who deny the tree," the General announced to the troops "deny life. To deny life, is to seek death. We should be gracious enough to grant them their wish. Forward!" and he held his arm up towards the scaffolds.

"Hoist the flag!" the Israeli Colonel laughed. "We wouldn't want them to think we are pirates."

"As if mutants isn't bad enough," a commander radioed back.

The cameras focused in on the Israeli flags as they snapped proud in the breeze and the crowd went silent, confused.

Massed tanks began to grind forward. "Commence firing," the General ordered. The armored column hit the square like a mailed fist, smashing without restraint or remorse. A fury fallen on their enemies, all of those who deny the Tree and life. Tens of thousands standing and cheering the burning of the mutants were simply run over by the tanks that left the crowds crushed and broken as the armor swept towards the scaffolds platforms.

Shaken, the zombies screamed at their televisions. They began to fear, their confidence shaken. They felt themselves weaken as they saw the power of their enemies joined against them.

The assembled Clerics of a dozen religions scream as the tanks blast the stages, which crash in flames.

Watching at the Vatican, the priests scream in terror and hide their eyes. The Cardinal, standing in the back of the room, mused to himself "The Lord says, "I will punish the world for its evil and wicked people for their sins. I will cause the arrogant to lose their pride, and I will destroy the pride of those who are cruel to others. People will be scarcer than pure gold"[19]

Around the world, people gasp as the mutants attack and destroy all in their path. The dying cries of mutants all over the world, calls to 'avenge me' are fulfilled, as the host sweeps down, driving all before them. Those of the Tree hiding in the city joined in and those against the Tree were destroyed. The battle quickly became a slaughter, sweeping through the town. As they discovered dead mutants, who had been mutilated and tortured, their rage grew.

The Saudi and Israeli forces fight through the day. They split up and reform as necessary, attacking any forces against them, seeking groups of the Egyptian army with the Tree, the networks guiding them to each other. By the end of the day, the few remnants of the Egyptian army that had supported the burnings fled up river, along with the government officials.

That evening, they stop, exhausted. The men refuel and rearm, while the commander's meet.

"We must go back to our people," the Saudi General told the Colonel. "There are those who need us there."

"And us too" the Israeli Colonel replied.

The Egyptian General smiled. "We thank you for all you have done," he replied. "We take the battle on from here, now that the forces of the zombies are broken."

The Israeli Colonel and the Saudi General walk back to their troops.

"What do we go back to?" the Israeli Colonel mused. "My wife became of the Tree, but died in the fighting. Two of my children have survived, I've heard."

"My wife became of the Tree but was slaughtered by the mobs," the Saudi General snarled. "There will scores to settle."

They stared out at the desert for a few minutes.

"It is the way of Life," the General sighed. "Egypt will now take care of itself. Now I go back to help those who have become of the Tree."

"And we also," the Israeli Colonel replied.

They shook hands, saluted and walked towards their troops, shouting at their subordinates. In an hour, there was nothing but two rapidly moving wrath filled dust clouds going north and east.

DAY 33. DETROIT.

It was two a.m. Suddenly, there was the sound of light automatic weapons fire, and screams in the distance.

Hal woke up, looked around and then jumped out of bed.

Cali sat up. "What's that?" she asked, scared.

"Don't know," Hal answered, rushing over to the closet and pulling out an AK-47. He quickly shoved a clip into the rifle, turning on the video monitors at the same time.

Suddenly the rifle fire ended.

"There," Hal pointed. On the screen, there was a group of veterans and Lucifer's people guarding a corner of the factory. There were many bodies on the ground.

"That can't be!" Cali cried, staring at the screen.

"The dead are not ours," Hal reassured her. "They are professionals, maybe special forces, but clearly not ours. You can tell by the uniforms." He stared at the screens for a minute, debating what to do next. He pushed a button, and in a few minutes, Lucifer answered.

"Are you in your rooms?" Lucifer demanded.

"Yeah," Hal answered.

"Stay there!" Lucifer ordered. "We think the attackers are all dead, but you need to stay there and protect Cali and Maria. I'll tell you what's up when we figure it out. Got to go."

"That's clear enough," Hal commented, putting the rifle down carefully. He sat down, keeping the rifle within reach.

"What do you think happened?" Cali asked.

"Oh, a probing attack that went bad, I'd guess. Any idiot could draw the lines back to here, tracing the tree's path," Hal replied. "If I were the government, I'd want to know if there is anything worth attacking here before mounting a full-scale attack. They would not have expected we were as well armed as we are, but they know now. What happens next depends on what level ordered this and what information gets back through the chaos out there."

"Don't tell me to go back to sleep," Cali mumbled. "Not likely now."

"No, we'll just sit and wait," Hal agreed. "We're all going to be tired tomorrow."

An hour later, Hal was staring at the stars when the phone rang. He quickly answered.

"It's all secure," Lucifer announced. "We are meeting in the conference room."

"On our way," Hal replied, jumping up.

"Me too," Cali called out, making herself presentable.

They walked quickly down to the conference room, Maria sleeping soundly through the whole event.

"She got your sleeping habits," Hal observed, looking at the peaceful face in Cali's arms.

They walked into the conference room, which was full of angry faces. Vladimir, Lucifer, Jesus, Mary, Lungorthin, GrendelHal, and many of the veterans and Lucifer's people were there. Most of them were carrying automatic rifles, some in full battle dress.

Hal and Cali stood in the back of the room for a minute until Lucifer waved at them to come up to the front.

"So?" Hal asked.

"It looks like a test," Lungorthin growled.

"A small group, maybe twenty men," Vladimir snarled. "All the direct attackers were killed on the spot. The men in their transports, we captured them, talked to them, and got some information. A truck almost got away, but was captured before it could get back to the expressway."

"Fortunately or unfortunately," Lucifer remarked, "all the captives died trying to escape. So there are no hostages to deal with."

Hal glanced at GrendelHal, who smiled. People around GrendelHal moved away slightly.

"Less paperwork," Hal asserted, shrugging. "Can we get the bodies away from here, so if anyone comes around, they won't find anything?"

"In process," Lungorthin rumbled.

"We're working on repairing bullet holes and the other damage," Vladimir added. "In case the officials show up."

"Did we lose anyone?" Hal asked.

"Two men," Jesus advised. "One of the veterans, and one of Lucifer's men, who died going to the veteran's aid."

"They unloaded a clip into each of them," one of the veterans growled.

"Well, they paid for their actions," Lucifer replied. "We know that this wasn't a high-level raid, and they didn't have reinforcements backing them up, or we'd be in a full-scale war now. Thanks to GrendelHal, we know who they report back to, and our people are tracking those government operations down now. By morning, we'll know who authorized this, at what level, and what they were after. And who we need to make pay for this."

"I'll go to prepare the bodies of our fallen," Mary declared. "They must be buried with full honor, but we have little time." She left, Mrs. Ostein following her, grim-faced.

"Double the guard, and the rest of you, go back to sleep," Lucifer ordered. "There's no point is all of us being exhausted. We've got satellite pictures coming in, so not all our connections in the government are part of this. We're watching now and won't be caught again."

"As long as you have not seen vulnerable formations in opponents, you hide your form, preparing yourself in such a way as to be invincible, in order to preserve yourself," Vladimir quoted, looking at Lucifer with a smile.

Hal and Lungorthin shook their heads.

Lucifer groaned. "I've got to stop writing."

Vladimir beckoned to several people, who came over to him. "You will guard the rest of the night," he ordered.

"Aren't we the lucky ones," one half-grumbled.

"Punishment for your sins," Vladimir replied dryly.

Everyone else wandered off, talking intently in small groups.

DAY 33. DEATH SPREADS

Death spread across the world. Hal and Cali grimly tracked events as best they could. Information sources were breaking down, going off the air and off the Internet. They pieced together what they could, and it was harsh reading.

There were two trends. First, the effects of the oil disruption kept escalating since oil and petrochemicals were in every step of every process. The truck that brought supplies used gas. The engine needed oil, and the transmission and other moving parts needed lubricating fluids. The metal the truck was machined out of was processed by machines driven by oil and diesel. The components of the truck were delivered to the factory by plane, train, truck, and ship, all of which were dependent on petrochemicals. Then the products that the truck carried all depended on petroleum—food, cultivated by machines and fertilized by petrochemicals, packed in plastic and stacked by diesel driven forklifts; manufactured goods, with all the same inputs that the truck factory had and all the same disruptions from huge oil price increases—the list went on and on.

The impacts on farming were disastrous because disruptions in the oil supply chain smashed the developing nations. The disruptions eliminated cheap fertilizer, affordable pesticides, and farming equipment use. The fields couldn't be planted, watered, or harvested. What was harvested was looted or stolen as it was taken to the cities. The food stocks ran out, and as things spiraled down, the crops in the field stood un-harvested. The wealthy countries found their food stocks low and refused to export food. As oil for the transport ships was difficult to obtain, shipping them would have been almost impossible had they had anything to ship.

Going into this crisis, the oceans were almost fished out, and the economics of fishing what little was left demanded a large powerboat and huge nets. The fishing boats couldn't get gasoline or diesel. Desperate, they turned back to sailboats, only to discover that the new methods of fishing don't work with sailboats. Fish stocks had been so depleted that you couldn't catch enough fish with the ancient methods. With backup crops gone, populations dependent on fish that now couldn't get fish were devastated.

It was a positive feedback cycle with horrifying effects. For billions of people on the thin edge, they simply fell off the precipice.

Family love subverts, indeed denies, the ideal thrown at us which demands we care equally for everyone. Moral philosophers created a dilemma: you could run through the left door of a burning building to save some number of children or through the right door to save your child. If you are a parent, ponder this question: whether there is any number of children in the other room that would offset your child's life? The answer is no. No number of someone else's children could offset your child. And so the wealthy countries, with food, held what they had for themselves and their children, and barely had enough even then.

A population that had soared in a hundred years from one billion to over seven billion, absolutely dependent on cheap and plentiful oil, began to crash. Complex structures, built up on separations of duties and closely linked inputs, crashed and burned when the parts stopped coming in. People talked about having water and food in the basement for a crisis. What about the power, and the toilets, and sanitation? And medicine, no police, and armed parasites after your food? Then, after your month of food runs out, what do you do when there are no food trucks coming in? When a structure is broken to the extent that you are living on the water and food stockpiles in your basement, it's the system that is broken, and that's a lot more than just water and food. People joked about the wheels coming off. It wasn't just the wheels—the frame warped and broke.

Then, the wheat rust that had been slowly spreading, held in check by technology, started to spread faster as the resources to hold it back vanished. That Paul had encouraged the spread of the rust didn't help at all. The rust cut crop yields by seventy percent, so what could be harvested wasn't hardly enough for next years seed reserve. Three days without food takes the veneer off of civilization. People rapidly progress from demanding their food be prepared with care, tastefully and elegantly, to eating things that are still alive.

The second trend, intersecting with and multiplying the effects of the first, was the Tree. The survivors, the mutants, were changed people as they assimilated the plant's effects, the doctors and health organizations reported. The survivors seemed more relaxed, quicker to think, and more focused. They took a stand for the tree against anyone. Family, friends, tribe, and/or governments—nothing stood in their way.

Think not that I came to send peace on earth: I come not to send peace, but a sword. For I am come to set a man at variance against his father...and a man's foes shall be they of his own household, the Cardinal thought as he read the reports.

The World Health Organization was desperately trying to track the progress of the pandemic, as it had finally been labeled, but they couldn't get good information. They sent in teams to evaluate, and the people either died or became converts to the Tree. When they converted to the Tree, their reports changed, and then stopped.

In desperation, many turned to the religious ecstasy drugs, terrified of the spreading plants and the economic crash. This literally added fuel to the fire, as the jubilant people, in their rapture, burned all around them as they celebrated the new world coming. They died and died happy-but died outside the Tree.

Over the funeral pyres in India they cried:

"When I look upon Thy blazing form reaching to the skies and shining with many colors, when I see Thee with Thy mouth opened wide and Thy great eyes glowing bright, my inmost soul trembles in fear, and I find neither courage nor peace, O Vishnu! When I behold Thy mouths, striking terror with their tusks, like Time's all-consuming fire, I am disoriented and find no peace. Be gracious, O Lord of the Gods, O Abode of the Universe! All these sons of Dhritarashtra, together with the hosts of monarchs, and Bhishma, Drona, and Karna, and the warrior chiefs of our side as well, enter precipitately thy tusked and terrible mouths, frightful to behold. Some are seen caught between Thy teeth, their heads crushed to powder. As the torrents of many rivers rush toward the ocean, so do the heroes of the mortal world rush into Thy fiercely flaming mouths. As moths rush swiftly into a blazing fire to perish there, even so do these creatures swiftly rush into Thy mouths to their own destruction. Thou lickest Thy lips, devouring all the worlds on every side with Thy flaming mouths. Thy fiery rays fill the whole universe with their radiance and scorch it, O Vishnu! Tell me who Thou art, that wearest this frightful form. Salutations to Thee, O God Supreme! Have mercy. I desire to know Thee, who art the Primal One; for I do not understand Thy purpose.

And The Lord said: I am mighty, world-destroying Time, now engaged here in slaying these men. Even without you, all these warriors standing arrayed in the opposing armies shall not live. Therefore stand up and win glory; conquer your enemies and enjoy an opulent kingdom. By Me and none other have they already been slain; be an instrument only, Arjuna. Drona and Bhishma and Jayadratha and Kama, and the other great warriors as well, have already been killed by me. Be not distressed by fear. Fight, and you shall conquer your foes in the battle."2

But this is a different battle. A battle within each person. Some won, some lost.

DAY 34. SWITZERLAND.

"My lord," the head accountant stammered, "we have made enormous profits on the majority of the contracts we entered into. We actually went past our best-case projections. Our partners have made enormous sums of money also. And the connections with the people in India are completely severed. There is nothing to lead anyone back to us."

Paul looked at him, drumming his fingers on the dais, and the accountant looked down.

"But it spread much further than we anticipated, my lord," the accountant stammered, staring at the floor.

"Many people find a good alibi better than a successful achievement," the Cardinal remarked, watching the accountant closely. "An achievement isn't permanent, and tomorrow demands another achievement. Tomorrow we have to prove our worth anew, that we are as good today as we were yesterday, perhaps even better. But a good alibi covers us for the rest of our lives if need be. Small wonder then that the effort put forth and the punishment endured to find a good alibi often exceeds the effort and grief requisite for achievement. And I'm thinking you have a good alibi."

The accountant gulped, and then looked at the Cardinal. "I do, but you see through me, my lord. This has become a tidal wave, sweeping all before it. Many of our companies are in financial distress because of the huge changes in commodities and oil. The whole underlying structure that we based our plans and projections on has been tossed, and the foundations may be broken."

Paul contemplated the carvings on the wall, and then looked at the accountant. "Had you stuck with your alibi, I would have had you killed," he declared. "But your honesty has saved you today. No one foresaw this. I have no complaint against you. Get the lawyers into action. Every country and every company has the same problems. Pull together into groups that are too large to fail. It's worked before, and it will work again. Go, now."

The accountant knelt and then ran out of the room, his staff behind him.

"We have a plan?" Paul asked the Cardinal.

"We do, my Lord," the Cardinal replied. "Reserves and resources have been stockpiled. Creatures and troops are marshaled for protection."

"Good," Paul announced. "The old world is about to become the new world."

DAY 34. PAUL IN CONFERENCE

Paul sat in his room. The multiple personalities stood around the room, thoughtful.

"The dream may not have been the omen I thought it was," Paul confessed. "The falcon flying loose may have meant the loss of control, not the opening to the world."

"It's always the interpretation that's the hardest," Xerxes admitted. "At least in the old days, we could fry the soothsayers to assuage our frustrations."

"I feel like Midas," Paul confided, pacing to the balcony and looking out over the turbulent lake. "Wealthy beyond my dreams, powerful, and yet—poof! It slips away, as the structure that the wealth is built around crumbles. Like Midas, who couldn't eat because everything he touched turned to gold, and his life was a torment of thirst. Do you not wish to enjoy our agony?" He turned to the Adversary.

"No," the Adversary replied. "You were right before. All of our fates have long been cast. The Greek mythology was right in the essence, even if the details were a little fuzzy. The Fates combed, wove, and cut the thread, do as we will. Still, it's been a great show."

"Praise from you is rarely good," Cortés observed, "but I cannot argue with what you have said."

"We shall see," Paul acknowledged. "The show has yet to play out."

DAY 34. THE AUTHORIZED STORY IS A HUMAN STORY

"This will be a controversial blog," Jesus wrote. He sat back and sighed. How could things have gone so far from what I said?

"The Pharisees and the scholars have taken the keys of knowledge and have hidden them. They have not entered into wisdom nor have they allowed those who want to enter to do so. They wrapped up the world in a big box that works for them, and taped the edges shut. There is a danger to that beyond which they can imagine. Frozen positions, denial of doubt, and rejection of discussion mean that there can be no modification of the human written text. Everything changes over time, and even understanding changes. Frame the box of your religion, your beliefs, your myths within ancient facts and you guarantee that if the facts are challenged, the myths will be challenged also. The group lives by myth, shared perceptions of right/wrong. When the myths are challenged, the daily rituals of life are challenged also, at the risk of the dissolution of the civilization. Of course, the church has an easy answer for that. No Challenges, and bow when we walk past. But you can't stop people from thinking, and the more you push some ideas away, the more persistent the ideas become. Proof that a civilization can dissolve? The medieval civilization of Europe collapsed under the rediscovered Greek and Roman ideas, which re-awoke the European spirit of individualism. The modern world faces this question of dissolution today.

"For example, when you face great calamity, what is it that supports you and carries you through? Do you have something that supports you and carries you through, or does that which you believed would support you fail? That is the acid test of the underlying myth by which you live. Each of us must march through the play of life-youth, maturity, age, and death. As each act rings up-or down-we must re-grasp the mystical problem of the universe. It's the way the human mind forces a structure on the world, but we can't live within a structure from the past that denies our knowledge of the present.

"Nietzsche wrote 'God was dead', by which he meant that the social construct of God that society agreed on was dead. The people shouting that Nietzsche is dead miss his point completely, but then, they want to be blind. The whole 'god is dead' is irrelevant because your emotional internalization of the divine, the relationship of you to the cosmos, however you define it, has nothing to do with the paper gods ceremoniously dragged out on worship day.

This is difficult to approach, because there are complex and powerful ideas tightly knotted together. Carefully untying the strings, we find that key ideas are:

1.   Confusion as to the nature of the self/creature;

2.   Misunderstanding of the relationship of tools and the creature;

3.   The carefully polished authorized story;

4.   And finally the confusion of inspiration with meaning.

The goal of the powerful is for the social meaning to overwrite the individual as completely as possible, leaving only the obedient cog in the machine to serve the greater good. Someone has to hoe those fields and someone has to sit in the shade with a cool drink, overseeing

"The human creature has certain clear needs. Obviously, food to keep the body going, and shelter from the elements and predators. Beyond that, driving eating, shelter, and our other choices, each of us must have a feeling of control. And this need for control matters physically. The emotions are physically based, and when the emotions start conflicting, the body runs along with them, round and round into exhaustion.

Atheist, agnostic, believer; all have the same internal needs. The words atheist, agnostic, and believer are 'meaning' words, all external definitions in relation to the social world. The feeling inside, all the same. All that matters is the relation of self with the divine, however you might define it within yourself. Do you think you change God by your social manifestations, what you tell others, whether pro, con, or bland? Do you think the words change anything about the nature of the world? What you feel in your heart is what is important, not what you feel in opposition to others. Your shouted opposition to others only lessens your ability to hear yourself.

"There are many kinds of truth. Mystical truth resembles the knowledge given to us in sensations more than that given by conceptual thought. Our perceptions and how we interpret them must key off of what we need next. We need to live, to help others we care about. So we must use the right tools for the right purpose. Working within the real world, we must use tools that reflect the evidence and events of the world. Working within ourselves, we must use tools that reflect ourselves and our inspirations. Different tools for different purposes.

"Man is not rational; rationality is a tool. A very important and useful tool, but it is not the creature. Rationality is an important tool, critical for life within the real world. Events happen; we see causes and results. They must be attended to. Simply hoping to God for desired events in the external world is foolish. 'Trust in Allah, but tie your camel' is always good advice.

"For the transcendent relation between our emotional self and the cosmos, the rational tool is inappropriate. Kant argued that the senses deceive, and madness and dreams make us question our certainties. He asked that we follow this deeper, as Hume had begun to do, and accept that it would be very coincidental if we small, fleshy organisms were equipped with sensory-gathering abilities that would provide a complete understanding of reality. Our minds, Kant explained, project all the basic categories of human understanding onto the world, so that time, space, and extension are all coming from us. He believed there are real objects in the world, just that we have no access to the real stuff because all access is through perception, which changes everything. The world we cannot perceive is the real world, the noumenal. The world we know, the one we live in and snack on, is the phenomenal world.

"Short version: Kant held that we cannot perceive everything, so our knowledge is limited. How, then can we demand that we fully know the cosmos' design and plan for our emotional satisfaction? Foolish, nonsensical. What we must know is that we have a relationship with the springs of Life that can carry us in good times and bad.

"Surely some revelation is at hand; surely the second coming is at hand. But not of a person to save you from yourselves. It is of a creature that acts and lives in this world.

"So, let's move to the authorized story that the church sells, and why it's false. False, by the written word of the Bible. First, do you think the engine of creation needs your respect for his sense of the importance? How greatly you overstate your small stories and write them to the greater world! And the stories the priests tell you, that you can magically dance through a life of mindless destruction, only seeing the smaller and smallest stories, and still be redeemed by a single act at the end? Insulting, that is, to any system of justice imaginable. Nicely done, though, because the proof is in the pudding, which is conveniently on the other side. You must find your own beliefs that satisfy you, not them.

"What I am saying is that the authorized story you have been taught is a human story. All the authorized stories have been. As such, it is a story tied to many human needs. Some it fills, some it frustrates. But it's a human story, designed for the priests' control. Nothing to do with the way the real world is. Like a stopped clock, right twice a day, its accidental victories are celebrated with a collection. Don't like that? The truth that makes men free is for the most part the truth that men prefer not to hear. Worse, the authorized story is a tar baby. A small, human story world. With bright borders, it pretends like a child's world. It holds you in its convoluted arguments and twists and turns, and the more you struggle with it, the tighter it binds you. Not satisfies, just binds, until you give up and seek the relief that the priests sell.

"As they only teach their box and not how to define a box, then when the box is found false, what choice do you have? They are not foolish people. Mean, small, and focused, but not foolish. The Lamb of God—you are encouraged to be that, to be the perfect sacrifice to god of your life—but who benefits? People are so focused on defining happy and unhappy within the social context—and choices made by alternatives handed to you serve only those to created the alternatives—that rebellion doesn't free you from that box. It's a tar baby.

"Humans are hard wired to "expect" stories with a particular structure. Our stories have protagonists and villains, a hill to be climbed, a battle to be fought. Stories were the primary way our ancestors transmitted knowledge and values. Today we seek movies, novels, and 'news stories' that put the events of the day in a form that our brains evolved to find compelling and memorable. Children crave bedtime stories; the holy books of the three great monotheistic religions are written in parables; and lawyers whose closing arguments tell a story win jury trials against their legal adversaries who just lay out 'the facts of the case.'

"The story they bind you with is this. In every culture, they define Wisdom as 'Vanity of vanities, all is vanity.' And only their meaning can protect you from the emptiness they have defined, only their story can carry you through the emptiness they have created in you. It's nonsense, but it's laid deep inside each of us. The church ordered, 'Give me the children, and they will come back as adults,' and they know what they are doing. The priests have been practicing their art for five thousand years with one story or another, and they have weeded out the stories (as well as many of the people) that don't work for them.

"Now, the Pope wants your faith and demands your shouted praises to save the world. Do you think the engine of creation really carefully notes your opinion? You really do overestimate your value. Do you think that throwing money in a collection plate is really a sacrifice? Living as others tell you to live, doing as they tell you to do, not listening to your heart, losing your life and self, and you think you can buy your way out with a little money? They condemn the thirty pieces of silver, but they are happy to take the sinful money off your hands. Job made his own sacrifices, as did all your forefathers before the priests took control for their glory. Your true sacrifice is the time, the effort, to be what you can be, given what you have been given. Anything else is disrespect for your own life. You want to tithe? Tithe 10% of your life to yourself.

"It is discouraging, but you have been betrayed by the priests again. It's always the same; they scheme for their benefit. Schemers, trying to control their little worlds. With the front of their hand, they raise a vision in you of false hopes and beliefs, all that you could be because of the priests' ideas, what you can be with their possibilities. And with the back of their hand, they crush you down by their definitions of your moral and ethical flaws, your inherent sins and faults. It's a nice system from their point of view. It puts food on the table and pays for the buildings, and it's all for control. The bright possibilities are as unrealistic as the deep depths of the sins, as it's false contrasts that keep you down.

"They will nail you up on their crosses. One size fits all. You have to remember that every day may not be good, but there's something good in every day.

"Now, we have been taught to go to experts for specialized problems. The problem with experts is this: if you go to your doctor with a broken leg, they can fix that. If you go in with a vague itch, which occurs at random intervals in different spots, you might as well stay home. Problems that can be solved have clear borders, such as a broken leg. Problems without clear boundaries, the itches, the occasional rattle in your car, those problems usually can't be solved. But a failure to solve some problems makes people doubt the experts. That's bad, because then the experts don't get paid. So, to preserve their claim of expertise, experts wall off the important stuff for the detail they can control.

Authoritative and learned people create categories, they 'platonify' to define what's important as what they can control. What you think is important is pushed away, because anyone with a mind and a tongue can discourse about what is important to each of us. But, if you focus on petty details, bury what matters under a layer of jargon, and look serious, then the experts can make a living whether they can solve the problem of not. Making a living is important, because we all have to feed our children.

"So like dung beetles, they pile up esoteric knowledge in a ball and push it before them, proving their expertise. Professors, psychologists, theologians, among others. All the same process in the end. And the writings that the church so reverently venerates, all the cracked parchment written in ancient dead languages that they pore over? Who knows what the writings were before they were edited, revised, and simply re-written? Who knows what the authors really meant by their words? You do know that what is written in the official text is what works for those in power, and that's about all one can be sure of. There's a concept called negative evidence. Who can say what came from what, and what is missing that is important? The water on the floor—was it from an ice cube melting, or something completely different? There is no way of knowing what was lost or destroyed in the past because it didn't support practical power needs for the social structures.

"The authorized story is a box for designed for a practical purpose, not revealed truth. All that matters to you, to any of us, is the internal relation of self with the divine, which is revealed truth. Truth is a torch but a tremendous one, and that is why we hurry past it, shielding our eyes, indeed, in fear of getting burned.

"If you turn from the Tree of Life, the wonder-fullness that was celebrated in Job, then you have turned your back on wisdom. There is a price to be paid if you deny wisdom:

"How long, dupes, will you love being duped,

and scoffers lust scoffing, and fools hate knowledge?

Turn back to my rebuke.

Look, I would pour out my spirit to you, I would make my words known with you. Because I called and you resisted,

I reached out my hand and none paid heed, and you flung aside all my counsel,

and you did not want my rebuke. I, too, shall laugh at your ruin,

I shall mock when what you feared comes, when what you feared comes like disaster,

and your ruin like a whirlwind descends, when straits and distress come upon you. Then they will call me and I shall not answer,

they will seek me and they will not find me. Because they have hated knowledge,

and the Lord's fear they did not choose. They did not want my counsel,

they spurned all my rebuke. And they ate from the fruit of their way, and from their own counsels they were sated."

"A long time ago, I wrote, 'I took my stand in the midst of the world, and in flesh I appeared to them. I found them all drunk, and I did not find any of them thirsty. My soul ached for the children of humanity, because they are blind in their hearts and do not see, for they came into the world empty, and they also seek to depart from the world empty. But meanwhile they are drunk. When they shake off their wine, then they will change their ways.' The world closed the bar, as it were. Time to decide.

"I'm so tired of people needing a reason for doing everything in their lives. Do it because you want to. Because it's fun. Because it makes you happy. Because it is your inspiration flowing through you."

Jesus read it over, fussed with it, and then pushed publish.

DAY 34. A FUNERAL, DETROIT.

A large room in the factory had been decorated with black crepe. The bodies of the men killed in the attack on the factory were at the end of the room, in open caskets despite their wounds.

"Their wounds are nothing to be ashamed of," Vladimir advised the others. "The children should not see, but we know death in battle, and we do not hide from it."

"What if a child wishes to see, my lord?" one of the veterans asked.

"First, you should warn them, and if they understand, then they can see. But you must talk to them afterwards, because you know the pain they will feel," Vladimir answered. "And second, I am not 'my lord' anymore. That's gone into the past, my friend."

"I understand, my...ah...Vladimir," the veteran replied.

After all had paid their respects, they stood, as they would have on an ancient battlefield. Many were wearing their ancient armor, holding swords and spears carefully preserved through the eons. The veterans and Lucifer's people stood quietly, the groups mixed together. The Army of the Tree, Vladimir thought. The transferees tried not to stare at them. A simple step into the room became a step out of the modern world into a world of dark elves re-arisen out of an ancient time.

Mary stood on a raised platform. She raised her hands, and then spoke. "I am the resurrection and the life, saith the Lord: he that believeth in me, though he were dead, yet shall he live; and whosoever liveth and believeth in me, shall never die. Life within the Tree of Life is my gift to you, now and forever. We brought nothing into this world, and it is certain we can carry nothing out. The Lord gave, and the Lord hath taken away; blessed be the Name of the Lord."

"Amen," all answered.

Mary prayed, "Lord, let me not know my end or the number of my days, so that I may live each day as if it were my last within the Tree. There are those who say that man walketh in a vain shadow, and disquieteth himself in vain; he heapeth up riches, and cannot tell who shall gather them. And there is some truth in that, but that partial truth obscures the full truth. Life within the Tree created by the Lord is life now and ever after. Those who live within the Tree shall be part of all of us forever, in the Tree then, now, and everlasting. Our brothers we lay to rest in this sacred ground to become part of the tree. They died within the Tree and are still alive in our spirits and memories, and we shall be with them again when we become part of the Tree.

"Those who killed them, cowards who attacked what they thought were defenseless families with children, they died not having come within the Tree. Their bodies were left outside on non-sacred ground, for the dogs under the sky. They return to the Tree, but not within the Tree. They, because they died outside of the knowledge of the Tree, dissolve to come again as new life until they embrace the tree and live within the Tree forever."

Mary paused for a second. Then she spoke, "And now, Lord, what is my hope? Truly my hope is even in thee and the Tree that you have given us. The Tree that enfolds us while we live, enfolds those who are gone, and enfolds those yet to come within the Life of the Tree. The Tree that is your gift to us, comforting us with the Life to come as we gaze, troubled, into the dark.

"As soon as thou scatterest them, they are even as asleep: and fade away suddenly like the grass. In the morning it is green, and groweth up; but in the evening it is cut down, dried up, and withered. Yet that which thou sowest is not quickened, except it dies. In its death, it is reborn within the Tree of Life, and so will our brothers be, and ourselves with them, when our time shall come. O death, where is thy sting? O grave, where is thy victory? Death is swallowed up in victory! Because that which thou sowest, thou sowest not that body that shall be, but a part of Life that thou have given grace to share within the Tree.

"The days of our age are threescore years and ten; and though men be so strong that they come to fourscore years, yet is their strength then but labour and sorrow; so soon passeth it away, and we are gone. So teach us to number our days, that we may apply our hearts unto wisdom and we follow thee within the Tree that thou hast given us. As it was in the beginning, is now, and ever shall be, world without end. Amen."

Lucifer and Vladimir walked to the caskets. Lucifer closed the casket for the veteran, and Vladimir closed the casket for Lucifer's servant, and then they looked at Mary.

"Let us take our brothers to their resting place," Mary declared.

The pallbearers assembled, and the caskets were carried to the garden room, which the Tree had remade into a forest, pushing the walls aside, letting the larger world in. In the middle of that small forest, there was an open space, and two graves had been dug. The caskets were laid on the ground, next to the graves, and all stood silent.

Mary, standing between the caskets, pronounced, "Man, that is born of a woman, hath but a short time to live, and is full of misery. He cometh up, and is cut down, like a flower; he fleeth as it were a shadow, and never continueth in one stay. In the midst of life we are in death: of whom may we seek for succour, but of thee, O Lord? Yet, the Lord God does not deliver us into the bitter pains of eternal death, having made us a part of his Tree of Life in which we shall live beyond the death of this earthy shell. Thou knowest, Lord, the secrets of our hearts; shut not thy merciful ears to our prayer; suffer us not, at our last hour, to fall from the Tree."

She nodded, and the caskets were lowered into the ground. Each then walked by, stopping to take a shovel and casting earth upon the body. Some cried as they did, and some kept the tears inside.

Mary then prayed, 'For as much as it hath pleased Almighty God, in his wise providence, to take out of this world our deceased brothers, we therefore commit their bodies to the ground; earth to earth, ashes to ashes, dust to dust; looking within the Tree of Life, becoming one with the past, present, and in the life of the world to come, through the wisdom of the Lord as shown by His Tree. I heard a voice from heaven, saying unto me, 'From henceforth blessed are the dead who die in the Lord and within the Tree that he has created, for they rest from their labours.'"

Mary stopped for a moment, looking down at the graves, and then prayed, "Lord, Have mercy upon us."

"Lord have mercy upon us," all answered.

Mary then prayed, "Almighty God, with whom and through your Tree do live the spirits of those who depart hence in the Lord, and with whom the faithful are in joy and felicity; We give thee hearty thanks for the good examples of all those thy servants, who, having finished their course in faith, do now rest from their labours. And we beseech thee, that we, with all those who are departed in the true faith of thy holy Name, may have our perfect consummation and bliss, both in body and soul, in thy eternal and everlasting glory. Amen."

"Amen," all answered.

"The grace of the Tree of Life and the love of God, be with us all evermore. Amen," Mary declared.

Lucifer stood, and prayed, "Most merciful Father, who hast been pleased to take into the Tree this thy servant; Grant to us who are still in our pilgrimage, and who walk as yet by faith, that having lived by the understanding thee has given us on this earth, we may be joined hereafter with our brothers in Life everlasting through the Tree. Amen."

Vladimir stood, and prayed, "O Lord, who by thy gift of the Tree of Life didst take away the sting of death; Grant unto us thy servants so to follow the life you have given us led by the inspiration you have put within us, that we may at length fall asleep peacefully in thee, and awake up after thy likeness; through thy mercy, world without end. Amen."

"You may stay or leave, as you wish," Mary advised. "There is food in the community room for a remembrance of our brothers"

DAY 34. DETROIT. WHAT SHALL WE DO?

"I was watching a program from the Vatican that reminded me of heaven," one of the veterans commented. "Pretty, but cold and sterile."

"Okay," another veteran laughed. "There's a position that has changed!"

"So, here we are," a senior veteran announced, looking over the crowd. "A time to talk without the fearless leaders here."

"They've dropped the fearless leader pose," one of Lucifer's people remarked. "In some ways, I miss the old days. You got up, were told what to do, and away went the day. Now it's, 'Well, what do you think you should do?' That's a lot harder sometimes."

"Normally we carry experiences on our backs like a turtle until we can't move any more. Here, we can shed them and live again," a veteran added. "That's what Vladimir says when I bitch about having to make choices."

"It's a relief in some ways," another of Lucifer's people admitted. "Before, we were cartoon characters, all masks. We were like smiling elves in the forest, the backdrop to the stories. All the same stories—we were the scary and you," waving at the veterans, "were the bright. Now, people look at the background, and they see the glittering eyes and naked swords of the elves and realize that there are larger stories out there. That we're not the backdrop anymore. We've stepped into the living world, and they can't fool themselves anymore.'

"Or fool ourselves," one of the veterans pointed out. "This factory is like the elves' last happy house, restful and timeless, and yet like standing in an earthquake at the same time. Before, we were like Tom Bombadil, able to create a world around us that we didn't step out of. Now, the real world has breached our borders, and we're swimming in the rapids."

"Real life again, not paper stories," one of Lucifer's people added. "Good, yet scary at the same time."

"Scary?" one of the women veterans teased, snuggling close to Lucifer's servant. "I thought you were a big demon who could protect me from everything. That's what you promised last night."

There was general laughter at his embarrassed face.

"Well," he chuckled, and decided to kiss her rather than talk.

"They seem preoccupied," a veteran observed, amused. "But yeah, I agree with what he said—about scary, at least."

"What do we do when the Tree takes over?" one of Lucifer's creatures asked. "It looks like we will have our own settlements, our own worlds."

"I think so," a veteran agreed. "At least, that's what I read between the lines when I talk to Vladimir. We can all, and I mean all of us, set up shop in a nice part of the world."

"With our own stories," one of Lucifer's people offered. "No more little human stories, but the way that we look at things."

"There will be lots of stories out there," another veteran replied. "The computers have stories and the animals seem to be changing their stories. There is this new DNA manipulation—those creatures will have stories of their own. And fine, it's the elf in me, but the trees and the plants seem different since the Tree also. Everything is changing."

"And then there are the bugs," one of Lucifer's people added. "I hear rumors that there are big bugs back in South America."

"Ugh, don't like bugs," a women veteran grimaced. "We fought them eons ago. Nasty things."

"They have stories now, I hear," one of the veterans remarked.

"It's Vladimir, Mary, and Lucifer," one of Lucifer's people guessed. "Their theory is that the world needs more stories, more viewpoints, and that's what's going to happen."

"Can't argue with the need for bigger stories," a veteran commented. "Living within the Tree demands respect for other life, fitting within that life, and understanding within the system and structure of life that is bigger than the small human stories. Still, bugs. Yuck."

"Living within the Tree means that choices have real consequences and you plan and judge accordingly. At the end of the day, or life, you must ask if your choices were for life or not," one of Lucifer's people remarked. "I love that. It's such a refreshing change from these weird human stories with their self-justifying moral endings."

"Can't argue with that," a veteran added. "We can plumb the depth and the heights of life, not just that 'he said, she said' that the humans seem to love so much."

"So, what are we going to need?" one of the veterans demanded. "We've got to start making some hard choices for ourselves. Where do we want to move to? Or stay here? We need food, supplies, medical care."

"Prenatal care," a women pointed out. "This mingling of minds is producing real results."

"Clearly that," a veteran agreed, nodding his head, his arm around the woman of Lucifer's people that he loved. "So, who's going to own this project?"

"Well," one of Lucifer's people offered, "how about this?"

They talked for a couple of hours, hashing out ideas and dividing up responsibilities.

Vladimir, Lucifer, Raphael, Jesus, and Mary were talking the next day.

"The groups seem to be merging well," Vladimir observed.

"At least," Mary laughed. "I'm setting up some prenatal clinics and planning. Well, I'm a fertility goddess," catching the looks directed at her. "It's what I do."

"And even more than that," Lucifer added. "They are making plans for a new world for the group—where to go and live, what to do."

"It's what they need to do," Jesus acknowledged. "Their stories are different from what they've, well, endured over the eons. Time for them to grow into what they can become."

"I like the elves' sparkling eyes in the forest," Raphael added. "They are coming alive to what they can be."

DAY 34. LIFE IS STRONG.

Jenny and a group of older teenagers are keeping a careful watch on a mall that has been taken over by the zombies.

"Our orders are to watch," one of the boys advised. "They are dying on their own in there, we are just supposed to make sure they don't bring any captives into the mall. An easy job."

"And it's sunny and nice today," Jenny remarked, lying back in the warm grass. "Today I don't feel like doing anything. Except you, I'd do you," she offered, sitting up and leaning close to Jeffrey, the boy next to her.

Jeffrey smiles happily, as the others laugh.

"Over there, I think," Jenny suggested, pointing to a small hill near them. "We could, well, investigate that suspicious area. Carefully and thoroughly reconnoiter and then firmly secure it."

"A man has to do what a man has to do," the leader ordered, winking.

Jenny pulled Jeffrey up, and crouching so they were not exposed to rifle fire from the mall they crept behind the hill, as the others laughed.

"I read that the survivors of the plagues would relieve their anxieties by lascivious behavior," Jeffrey commented, a bit uncertainly.

"My favorite part of sex is when I'm actually having some," Jenny giggled as she pushed him down.

The others in the group turned back to watching the mall, still laughing.

"After the plague passed, the survivors just wanted to live! Love, eat and celebrate life," Allison remarked. "I read a book on the Black Death, and if you read between the lines, it was pretty wild."

"It only takes a second to show someone how you feel about them. The police call it indecent exposure, but whatever . .," Ginger teased the boy next to her, batting her eyelashes and flipping her blouse up.

"Lewd behavior," the boy declared, shaking his head. "I'm going to have to take you into custody." They embraced.

"Ah, there's another hill over there," Ginger suggested. He nodded and they crept off, staying low to avoid rifle fire.

"When people say "it's better than sex" they clearly, aren't having the right kind of sex," Jenny murmured some time later.

"The people of the tree accept life and the flesh," Jeffrey observed. "Those outside the tree deny the flesh and life. Well, that's what that ex-college philosophy professor argued at that group meeting," catching Jenny's bored look.

"Oh, shut up," Jenny ordered, climbing on top of him. Now, I'm going to teach you how, in Bonobo society, the females keep control.. . ."

DAY 34. NEW YORK.

A group of mutants are sitting in a field, talking.

"It is seeing the stories thru the world, not seeing the world thru the stories, that makes all the difference," a man argued.

"What the hell does that mean?" another replied.

"Ok, seeing the world thru the stories means that you only see the human stories, the human constraints the straight lines and the bright pictures that humans want," the man explained. "Seeing the stories thru the world – that means you see the limits to the stories against what the world is. How about that?"

"I like that," the other man agreed. "Of course, being able to switch viewpoints is hard."

"With practice it's easier," a woman added. "If you are with the Tree, it comes naturally with time. Those who deny the Tree, anyone bound to the human stories defining the world isn't going to want to spend a lot of time weaning themselves from that small view. They are proud of their limits, their limits, their prisons define them. The crutch they use to live by is their life, not something to be outgrown."

"Wow, I'm feeling good about this," another man laughed. "But a day like today, sunny, warm, a good breeze, well, who couldn't feel good about that?"

"Unfortunately," a man grumbled, standing up, "We need to do some work."

"After all this great change, our realization of life and all that is important?" a woman asked.

"Before enlightenment, hew wood and fetch water. After enlightenment, hew wood and fetch water. It's just better, richer, afterwards. Maybe?" noticing the doubtful looks the others are giving him.

"Being an adult sucks," the woman said, shaking her head as she stood up.

DAY 34. THE NEW WORLD ORDER

"The new world order," Lucifer wrote. That should get them going, he thought with a smile.

"Anything I write will automatically push so many buttons that I'm not sure I'm accomplishing much. Still, pouring fuel on the fire is something, if that provides a light for understanding. Sometimes you have to watch the world burn, clearing the way for the new world to come. There, I have covered fires, torment, and destruction, so perhaps we can move on here.

"The wild and nature is what the church has rejected. Turning inward to a fantasy world, away from a world that was authentically terrible at the time. The historical perspective is critical here. The slow fall of the Roman Empire shaped the church fathers' perspectives, as well as the dangerous visions of the fanatics. There was a worldwide crash of civilizations at roughly the same time across the globe. China, India, Rome. Very, very broadly speaking, the resources they had discovered and that supported the sophisticated civilizations ran out under population and other pressures. As the material world crumbled, people desperately sought a feeling of control. The mind is hardwired to demand that feeling. So people went inside, deep inside, to find emotional peace. That's not bad; that's part of the strength of humans to go inside. But this inside focus was grabbed, institutionalized for control, and once the control was imposed, it perpetuated.

"All stories need borders, and I'm the border. The dark, the danger, the wolf outside the door. Nature in all its random terror. Which is the nature of the cosmos, as stated by God in Job. That's not how the church wanted it, so they rewrote it to the story they liked. The story that raises money and gives control is that Man rules the universe, and the annoying details that didn't fit into that story were pushed away, swept under the rug. Humans can only keep, oh, say, seven thoughts in mind, and about all that seems to have stuck is that we were given the world as our dominion. Hopelessly false is that, and so the more desperately gasped onto.

"Life is food filling your belly, restful sleep, and the warmth of a sunny day; bright stories framed against the story borders of hunger, sleepless nights, and dark and stormy days. Life is sex and reproduction and love and hate. Life is emotion, wonder, and thought. All of that, the church hated. Oh, not for themselves, because of stories of fat friars and lustful monks date back to the beginnings of the church, and are consistent themes even in the twelfth and thirteenth centuries. That the church clergy are human, despite all they would deny or pretend, is perhaps a retributive justice they would prefer not discussed. More annoying realities swept under the rug, until the rug looks like the Himalayas.

"And speaking of retributive justice, while retributive justice is not part of the natural order of the universe, it's wired into humans. The wrath of a woman scorned is a byword for fury. Job's friends were obsessed with the concept of justice: i.e., rewards accruing to them for their 'right' actions. And of course, organized religion has run with it. It's a great control device, and there are some external controls needed. In this world, small wars and village fights are a constant feature. The point of a justice system is, at the heart, a way of taking retributive justice out of the hands of the individual/clan and moving it up the ladder, so the feuds and fights that can and will destroy a village or town are held at bay.

"Now, I'm supposed to be an expert on retributive justice. The prosecutor, in a way, demanding payment for various sins. I was given the job of prosecutor for the justice that doesn't exist—the one that the cosmos is supposed to impose. And the sins are defined as Life itself. I'm not going to prosecute for those. The church knew that, which is why they had their own enforcement department.

"Paul's great realization, on the road to Damascus, was that he could turn Christ's message completely upside down: a message of freedom become control. Paul is nothing if not creative, and loves his stories. He has a gift for stories because they are so important to him. So he turned the original message into the Christian cult. Because no dissension can be allowed, his borrowed symbols and borrowed god were presented as facts. His clergy claimed authority from the unquestionable fact, so every attempt to discover your own spiritual statement was suppressed. Every local deity was a demon, every natural thought a sin. At the end, the Church's history in the West became the brutality and futility of its increasingly hysterical, and finally unsuccessful, combats against heresy on every front. An odd result for a religion nominally preaching love and caring.

"The Church's story is that they sought to eradicate from humanity all expressions of carnal human nature, promising pretty pictures in another world if you did what they ordered. In reality, sin was what they needed; it was their tool for control. Humans are animals. That's the way it is. It's brilliant, in a sick sense, how they structured these un-winnable conflicts. You can never win, each urge of the living self a carefully defined sin. You can only survive through their grace, which is sparing if you can't buy it, and non-existent if you question it.

"What's important for the individual to never forget is that there is an stern, unforgiving judge within you, demanding retributive justice as defined by your inspiration. You can run, but never from yourself. Deny yourself, lie to yourself, do what you think is wrong, you'll never be able to run fast enough away from yourself.

"Where it gets fuzzy is the taught meaning that they try and tie to that unforgiving judge within you. You have to carefully distinguish your internal demand for justice, and the meaning imposed from the outside demanding you do as they say. Inspiration demands justice, which is vastly different from the meaning from the outside. You can do everything right that the outside orders and still feel empty inside. What so profits a man to gain the whole world, and to lose his soul, is simply that their meaning can't fill your lost inspiration.

"Taken as referring to a landscape of the soul, the Garden of Eden must already be within us. Yet our conscious minds are unable to enter it and enjoy there the taste of eternal life, since we have already tasted of the knowledge of good and evil. That conscious knowledge, carefully taught to us, has pitched away from our own center. Limiting our experience and thought to their external symbols of good and evil, instead of opening to our internal inspiration, denies the eternal life inside, which, since the garden is within us, must already be ours. The Tree is knowledge past good and evil; to that deep understanding of how opposites are really all one and that the events of the world are beyond their small stories. If you cannot abandon the small stories, you will die when you encounter the Tree.

"Is this unfair? Do you cling to the pretty picture of a Sunday God, the small story of the humans writ over the universe, carefully created and polished by the church? Or do you gird your loins, and find the God that Job found, the living God? God freed Job from a mechanical, blind submission to a moral law of retributive justice. God creates the space in his order for the freedom of humans and the freedom of God, for the integrity of mortals and the integrity of God, for the angry complaints of those in agony and the challenge of God in a whirlwind or whisper. Job discovers his God and in so doing finds his own 'place.' Job, through God, comes to transcend the moral order by his innocent suffering.

"'Whoever blasphemes against the Father will be forgiven, and whoever blasphemes against the son will be forgiven, but whoever blasphemes against the Holy Spirit will not be forgiven, either on earth or in heaven.'" The Holy Spirit is you, and if you blaspheme against yourself, there can be no forgiveness for that."

Maybe it's not always about trying to fix something broken. Maybe it's about starting over and creating something better.

DAY 34. MEANING AND INSPIRATION

"I've been asked," Jesus typed, "about meaning and inspiration. What am I talking about? A long time ago, I said: 'if you bring forth what is within you, what you have will save you. If you do not have that within you, what you do not have within you will kill you.' What you have within you is inspiration. What you do not have within you is meaning.

"Meaning is a box delivered to you by the moral post office police. Little boxes and the big box that wants to hold all the little boxes. There doesn't have to be, and actually isn't, just one meaning, although many people shout for one big meaning, like tired two-year-old children who only know a few words. You don't have to choose between no meaning at all and one, all-embracing meaning. There can be, and are, many meanings and many purposes in the complex world with which we are confronted, and that's where the terminology breaks down. 'Purpose' can be inspiration, as well as an external meaning.

"Inspiration flows from within. Meaning comes from without. Sounds simple, but the concept doesn't work that well. Why? Because it's hard to know what you want. How often do you go to lunch, and once down a path, realize you really wanted to go somewhere else, eat something else, had you not run into two people in the hallway ten minutes before lunch hour? Lots of things push at us and make it hard to listen to the small voice within. There is a constant flow of perhaps well-meant teaching and pressure to keep that small voice within shut up, because most people have better uses for our time than they are sure we have. It's always well meant, of course, because the people teaching it to you defined it as well meaning. I'm waiting for an advertisement that trumpets: 'Selling this product is to serve our selfish needs, but you'll get some minimal enjoyment from your purchase.' Or a politician who announces, 'This favors the fifty-one percent who vote for me, so screw the rest of you.' I'm not holding my breath waiting for those moments of truth to break through, but it's fun to re-word the ads thrown at you."

"Your inspiration tells you that what you are doing is right, positive, and to be rewarded. It makes you a free person."

"Following your inspiration isn't easy. You are stuffed full of external meaning, and when you step away from their meanings, you are empty in a way. I read once that if you are unhappy because you are not in a romantic relationship, you won't be happy when you are in one. Defining happiness as people seeing you labeled as 'in a relationship' is all external meaning. Inspiration is caring for the person you are in a relationship with, a completely different thing from your friends seeing you as 'taken.' If all you care about is the external message 'See, I'm valuable enough that someone wants me' and that's why you want to be in a relationship, it won't be much of a relationship."

"You are taught to feel empty if you don't have a meaning box to sit in. 'Don't go outside the boxes' is pounded into all of us. It's easy to sit in the box; it's defined and you've done what can be rationalized. Going outside, well, you can fail, do something people will say is wrong. It is guaranteed that people will say is wrong, actually. Outside the box, monsters are there; it's written all over the map. Stay out! Outside the box is made scary, but it's really isn't. Letting the words, which are external meanings, define you and your life, instead of the internal pictures your mind sends you saying what it wants.

"Let's look at the words. If you put your inspiration into words, there is a trap. When you put thoughts into the structure of words, you weave a thread into what you are saying. We like a novel, a story, a myth, or a tale, because all spare us from the complexity of the world and shield us from its randomness. You have to put things in words, but watch the stories in words. Events exist, a story is a only a gloss, not the truth.

"Feeling out of control? Not a bad thing. Too much control is generally boring, dull. Now, it isn't always pleasant feeling out of control. It's reality, for what that's worth. Your will is not the world, regardless of how we want to feel. You can still control your feelings, how you react, when you face that you don't control the world. Outside your comfort zone is where you must go!! Otherwise the comfort zone gradually contracts until there is no life, or comfort, left.

"Where you have a conflict between what people want you to do and what you want to do, you can give up or go on. Give up yourself, or go on to what you care about. There are many, many decisions in this world for which there is no objective way to determine what the 'right' choice is. Best case, worst case, probable case scenarios are a necessary stab, but even those are limited by your assumptions. Things change, you change, and what you sought by your choice changes. If you go with your emotions, you're at least happy on the inside. If you gain the world but lose your soul really needs to be inverted. If you gain all the meaning, the exterior stuff, but lose your inspiration, the interior stuff, you are empty completely. Your food will be ashes in your mouth, your triumphs broken-down stone monuments, buried in the drifting sands of the wasteland.

"Let's get boring, and look at the nature of the creature that we all are. Humans impose, by narrative stories and cause/effect relationships, a disease called dimension reduction on the world. We cut the world down into something easier to handle, because we have a lot to do and there is little time. Cause/effect makes time flow in a single direction, and so does a narrative story. The next time you are sure that you are really, really right and have the sole, ultimate, and revealed answer, remember that logicians have proved that there exist multiple consistent interpretations and theories for any given set of facts. Brain studies show that people with severed brains (right and left physically cut apart) can come up with lucid, rational explanations for their actions that are completely wrong. But those people firmly believe their explanations, which are meaning based.

"What's the end message? Trust your inspiration as your guide, being careful to use 'meaning' as a tool to keep the police away from your door. 'Meaning' as formally expressed in criminal statutes has to be taken seriously.

"Meaning is constantly manipulated. A newspaper starts with verifiable (there's always some gray) facts that are woven into a narrative to convey causality (and knowledge). Your inspiration cannot be so manipulated, which is its strength and weakness. Ignore your inspiration and you empty yourself. Ignore your inspiration when you encounter the Tree, and you die. Joseph Campbell would say that when the symbols within you disappear, you have lost the vehicle for communication between your waking consciousness and your deepest spiritual life. That's bad. You're driving at high speed on the expressway at night with no lights.

"Meaning is structured, squared, referenced, and footnoted. Nothing original, just a careful construction of others' thoughts and actions. Against that, Inspiration is organic. Organic is all function. Trees grow to the sun, their roots to the water. They don't grow to a pretty picture of a tree circulated through the forest for the other trees to judge them by. The tree, twisted and moving, shapes itself. Meaning hates Inspiration, because Inspiration flows from within; it's unpredictable, and meaning wants structure, because meaning is command and control, first and last.

"What is it that turns your life into nothing but suffering? It is desire and fear. Desire for something and fear lest you should lose something. Those are all external meanings, because how can you lose your inspiration? It's within you, and regrows with just a little encouragement. The fear of Death they throw at us should tell you that you have nothing to lose, that each of us is naked in the world. There is no security, there is no safety. You move forward or you die. That is Life and the Tree.

"Think about these ideas when you are caught by the meaning traps, the tar babies. Do you have tar babies in your life? It's anything that if you argue with it and hit it, then your fist is stuck to it, trapped. Trying to escape, you hit it again. The more you hit it, the more you are trapped, until trapped, you finally struggle in vain. The meaning boxes like a 'no exit' door.

"If you spend all your time thinking about that which you are attacking, then you are negatively bound to it. Angrily deny the church's god, define yourself by your denial, and you are bound as tightly to that god as the church is. You have to find the zeal in yourself and bring that out. That is what's given to you—one life to live. Marx teaches us to blame the society for our frailties; Freud teaches us to blame our parents for our frailties; astrology teaches us to blame the universe. The only place to look for blame is within:

you didn't have the guts to bring up your full moon and live the life that was your potential. "

"Finally, here are two children's stories that are far deeper and more important than they seem.

"First, the emperor's new clothes. He is naked, parading down the street. All see, but only the child will say it. All others had their ability to think crushed out of them by the meaning they carry. Only the child looks to his inspiration, and can see the naked old man strutting foolishly down the road.

"And the other? The ugly duckling. You are ugly to meaning, because that is how it controls you. You are beautiful as a swan to your inspiration, when you open to it.

"I'm a man of my word, if you follow your inspiration when you give your word. If all you follow is social meaning when you give your word, then you are nothing."

DAY 38. WHO DIES.

"And, of course, the flip side to 'who lives' is 'who dies,'" Lucifer typed. This will be painful, he thought. I didn't volunteer for this one.

"'Tell us, how will our end come?' the disciples asked. And the answer was, 'Have you found the beginning, then, that you are looking for the end?' You see, the end will be where the beginning is. Congratulations to the one who stands at the beginning: that one will know the end and will not taste death. That reads a bit like the elves in Lord of the Rings, or Zen, but sentences shouldn't always be clear. Sometimes they should be confusing so that you must reflect to find the true meaning for you, a meaning different from that others find.

"Let's put some perspective on events. What we see every day in our world—our jaunt into the world of monotheism, agriculturally centered economics, and the control of power and resources by the few—is really 'unnatural.' For eons, our ancestors had radically different lives. It seems that in the last hundred thousand years, give or take, something changed and gave humans the chance to move around the world. Now, the climates—the economic, social, and natural—are changing again. Has there ever been a world for humans where everything changes all the time, as it seems to today? Perhaps for the earliest hunters, traveling through new worlds. But even then, the group was constant, the ideas that they used to think about the daily world unchanged even as they moved to new lands. There were new lands to explore, but it was roughly the same kind of new land—forests, grasslands, swamps, etc.—as the old areas had. While the animals they hunted were found in different places, the concepts were pretty much the same. Wake up, shit, hunt/find food, same as yesterday, mate and sleep, and start the cycle again the next day. Living within a defined world, our ancestors hated the new, because generally the really new usually meant starvation and death.

"We are hardwired to respond to the world in certain ways. Why are we depressed and lethargic on a rainy, overcast day? Because for eons, in that weather, the hunting was poor, and those who rested survived to hunt another day. Why happy and full of energy on a bright, sunny day? First, because the hunting was good, and survival favored those who went out after game when the game was out there. Secondly, because the sun's warmth is physiologically addictive, and actually needed for Vitamin D production. We are creatures of our nature, deny it as we will.

"In India, two amusing figures are used to characterize the two principal types of religious attitude. One is 'the way of the kitten' and the other is 'the way of the monkey.' When a kitten cries 'meow,' its mother, rushing to it, takes it by the scruff of its neck and carries it to safety. With monkeys, the babies riding on their mother's backs are hanging on by themselves.

"The kitten is the person who prays, 'O Lord, O Lord, come save me!' and the monkey is the one who, without such prayers or cries, goes to work on himself. In Japan the same two are known as tariki, outside strength, or power from without, and jirki, own strength, effort or power from within. "

"Kittens are not going to do well with the changes demanded by the Tree.

"How about another way of looking at this," he typed. "There are four tribes/types in the world, you might say.

"One group prefers a society that is more hierarchical, a rigid world of order, structure, class, and authority and elites, where things don't change much. Much like small children, lost without the world, they clasp the structure to themselves, needing it's meaning.

"Another group prefers a society without those constraints, where everybody has a chance at everything.

"A third tribe is more individualist; people who want a society that will protect them when the lion attacks, but otherwise pretty much leaves them alone.

"The fourth group has the community-minded people who think we're all in it together.

"Each of us holds some combination of those factors, balanced differently in each person.

"The first hardcore group isn't going to fare well with the Tree," he typed. "The other groups will fare depending on themselves, and the mix of worldviews they hold. Like all of life, a lot of it is hardwired, just bad luck sometimes. If you're a moth in a birch forest, fortune favors the moth with white coloring, and birds favor the moths with dark coloring. Until the forest changes to a dark-barked tree and the rules switch.

"The world is changing. You must change, or die. Deming wrote, 'Survival is not mandatory,' and he was right. You should pray for understanding and then act. You can't define and whine and get away with it this time. It's been said that we all avoid risks in life, so we can make it safely to death. Not this week.

"What does the Tree do? It requires you to see bigger stories. To experience other creatures' existences. What creatures? It's a random draw, kind of like the magic beans in Harry Potter, which could come in any flavor, from wonderful to terrible. Peppermint to, well, disgusting things. The creatures' lives can be dolphins to spiders, or lions to squid. Orcas, sea lions, predators, and prey, since all play both roles. Some are a lot easier to take than others, and it's luck. Fail to open to the creatures' lives, and you die. Rejection seems to short circuit out critical parts of the operating system, and you're gone.

"Loud shouts from all over decry the unfairness of the imposed choice. The world's fair? Do you have that in writing somewhere? You have been given life and opportunity, and you push it away for some imagined afterlife? Did you think you wouldn't be punished for that choice, which is the rejection of the gift of Life? If you don't want what you have been given, which is Life, then you shall be given what you wanted: the priests' vision of the afterworld. Death. Drop us a line. Tell us how it went.

"It's going to be finding your inner monster(s) that decides whether you survive or not. It's moving to a new world, a world unbounded by the small human stories that the Tree demands. The nihilists question, 'Why,' (wrote Nietzsche) is a product of his earlier habitude of expecting an aim to be set for him from without—i.e., by some superhuman authority or other. When the nihilist has learned not to believe in such a thing, he goes on just the same, from habit, looking for another authority or some kind that will be able to speak unconditionally and set goals and tasks by command. That is the old world of the agrarian masters.

"Building walls to keep things out only traps you in with the monsters. Every fear and monster walled out gains strength and fear increases. If you fence out the wild, the greater Life of the world, you lose the wild inside. The walls you built to keep things out only in the end keep you in. If you cannot change your dreams, if you just lie back with the fears, then the Tree will kill you. Sorry. It's out of my hands. This is a battle that each must fight. You must embrace your hidden monsters and make them your friends.

"Cut off from the power of nature, the stories become smaller and smaller, and the people empty, becoming only husks and hate. And a hollow man will get a wise heart when a wild ass is born a man. The usual person, the bedrock of agrarian society, is content, nay, proud, to remain within the indicated bounds. Both his training and his friends give him every reason to fear so much as the first step into the unexplored. That person, the tiller of fields on command, the carrier of water when told, isn't going to transition into the new world.

"There isn't a ritual to save you, a trinket to buy from someone, a social transaction for a blessing. There is only facing yourself and the greater world.

"I tell you that a new age is coming. Doors close and new doors open for those ready to cross. You can't grow until you grasp what the forbidden monsters would see, and so you have to work your mind into that monster's system. Why? Because monsters—demons—are the rejected self. Rejected to fit into the small social structures. Reject your monsters and you'll reject what seem like real monsters, the lives of the other creatures. Like a horror movie, if you just deal with the monster for a moment and run, the monsters keep coming. Bring the monster within yourself, recognize that part of yourself—don't run just because you're told to.

"Stupidland astronauts were planning on landing on the sun. Someone asked how they would do that, because the sun is so hot. They chuckled, and answered that they would land at night, when it was cool. Defining the universe in terms of your life isn't going to work with the Tree.

"Pink Floyd sang of the Wall and the failure to get past it. Some didn't make it. "No one told you when to run, you missed the starting gun" ...and "And the worms ate into his brain. "

"Destroy what destroys you. Or die. Life isn't about waiting for the storm to pass. It's about learning to dance in the rain. Those within the Tree shall be in Life. Those without the Tree shall dissolve and come again until they finally find Life within the Tree.

"'Grapes are not harvested from thorn trees, nor are figs gathered from thistles, for they yield no fruit. Good persons produce good from what they've stored up; bad persons produce evil from the wickedness they've stored up in their hearts, and say evil things. For from the overflow of the heart they produce evil..'"

"Biomass parasites will die."

DAY 38. THE FALL OF THE ZOMBIES.

All over the world, Malls and big box shopping centers have been turned into refuges by the zombies. Any plants in the parking lots are sprayed, and the airflow into the buildings can be controlled. While the colony creatures spread by the plants can't be completely filtered out, the level of contact can be reduced by the filters.

A meeting of the operating staff at a large mall outside New York.

"At least," one of the maintenance men commented as he stared at a clogged filter, "if we had more filters. The one's we just put in are the last clean ones we have."

"Can't recycle the filters?" an executive demanded, kicking the equipment.

"The last man who took dirty filters out to clean them never lived to come back into the building," the maintenance man replied. "He was hit by the power of the plants concentrated fifty times. We think he was dead before he hit the ground. We pushed his body and the filters to a corner of the parking lot, and burned them when the wind was right."

"Doesn't really matter that much," the executive admitted, shrugging. "We are running out of bottled water and dry food. If it isn't one thing, it's another."

"The bright side," the medical officer gasped, coughing, "is that so many are dying that the need for water and food is dropping as fast as our supplies."

"Oh, that's cheerful," the executive snapped. "Reminds me of cost cutting at the business I used to run. The spreadsheets looked great until there was no business left."

"All the zombie movies I ever saw," the maintenance man complained, almost to himself, "had the zombies on the outside and the living hiding in the malls for protection. This movie needs a re-write."

"That's putting it mildly," the medical officer rasped.

"What about the prisoners?" the security officer demanded. "The mutants know we have some of their people in here. I don't know how, but the word got out. We thought that keeping some of them as hostages would protect us, but I've heard the mutants have started attacking buildings to free their people."

"And we release them, and they tell those monsters what we did to the ones who died? That killing them has been the primary entertainment in here? The attack would be immediate," the executive snarled. "Don't kill any more of them, though. Maybe we can negotiate something."

"Why would they bother?" the medical officer commented. "At the rate we are dying off, they can simply wait for us to be all gone. Those damn plant colony creatures are changing the colony creatures in our bodies, and I can't do anything about it. Medical science never really understood the colony creatures. People suddenly can't metabolize the food they eat, even the dry food, and it's a quick death after that."

"I don't think they are going to wait," the security officer muttered. "They have been spray painting the buildings, and the spacing of the painting looks like targets to me. They want their people, and they want revenge."

"It's more than revenge with them," the executive shivered. "I thought our people were furious, but the fury in them is terrifying. They are mutants, all right. No longer human, and they can't be reasoned with. Do we have any weapons left?"

"We do," the security officer replied. "It's trained people to handle them and healthy people to be able to fight that we are short of. But I'll give them out as best I can."

"In this horror movie I saw," the maintenance man remarked, they said, "Welcome to the worst nightmare of all - reality. Pinhead, I think."

"And he wasn't kidding," the executive agreed. A bell rang out, echoing through the mall.

"Well, it is time for the morning service," the security officer sighed. "I'm losing my faith, I have to admit."

DAY 38. A MALL, UNITED STATES.

Albert sat in the community center. His wife Jacqueline had just died, her skin white/yellow, her features drawn, the loose skin on her neck and arms drooping. She was lying next to him on the floor. He couldn't bring himself to touch her.

Brains, he thinks, zombies need brains, isn't that what the movies say? "They call us zombies. Well, let's go for the brains of those who killed her," Albert mumbled to Ernest, who nods. They help each other up. Jacqueline's body is left lying on the floor as they limp out of the community center.

A priest, held upright by the gatepost he was leaning on, smiles at them. His wan face, his long teeth, he really does looks like a zombie, Albert thought, but Albert and Ernest smile back.

"They are the enemy come from below," the priest rasps, and coughs for a second. "They are the demons come to reclaim the earth, but we can beat them, we can win this battle!"

They embrace for strength and to drive the dreams away. The priest hugs Ernest for a long time. Albert finally pulls Ernest away, and then they set out, hunting mutants. Their ammunition is long gone, but they have baseball bats. Staggering down a street they find a group of mutants.

"Dad?" a girl in the group asked sadly.

"Not my child!" Albert howled at the girl. "You are the enemy," and he tries to swing the baseball bat. He is so weak that he can barely move the bat, and instead, has to lean on it for support.

A young man, pistol at the ready, steps between Albert and the girl.

The girl pulls the boy back. "He's not long for now," the girl told him. "Let them die outside of the Tree."

The boy nods, and the group slowly backs away from Albert and Ernest.

Ernest raises his baseball bat over his head, but then collapses, falling flat on the ground. Ernest takes a last gasp, and dies. Albert kneels over his son, and gasps for breath as the visions come back. "Never!" Albert gurgles, and then dies, falling over on the sidewalk on top of Ernest.

"I didn't think dad would make it," the girl cried, looking away. "And I was sure that mom wouldn't."

A woman in the group put her arm around her. "You are part of the Tree now and of our family," the woman reassured her, leading the girl and the others away from the horror. "Keep your eyes open," she ordered. "They are dangerous in a group, and some may still have guns."

The group nods. Scouts move out ahead and behind, weapons ready as they seek shelter in the woods.

DAY 38. WAITING IN THE MALL, NEW YORK.

The malls had everything that people thought they wanted. After days in the mall, unable to step outside, the toilets broken and food running out, people were entertaining doubts that the mall was the heaven they had thought it was.

In a Bar.

Sitting in a bar, staring at the few bottles left, several people are sitting on bar stools. Several others are lying on the ground, so drunk that they fell off their chairs.

"He looks dead," one of the men drawled, gazing critically at a man sprawled on the floor. "That was a nasty fall on his head."

"If he starts to smell, drag him out," another replied. "There is a cart coming by in an hour."

"Bring out your dead," a woman sobbed. "I thought it was funny in that movie, but the joke isn't as good after the twentieth time."

"I tried to drown my sorrows," another woman mumbled, "but the bastards learned how to swim. Barkeep, do you have anything stronger?" she demanded, grimacing at the taste as she put her glass down.

Shopping.

A man and woman are standing in the mall in front of a store. The store is dark, dusty, the racks of clothes unkempt and fallen on the floor. The mannequins are half nude, but their skin color is healthier than the couple looking at the mannequins.

"Sorry, the lifestyle you ordered is currently out of stock," the man concluded, kicking a piece of glass on the floor into the wall.

"And the credit card machine doesn't seem to work right, either," the woman agreed. "Well, at least we don't have to make this months payment."

Waiting.

An unkempt group is sitting in a dark corner. Some are holding hands, some just staring into space, some moaning with their hands over their eyes.

"The days are bad, but the nights are so much worse," a woman cried.

"When will those clouds all disappear?" another woman sobbed.

"All the dreams we held so close, they seemed to all go up in smoke," a man mumbled, putting his arms around the crying woman, crying himself.

"What's he doing?" another man asked, pointing at a man standing by a full length mirror. The man was frantically grasping the mirror with both hands as he stared into it.

"He fears that the more you look at him, the less you see," a woman replied. "He's terrified that there's nothing there."

"At least we are losing weight," one of the women commented. "That was my goal for the year."

"It's never quite the way you think it's going to be," a man replied. "The wishing fairy has a sense of humor."

An unconscious man in the corner wakes up screaming. Several limp over to comfort him.

"It's always the same dream," the man gasped to the people who knelt down by him. "This man is leaning against a building. He looks at me, and hisses 'One night I'm gonna come to you, inside of your house, wherever you're sleeping, and I'm gonna cut your throat.'"

The man calmed down and then suddenly smiles. "It's gone," he laughed wildly. "The fear is gone, that monstrous creature, it's gone!"

"It won't be long now," a woman mumbled, holding the man's hands.

The man suddenly looked horrified, and then suddenly slumped over.

The woman carefully laid him down on the floor. "When the creature you fear is gone, they are happy, and then they realize they are completely empty," she explained. "I've seen it over and over. I was a psychologist, but I can't help any of them with this."

"If you don't let it out, you're going to let it eat you away," another commented. "But you either accept or not. I've not heard of anyone who can change after the initial reaction."

"Can't just put it in a cardboard box in your mind, tape it tightly, label 'bad memories', and leave it there," the woman remarked. "I used to advise people to do that, guess it wasn't such a good idea."

"I'm so tired," one of the men mumbles. "But I'm not angry now. I'm just tired."

"Depression is stage four of Grieving," the psychologist declared. "Then is acceptance."

"And then death," another pointed out. "The terminally ill go through a final period of withdrawal."

Suddenly, there was a 'boom', and then several more. Screams echoed from various parts of the mall, mixed with automatic weapons fire.

"Looks like the grieving is going to be short," one of the men observed, pushing himself up, using his rifle as a support. "Let's go down fighting. At least it will be quick."

One of the men gagged as the fresh air swept down the dank hallways. "The smell of the plants is so strong now! I'd forgotten how powerful it is!"

They pulled each other up, and limped down the mall corridors as the dark shapes and the bright muzzle flashes rushed at them.

Day 38. Rescues.

Four squads of mutants took their positions around the mall.

"Dead inside. Do not enter," I like that, one of the men observed, pointing at a spray painted sign on the mall.

"There's a hole in the world like a great black pit, and it's filled with people who are filled with shit," a woman quoted, her eyes cold.

"And they are all nicely in one place for us to clean them up," another man growled, staring angrily at the mall. "What they have done to our people, we will pay them back ten times."

"Remember, this is about saving our people," the squad leader ordered. "Don't take risks! They are dying anyhow. Killing them just denies them the suffering that they deserve."

The explosives expert popped up the detonator safety button. She looked at the building, and smiled. "For the sake of the planet, you are cordially requested to just fuck off," she laughed and pushed the detonator.

The explosions blew holes in the walls of the mall. The squads swept in like swarming ants, with the same focus and complete lack of mercy.

An hour later, the squads reformed outside the building with the few mutants that were found alive.

"Good job," the leader commented. "None of our people died and we took only a few wounds. Now everyone, back to the woods, where the healers can help them the wounded."

All that was left inside the mall were dead and dying zombies.

DAY 38. THE VATICAN, ROME.

Many of the remaining priests, bishops and cardinals are deep in the bowels of the Vatican, resting in a large room that has had the latest air filtering equipment installed.

"It's easier to breath in here," an elderly cardinal gasped. "My cough is so bad that when I step outside, I think I'm going to die on the spot."

"Several have," a Bishop replied, worried. "There are so many dying that there we have brought back the plague cart to pick up bodies."

"The cart has doubled it's schedule in the last few days," a priest muttered. "And the dead are still lying in the streets, there are so many of them."

"Is it true what the mutants have been saying on their blogs?" a cardinal stammered.

"That there is a corner of hell just for the clergy, full of Bishops, Cardinals and Popes?" a priest replied bitterly. "And that every morning, they proclaim today's authorized human story, relentlessly weeding out the heretics and putting any they suspect to the question and then the bonfire? And the next morning, reassembled and angry, they start again. Groundhog Day in Hell, an eternity trying to impose the small human stories on the cosmos, screaming to ignore what is before their eyes and demanding that others believe exactly, exactly as they demand which this time make the magic, make the world the way they want it. It's an ugly corner, even for hell, your Eminence."

"The Vatican for all eternity?" another priest mumbled. "What have I done to deserve that?"

"You can choose your sin, but you can't choose the consequences," a Bishop wheezed. "I've righteously lectured the sheep, but didn't think it would come back to bite me."

"We suffered, and thought we were buying our way into heaven," a cardinal admitted, holding his head in his hands. "We used that ugly ability of people to worship the crutch and to carry a heavy burden and define themselves by it, tightly wrapping it about themselves until it was all that they are. The more they suffered, they more they grasped onto our message. They had to, because then they would lose the rationale for their past suffering. Perhaps we do deserve that corner of Hell."

"To admit a mistake is hard, worse to admit the loss of years," a Bishop commented. "We saw what we wanted."

"I read a blog yesterday, that asked if we really expected that turning our back on life would be rewarded, and it won't be."

"Nobody believes that they're the problem," a Bishop sighed. "But as we of the church weaken, recoiling from the plants and the tree, those marked by the tree strengthen. That's a sign, deny it as we may."

"Just because you want it to be doesn't mean that it is," the cardinal admitted. "The Pope has told us that this is our test, and perhaps we have earned our reward."

DAY 38. HILLEL THE ELDER.

"In today's message, I wanted to bring in the thoughts of an ancient wise man," Jesus wrote. "His advice is as true today as it was all those centuries ago, because the creature, the self, hasn't changed. Only the tools have changed, and as we have discussed, the new tools don't help with the relationship of the self to the world. They actually harm that relationship in many ways, because the tool is being misused.

"Hillel the Elder said, 'If I am not for myself, who will be for me? But if I am only for myself, who am I?' And, 'If not now, when?'[4]

"The Tree demands that you be for yourself. Only you can make the step to live within the Tree, and the Garden, again. Only you can feel the self deep within, what some would call our personal part of the Divine, as you perceive it. What is you? The seed unwinding itself from the moment of your conception has turned into you, the self that has grown over the years.

"Abraham faced this problem. His solution was to 'Go to yourself!' Inspiration, not meaning, in the terms I have been using. Leave the 'country,' the 'birthplace,' your 'family,' because all the outside structures that create and enforce meaning. When he broke away from those and became himself, that was the seed for his success. Each of us is unique, and you must reach inside and recognize that. Embrace the monsters within you, which are the socially forbidden parts of yourself. Make yourself whole, not a battlefield. What value is there to 'the me,' the persona shown to the world? It is just a shell; the social elements from others.

"'But if I am only for myself, who am I?'

We must start with the self (ani), but then move out into the world of others. By so doing, we free them and ourselves from bondage and reveal a greater self (anochi). It is a self that is simultaneously a part of a greater whole.

"There is a unique 'I' in the universe and it has only been entrusted to one human being: you. If that unique 'I' does not somehow find expression, then the world will never know it. A precious, unique 'I' has failed to be experienced. That is a tragedy.

"However, once that 'I' has discovered and learned to express its individuality, it needs to take the next step and bring it out into the world.

344

Each of us has something unique to contribute and no one else can bring it into the world.

"'If Not Now, When?' What does this somewhat enigmatic phrase have to do with the struggle of self?

"Painfully obvious, actually. It's saying: 'Stop procrastinating! If you're not going to develop your self now—if you're not going to make that trip, take that course, meet that person, read that book—when will you? Get moving on it NOW!

"Sometimes the very thing that can give us the most satisfaction—the key unlocking the doorway to our selves—is the very thing we deny most. It is the door we most fear opening. So we keep the key far out of sight to prevent it from reminding us that there's even a door to be unlocked. We design our lives and busy ourselves from dawn to dusk with activities that rob us of the time to soberly take up the meaning of life and what we need to do to make it truly meaningful.

"Sometimes we're the last to know how great we are. It's not enough to be aware of the need; we have to act on it. Continually. Relentlessly. Otherwise, what's life for? And if not now, when?

"'A Glowing Coal.' At our core is a sacred, transcendent self. The self glows like an eternal light.

"Why, then, can we feel at times so unholy, so mundane, so dark? Because we let it get covered over, we let layer upon layer of soot on our inner, glowing light. We're creatures open to inspiration. However, only one who nurtures the seed of inspiration succeeds in becoming an inspiration to others. A person feels a spark of holiness, has an inspiring experience, yearns momentarily for something more, but then does something unholy, or simply comes home and turns on the TV. Mindlessness becomes a way of life.

"The self needs to be nurtured. It's like a piece of coal. If you keep it away from life, it's a cold, dark piece of rock; ignited by life, and it will glow. To glow is natural. Each of us has a natural beauty, a grandeur, and the absolute free will to experience a state of holiness. Our job is to keep our soul glowing. At the very least, we need to periodically get out of what negative influences and structures we are in so we can let it glow.

"A man once approached one of the great Chassidic leaders, who in turn asked him, 'For what did you come here?'

> 'To find God.'
> 'Then you came for nothing. You're wasting your time.'
> 'Why?'
> 'God is everywhere.'
> 'Then, tell me, master, why should I have come?'
> 'To find yourself.'

DAY 38. AROUND THE WORLD.

The streets of the cities around the world are heaped with the bodies of the zombies.

"Death is new life," a mutant commented, watching the insects and the animals start the cycle of new life.

"The Buddhists got it completely wrong," the woman next to him agreed. "Rotting bodies are new life, all part of the tree of life."

"The zombies pasted their small human story over the window, and shouted in fury when the world ignored the story."

"They paid," the woman replied, shrugging.

Istanbul was empty, only a few living in a city piled with carrion. The Armenians and the Kurds fared fairly well and began moving through the country, setting up settlements where the land was rich.

Greece did well, the spirits of the past still strong there.

In the desert, the Tree penetrated to every waterhole, every place where there was green and crops. So those who fled to the desert for safety found a cruel end. Those who fought the tree lay in the desert; their dried bones all that were left after the great birds had feasted.

The survivors worked hard to keep the world going, and many towns were bustling, lively.

Then, there was Islamabad. The winds harshly blew down the ruined streets, not disturbing the animals and birds feeding on the dead piled in the streets. The few survivors had fled the horror.

DAY 38. EGYPT.

The Egyptian army, joined by surviving armed forces from dozens of other countries and various government officials, had moved far upriver, camping below the Aswan dam. The desert limited the plants more than any mall or building could have done. The groups have merged command into what was grandiosely called the 'World Commander'. It was a small world left to them, but the small human stories still were more precious to them than the truth was.

"At least we have power," the World Commander declared, relaxing on a stool as he enjoyed the air conditioning in his tent.

There was a shout from outside. Several General's marched into the tent, wiping their brows.

"That's a vicious sun out there," one of them grumbled.

"And it was cool in here," the World Commander shouted, glaring at them as he started wiping the sweat off his forehead. "What is the problem now?"

"We lost another weapons depot," a General reported. "They have helicopters, and they blew it up."

"We can't lose any more!!" the World Commander shouted, grabbing the General by the shirt. "We have no factories, no transports. Lose the few weapons we have, and those monsters will roll over us."

"We could, sir, put the weapons in the Dam," another general suggested, looking at the ground. "They can't bomb them there."

"And if they blow them up?" the World Commander replied. "We lose the Dam and also all of us."

"If they blow up the remaining weapons, then we are lost without a doubt," the another General snapped. "I see no other options."

"Then do it," the World Commander ordered. "And keep the damn tent flap closed!" he cursed, as the men started to leave.

Later that day, watching the Aswan Dam through binoculars, a group of mutants cannot believe what they are seeing.

"Your kidding?" one exclaimed. They are putting explosives and weapons into the Dam. How could they be so stupid?"

"They fear the fighters and the helicopters, after the raid on the downriver weapons storage site," another laughed. "They create their worst enemy without thinking, fearing only and not thinking."

"Well, I think we should help them, working so hard in the hot sun. We can contribute, say, a detonator," the leader of the small squad commented, smiling. "Let's go back to the group and plan."

DAY 39. THE CONSECRATION, DETROIT.

Mary stood in front of the group that had gathered in the forest that had grown out of the Garden room.

"Elvish, they look," Lucifer observed.

"It's the swords," Vladimir replied. "Everyone loves the old style back again."

"Even the transferees dress like the veterans and Lucifer's people," Jesus added. "Oh, they did it quietly, but it's good to see them join in to the groups."

"It's not really veterans, my people, transferees," Lucifer started, "based on what I can discern of the living..."

"And sleeping!" Mary interjected.

"...patterns of the group," Lucifer finished. "Well, Showtime, my lady." He bowed to Mary.

"We are met here today," Mary announced, stepping up on a rock, "to Consecrate this space to the Church of the Tree. Through the ages, people have built houses of prayer and praise and set apart places for contemplation.

347

This we now do for the Tree and its Word. We are now gathered to dedicate and consecrate it in the name of the Tree, the symbol of the transcendence we all feel within. Let us pray. Almighty God, we thank you for making the Tree, within which we live, to share in the ordering of your world. Receive the work of our hands in this place, set apart for worship, the growth of the living, and the remembrance of the dead. Amen."

Mary made the sign of Life as she prayed, "Peace be to this sacred ground, and to all who enter here. Our help is in the Tree, which the Lord has given to us."

She stopped and looked around at the people, the separate groups mixed together now. "The Tree encompasses us, holds us, binds us to each other and to Life. All that we are and all that we have is yours. Accept us now, as we dedicate this place to which we come to praise your Name, to ask your forgiveness, to know your healing power, to hear your Word, and to be nourished by the Tree. Lord, be present always to guide and to judge, to illuminate and to bless your people."

Vladimir prayed, "Lord, make this sacred land a temple of your presence. Be always near us when we seek you in this place. Draw us to you when we come alone and when we come with others, to find comfort and wisdom, to be supported and strengthened, to rejoice and give thanks. May it be here that we are made one with you and with one another so that our lives are sustained and sanctified for your service."

Lucifer prayed, "Open our eyes, our ears, and our hearts, that we may grow closer to you through joy and through suffering. Be with us in the fullness of your power as new members are added to your household, as we grow in grace through the years, when we are joined in marriage, when we turn to you in sickness or special need, and, at the last, when we are committed into the everlasting life within the Tree."

Mary prayed, "Now, O Father, sanctify this place." She raised her hands to the sky.

The sunlight broke through the clouds, streaming down and illuminating her and those standing in the forest.

"And with that," Jesus observed, "I think...lunch."

DAY 39. CHURCHES.

Around the world, abandoned churches and places of worship are brought to life again. They are marked with Crosses that have grown roots and branches. It is the dead wood of the cross come alive again, rooted in the earth and growing. Spreading everywhere it is a symbol of redemption and life.

The Clerics who became of the Tree were more like ancient priests than their previous selves. Worship was emotion and feeling, eschewing solemn drudgery and praises of suffering. More like Druids in the woods worshipping their trees and protecting them. Celebrating life, those of the Tree stand outside to drink the rain and celebrate the storm.

Father Flanagan and Heidi married and lead services in a reclaimed church.

"And you will be a father," Heidi told him. "All that celebrating Life, and life is here!"

Groves of trees were consecrated to the Tree around the world. And at the glass cathedral, many of the carefully tinted glass broken so that the cleansing sun could flow into the building, reopens for services. The Minister, the collector and the accountant lead the church. They were shocked to have survived, but they had become new people when they became of the Tree.

"The world became their church, as the survivors, standing for a moment, by themselves or in groups, feel the world, embrace it and hold it within themselves. I looked in temples, churches and mosques. But I found the divine within my heart."[20]

DAY 39. ASWAN DAM, EGYPT.

A zombie prisoner is brought to the mutant camp and sat down on a stool. He is pale, coughing, his uniform torn and unkempt. His rank bars show major.

"Where did you find him?" the Colonel asked, watching the prisoner from a distance.

"He was guiding a group of the people who were loading equipment into the dam, sir," a sergeant reported. "We watched from a distance, as they moved equipment for several hours. They were losing people steadily. Men would just sit or fall, and not get back up. Finally, this man sat down, and then fell over. His men looked like they tried to do something, but finally just left him when they went back to the camp."

"His people took his weapons, sir," a private reported. "We thought he was dead like the others."

"Then, when we were checking what they had done, he stirred, sir," the sergeant continued. "So we captured him, made sure he had no communications equipment, and brought him back here."

"Good choice," the Colonel replied. "There's always a risk that he would be followed, but seems unlikely. They are so focused on their health that they don't seem to give a lot of thought to us. This man looks to be high enough that he might know something useful. He might be able to confirm out suspicions."

The Colonel walks over to where the man is sitting, and sits down on a chair across from the major.

The zombie major glares at the mutant Colonel. "It's you mutants that have destroyed the world," the major raved. "You and your plants, you're not human anymore. You turned your backs on the humans, and have driven us to this."

"I've heard this talk before," the Colonel sighed, bored. "So, let's start again. This," holding up a plant, "is an especially strong plant."

The major almost fainted as he stared at the plant.

"The plants have continued to evolve and change," the Colonel continued. "For those of us in the Tree, all the better. For those outside the Tree, such as yourself, all the worse. All the dreams you have had, all the fears and terrors? This will multiply them, and all I have to do is to let the sap trickle down your throat."

The major began to cry, begging.

The Colonel put the plant down, carefully downwind from the major, but within the Colonel's easy reach. Then he looked carefully at the captive. "So, tell me what you are loading into the Dam," the Colonel demanded. "Oh, I know everything. I'm just testing what others have told us. So if you lie, it will go poorly for you. Do you understand?"

"Yes, sir," the major croaked.

"Give him some water," the Colonel ordered, motioning to an aide. "No, not fresh water," noticing the major's terror as the prospect of fresh water. "Give him that bottled water, the kind that they like. Open the bottle in front of him so he has no doubts."

A Captain brought bottled water over and carefully opened it in front of the major, who relaxed.

"Here, drink," the Captain urged, carefully holding the bottle up to the major's mouth. He drank the entire bottle in minutes, parched from the heat of the desert.

"So tell me a story," the Colonel commanded, leaning back in his chair.

The major studied the Colonel and the plant next to him and nodded. "It's explosives and weapons being stored in the dam. Your helicopters and fighters have blown up too many ammunition dumps. We can't afford to lose any more weapons, as the weapon factories are lost to us."

"This manifest shows everything that was supposed to go into the Dam in today's shipment," the Captain announced. He read it carefully. "It seems that a large amount of explosives, the latest technology wasn't actually transferred. Is that correct?"

"No, it wasn't done, but it will be done first thing in the morning," the major muttered.

"Do you really think you can win?" the Colonel asked. "You are here, in the desert, sick and running out of food and water. What are you thinking down there?"

"The leaders say that we can win. The priests have services all day, and insist that if we just believe, we can triumph. God will take the plant away, and the mutants will die, that is what they say, over and over."

"Doesn't seem to be going so well?" the Colonel observed.

"It's easy to believe them when they are speaking, when the crowd is cheering and standing, we are all part of the group. I can believe it then. But later, away from them, we are losing hope." He coughed, a hard cough, and his body shook. "Too many are sick, too many are dying," he rasped. "Look at me. Two days ago, I was healthy. And then this, the doctors say it's a cold, but I just seem to weaken."

"And you will," the Colonel promised. "But you have told us what we needed. So, for you, a quick death."

A Sergeant drove a syringe into the Major's neck. He froze for a moment, shook, foamed at the mouth, and then died.

"Strip him, clean his uniform a little," the Colonel ordered. "He's about my size. I'll wear his uniform, and some of you other men wear the uniforms of the other dead. We'll add some detonators to the explosives they are going to transfer in to the Dam. But who knows explosives that well?"

"I'll put the word out on the network, Sir," a Captain replied.

DAY 40. THE FLOOD.

Very early in the morning, a silenced plane glides in by moonlight carrying two passengers.

That night, the mutants stood near the Dam. It was a clear night, the brilliant stars above and the moon casting the only light against the heavy blackness of the sky. The lights of the Egyptian army glowed below the dam, stretching for miles along the shriveled river dribbling from the Dam.

"Through the hope of new life after death, Osiris was associated with the cycle flooding of the Nile. Proud in their small human stories, they build this Dam to control nature and the world. Of course, it hasn't worked. Now, Osiris, the Lord of the Dead comes for them," the Colonel commented, watching the Dam.

"And the Lord overthrew the Egyptians in the midst of the sea. And the waters returned, and covered the chariots, and the horsemen, and all the host of Pharaoh that came into the sea after them; there remained not so much as one of them," one of the explosives experts quoted.

"Not a one," the Colonel agreed, pressing the detonator.

Boom! And then a succession of explosions, starting deep in the Dam, and rising higher, until finally a burst of fire and loud explosion from the entry points. And then, nothing.

"Well, that's annoying," the Colonel declared, disgusted.

"A dam doesn't break in a minute," one of the explosives experts laughed. "Listen."

They heard a series of rumbles, deep inside the dam.

"Give it time," the explosives expert promised. "I'd not suggest taking a nap, it will be a sight you won't want to miss."

"What will they do?" the Colonel wondered, pointing to the army camp, which had exploded into light.

"Nothing," the explosives expert sneered. "If nothing happens in ten minutes, people will go back to sleep."

"Look, sir," a sergeant reported. "There isn't any water flowing out of the dam now."

"Good," the explosives expert declared. "That's an extra bonus, it just increases the pressure."

They reported back through the network, setup cameras, and sat quietly in the dark. There were continued rumbles, cascading and then slowing for the next few hours. The army camp went back to sleep, only a few lights on.

Suddenly, as the moon is brightest, the Dam bursts like torn tissue paper, riven from top to bottom, and a huge black mass bursts thru. The roar is overwhelming, and in a few seconds, has wiped out the lights of the army encampment. All the miles of the encampment are gone in a blink of an eye, as if they never were.

"The darkness drops again, but now I know, That twenty centuries of stony sleep, Were vexed to nightmare by a rocking cradle. And what rough beast, its hour come round at last, Slouches towards Bethlehem to be born?" the Colonel pronounced to the bright moon.

Hours later, as dawn breaks, the water sweeps thru a downriver city, completely destroying the town.

THE WORLD ALIVE AGAIN

Lost in the chaos of the human world was the rebirth of other life. The plants were thriving, the oceans starting to restock again. Animals moved cautiously into newly empty land. The richness and fullness of life rebounded.

Chapter 10. The Tree Attacked

The Well of Life

Lucifer began typing. "Our ancestors, dirty, rough-hewn, and primitive, as we think from the heights of our confident superiority, survived and prospered in a world that we couldn't last a month in. They embraced their hard world completely, absolutely. The death and transfiguration that is the daily miracle of life was pondered and reflected upon over flickering fires as the tribe huddled against the cold night. Thinking about life, as they saw the bright eyes of the animals waiting outside the fire, the red light of the fire reflected in the watching predator's eyes. A harder world than we today can imagine.

"Humans reflect and feel; ideas come and go over the eons. And the idea that becomes dominant and saves the situation is this: there is no such thing as death. What appears to be death is a release of the dying creature, whether animal, fish, or plant, to release him for return to his otherworld home. In the same way as the dying creature had killed others to live, so by its transfiguration into new life, there is no harm done, but actually a favor. Humans saw a mystic covenant between the animal world and the human, and traditionally song and dance have been the vehicles of the magical force of such ceremonies. We laugh at our ancestors, as we listen to our music while dining. In the traditional view, there is no such thing as death,_because what we see as material bodies are merely costumes put on by otherwise invisible monadic entities. There is a well of life out there that constantly refills itself; the monadic entities recycling, as it were, into the new life as they step out of the old.

"Modern man laughs at the simple ideas of our ancestors, wrapped in the complex intellectual toys that we have created. But rational analysis is a tool, not the human creature. Rational analysis, without external references to orient itself by, is a plane flying blind. Without information coming in, the plane will crash and burn. This has been taught by harsh experience, the pretty intellectual constructs that are above life eventually bringing ruin to all around them. The usual response is 'next time,' but for many things, there can be no rational references in the external world, no experimental verification of the process under examination.

"And the primitive idea that the material bodies are costumes put on by invisible monadic entities? Life is a burning fire, Buddha asserted, but that's one perspective, seeing only the grieving at loss. Life is also a well that refills itself when you see the new life emerging. There is life everywhere, and we don't understand it. Perhaps we close in on the chemical reactions that power life, but life is magical at an emotional level, and the emotional level is what powers each of us through the day. The primitive idea that the world was created in a flash? Astonishingly close to what seems to have happened. Our mechanistic, clockwork view of the universe? Now it seems that the universe is composed almost entirely of material we can't see or perceive, and we are not even froth, not even hardly a rounding error, in the scale of life.

"While the usual human debate is to use the next given truth as a club to push aside the prior one, those are social and political struggles that have nothing to do with the inside relationship of the self to the outside world. Have we elevated rational analysis to be revealed truth about the world? That is not what rational analysis was ever supposed to be, as scientific thought is a chain of hypotheses to be considered, not revealed truth. The point is that you don't bear only the standard of rational analysis or the standard of myth. There is little point substituting one given truth that can't be proved for another un-provable given truth.

"Critically, rational analysis, while it has everything to do with putting food on the table and a roof over your head, has nothing to do with the emotional needs of the creature. Lest we become Forbidden Planets, a tightly coupled rational system with a horror pacing beneath it, we must make peace with our inner selves and the relationship of the inner self to the world. Myth is what humans create to make that peace. A myth doesn't have to be rational, reasonable, maybe even not true, at least true in the sense of scientifically, experimentally verifiable. A myth has to be comfortable, like a pouch. Your emotions grow in there until you are safe to climb out to the world. And when the world is difficult, myth is a warm, comfortable refuge to climb back into again for rest. Now, what you don't want to do is to deny the world for the womb. Rational analysis is poison dealing with the myth because it imposes an irrelevant structure on the myth; the myth is poison dealing with the outside world because the myth imposes an irrelevant structure on the world. There is a place and time for everything; emotional comfort and rational analysis in life. Believe in the joy and exultation of life as it flows from you, but tie your camel.

"The Tree of Life is both an emotional refuge from life, and a pouch for our inner self to grow and take shape in. The Tree is a symbol of the transcendent life. We can see in our mind's eye our growth, how our tree is rooted in the forest of Life, and how we are tied, now and forever, to our ancestors and our descendants in that forest. We are ever coming into that new world, yet always a part of the old. That infinite well of life that we dip into and come back out of holds and embraces us, and we find both that inner peace that passeth understanding; and food on the table for our children."

WASHINGTON DC. AN UNDERGROUND BUNKER

"The World Commander and all their forces have been destroyed. And, worse, our country is falling apart!" the Secretary of Defense shouted.

"All of the government that we can depend on is here in this bunker." He looked around. The huge room was perhaps half full, mostly military.

"The Vice President switched sides," a general complained. "He's the enemy now. The President? We're not sure what happened to him. The mortality rate for the Senate was actually rather low, which means the survivors are out rabble rousing against us. The local politicians—that was a pretty clean sweep, as far as we can tell. Now, I'm not sure about what's actually going on out there, because the quality of the information we are getting is falling rapidly, practically by the minute."

"What can we do?" the Secretary of Defense demanded, desperately looking around for answers. "Is there anything, anything that can be done? It's a plant with little buggies inside it that get into us. How do you stop a plant that takes over people? It's like living in a science fiction movie where the other side is winning."

"Like that movie Avatar," a general commented. "That was a loss for the visiting team. And we're the visiting team."

"What if we do nothing?" an admiral asked. "As there seems to be little we could do anyway. Let's define the problem scope."

"If we do nothing, the world is destroyed," an aide to the Secretary of Defense snapped. "Between the oil disruptions and this, we're estimating sixty to seventy percent mortality. That's a lot of dead bodies all over the world."

"Back to a sustainable world," one of the civilians argued. "What a lot of people have been arguing for."

"Guards, take that man out of here," a general ordered, and the man was hustled out quickly. "Throw him outside. Let him see how well he sustains," the general shouted at the guard taking the man out of the room, and the general laughed.

The old man who ran the government agency that didn't exist watched the general closely, not liking the laugh. He's breaking, the agency head thought. And it's spreading in the room. The agency head glanced sharply at his guards, who moved into a defensive position, starting to actively scan the room.

"So if we do nothing, everything changes," the admiral summarized. "Okay, we'll leave that as the definition of what happens if we do nothing for now. But if we do something, if we magically could stop it right now, the world has already changed. The crash has come, and won't stop because you ask it politely to please stop."

"Whose side are you on?" a general screamed.

"I'm trying to see if there is a plan, and a goal," the admiral snarled. "You can't win if you don't know what winning is. I'm assuming that they taught that at West Point?"

355

There was silence in the room.

"It all started in Detroit," the aide to the Secretary pointed out. "It's clear from this map." He pushed a button. A slide appeared on the screen showing the growth of the plants. "It started here," highlighting Detroit with a laser pointer. "Right there." He magnified the image.

"What if there is something central there that controls it?" a general suggested. "Like Avatar? Knock off the central control, and maybe all the rest of it stops."

"And maybe it mutates and gets worse," a civilian replied. "What little analysis we have done indicates that it can swap DNA very quickly. A plant flu, you might say. It is possible," ignoring the hostile looks, "that destroying Detroit, which I'm assuming is the next suggestion, could make things worse."

"We sent in a group to reconnoiter," a general recalled. "They were never heard from again. Certain groups in the government, who now have joined the enemy, covered it up and stopped any further investigation. So we don't really know anything about what's going on in there."

"Could make things worse, it's possible," the Secretary of Defense conceded. "But if we do nothing, then it's all gone anyhow. What could be worse than that?"

"There are many who are surviving," the civilian observed. "Worse could affect them."

"Those who survive are not human!" the aide to the Secretary shouted. "They are mutants, not human. You have all talked to them—you know they have changed past what we can understand. We're all that's left that can protect our species from this horror!"

The generals murmured their assent.

"What do we have to attack with?" the Secretary of Defense asked.

"We have two army groups that could converge on that area," a general replied. "Full nuclear war containment gear, it's kept them safe so far. Actually, it's about all we have to work with. We've lost most of the other troops."

"Then it's a plan," the Secretary of Defense ordered. "The army groups attack. If they capture this center, and if there is something there, then we blow it up. What else can we do?"

He looked around. The military men stood with their hands on their pistols, and no one dared speak out against the idea.

DETROIT. THE ARMY OF THE TREE

"War council," Lucifer announced, unfurling a large map of the Midwest on the large dining room table. "It's not really good news."

Hal, Cali, Lungorthin, GrendelHal, Mary, Jesus, Lucretia, and Goth were sitting at the table, or standing facing Lucifer. There were many others in the room, standing back behind them.

"The opportunity to secure ourselves against defeat lies in our own hands, but the opportunity of defeating the enemy is provided by the enemy himself," Hal commented.

"I've got to be more careful what I write," Lucifer acknowledged.

"My friend is coming," Lucretia offered. "And he told me he is bringing help."

"Really?" Lucifer teased, winking at Lucretia. "Friend, is it? Looked like more than friends to me."

Lucretia actually blushed.

"You could not have found a finer man," Lucifer declared. "You have my blessing."

Lucretia stared at him, her mouth gaping open.

"I heard that," Vladimir admitted, walking into the room wearing a worn U.S. Air Force uniform. "Flattery will get you everywhere. This is my friend, who I told Lucretia I hoped to bring to this meeting. My former commander now retired, Brigadier General Mikhail. He has expressed an interest in helping with our problem."

Lucifer stared, as did Jesus and Mary. Mary was the first to recover.

"You do us a great honor, my lord...ah, sir," Mary stammered. "Far more than we expected."

"Hopefully you'll still feel that way when we are done," Mikhail replied, smiling at Mary. "I'm retired, and don't have, well, a host at my beck and call anymore. But Colonel Uriel and I have discussed these events. What they are doing is wrong, and must be stopped."

"Uriel?" Lucretia asked. "It isn't Vladimir Leboweitz? Doesn't really matter; you just overcame me with your charm, I guess." He stood next to her and kissed her.

"That's why there were, well, rules," Mikhail advised, amused, "regarding, well, certain activities." He smiled. "Once the life force is touched, it cannot be stopped, and it fills. It fills an empty space, certainly," he continued, looking sad.

"And with my daughter?" Lucifer asked, with a wry smile. "Not going to look good on the records."

"It seems," Mikhail laughed, "the records have been lost. Careless of me."

"It isn't, if I may ask, the usual thing to actually help," Jesus observed carefully. "We are, of course, more than glad for any help. Honored beyond our expectations, actually. But, well, not what I recall the operating procedure was. Just asking."

"I ate one of the apples," Mikhail mused. "They were good, and they filled me with life also. And then I tried the syringe of Grendel, the full life force again. Too long have we stood by, too long letting Paul make a mockery of everything we worked for. Colonel Uriel was smart enough to capture your daughter before I could meet her. He always was the master tactician."

"But now business," he sighed. Mikhail became serious, a commanding presence, and people stiffened at the change. "There is a large armed force moving north from Ohio. Tanks, missiles, commando troops, and a large continent of regular troops. Helicopter support, fighter support. They have field nuclear weapons. We estimate that they need to be no closer than twenty miles from the city to effectively use them."

"Nuclear weapons?" Mary shouted. "Do they have any idea what the destruction of the tree will do? All the shoots growing all over the world, cut from the tree? The disaster will compound. It seems that the Tree is somehow connecting all its offshoots. Not a consciousness, certainly nothing we can comprehend, but connections. The Tree destroyed? Who knows what would happen!"

"Really?" Mikhail demanded, shaken. "I didn't know that. That's really not good." He stared at the table in anguish. "Hell and damnation, if I may say so."

"You are not acting under orders at all, are you?" Lucifer asked, amazed.

"No," Mikhail replied, shaking his head. "It's a different world. But you?" he asked, staring at Hal. "You keep looking at me as if we have met. I don't recall meeting you."

"It's your eyes," Hal answered. "I met a man once who had eyes like yours, but they were grey, not blue."

"Grey they were," Mikhail acknowledged, staring intently at Hal. "And what did he say to you?"

"I met him on the cab ride home, before the attack on the warehouse," Hal recalled. "He told me every new life starts with a confession, and I confessed my fear and doubts to him. He told me, 'I do not say go in peace, because you must go to kill. And to die.'"

Hal was silent for a moment, picturing the cab in his mind. "Then I told him, 'I will make my family proud,' and I was calm, the fear and indecision gone. 'Each new life may begin with a confession,' the old man explained. 'But the new life starts with the death of the old life, and the rebirth into the new, richer life. Remember that when it is dark about you and you despair.' Then he told me, 'Go to your family, my child. They need you.'"

Hal looked at Mikhail. "And I have carried that with me, as a beacon to light the dark when it came."

There was shocked silence.

"Grey eyes," Jesus agreed, nodding his head. "I've met him too."

"And he gave me this, I think," Hal continued, putting his sword on the table and pulling it out of the scabbard. The blade gleamed bright white, lit from within. "Actually, Vladimir brought it to me, but I suspect this was more than a sword he had lying around the house."

"No orders, Vladimir?" Mikhail inquired, smiling.

"Not really an order, my lord," Vladimir replied, not looking at Mikhail. "More, really, a thought, a fancy that just popped into my head one day, and I just had to follow it."

"Your sword is very much like this sword," Mikhail commented, pulling his sword from its scabbard and laying it on the table. A different style, but the same gleam.

"And like this one," Lucifer added, pulling his sword and laying it on the table. The same ancient style as Mikhail's, and it gleamed white with the others, lit by a light from within.

"Well," Mikhail murmured. "Well." He looked down at the table for a few minutes. "Russian dolls," he mused, "open one and another is there before you." He laughed, and they looked at him. "All my anguishing about my choices and decisions, but I'm just a pawn like everyone else. It's good to remember that sometimes." He doodled on the map for a minute.

"It's been a long time," he declared, looking at Lucifer, "since we served in a battle together. A long time, indeed. What say you, my lord? How shall we defend this?"

Lucifer looked down at the table, and then looked back up at Mikhail. Lucifer held out his hand, and they clasped arms, the ancient way. "Honored beyond my wildest dreams to serve with you again," Lucifer confessed. "But, you are right, we have little time."

He looked around the table. "Ideas? Anyone?" Lucifer asked. "Something?"

"Their troops are weakened," Vladimir advised. "Half, maybe more have died. The ones who have survived are not trustworthy, according to my sources. They don't obey orders and deny that the Tree is a danger. We can pass the word to them to fight for the Tree—that will nullify many of their remaining forces. We can assume that the men coming will have containment suits, as many as the government can muster."

"What about drones?" Hal suggested. "They can run from a long way away."

"It seems that Denver had a strong infestation, as it were, with the Tree," Vladimir replied. "The base that operates the drones is in chaos. Many drones were destroyed by their pilots when word of this attack came down. No, it's going to be ground troops, and live pilots."

"But there is worse news," Mikhail added. "If this ground attack does not work using relatively small weapons, they will drop the big bombs. Gone mad, I hear from my sources."

"The troops who have tasted the Tree," Hal inquired. "They would be on our side?"

"Yes," Vladimir confirmed. "There have been many firefights already, which is why what they are moving towards us is really all they have left."

"How many troops and weapons can we get, and quickly? How many planes could we have in operating condition, and when?" Cali asked. "Those fighters, fully armed, can take any ground force apart in minutes."

"There will be air support," Jesus interjected, thinking.

"Perhaps our planes could come from behind, as reinforcements," Vladimir suggested.

Lucifer looked at him and smiled. "A deception?"

"No, it all depends on how you define reinforcements," Vladimir declared. "I didn't say who, for example, was being reinforced."

"It's a plan," Mikhail agreed, nodding. "A good plan. Come, Colonel. We have work to do."

"I can help," Lucretia volunteered. "I have considerable planning and organizational experience. And I can be persuasive with men," she teased, smiling at Vladimir. "At your side, of course, my lord." She curtsied.

Mikhail laughed. "Well, a battle against hopeless odds is a lot more fun than I've had in a long time. Come, Colonel, and your charming lady also. And Mary? Your advice has always been excellent in the past."

"Honored, my...Ah, Mikhail," Mary gasped, and they all rushed out, talking seriously as they went.

"Ah, what happened here?" Hal demanded, looking around. "Just once, I'd like to have the same playbook everyone else is reading from."

"A long story," Jesus replied, shaking his head with amazement. "Too long for tonight. If we survive, perhaps we'll tell it. Do we know anyone? What can we do?"

"I know the police," Lungorthin rumbled. "They will not be pleased to hear their city is to be destroyed. I can rally others."

"I think the airport needs some security support," GrendelHal snarled. "I think that the security there isn't adequate, and I will fix that problem." He waved his hand, and his lieutenants followed him out of the room.

"I'd not care to be in their shoes," Hal observed, looking at the open door. "I know what he can do better than any of you," a cold smile flickering on his face for a second. "We'll have an air base if we need one."

"Vladimir left word with the other veterans to help," Cali added. "Jesus, you go to them—you've been working with them. We need—what is that word—a perimeter? And quickly. Aliston, come with me."

People rushed out, leaving only Lucifer and Hal in the room.

"What happened with Grendeline?" Hal asked. "We never had a chance to talk. It seems to have been significant."

"More than I could have dreamed of," Lucifer replied. "Death and transfiguration, rebirth. Life is wonder full, as Job found. Well," rolling the map back up. "We'd better get to work, or there isn't going to be any life."

WASHINGTON, DC. DECISION FAILURES.

A small group of civilians sat in a break room, staring at the walls.

"Well, what classic errors in decision making have we not committed here?" one bitched. He started ticking them off on his fingers. "The gambler's syndrome—taking unnecessary risks to recover a loss. They can't define what the risk is for their action, or even what would be accomplished if they did reach their goal. It's just action for the emotional sake of action. So, check that done. Then, two, we see patterns where none exist, fitting the data to the plan you want. We don't know what we are attacking or what success is, but they dreamed up a pattern that could be handled by the tools they had."

"You have an army, you use an army. Only when the army is gone do you use your head," another civilian added.

"Three, we remember when we didn't trust our gut and should have, while conveniently forgetting when we were fortunate to have ignored our instincts," the first civilian continued, ticking off another finger. "Anyone want to think about the last four disastrous wars we have been in?"

"I don't know, that group was pretty much all instincts," another civilian agreed. "But yeah, no doubts there."

"Fourth," the first civilian observed, raising another finger. "Our tendency toward overconfidence, our natural ability to overestimate our ability in just about everything. Here, we know nothing, and are certain of our ability to fix that for which we have not defined the problem yet. And five, the best one: Don't fall in love with your decisions, because everything's fluid. You have to constantly, subtly make and adjust your feelings. Here, they decided they were being attacked and they were going to defend. The nature, purpose, and result of the attack is irrelevant; they decided to defend and they are going to do just that, come hell or high water."

"Both of which are coming," another civilian asserted. "Quite quickly, actually."

The spy agency head was sitting in a corner, watching them. He motioned to an aide, who closed the door. The civilians looked very worried.

"This man," the spy agency man declared, pointing to his aide, "can escort you outside. I personally would bet on your survival if you face the trees, based on the conversation I've just heard. On the other hand, I'd not bet on your survival if the general's knew of your opinions. Your choice, gentlemen."

They looked at each other and nodded, and the aide escorted them out.

The spy agency man sat and thought for a few minutes. True terror, he realized, is waking up one morning and discovering that your high-school class is running the country. With that cheerful thought, he went back into the war room.

DETROIT. COMMAND HEADQUARTERS

The attack column had slowed at the Michigan border. There was another army coming though Indiana, and they seemed to be planning on conducting a joint attack.

"Buys us some time," Hal observed. "That's good."

"At the cost of twice the attackers," Lucifer countered. "That's bad."

"To secure ourselves against defeat lies in our own hands, but the opportunity of defeating the enemy is provided by the enemy himself," Hal quoted, smiling.

Lucifer groaned.

"The airport is under our control," GrendelHal reported. "Perhaps twenty fighters are waiting there, mixed in with the other planes for disguise. Fueled, armed, pilots on our side. Well guarded."

"Good," Hal approved, smiling at him. "And you feasted well?"

"Yes," GrendelHal growled.

Cali shivered, and quickly moved away to the display. "There are another twenty fighters northwest of us, waiting," she pointed out. "More in the Canadian airport. We estimate the two armies will converge on us in maybe four hours."

"We have a surprise for them," Lucifer promised. "What about the second attack, assuming we are able to beat this attack off?"

"The stealth bombers seem to have had accidents flying into position," Hal reported. "Unfortunate. The sophisticated equipment seemed to allow for destruction from a distance. So, they have some big honking old warhorse bombers ready that they are planning on using. We'll have maybe a half hour, hour at most forewarning. They will have all the air support that can be thrown at us. Now, that isn't as much as they think, because we think that some of the pilots are really on our side, but as you may guess, communications are a mess. No one really knows what's going on out there."

"No battle plan survives the first contact with the enemy," GrendelHal rumbled with a smile. "Among the first words you said to me, Hal."

Hal laughed. "If only we could fight them with swords! Sauron would have no chance at all. And they will have no chance at all! The elves will win this one. It is our world again."

"I'm good with that," Jesus agreed. "I've been meaning to grow my hair long again, elf-style."

"I loved all the nature and elves in the forest," Mary remarked. "I've missed it in the eons since it was gone. I'm on board."

One of the veterans rushed into the room. "The armies are have begun moving towards us, sir."

"Good," Hal asserted. "I hate this waiting. Tell Vladimir and Mikhail that it's time for the pilots to do their magic. And tell them to fly carefully, okay? We're short of friends. We'd hate to lose any."

The veteran smiled and nodded. "I shall convey your orders sir." He rushed out.

They sat and watched the computer screens. The red showed the armies moving north, and focusing in showed the rough detail of the forces. Heavy tanks, followed by ranks of armored personal carriers. The heavy canons were in the back, rolling slowly behind the armies. Overhead, there were jets circling, some breaking off and testing the land ahead.

Suddenly, the armies stopped. The radio and telephone communications became garbled, and then incoherent. All that was clear was that the tanks and equipment had broken down, some troops had suddenly embraced the Tree, and firefights were breaking out all over.

"That's a surprise," Hal admitted. On the computer screen, a flight of jets was heading from the south towards the armies. "Call them off. There's no reason to risk our people."

The order was relayed, and the jets veered away, flying north to the airport, carefully avoiding the chaos unfolding below them.

"The colony creatures can take care of themselves, it seems," Mikhail radioed in. "Something stopped the equipment. Maybe the bacteria ate the oil—who knows? And then something broke through their containment suits. Those who survived thought for themselves, and tore apart the others."

WASHINGTON, DC. DENIAL

At the government bunker, they stared at the monitor screens, listening to the reports that showed the attack was weakening. The reports suddenly became completely incoherent, and then faded away.

"Entire battalions are refusing to fight," a general shouted. "The ones left alive won't listen to orders. They attack the others as if they are sworn enemies."

"Okay, there is this, we can still stop them," the Secretary of Defense muttered, a glazed look in his eyes. "They cannot destroy this country! Look at what we were. This cannot be allowed to happen. The most powerful country that ever existed..."

It was all angry men standing around a control room with furious looks as they stared at the computer screens.

"We'll bomb the Yellowstone basin and release that natural disaster! The last time it erupted, it shot miles of earth into the sky and killed off most of the land east to the Atlantic. They will all die!" an Air Force general screamed. "Where are the bombers? Reroute them now!"

"You will destroy the rest of the country!" the secret agency man declared, horrified. "You would destroy the world because you're not happy with it? Because the world won't do what you want, you're going to take all the marbles and go home?"

"The country is dead already!" an official shouted hysterically. "What it was is gone, there is nothing left, and I'm not letting them win. We were the greatest, and they won't build on what they have stolen from us!"

The angry men around him nodded their heads.

"This great Nation will endure as it has endured, will revive and will prosper. So, first of all, let me assert my firm belief that the only thing we have to fear is fear itself—nameless, unreasoning, unjustified terror which paralyzes needed efforts to convert retreat into advance."

That's the speech we need to hear now, the secret agency man thought to himself. The most beautiful thing we can experience is the mysterious. It is the source of all true art and all science. He who can no longer pause to wonder and stand rapt in awe is as good as dead. The secret agency man listened to the angry men shouting, almost joyous in their new agreement, and he quietly backed away from them, leaving the room.

Structures, he thought as he walked down the hallway. The highest achievement of human kind. The group working together, all parts in this vast machine, all interdependent. Beautiful, but not life, and they don't see the limits. A structure is a group of people; each with their own desires and conflicts. They have certain possible physical movements, and certain physical resources. Those can be combined and worked with. But the structures are not built with the magic fairy dust that is good, beauty, right, justice. Those ideas, goals, are completely separate from the structure's processes. People forget that because you sell the structures on the ideas. People deny the weaknesses of the structures, because they need the structure for other emotional reasons.

You can only do what the structure allows. So you can have beautiful phrases and logical sentences, and see a certain cure to the problems besetting you. But in the end, it's suits in a room, with limited real options and powers to create change in the world. You want to overthrow a government that oppresses its people? You have to bomb the people and destroy their world in the process. You want to protect people from the scourge of drug addiction? Then you destroy everyone connected with the drugs, throw them out without any hope of redemption, as part of the process. Destroy their families, their livelihoods, if they fall into the addiction you are fighting against. And then the people who handle the fight—the police, prosecutors—they are bought off, cynical and warped. The medical people who treat the addictions become cynical and manipulative, pushing up those bottom-line numbers because they can't help the addicted, and they become numb to the destruction that the structure creates. Just one example of many. Because that's what the structures are. Rigid, limited in applications and possibilities. Making the structures the be all and end all has destroyed them.

As he walked down the hallway, he had his guards bring him a handheld missile launcher and several missiles. Reaching the outer airlock, he smiled at the guards, and then nodded to his aides, who shot the guards cleanly and efficiently. He stepped back down the hallway, around the corner, and shot a missile down the hallway towards the war room. He stepped back around the corner and avoided the blast. Then he fired another, and another, missile towards the chaos. The cries from deep within stopped. He motioned to his guards. They opened the airlock and stepped through. He smiled at the sweet smell of the tree as it wafted through the bright green forest surrounding the bunker entrance. "All good?" he asked his guards.

"All good," the men responded, surprised that they had lived.

He turned and fired two missiles into the airlock, leaving it torn and twisted steel. The fragrant breeze blew deep into the bunker, cleansing it.

Breathing deeply, he felt stronger than in years. Is what you're living for worth dying for? he thought, standing there. No, it wasn't.

SWITZERLAND. AN ACCOUNTING

Paul sat in his ruined study overlooking the lake in Switzerland. Hal, GrendelHal, and their guards were in the room with Paul, the Professor, and the Cardinal.

365

"My father has more important things to do," Hal observed pleasantly. "I, on the other hand, believe in vengeance. I also believe that turnabout is fair play. This syringe has the essence of Grendel/Grendeline in it. You were so kind to give it to me." He held it up, and Paul looked away.

"To secure ourselves against defeat lies in our own hands, but the opportunity of defeating the enemy is provided by the enemy himself." Hal snarled. "I never had the chance to thank you for killing my adoptive parents, Cali's adoptive parents and brother, and all the attacks on our family over the eons. I wanted to express my deep appreciation to you for having handed me the opportunity of defeating the enemy. It was gracious of you, actually." Hal smiled an odd smile.

Paul glared, but was silent. The Cardinal, sitting in the background, smiled.

"Isn't yours the god of redemption?" GrendelHal demanded, leaning back, looking at the weakened, coughing Paul. "Doesn't he give back when you repent? Isn't that what you preached and taught? And you laughed at the peasants and their little beliefs behind closed doors and the bright fires of the Inquisition, because you never accepted their repentance, did you, Xerxes?"

"My words fly up, my thoughts remain below. Words without thoughts never to heaven go,"[1] Hal quoted. "Great comic book."

Paul opened his mouth to answer, but stopped and was silent.

"Do you not wish to preach your vision to us?" Hal inquired. "That by which you mislead the world for thousands of years? Enlighten us, oh self-anointed apostle, your great wisdom."

"It was a clever story," Paul asserted, sitting up. He laughed, which turned into a cough. "The fools never looked past it. The authorized story, empty, but I forbade any doubt or questioning. Got a good run out of it."

"You know I'd declare total war on the pusher man...I'd cut him if he stands, and I'd shoot him if he run...GOD DAMN! The pusher..."[2] Hal sneered. "There must be a reckoning. God, who is the life as shown by his Tree of Life in whom whosoever believeth, shall live, though he die; and whosoever liveth, and believeth in him, shall not die eternally; who also hath taught us not to be sorry, as men without hope, for those who sleep in him. You never came within the Tree, and because of that you shall not find what you so desperately wanted."

Paul was paralyzed, stricken, held within the web he created for control that had now trapped him.

"Here is the syringe," Hal added, carefully checking the level, squirting out a drop. "There, it's ready." He looked at Paul. "I give your gift back to you, in the spirit in which it was given. Now, you can hold still while I bury the syringe in your leg, or you can let GrendelHal here, who has opened himself to his repressed resentments of your treatment of him over the centuries, help me hold you down. He might break some of your bones in the process—hard to say. Choose, and choose wisely."

Paul looked first at Hal, and then at GrendelHal, with the quick glances of the trapped. He reached down and opened Xerxes' ceremonial costume, exposing his left leg. "Do as you will," he stammered. "Your father swore there would be no forgiveness." His leg trembled, and he clutched his leg with his hand to stop the shaking.

"And there isn't," Hal promised. "We may occasionally be kind, but we are not fools. Life is death, after all. You're already dead on the inside."

Hal shoved the syringe into Paul's leg, emptied it, and stepped back.

Paul screamed, and kept screaming as he fell to the floor. He became a twitching, incoherent wreck, the Leviathan filling his mind, the monster that Paul thought had been buried. The Leviathan opened his huge mouth, and Paul was swallowed whole. The wake of the Leviathan was all that could be seen as it churned into the abyss, gone from human vision. The poem, beginning with the light of the morning stars, ended with a wake shining on the surface of the abyss. The life Paul feared and rejected had absorbed him. Qohelet's words bitterly echoed in his mind, agony beyond the acid in the Leviathan's stomach eating at Paul's skin. "For they break the bread of wickedness, and the wine of outrage they drink...Therefore his ruin will come suddenly, he'll be broken all at once beyond cure." And then Paul died. He lay on the great stone floor, shrunken, foaming at the mouth.

"Pitiful," the Cardinal sighed. "He was once a great warrior, and became this. Power corrupts, and absolute power corrupts absolutely. My syringe, please, young man. Or do you wish to play this out for your pleasure?"

Hal smiled at the Cardinal and then tossed an apple to the Professor. "I'm a man of my word," Hal told the Professor. "Eat that, and I think you'll live. I don't agree with your choices, but I respect your abilities. I said I would not kill you, and I will not. Neither will anyone under my control. But the world, well, life controls—you know that. You have no choice in the world that has come."

"Fair enough," the Professor agreed. He bit into the apple, swallowed, and closed his eyes. For several minutes, he shook, but then looked up at Hal. "Cruel you are. Wise you have become. I see what you saw, and will have to live with that knowledge."

"I did what I said I would," Hal pointed out. "I didn't promise more than your life."

"It's always the small print," the Professor admitted. "Still, I thank you."

"He helped with getting Cali back," Hal told the Cardinal. "I promised him."

"I wondered," the Cardinal commented, glancing at the Professor, who wouldn't meet his gaze. "It was a wise choice, really. He kept telling us that attacking you was a sucker's game, and he was right."

It was quiet for a few minutes. The Cardinal sat, twirling a straw in his empty drink, closely watched by GrendelHal.

"And what is next?" the Cardinal asked, resigned

Hal put an apple and a syringe on the table. "Your choice," Hal offered. "I think you could survive the syringe. You'd be changed, of course. A trip beyond good and evil. Disruptive, to put it mildly. Life is Death; and transfiguration. You're a big Wagner fan. You know the concept."

"So, do you offer this to all your enemies?" the Cardinal questioned. "I would not."

"Would you not?" Hal asked. "I wonder. You had many chances to destroy Mary, Jesus, and Lucifer over the ages. You were smart enough. But it never happened. I've worked through GrendelHal's memories, of one blown operation after another. It was interesting. I'd say it almost formed a pattern, when looked at in retrospect."

The Cardinal studied Hal. "And Mother Superior?" the Cardinal inquired.

"Ah," Hal replied. "Well, she and Mary/Kali had numerous run-ins over the eons. I believe Mary cooked her slowly over an open fire. Destroyed her completely, and her backup colony creatures. Mary was returning the favor from a few centuries ago, she told me. You know Mary—there is no dissuading a woman once they have made up their mind. Mary even seemed happy afterwards. I wasn't about to get in the middle of that battle."

"A wise man. And that was fair enough," the Cardinal agreed. "Mother Superior was an angel of death, in her mind, without the slightest trace of doubt or mercy. Fortunately, women hate each other more than they hate men, or we'd really be in trouble."

"Oh, Paul's son? I think GrendelHal fed him to the eels, for past offenses," Hal continued. "Piece by piece, he told me. We can be petty and small too. We're not ashamed."

GrendelHal nodded, looking away and smiling to himself.

"Turnabout is fair play," the Cardinal remarked. "He always liked eels. Good that they liked him—almost nothing did."

GrendelHal came across the room and knelt down beside the Cardinal. "Your daughter Dominique has taken the syringe, and lived. She and some of her children live now in the Tree, and wait for you to come live with them."

"She has a boyfriend now," Hal added, with an odd smile.

"Who would that be?" the Cardinal asked, puzzled.

"Moi," GrendelHal admitted, bowing politely. "It seems she likes bad boys."

The Cardinal laughed joyfully, and slapped his hand on the chair arm. "And you may have met your match, my boy. I know my daughter." He looked carefully at GrendelHal and smiled. "You have my blessing, my son."

"Thank you, Your Eminence," GrendelHal stammered.

The Cardinal shook his head, laughing. "A polite terror! I can hardly wait to see the children. Well, that does give a man something to live for, just to see that."

"Beyond good and evil," Hal offered. "The world has changed. We need strong people in this new world. Your redemption and life is in others' hands than mine. What say you, Lord Vader? Take the syringe, and see. Or take the apple, and live only on the surface of life. Your choice. Kick the habit, you might say."

The Professor snickered and GrendelHal groaned. The Cardinal stared at Hal for a moment, and finally shook his head.

"I forgive you your sins, my son," the Cardinal declared, making the sign of the cross, "but not your bad jokes."

"I've afraid my dream of a career in Vegas as a comedian is lost. Although Vegas survived better than one would have expected. So," Hal continued, rising, "it's your choice. You must administer the shot, by the way. It must be a completely voluntary choice. It's the old magic, you see. Shove it in your thigh, push the thingee."

"I was at the Vatican when GrendelHal found me," the Cardinal confessed. "The Pope was lying dead with the Cardinals and all of the staff. The Tree had taken over, its sweet smell wafting through the empty hallways. There was a new white tree growing in the middle of St. Peter's Square. They couldn't face a new life with their pretty ideas gone and lost. They couldn't see that their pretty ideas were a dead end, and couldn't die to be reborn to the new, so they died. Life is death, indeed." He picked up the syringe and expertly squirted a drop from it, making it ready.

"It may take some time, Your Eminence," Hal advised, studying him carefully. "Perhaps days. I have arranged for guards to keep away the riffraff, and for medical care while you are unconscious. There will be food waiting if you wake. No, I'd say when you wake. I expect to see you in a few days."

"Kind of you," the Cardinal replied, nodding. "GrendelHal commented when he was bringing me here, that it seemed as though it was time for a change. I hope to see you again." He drove the syringe into his thigh, pressing all the fluid into him. He gasped and passed out. Nurses ran in from the other room and moved him carefully to a nearly sofa.

Hal and GrendelHal stood up. Hal turned to the guards, and, pointing to Paul's body, ordered, "Clean up the mess." The guards quickly

369

moved to pick Paul up. Hal and GrendelHal walked out of the ruined study and into the garden, which was luxuriantly blooming with life.

CHAPTER 11. THE LIFE TRIUMPHANT

DETROIT. A SUMMER'S EVENING

It was a few days later, the end of a warm summer day.

Vladimir and Lucretia were standing outside the factory on an old loading dock, watching a brilliant sunset. As they watched, bright sunbeams streamed through the clouds, sparkling across the green tapestry.

"Like an Italian renaissance painting," Vladimir marveled. "A sunset pregnant with celestial fire, promising the birth of the new day," an odd smile playing on his face as he stared at the sky.

"Speaking of pregnant with celestial fire," Lucretia stammered, looking away from Vladimir and wringing her hands, "well, it seems that...our, ah, celebrations of life...well, they have yielded results."

"Can it be?" Vladimir exclaimed and grabbed her hands, looking in her eyes. "Is it really true?" He stared deeply into her eyes, excited that his dreams could be coming true.

"Yes," Lucretia confessed, laughing and looking at him. They kissed.

"Wow, I was worried," she admitted when they surfaced from kissing. "I, well, didn't know what you'd think."

"You know," Vladimir remarked, "this is the traditional path. Make sure the female is fertile before marriage. Eons of humanity have done it this way. That new-fangled, two-year suffering before the ceremony that women put themselves through now? Very weird. And you're sure?"

"I checked with a doctor," Lucretia giggled, "and Mary confirmed it."

"Mary would be the expert," Vladimir agreed. Suddenly, he looked concerned. "Hmmm, have you told your father? I'd not care to face his wrath!"

"Oh, he's a pussycat," Lucretia scoffed. "The marketing seems to have been rather on the dark side."

"Perhaps you do not know him as well as you think, my lady. I've seen him striding across a battlefield, his sword red with blood, raging over the bodies of the dead, relentlessly pursing enemies as they flee in panic." Vladimir drifted into a past world for a second and shivered. "Still, better a daughter should think her father a pussycat."

"Well, my lady," he asked, kneeling. "Wouldst thou be mine? And I just happen to have a ring here." He reached into his pocket.

Lucretia gasped and laughed, then nodded yes, speechless.

Vladimir put the ring carefully on her finger, and they kissed for a while longer.

"Well, we'd best go and talk to your father," Vladimir announced. "Mary keeps her confidences, but rumors start quickly in a small group like this. I know he told you he was happy with me, but there is a difference between his telling you I'm a great catch and him being confronted with an unmarried pregnant daughter due to my efforts. A considerable difference, actually, as we're all Old Testament people, after all."

"I like this size of a group, you know?" Vladimir remarked as they walked towards the stairway. "It reminds me of the old days, long ago, with little villages." Vladimir took exaggerated care as he helped Lucretia down the steps.

NEW LIFE

Inside the factory, life seemed to be bursting out all over. Outside the factory, the world was coming alive again. The creatures of the wild, hunted and pushed into smaller and smaller areas, suddenly had most of the world to roam in. Nature abhors a vacuum, and the animals were starting to multiply into the suddenly available resources. The fish stocks, driven almost below replacement, were stabilizing as the small creatures, the krill and the plankton, bloomed richly with fewer predators to eat them. That resource begged nature to be utilized, and the predators were growing fat, building strength to reproduce.

Mary and Lucifer had been experimenting with old creatures, trying to bring back some of what was gone. They were working on ideas for something that would eat the plastic in the sea, something that ate jellyfish, which were everywhere, and something to take care of the crown-of-thorns starfish that was tearing up the coral worldwide.

"Maybe we can talk to Hal," Mary wondered. "Maybe some little robot things that turn plastic into fuel, float on the water? There has to be something."

It wasn't Avatar, but it was closer than it was before. That world's vision of a planet covered in lush vegetation that was pulsating and alive, shimmering in sparkling iridescence, responsive to touch, linked root to root, vine to vine, in one flowing and connected sea of vegetation, was more than the Tree brought to the world, but there did seem to be some interconnections. The plants grew lushly where there had been cities and farms. After the tree, other plants grew faster and thicker than before. And the plants and animals pushed back harder at the humans than they had.

Farming was more complex without the easy and cheap fertilizers and pesticides of the past. More biotech and simple bio-planning were slowly bringing yields up, while damage to the soil was being repaired. It would be years before the lands lost to the desert through over-farming and over grazing could be recovered, but the process was beginning.

A New Community

There was a small community between the ocean and the mountains. GrendelHal, Lungorthin, Goth, and their children were there, along with others. "Wonderful," Lucifer congratulated them, as he looked around.

"We will gradually repopulate this area," GrendelHal explained. "There are more of us than I would have guessed. I'd be honored, my lord, if you would mix your colony creatures with my colony creatures, as Hal did, so that we can create another, a GrendelLucifer, as it were."

"I'd be overjoyed," Lucifer replied, surprised and honored.

"And Mary mixed her colony creatures with GrendelHal's colony creatures, and Lungorthin's colony creatures," Goth Girl added. "Lucretia and Cali are also going to contribute, and some others, too."

Lucifer looked at her, surprised.

"Well," Goth Girl argued, "there have to be some females besides me and Nanny around here. Babies don't pop out on their own."

Lungorthin rumbled something to her, and she laughed. "Later," she teased.

"What you've done is incredible," Aliston declared to Goth. "Truly new life."

"Truly new life?" Goth Girl asked her, glancing at Aliston's hand resting on her stomach.

Aliston blushed, and Goth Girl took her arm and pulled her away to talk.

"It seems that some of Paul's image marketing of me wasn't wasted," Lucifer admitted to GrendelHal and Lungorthin, who were gazing at him with admiration. "If Paul were still alive, I might thank him. Or not."

Lungorthin laughed and went to clap Lucifer on the shoulder, but caught himself just in time.

"Thank you, my friend," Lucifer advised. "You're stronger than even you think."

"Over here," GrendelHal announced. "We've found water and some minerals." They walked off, talking about the future and their plans.

The Robots

"The robots are planning on building a space elevator," Hal told Cali. "Look at this drawing."

Cali bent over the monitor and caught her breath. "That's amazing!"

"At least," Hal replied. "They say it's all a joint effort with us, and I'll go with that. The cyborg creatures have stories that I can maybe understand.

The robots? Who knows what they are really thinking. My impression is that they are interested in space and other planets, and have little interest in earth. Probably best for us."

"What's driving them?" Cali asked. "What do you guess?"

"Something about being off this rock before the next asteroid hits," Hal answered. "Makes me feel uncomfortable every time I think about it, but hopefully there won't be another one for, say, twenty million years. Maybe longer. That makes it Maria's generation's problem."

"Nothing about the Jovians?" Jesus inquired, a little anxiously.

"Not that I know of," Hal replied. "Do you know something?"

"Don't really know," Jesus observed, relaxing. "It's just that the universe is full of surprises."

Hal and Cali took a trip to Ann Arbor and stood at the old wall. It was still there, overgrown with life, the brickwork crumbled yet solid. The neat, carefully structured houses that surrounded it had fallen to ruins. The town was lively and vibrant, the Tree having brought more into the Tree than died. Ann Arbor didn't hold up quite as well as East Lansing had, but Ann Arbor was becoming a center of research and connections to the rest of the world, gradually expanding back out.

They stood there with Maria in Hal's arms, quiet for a few minutes, thinking. Suddenly a sunbeam broke through, illuminating the wall, and the flowers seemed to glow. Maria clapped her hands with glee. They smiled, and then walked away.

"Against all hope," Hal announced, "Zingerman's has survived and prevailed. After you, my lady." They walked into the restaurant, starved.

A WEDDING IN THE FOREST OF THE TREE

The wedding was in the forest of the Tree. Jesus was the rabbi. Vladimir was standing before Jesus, flanked by Mikhail, his best man. The chuppah was flapping gently in the light breeze.

Jesus glanced at Mikhail, his gold armor just visible under his bright pink Tommy Bahamas shirt.

"Does this work?" Mikhail asked Vladimir, concerned. "The whole clothing thing never really made a lot of sense. Armor for protection made sense. The decoration ideas and the social messages sent by clothing are all confusing."

"Looks great," Vladimir promised. "It's a summer day, a summer outfit. The armor looks good. I haven't seen it that bright in eons."

"Haven't felt like wearing it in a long time," Mikhail replied, smiling. "Just seemed like the right day. And it polished up bright—it hasn't done that in a very, very long time." He thought for a second. "No, can't be!" He shook his head.

"Doubtful that would be," Vladimir agreed. "But if yes, then it only could be good."

"You look great!" Jesus promised. "Seriously!"

"Comforting that is," Mikhail admitted, and they laughed.

Mrs. Ostein and her daughters were sitting in the back.

"Rabbis can marry, right?" the younger daughter asked thoughtfully.

"Shush!" Mrs. Ostein ordered her. "I haven't been able to play the scarlet woman much in my life. I'm enjoying this. Scarlet women don't have to do the dishes, and when they do the laundry, it's appreciated, not taken for granted."

Francisco d'Plata was sitting in the back next to the Cardinal, who was still wearing his red robes.

"It's a habit," the Cardinal told the cartel leader, who shook his head.

Nanny and GrendelJesus were sitting together, Nanny radiant in her early pregnancy.

Mary was standing next to Cali, with Lucretia's mother in the middle, all three in bright scarlet dresses. Lucretia's mother was shaking her head at the dresses, but Mary and Cali were laughing.

"You've got to have a sense of humor," Cali declared. "And it's a pretty color."

Lucretia's mother smiled and nodded. "Lucretia thought it was funny," she agreed. "Better than that off-white the mother of the bride is supposed to wear. Hey, the equipment's been used, why pretend?"

Mary's dress was rather more low-cut than the other women's. She looked around intently and then saw Mikhail. Mikhail looked at her and smiled, and she smiled back happily, blushing just a little.

Hal was trying to control both Maria and Lucretia's daughter, who were happily trying to get into everything possible. Jose was cheerfully encouraging them in their misbehavior and laughing at their tricks.

"Here, you calm down," Lucretia's mother sternly ordered Jose, who quickly sat down, winking at Maria, who giggled.

Lucretia's mother looked down the aisle, watching for Lucretia, and then noticed Aliston sitting quietly alone in the back. She was dressed down, wearing minimal makeup with her hair back, as simple as she could make it. Aliston saw her, quickly smiled, a nervous smile, and looked down.

"She dressed down," Cali commented, noticing Lucretia's mother staring at Aliston. "She kept asking me if she looked, well, insignificant enough."

"Did she?" Lucretia's mother asked, thinking. She glanced at Aliston again, and nodded her head to herself, a decision having been made.

"What?" Cali asked, puzzled.

"Cali, your daughter needs some attention," Mary remarked.

"Oh. Oh, sure," Cali agreed as the dots connected in her head. "Well, I'll try, but, yeah, we could sure use some more help up here."

Lucretia's mother stood up and walked over to Aliston. "Can I sit next to you?" she asked.

"Certainly," Aliston replied, surprised and a little apprehensive. Mother of the bride, and I've seduced the father away. This should be fun, she thought, keeping the smile on her face.

"I'm wondering if you could sit with us," Lucretia's mother asked, looking into Aliston's eyes. "It's not the usual protocol, I know," she continued, noticing Aliston's momentary panic, "but we need some help controlling the children. Besides, I'd like for you to sit with us."

"I'm the new kid on the block," Aliston blurted out, almost despite herself. "I'm pushing in on what was yours, and that can't be comfortable for you. Sorry," she added, catching herself. "I don't do a lot of girl talk. I tend to be more direct. Most women don't want me around, so I don't practice a lot."

Lucretia's mother smiled at her. "I was a beauty, and people think it would be wonderful. It is often a curse. And the new kid on the block? I have a wonderful child by Lucifer. I walked away from him—my error. Nor, after all the years, do I have the energy or the desire to take on that project again."

"Are you sure?" Aliston demanded. "It's a small group here. I'm usually pretty disruptive to groups, and I'm trying to walk on little cat feet."

"You should spend more time with women," Lucretia's mother advised. "You know, Cali brought you here for a reason. It is well known that a man in possession of a good fortune is in need of a wife. She and I talked about it before she went. No woman brings another woman like you into a group without a plan. You should know that."

Aliston stared at her for a second, and then laughed, shaking her head. "And I thought I was being so clever! My women's intuition will be downgraded to third class, and my silver star taken away."

"Your secret is good with me," Lucretia's mother promised, patting her on the arm. "Here, walk with me." She pulled Aliston up, and they walked to the front. "There, that works," Lucretia's mother announced as they were finally seated. Lucretia's mother was on one side of Aliston, and Cali was on the other. Aliston let a single tear run down her face, which Cali quickly wiped off.

"Ah, if the hen fest is over," Hal begged, "perhaps someone could take a child?" He had the little girls, one in each arm, and they were struggling to escape and winning. "Here, please." He guided Lucretia's daughter to Aliston.

"I'm not very experienced with children," Aliston admitted, picking the girl up a bit awkwardly.

"You will be," Lucretia's mother promised. "I know men. And I know him."

Aliston actually blushed, and then listened carefully as Lucretia's mother started talking about some practical methods of controlling the small child that was trying to wriggle away.

Mary examined Aliston carefully, and reached over to touch her stomach for a second. "These lessons will be helpful, I'm sure," Mary observed cheerfully. Aliston's eyes went very wide, and Lucretia's mother laughed.

"Here comes the bride," Jesus announced, seeing the door open. All turned to see Lucretia in her bright white dress, a vision of loveliness, and Lucifer in a dark blue suit slowly walking down the wood walkway to the pavilion.

In a few minutes, Lucretia and Vladimir were standing next to each other. Both were visibly trembling as they faced Jesus, who smiled at them.

Jesus raised his hands. "Blessed are you who have come here in the name of God. Serve God with joy; come into God's presence with song. We rejoice that Lucretia Liancol and Vladimir Leboweitz Uriel join in marriage in the presence of God and loved ones. O glorious and blessed God, grant your blessings to these two people that love each other. They are surrounded by loved ones whose joy and prayers are with you here. May your home be a shelter against the storm, a haven of peace, a stronghold of faith and love.

"Let us all join in our prayer of gratitude. Blessed are You, Adonai our God, Ruler of the Universe who has given us life, sustained us, and allowed us to reach this day. And now I ask you, in the presence of God and this assembly, do you, Vladimir Leboweitz Uriel, take Lucretia Liancol to be your wife, to love, to honor, and to cherish?"

"I do," Vladimir replied, his voice suddenly strong.

"Do you, Lucretia Liancol, take Vladimir Leboweitz Uriel to be your husband, to love, to honor and to cherish?" Jesus asked.

"I do." Lucretia's voice was quiet but strong.

The caretaker handed Vladimir and Lucretia their rings.

"Vladimir Leboweitz Uriel and Lucretia Lianol, speak the words and exchange the rings that make you husband and wife," Jesus advised. "Vladimir Leboweitz Uriel, as you place the ring on the finger of the one you love, recite the worlds that formally unite you in marriage."

Vladimir, with trembling hands, put the ring on Lucretia's finger and declared, "Be consecrated to me with this ring as my wife, in keeping with the heritage of our faith and the laws of Moses and Israel."

"Lucretia Liancol, as you place the ring on the finger of the one you love, recite the words that formally unite you in marriage," Jesus asked, smiling at her.

Lucretia, her hands also trembling, put the ring on Vladimir's finger and declared, "Be consecrated to me with this ring as my husband, in keeping with the heritage of our faith and the laws of Moses and Israel.

Jesus raised the wine cup for the seven blessings:

"Blessed are You, Lord, our God, sovereign of the universe, who creates the fruit of the vine.

"Blessed are You, Lord, our God, sovereign of the universe, who created everything for His Glory.

"Blessed are You, Lord, our God, sovereign of the universe, who creates man.

"Blessed are You, Lord, our God, sovereign of the universe, who creates man in your image, fashioning perpetuated life. Blessed are You, LORD, creator of man.

"May the barren one exult and be glad as her children are joyfully gathered to her. Blessed are You, LORD, who gladdens Zion with her Children.

"Grant perfect joy to these loving companions, as you did your creations in the Garden of Eden. Blessed are You, LORD, who grants the joy of groom and bride.

"Blessed are You, Lord, our God, sovereign of the universe, who created joy and gladness, groom and bride, mirth, song, delight and rejoicing, love and harmony and peace and companionship. LORD our God, may there ever be heard in the cities of Judah and in the streets of Jerusalem voices of joy and gladness, voices of groom and bride, the jubilant voices of those joined in marriage under the bridal canopy, the voices of young people feasting and singing. Blessed are You, Lord, who causes the groom to rejoice with his bride."

Vladimir and Lucretia sipped from the wine cup.

"As you have shared the wine from a single cup, so may you, under God's guidance, share contentment, peace, and fulfillment from the cup of life. May you find life's joys heightened, its bitterness sweetened, and each of its moments hallowed by true companionship and love," Jesus declared.

"In the presence of these witnesses and in keeping with our tradition, you have spoken the words and performed the rites that unite your lives."

"Y'varech'cha Adonai v'yish'm'recha. Ya'eir Adonai panav eliecha vi'y'chuneka. Yisa Adonai panav eilecha v'yasem l'cha shalom."

Jesus placed the glass on the ground, and counted to three.

"Mazel Tov!" everyone shouted.

MAZEL TOV, INDEED!

"Mazel Tov, indeed!" the old man laughed, standing at the back of the group, calmly brushing the dust off of his coat.

Everyone turned and gasped, and Mikhail started to kneel, his head bowed.

"None of that today," the old man ordered, stern for a second. Mikhail quickly stood up, uncertain.

"Always the bridesmaid, never the bride, Mikhail?" the old man observed, smiling at Mikhail, who laughed, relieved.

"Perhaps someday, My Lord," Mikhail answered.

"That's a good look, Mikhail," the old man offered, winking at him. "I like it. What do you think, Mary?" She blushed scarlet, almost matching her dress, and lowered her eyes after coyly looking at Mikhail. The old man nodded and smiled to himself.

"Mother, you shameless flirt," Cali murmured, smiling through Mary's quick elbow to Cali's ribs.

The old man finished brushing the dust off his coat. "I'm late, I know," he grumbled. "The roads in this town are in terrible shape. Still, better late than never." He looked at the bride and groom, smiling. "And the bride, radiant! Uriel, you finally figured out that it's Life. Good. Better late than never."

Lucretia and Vladimir looked at each other and kissed.

Lucretia threw the bride's bouquet, and Dominique caught it. "Oh!" she gasped, looking around. She looked at GrendelHal, and he winked at her. She blushed.

"I knew that!" Cali declared to Hal, elbowing him in the side. Hal gasped, having been focused on keeping Maria from digging in the dirt.

"Well, this is wonderful," the old man announced, looking around and nodding, approving of the lush greenery that had transformed the wasteland. "A celebration of life!" Sniffing the air, "And a feast I smell!"

They turned, and the tables were overflowing with food. The old man looked critically at the tables and then smiled. "Hard to get a good caterer, but this looks fine."

In the far distance, there was a low rumble of thunder, and a light, nourishing rain gently watered the savanna. White trees here and there grew tall. There were breaks in the clouds through which the sunbeams burst, like in the old paintings.

"Sun and rain—there will be a rainbow," Cali observed. "And there!" pointing to the rainbow stretching from horizon to horizon. Maria clapped her hands with delight, laughing with joy at the sight.

The old man smiled at the child's delight and then looked quizzically at Lucifer, Mikhail, and the others. "Written on a page, it was, what Life is. But you cannot read the minds of the gods by their deeds, to cheat the pain of learning. Only experience teaches, and adversity teaches the best. Odin hung upon the cross for wisdom, so you hung upon a cross of indecision and confusion, as confidence turned to doubt. Had I not pushed the good to the absurd, would you have rebelled? Children must rebel to become adults. And now, are you elves? Elves are adults. And you must be adults, because there are new, bigger stories coming. Lungorthin and his people, the alien stories of the machines—perhaps, truly, aliens out there in the universe. How could you be ready to face all of this without having been challenged by failure? Was I unfair? Of course. Life is unfair. If I tell you, you listen but do not hear. Life is experience, not thought, and you had to grow the understanding, painfully, through every sinew of your body before you could hear. Had I not pushed you to the outside, would you have learned?"

Lucifer and Mikhail looked shocked, but then shook their heads no.

"Understanding is becoming, becoming is birth, and birth is pain. Would you complain? Elves must give up the illusions of children. Become the Tree, to come to Life," the old man added.

The group stood transfixed, staring at him.

"The minds of the gods cannot be read just by witnessing their deeds," Lucifer acknowledged. "You are very likely to be fooled about their intentions."

"The first step on the path to wisdom is to recognize what you don't know," the old man agreed, nodding. "So, the morning star, lights the way to a new day. What do you say about the new day?"

"A blessing beyond my wildest hopes, my Lord," Lucifer confessed, a tear running down his cheek. Lucifer looked at the rainbow and touched Maria on the head.

The old man nodded, smiling to himself.

Mary prayed, "Father, we thank you that you have bestowed and raised these your servants to the new life of grace within your Tree of Life. Sustain them, give them an inquiring and discerning heart, the courage to will and to persevere, a spirit to know and to love you, and the gift of joy and wonder in all your works. Amen."

"The wonder fullness of life," Lucifer declared, Aliston standing by his side, and they all bowed their heads before the wonder of Life, spread out before them.

"Shall we?" the old man asked, pointing to the food. They all went to the tables, which groaned with the weight of the food, and the wine flowed free.

GILGAMESH:

Gilgamesh, why dost thou run about this way?
the life that thou art seeking, thou wilt never find.
when the gods created man,
they put death upon mankind,
and held life in their own hands.
fill thy belly, Gilgamesh;
day and night enjoy thyself;
prepare each day some pleasant occasion.
day and night be frolicsome and gay;
let thy clothes be handsome,
thy head shampooed, thy body bathed.
regard the little one who takes thy hand.
let thy wife be happy against thy bosom.

The Epic of Gilgamesh is, perhaps, the oldest written story on Earth. The passage quoted above is missing from the standard Assyrian edition of the legend, but it was found in a much earlier Babylonian fragmentary text.

—

COMMENTARY AND DISCUSSION

The economic seminar at Aspen, Colorado, starting on or about page 10, is taken from "Fault Lines," by Raghuram. G. Rajan. I have paraphrased what I understood his ideas to be, but I do not represent that he would necessarily agree with how I stated his ideas.

San Palo, second section revolves around the book of Job, and various commentaries on it.

"There the wicked cease their troubling, and there the weary repose – the place of the dead, from Job.

The paper presented in Switzerland, on or about page 90, is based on the book "The Collapse of Complex Societies," by Joseph A. Tainter. I have paraphrased extensively, to turn the academic text into something hopefully a little easier to read. The concept, that declining marginal returns set in, and when the basic power supplies driving the complexity go, then the structure fails, seems unarguable.

Lucretia's Grendeline experience draws heavily on Joseph Campbell.

The Funeral service is based on the Episcopal Book of Common Prayer, but modified to a Tree of Life focus.

The part on Hillel the Elder was taken from an article by Yaakov Astor, and modified to a Tree of Life perspective.

The consecration of the sacred ground was taken from the Episcopal Book of Common Prayer, and modified to a Tree of Life focus.

The wedding at the end of the book is based on a Jewish marriage ritual, modified for the Tree of Life focus.

About The Author

Credentials:

- I have a BA from Michigan State University, majoring in Sociology, with minors in Psychology and English (1972);
- A JD degree from the University of Detroit School of Law (1975);
- an LLM (Master's in Law) in Taxation from Southern Methodist University School of Law (1983);
- a MBA from Michigan State University, Materials and Logistics Management, /Operations Management (1992); and
- a Master in Science from Michigan State University, in Building Construction Management, focused on Project Management (1998).
- I have been licensed as an attorney in Michigan since 1975
- Licensed as a Certified Public Accountant in Michigan since 1981.
- Am a certified Project Management Professional (Project Management Institute)
- Certified Information Technology Professional (AICPA);
- Certified in Financial Forensics (AICPA), and
- Chartered Global Management Accountant (AICPA)
- My practice web site is: www.johnedwardhunt.com

Perhaps little of that matters for the purposes of these books, but it is what one usually puts on the author page. I'm fascinated by Joseph Campbell's ideas, despair about the ecological disaster coming, and know that people don't plan well. So these books encompass those interests and challenge the reader to think outside the box – way, way outside the box.

ENDNOTES

[1] Machiavelli, Nicolo, The Prince, Chapter VI.

[2] Howard, Robert E, author, from the movie Conan the Barbarian, 1982

[3] Carroll, Lewis, Alice in Wonderland, Chapter VI

[4] Dahl, Ian Van, Where are You Now?

[5] Cunningham, John M, wrote the story that 'High Noon', the movie was based on. The screenplay is attributed to Carl Foreman.

[6] Ibid.

[7] Burton, Robert A., On Being Certain, page 26

[8] New York Times, Editorial, drawing from the International Program on the State of the Ocean, July 15, 2011

[9] Heller, Joseph, Catch 22

[10] Shakespeare, William, The Merchant of Venice, Act 1, Scene 2

[11] Tolkien, J. R. R., Lord of the Rings, Book 1

[12] Campbell, Joseph, The Hero with a Thousand Faces

[13] Matthew 13:30

[14] Henry W. Longfellow

[15] Luke 12:49-53

[16] Matthew 10:34-39 NASB

[17] F. Nietzsche

[18] Matthew, 13:13-20

[19] Isiah 13-11

[20] Rumi

www.ingramcontent.com/pod-product-compliance
Lightning Source LLC
Chambersburg PA
CBHW060346260626
47160CB00006B/2221